LOCKSPELL

Phil Coleman

For Kit

Contents

PART ONE:

Tracer

1

~ Cinq ~

The air pulsed with drums, tambourines, shouts, and firecrackers. The noise danced through the sweltering air, mixing with the sweat and breath of costumed revelers. On this night, the town would laugh and cry in memory of the Pentarch. Three hundred years had passed since the Titans ravaged the world. Why not risk bringing them back?

Cinq frowned. This festival was a terrible idea. These people should be hidden away, tucked in the caves of the nearby mountains, or crouched among the dunes of the surrounding desert. To gather on the solstice was the worst kind of arrogance. They'd certainly draw the attention of the fey, if not the Titans themselves—though some would argue that was entirely the point. But Cinq had come too far to run now.

Lifting the brim of his wide, peaked hat, he scanned the rooftops. Since he and Nissa had arrived in the city, the sky had faded from burnt umber to twilight gray. Birds lined the ridges, dancing from side to side, waiting for an opportunity of a dropped piece of—anything.

"You see something?"

Cinq turned to the girl seated across from him. Nissa's skin was decorated from neck to toe in the runes of the wikken. Her clothes were a collection of animal skins strung with beads and draped in feathers. As she moved, her tattoos peeked out from underneath. The girl studied him with a practiced look that he had yet to decipher if mocking, or merely inquisitive.

She pressed, "Come on. What are you looking at?"

He shut the notebook in his hand, tucked away the nub of charcoal, and slid the book into his coat pocket. "The birds, Nissa. They seem like they're waiting."

The witch cackled. You always hear about witches cackling, but never a teenage one. And if Nissa was more than fifteen—conventional years, that is—then Cinq would be damned. And of course, "witch" wasn't the proper term. Anyone who used magic was called a witch these days. That meant a wikken like Nissa, the monks in the monastery above town, and—most especially—mages like himself. To those who used the word, they were all lying, dirty, nasty, greedy, underhanded witches.

Nissa rolled her eyes. "Of *course* they're waiting. They can feel it. I can feel it. Heck, everyone here could feel it if they just stopped for a minute." She smirked. "And *you* can feel it too. Don't listen for whispers on the wind when there's screaming in your face."

Cinq raised an eyebrow. "Now who's being poetic?"

A firework lit the sky in a viridescent burst; tendrils of smoke dissipated in the afterimage. The crowd cheered in appreciation. This wasn't just some kid with a banger, or even a merchant showing off. An explosion that size meant the parade had begun.

The procession would continue down main street to stop at the stage erected in the town square. Everyone would follow, even though most were too far away to hear the actors speak. On cue, the crowd began to move.

Cinq took a deep breath. "Of course, I feel it. But that's all. You're the expert on these things. Do you think it will happen tonight? I'd like to be in and out quickly if we can. Are the fey talking at all? Are they nervous because of the solstice?" He cursed under his breath. "Or because there are so many, many, many people here?"

Nissa leaned back and propped her feet on the table. "Which of those fifty questions did you want answered?" She sighed. "It's not a science. Pretty much the opposite. And just because I know more than you, doesn't mean I'm an expert. Hours? Minutes? A week? My bones say tonight—but I wouldn't bet on it. Not that we have money for betting. And even if I knew, so what? You think these people would go home? No one would listen to us."

"Some might," Cinq replied. "No. Probably not. After all, *we're* dumb enough to be here. Plus, we look like two more kids dressed for the party. I'd have to make a major show of magic to be believed, and I'm not in the business of wasting it."

"There's an understatement." Nissa rolled her eyes. "Plus, we don't *want* to get noticed."

A chill crept across Cinq's skin. He thought of the reavers—fanatics who'd sworn to hunt down and exterminate those who used magic. They called themselves "witch doctors," a tongue-in-cheek declaration that they were curing the world of witches. And their numbers were growing. Normally, being out in the open, and dressed as they were, was risky. But not tonight.

Cinq dropped his voice low. "You think the reavers are here? Now?"

Nissa looked surprised. "What? Reavers? Those clowns probably took the night off—all part of having no sense of humor or fun whatsoever. I was talking about your buddies back at Eastwind. Oooh! That reminds me, I got you a present." Nissa fished in her leather satchel. She removed a piece of folded paper and handed it to him.

Cinq laid out the poster to see his own face looking back at him, along with the words "eighteen years old, tall, thin, thievery, valuable, wanted, reward," and "not presumed dangerous." He crumpled the sheet. How shortsighted could the other mages be? They'd be arguing semantics until the Convergence. Cinq shoved the poster into his pocket.

Nissa grinned. "I know, right? Wanted posters. Who does that? At least they're taking us seriously."

Cinq waited until the flare of panic, embarrassment, and outrage passed. He steadied his voice. "*Us?* Don't be ridiculous. There is no 'us,' at least not as far as the Tower is concerned. Where did you even find that?"

"That? On a wall somewhere. Right next to—"

A large man in a brown monk's robe—possibly a potato sack—stumbled into the table next to them. The contents of his mug splashed up in the air, to his confusion and the entertainment of his friends. The drunk fumbled upright and tried to take a sip from his now-empty mug. Consumed with purpose, he charged back into the crowd.

Nissa rested her elbows on the table and propped up her chin. "I wouldn't worry about it. But it made me think. Are you considering going back to the Tower after this? Would three of us be enough?"

"No. I've made my decision. I either need to return with real proof or wait until it's bad enough they care on their own." He dropped his voice to a mutter. "Which might not be far off."

"Hah!" She smacked her hands on the table and broke into a grin. "Soooo dramatic. But I've found you out. You're nervous! The unflappable Cinq LeGarrec is nervous. All that talk of reavers and your old buddies was a distraction. You're worried about the Titans." She sat back in her chair and popped a salt cracker in her mouth. "Now, as for me, I'm kind of excited to see one."

He exhaled. "I suppose it will be exciting, but—"

Nissa interrupted, "But you'd rather skip that part. All right then. I know you're not here for the play, so can we get on with it? What's thingee say? Is our girl moving yet?"

Cinq was relieved to get back to business. Thoughts of the tower, reavers, and being called a thief… it was all too much. He liked his problems emotion-free. Clinical. He reached into the inner pocket of his long coat and removed the Tracer, a crystal sphere the size of an orange. He tapped the surface three times, and the inside filled with vapor, which swirled then coalesced. Within the depths, an ember of light split into five points. Two lights were so faint as to be nearly invisible, but of the three brighter lights, one darted to the side of the sphere nearest Cinq, while the other pointed at Nissa. The third—nearly as bright as the first two—moved to the far side, never quite settling.

Cinq jumped to his feet. "He's on the move."

"Or she," Nissa interjected.

"Or she. Not important."

"Of *course* it's important. If it wasn't important, then…"

But Cinq was already up and pushing into the crowd. With one hand he held the Tracer to his chest, while the other gripped his tall, inlaid staff. Cinq pushed through the crowd of mages, monks, wikken, scholars, and hermits. None of them real, of course. Just revelers costumed as one of the five stages of the Pentarch. Then again, a few *might* have been authentic. After all, wasn't he? An actual tower-trained mage in a sea of false ones? He glanced over his shoulder to see Nissa following behind. Scratch that. She wasn't following; she was dancing. For every elbow Cinq used to carve his way through the crowd, Nissa would duck and weave, tickling the chins of those she passed, sometimes whispering in their ears, and alternately smiling or scowling as she threaded between. Anyone who cared to look *had* to know that she wasn't just a farm girl in costume.

"Nissa, come on," Cinq chided. There was no animosity in his voice. They had been traveling together for more than two months. He knew she could be trusted to do the right thing. But always on her own terms. And always in her own time.

He turned forward and collided with—Nissa. How had she gotten in front?

"Bald kid, one o'clock." She paused. "And he's a he. One point for you."

"How do you…?"

"Check him yourself."

He glanced at the Tracer and saw that the third point of light was indeed pointing directly at the boy. Then Cinq noticed the subtleties Nissa had been quicker to spot. The shape of his cheeks, the set of his jaw. But most telling were the eyes. The steel-gray eyes, the left flecked with yellow, the right with green, were the same eyes Cinq saw when he looked in the mirror; the same he saw in Nissa. The rest of the boy was an afterthought. He was younger than Nissa, though the haircut—or rather lack of hair—made him look even younger. As for clothes, he wore a brown mendicant's robe. And this was no costume. The robe was frayed in all the right places to indicate time spent kneeling.

A monk. Of course he'd be a monk. That point went to Nissa.

The moment of victory was brief. Nissa fell to her knees, shrieking as she clasped her ears. Cinq stumbled as well. Energy built around him, an air of potential and possibility vibrating through every stone, rock, and grain of sand. It howled through the streets, the mountains outside town, and even in the wind swirling around the revelers. The electric current built to a fever pitch, drowning all sound in a piercing whine.

Then it stopped.

For a span of seconds, the crowd was silent. The force was so powerful, so overwhelming, it affected even those untrained in magic. But the moment was brief, ended by the sound of splitting mountains.

The thunder came first. Instead of rolling and fading, the rumble grew, roaring as it strengthened. The earth shook violently, jolting back and forth. The now-shrieking masses crashed and tripped into one another. People tried to run, somewhere, anywhere, but there was nowhere to go.

The quake continued. Cinq whipped around to check Nissa, before turning his attention to the monk. Miraculously, the boy remained standing, his body in a crouch and arms to his sides. His face was pale, his eyes wide. Cinq spun around to face the thunder, to look in the direction where everyone now stared.

His books hadn't prepared him. An entity emerged from a cloud of dust. Sand, rock, boulders, and debris billowed and churned as they piled atop one another. One hundred feet tall, two hundred, three hundred, the mass of rock transformed from a shapeless pile to take on a very real—and vaguely human—form: the Earth Titan.

When the ground quit shaking, screams filled the void. People were running again, and this time they had a clear objective: to escape.

Cinq felt a hand pulling on his shoulder.

"Hey, Cinq!" Nissa shouted. "Follow the kid!"

Nissa pointed to the monk caught up in the crowd. Cinq stole one last glance to see that the Earth Titan was, indeed, approaching. They took off in pursuit. This time Nissa was in the lead, but he was soon on her heels. Her smaller body was unable to force through the crowd. Cinq jammed past her and pulled the wikken into his wake.

The boy was gone, disappeared into a side alley and out of the flow of traffic. Cinq veered sharply, nearly trampled as he moved across the current of people. He held steady, keeping his staff crooked close to his body and his head down. They fought into an alley, where they finally broke free from the river of bodies.

Nissa slid around Cinq. She flinched as the boom of the Titan's footfall sent gravel and sand raining down on them. "This way!"

The alley dead-ended after twenty feet. When Nissa reached the end, she disappeared. He rushed to follow. At the far wall, a narrow passage was carved in the bricks. Cinq pressed himself against the building and slid along an entry so narrow that both his chest and back dragged against the wall. He gripped his hat in one hand and staff in the other until he emerged on the far side.

When the passage opened, he stood in a small courtyard, bordered on four sides by brick walls that opened to the sky above. There were no breaks in those walls, neither window nor balcony, insinuating that the chamber might be a mystery to those who lived in the surrounding buildings. Cinq looked first up at the sky swirling with red-brown dust, and then to where Nissa perched over a ring of bricks rising from the ground. The wall was two feet high, with a wooden arch above it and a metal pole disappearing into the pit below.

"Well? Or bunker?" Cinq asked.

Nissa shrugged. "A way out."

"After you."

"You're bigger," she countered. Her words were punctuated by another immense footstep, eliciting a scream from the crowds and a few bricks toppling from above to land beside them in the courtyard.

"Fine." Cinq gripped the pole with one hand and hooked his legs around it. He clutched his staff to his body and disappeared into the darkness.

2

~ Cinq ~

Cinq gripped the pole just tightly enough so as to avoid a complete freefall. After sixty feet of descent through the dark, he collided with spongy ground littered with rotting food, feathers, and general debris. His legs buckled on impact, the left knee striking him hard in the chest. He toppled to one side where something damp and fetid seeped into his clothes. As his eyes adjusted, the outline of a domed corridor took shape. Firelight from iron braziers cast an orange glow against the stones, while shadows etched lines between them. Cinq regained his feet and limped away from the pole. A moment later, Nissa landed beside him with a wet thud.

"Well, that was fun," she whistled. "Unless, of course, we have to climb back up. That would suck." She paused, her nose wrinkling. "Uggh. It's awful down here. But… maybe safe? Do you think we're deep enough to be safe?" She looked around. "Where's the kid?"

In response, a heavy pulse reverberated through the tunnel, followed by another louder, and then another louder still. The walls echoed with each boom. Dust, gravel, and rocks rained down.

Panic rose in his chest. "Nissa, we need to go. Now! Don't stop!"

She dashed forward, her head tucked low. Cinq raced after, fighting the urge to pull a torch from the wall out of respect for those who might follow. Another thud from the Titan's footfalls, and the corridor disappeared in dust. Cinq kept running. Moving blindly was less dangerous than lingering. He felt stupid thinking of all the times he'd boasted about what he'd do if he saw a Titan. This was the leading edge of a nightmare, and they weren't free yet. A Titan could—and often would—grind a city to rubble. The farther they could get away, the better. *No, no, no, no!* Cinq chided himself. This wasn't about escape; it was about finding the monk.

Suddenly, the ground dropped away. Cinq flailed as he fell, arms windmilling until he plunged into icy, black water. His breath exploded from his chest from the shock. He struggled to swim upward, his long coat weighing him down. Though awkward, he clutched his staff with one arm, while kicking with his feet and clawing up through the water. As Cinq broke the surface, he came face to face with a smiling Nissa. They were in a half-submerged cave with torches circling the walls on all sides. What's more, they were no longer alone. Dozens of others, who also had the good fortune to escape, treaded water around them.

Thud. Another reverberation, but this time the shock was insulated by the trinity of depth, rock, and water. Whoever had constructed this bunker had shown both foresight and ingenuity.

Nissa swept her dark hair out of her face, where it clung in wet tendrils. "Let's move it," she sputtered. "We're in the drop zone." She turned and swam toward the closest wall, where several other people clung to rocky pillars. The glossy, water-smoothed stone provided handholds for anyone too tired to swim but unwilling to leave the safety of the pool. The refugees cringed with every footfall of the Titan. And yet none were petrified with fear. They'd had enough wits to make it this far, which was saying something. Those less clear-headed would be cowering on the city streets, or already dead.

Cinq swam to Nissa. Staying afloat with his clothing saturated by the frigid water was laborious, though manageable. "You think there's a way out?"

A man with a shadowed face curtained by thick sideburns and a heavy mustache spoke. "A way out? Of course there is. With luck, it won't be caved in. But stay where you are for now. If you're in the pool, bucking rock won't break your legs."

Nissa lit up at the sound of a friendly—and distinctly rational—voice. She beamed back at the man. "You seem calm enough. This doesn't make you nervous? My name's Nissa. From out of town. You… probably know that part already."

The man grinned back, baring teeth made of at least six separate types of metal. "Call me Hollinder. And I'm not that brave. I'll be shaking once the rush wears off." He paused. "Some folks are there already."

Cinq nodded. The small cavern reverberated not only with the footfalls of the Titan, but the sobs of the survivors. Perhaps there were other bunkers, other means of escape not so carefully hidden. And maybe others would simply be lucky. But many would die.

Another echoing footfall. And another. Each pulse sent shocks through his chest and ripples of magic through his mind. When the Titan moved, his presence was felt in both the physical and spiritual planes.

Nissa mused, "That one was softer. I think it's moving on. Or possibly…" she tilted her head.

Hollinder grinned. "Or maybe it just—"

"Shhh," Nissa snapped.

Cinq strained his ears, but there was no sound echoing from above, only the slosh of unsteady water against the walls of the cavern. The muffled sobbing diminished as they waited. When the seconds stretched on, Nissa spoke.

"He's gone," she whispered. "The Titan's gone." Her eyes widened. "But they've found us."

"Who found…?"

Cinq was interrupted as a muffled shriek echoed through the bunker. The sound was high-pitched and yet gurgled and rasped like an injured cat. The first shriek took the room to silence once more. And the second, even louder, sent everyone into a frenzy. Screams of "Banshees!" filled the room. The calm was replaced by the thrashing of men and women swimming to the exit.

Hollinder, the metal-toothed man, climbed from the water to where the room ended in a teardrop flanked with torches. He waved to the others, pulling them up and out, one by one. "To the exit! This way!"

Cinq and Nissa swam alongside the rest of them. Behind Hollinder, a rock passage twisted away and out of sight. The water frothed with the fury of swimmers. Desperate hands reached for purchase, but just as often found the clothes and shoulders of other people. Cinq fought along with the rest, until he and Nissa reached the shore. They clambered onto the rocks. He was vaguely aware of bruises and scrapes covering his knees, shins, and elbows, though that was just a distraction. He turned back to the pool teeming with swimmers. He gripped his staff in both hands, the front end held low above the water. He clenched his jaw in concentration. Beside him, Nissa helped pull people ashore. The stream of refuges poured around them and into the tunnel behind. In less than a minute, they were the only two left at the water's edge.

Cinq didn't budge. "It's not over."

Another shriek, this one deafening. An inhuman shape plummeted through the apex of the cavern, screaming as it fell to crash into the water. The piercing cry cut to a whine as the banshee submerged. Cinq released the pent-up energy. Magic surged up his arms and into the staff, focusing at the tip as he dipped it into the water. White light flooded the chamber. His ears filled with splintered cracking as the surface froze solid, trapping the banshee beneath. The creature slammed itself against the ice. Each collision resulted in shooting cracks and glimpses of wings, talons, and reptilian teeth. Its jaws snapped, but it couldn't bite the smooth surface. The thrashing stopped. Only to be followed by a second shriek from above.

Nissa tugged at his shoulder. "Let's go!"

He scrambled to his feet and sprinted after her. At the end of the tunnel, Nissa darted through an ironbound door held open by Hollinder. Cinq crammed through the opening just before it slammed shut. Several men struggled to drop crossbars across the entryway, which slid into place with a satisfying clang.

Cinq dropped to one knee. His heart pounded in his chest. The momentary silence was banished as something very large, and very heavy, threw itself against the door. On the other side, banshees wailed in fury. The creatures attacked the door, over and over again.

He watched the door, bracing himself for the next blow, praying the iron would hold strong. It didn't come. He waited alongside the others, keenly aware that their eyes were on him and the door in equal measure. But he didn't move. He held off as long as possible before the itch of curiosity overtook him. Cinq reached into his pocket to examine the Tracer. He cradled the sphere between his thumb and two fingers, satisfied that it was intact. The dancing lights drew his eyes to the far side of the room. For just a moment, he wondered if he wasn't rushing things. Could this wait for another day? That monk wasn't going anywhere, or at least not fast. No. He shook his head. He refused to wait another moment. He'd waited long enough.

Cinq stopped. Just to the side of the door, against the wall and with arms wrapped around her knees, Nissa sat shivering. Her eyes were clenched tight, and she mumbled to herself. Her dripping knees, legs, and forearms were streaked in mud and scratches. He crouched beside her. He laid his staff on the ground as he placed a hand on her shoulder.

"Nissa, are you hurt?"

Her eyes snapped open, the pupils wide in the dim light. "I'll… I'll be ok. It's just. Those things are really, really loud." She tapped her head. "I just need a few minutes." She forced a smile. "Go ahead, I know you want to. Just try not to scare him off."

Cinq stood and surveyed the room. In front of him, the chamber stretched into a high-ceilinged expanse festooned with stalactites. Man-made columns stretched from the ceiling to a cobbled floor. The walls were defined in halves as regimented brickwork gave way to natural stone. The juxtaposition of rough cut and masonry complemented one another. Apart from the columns and the brickwork, the only man-made things were wicker baskets jumbled against one wall, and the heavy doors leading both in and out. Around the chamber, huddled in small groups, were the refugees. Cinq counted around forty people in a room that should have held hundreds. Perhaps the bunker's architect had been too optimistic about its usage. Perhaps the entrance had been too well hidden. Perhaps the Titan had come too fast.

Cinq ignored the eyes studying him. As he crossed the room, he heard a stew of comments and questions float around him, permeated by fear, cries, and whimpers. Others spoke in excited bursts as young men told and retold their stories. Below those voices, in mumbles and whispers, were those who spoke of magic. A real mage? Here? What should they do? Cinq gritted his teeth and set his eyes forward. Ahead, the young monk was hard at work splinting the leg of a refugee. Bandages, both neatly rolled and loose, surrounded him. On all sides, wounded people waited their turn as they clutched their bleeding sides and bruised heads.

As Cinq approached, the monk scrambled to his feet. He slid the pile of unused wrappings to a woman beside him and met the mage expectantly. The boy was sodden, his skin streaked with mud and scrapes covering his forearms. His robe had been cinched up around his waist. His canvas pants and soft shoes were smeared with dirt and drying blood.

The monk's eyes were bright. "You're a mage, right? A real one?"

"That's correct. Cinq LeGarrec, of Eastwind Tower." He tilted his head in greeting. "This might sound odd, but—"

"So you can heal." The boy glanced to the waiting queue. "A couple of these folks could use it. Some major breaks. There are some supplies, but it's not enough. Now that you're here, we can… what are you looking at?"

Cinq shifted uncomfortably. "Healing isn't my discipline. I'm here because—"

"Then I need to get back to work." The boy lowered his eyes. "No disrespect, sir. But these people need help. The masters say that…"

The monk prattled on about responsibility, and kindness, and any number of other things—Cinq wasn't listening. He let the wash of words drift by as he studied the boy. The similarities in their appearances were remarkable. Face, jaw, shoulders, skin tone, and of course, the eyes. They could have been brothers. Maybe they were. The monk was shorter, but perhaps only because he wasn't done growing. Even so, he had the lean, agile look of an athlete. When at last the boy stopped speaking, Cinq wondered if he'd missed a question.

Cinq said, "You didn't tell me your name."

"I didn't? It's Yon, of Open Eye. Is there… is there something else?"

"Yes. I've been looking for you." Cinq clenched his jaw. This wasn't going the way he'd anticipated. Then again, he'd expected someone else. Or maybe he hadn't. He didn't know what to expect.

Yon winced. "Because of the Titan?"

"No. Not exactly." He folded his arms. "I think the Titan was just a coincidence. Most likely, at least. Either way, it's not important for now."

The boy's cheeks flushed. "How can it… not be important? How is this not the most important thing ever? What about the town? My friends? The elders?"

Cinq shook his head. "A poor choice of words. Clearly, the Titan is *important*, it's just not relevant to why I'm here."

"To look for me?"

In a moment of reflection, Cinq considered his own appearance. Soaking wet, covered in mud, still dripping with the dank and cold from the pool, and likely stinking of adrenaline and fear. There was no "respect for the hat" here, and he couldn't offer the one thing requested. Another approach then. Cinq reached into his pocket and held out the sphere. He cradled it so that only the tips of his fingers made contact. "Do you know what this is?"

"No." Yon shrugged. "Something magic?"

The response struck Cinq as funny, but he kept a straight face. "Yes, actually. This is a Tracer. And it's very, very old. It's used to find lost things." Cinq twisted it in his hand. "Tracers are attuned to things of importance. If you follow the light, you find what was lost."

Yon studied the Tracer. "So, I'm a lost important thing?"

"Not anymore," a cheerful voice interrupted. Nissa poked her head around to smile at the two of them. Cinq did a double take. She'd been huddled in the corner only minutes ago and now she was smiling? If not for her puffy eyes, and her tear-streaked cheeks, Nissa looked practically cheerful. Either she recovered quickly, which he doubted, or she didn't trust him to handle this conversation. Cinq made a mental note to discuss it later.

Yon asked, "I'm not lost, or I'm not important?"

Nissa winked. "Lost." She clapped a hand on Cinq's shoulder. "My name's Nissa. You two getting along?"

When the monk didn't reply, Cinq offered, "This is Yon. We were discussing the Tracer."

The boy looked suspiciously at Nissa before turning back to Cinq. "Why is it tracking me?"

Cinq said, "That is exactly the right question. And it's the one I've been trying to answer. You can hold it if you want. Just please, be careful." He passed the sphere to the boy. "This Tracer has more than one thing linked to it—it has five. It's not just attuned to you, but also me, and Nissa here." Cinq removed his hat to scratch the top of his head. "I've been following where it led. I found her first. And now you. Two to go and we have all five."

Yon hefted the sphere first in one hand, then the other. As he swung the orb and twisted it, the three bright lights remained fixed on them. The other lights stayed dim. He asked, "All five of what?"

"He doesn't know," Nissa chirped. "Well, you don't."

Cinq said, "I don't know yet. In theory, if we're all together, the puzzle is solved. Or at least easier to solve. I do have theories."

Nissa reached forward to tap the sphere in Yon's hand. The lights were sent swirling before they settled on their targets once more. "Just so you know, Cinq hates secrets, especially any involving himself. Which is kind of why we're out here. Or down here, rather." She cocked her head. "So, are you in or out?"

Yon replied, "In or out of what?"

Cinq muttered, "Nissa, don't make this more than it is."

She ignored him. "Oh, come on! It's been a big day—biggest anyone here has ever had. And *this*, Yon my friend, is adventure knocking. A wikken and a mage just showed up on your doorstep—alongside a Titan for flair—and are asking you to go on an adventure to unravel a mystery! Now, are you coming with us or not?"

Yon looked back and forth between the two of them.

Cinq cleared his throat. "She's being dramatic. This is a legitimate scholarly endeavor. This Tracer has a catalog number and a record of origin. I'm working on my dissertation, not on a wild goose hunt."

Yon remained silent.

Nissa said, "Now Cinq, you are leaving things out on purpose." She turned back to the monk. "He forgets to mention that he stole it, and that the other mages kind of put a bounty on him."

"I *borrowed* it." Cinq dropped his voice to a mutter. "I even filled out the paperwork."

Nissa continued, "Sure, but you didn't ask anyone with, you know, words coming out of your mouth and all."

"Hold on! Stop it, you two." Yon shook his head. "Why now? Why here? Why are you here *now*? Don't you see what's happening? A Titan came… a Titan! It destroyed the town, and maybe more than that." He clutched his head. "And you want me to run off with you? Look around. Look at these people. This is *not* the time for this. I can't run off now. My teachers… my friends…" He trailed off.

Cinq cleared his throat. "As I said—"

Nissa rolled her eyes. "Stop it, Cinq. Yon is being—say it with me now—*empathetic*. It wouldn't be right for him, *or us*, to just dance off in a tragedy." She turned back to Yon. "Don't think I'm not shaken too. It's just, you know, sometimes you put on your best face. I was just a puddle earlier while you were over here helping. So, which of us is braver?"

Cinq looked at Nissa. He forced his voice to sound even calmer and more reasonable than what he considered his ordinarily calm and reasonable self. Fine. He'd try compassion. "Ok. Nissa's right. And I'm not saying we abandon anyone. I'm simply observing that nothing gets solved by staying still."

Yon scowled. "You mean helping others?"

Nissa placed a hand on both of their shoulders. "Listen, you two, it's going to be a long trip if you're going to pick at each other. How about this? No one is deciding anything for now. Let's go up top and see what's left. Mr. Yon can check on his friends, and maybe, just maybe, the wise old monks know something about this Tracer that the wise old mages didn't. Then he can make up his own mind. Deal?" Nissa held out her hand.

Yon dropped the Tracer into her palm. "Deal."

Cinq smiled, satisfied. A sense of rightness settled on his shoulders, as though having the three of them together scratched some itch in the back of his mind. Better than before, even if not quite complete. Certainly, Yon hadn't agreed to anything, but he would. Something wanted them together; the Tracer was just a part. Cinq wondered if soon things would start to make sense.

The feeling lasted for six seconds.

3

~ Cinq ~

The half-hewn, half-constructed walls of the bunker both amplified and deadened sound at once. Because a whisper on one side of the chamber was easily heard on the other, it was like being in a crowd. Noise was nowhere and everywhere. As such, Cinq heard the reaver at the last possible moment.

Hear was not even the right term. He felt a pulse in the fabric of magic. He glanced over his shoulder to see a man in dark clothing sprinting toward him. The man's hand was upraised, and a long, curved knife gleamed in his fist. Cinq flung out his staff in defense a moment before the man knocked him to the ground. The stone floor slammed against the back of his skull. He let go of his staff to wrestle against the attacker, fighting to keep the blade from finding its target.

"Death to witches!" the attacker screamed. Phlegm sprayed across Cinq's face. The man straddled his prey, straining to bring the knife down while Cinq resisted. The reaver was much stronger than him, and Cinq hadn't a scrap of magic remaining.

Yon collided with the reaver in a blur of brown. The man was thrown aside, only to come up snarling. Cinq snatched his staff and scrambled backward. Yon placed himself between them, hands up and ready. He looked fiercely determined, despite being so much smaller than his opponent. Nissa crept up from the other side. She held a knife in each hand.

Cinq gripped his staff, one end pointed at his assailant. The reaver darted his eyes between the monk, his target, and the wikken. The crowd closed around them. Hands wrestled against wrists and shoulders; arms wrapped around necks. Cinq's staff was wrenched from his grip. In a matter of seconds, the reaver, Cinq, Nissa, and Yon were all held fast. Hollinder strode through the crowd. He held a cudgel in one hand which he slapped against his palm.

"Let those kids go." Hollinder turned to the reaver. "But keep him held."

Cinq, Yon, and Nissa were released. Hollinder stepped between them, inspecting each in turn. "You kids ok?"

The reaver lurched against his restraints. He glared at Hollinder. "You're defending them? They're witches! They brought the Titan here! Them and their magic." His words dripped with hatred.

Hollinder took a step toward the man. "I don't need this right now. There's a situation outside—if you didn't notice." Hollinder turned back to Cinq. "That true? About your magic? Did the Titan follow you?"

Cinq straightened. "*My magic* kept the banshees away."

Nissa tilted her head. "And the big doors helped too. Give the doors some credit."

Hollinder looked at the reaver, then at Cinq. "Yeah, I saw that. But how did they find us?"

Cinq smoothed his still-soaking coat with as much dignity as he could muster. Right now, he felt a lot less like a raised journeyman mage than a water-logged kid. "I don't know. Otherplane creatures may be attracted to magic, but I didn't use any until *after* they arrived." He cleared his throat. "As for the Titan, I suspect it was the crowd."

Hollinder frowned. He looked between the three of them—mage, wikken, and monk. "We'll talk more about this later. You helped, and I saw you help. So, I'll believe you." He pointed to the reaver. "Someone do something with him. Figure it out. And you three," he turned back, "I don't want any more of this. Lay low." He stalked away.

The crowd parted as Hollinder's companions dragged the reaver to the far wall. Nissa clamped down hard on Yon and Cinq's shoulders as she pulled them close. Her eyes shone wildly.

She said, "We need to get out of here. Right now."

Yon protested, "We? I'm not even a part of your—"

"Just a second," Cinq interrupted. "Nissa, what's this about? Do you hear anything? What do your friends say?"

She cocked her head to one side to listen. Cinq listened as well, though apart from the murmur of the crowd, he heard nothing but the drip of water, heavy breathing, and the occasional whimper.

Nissa said, "I don't hear anything. That's not the issue. It has absolutely *nothing* to do with the fey and *everything* to do with us nearly getting stabbed. We found one reaver, but are there others? I don't know. We aren't wanted here. And don't forget you're a perfectly respectable mage, not some nasty little wikken. If everyone wasn't in costume, I'd have been burned at the stake six times over. So can we go or what?"

Cinq pursed his lips. Sometimes he forgot about the mistrust common people had for the wikken—far more so than other magic users. Perhaps this was because a mage fought in tangible ways. Or perhaps because the wikken weren't well understood. Nissa had her own theories, with simple misogyny being only one of them. The wikkens knew about Titans; Titans were the enemy. Guilt by association.

In theory, they should all be respected. Mage, wikken, monk, scholar, hermit. All five of the great disciplines were an aspect of the Pentarch. And if the Titans returned in force, it would take all five to defeat them again. How could people idolize the Pentarch, and yet deny his parts? Cinq clenched his jaw. He knew the answer: people were terrible. They needed enemies, needed scapegoats. Fleeting moments of unity disappeared the second the threat did. These days, magic users had to deal with prejudice, and Titans, *and* reavers. He could use another Pentarch now.

Cinq turned to Yon. "Are you coming with us, or not?"

He watched the boy carefully, then looked past him to the other refugees. Amidst the still-present sobs and cries, emotion grew as thick as the stink from damp clothing and nervous sweat. The temperature of the room was rising again. Would another attack follow where the first one failed?

Yon shifted nervously. "I have to get back to the monastery."

Nissa nodded. "Of course. But that's later. What about now?"

"I'll... I'll do it." Yon clenched his jaw and breathed deep.

Nissa said, "Perfect. Just one last thing to do." She crossed back to the iron door through which they had entered. She studied it before laying a hand against the metal. She recoiled.

Cinq asked, "What is it, Nissa?"

"Banshees. They're still there, all right. Pale, hungry, angry. And they're just... they're just waiting. They know they can't get through. They're waiting for a mistake."

Cinq turned to the watching crowd. He cleared his throat. "You know what I am." He looked around, while at the same time avoiding direct eye contact. "That door," he pointed to the entrance, "should not be opened. Whatever you think you hear, no matter what the voices say, don't do it. Those are banshees on the other side. Not people." He turned and started toward the door on the opposite side, with Nissa and Yon close behind.

A woman with white-blonde hair stared him down as he passed. "Where are you going?"

"Out the other way," Cinq replied. He kept his voice calm. "There's nothing more I can do here."

"No!" The woman stomped forward, her face contorted into a scowl. "No one's going anywhere. Who's to say there aren't banshees through that door too?"

He glanced sidelong at Nissa who shook her head.

Cinq said, "Look, we all have to leave sometime. And I know not everyone wants me here. So, anyone who wants to join us is welcome. As long as you don't mind the company." He shot a challenging look around the room.

"I'll go," Hollinder called out. "To, um, supervise."

Cinq nodded. This was unexpected. "Of course."

Nissa grinned. "Us, too!" she called, presumably for the benefit of the room. She wrapped an arm around Yon's shoulders.

The blonde woman's eyes widened. "And if the banshees come back? Who will protect us?"

Hollinder cleared his throat. "Enormous iron doors."

"But how will we know when it's safe?" she protested again.

"It may never be safe," he snapped. "But I'll come back once I know it's clear. And if I don't," he shrugged, "there's your answer."

The crowd erupted in murmuring once more, even more frantic than earlier. The voices piled atop one another, running the gamut of angry, panicked, and despairing. *Enough of this,* Cinq thought. He raised his voice. "Everyone, please. If the banshees are out there, we don't want them to hear us."

The room snapped to silence.

Cinq asked, "Anyone else coming?"

No one spoke. No one moved. They simply eyed the four of them. Cinq felt them watching his hat, his staff, studying Nissa's tattoos, and assessing the boy in his brown monk's robe. These people wanted the witches gone.

"Then let's go." He put his hands against the door and pushed through.

4

~ Cinq ~

The iron door swung shut with a clang that echoed down the darkened corridor. The torch in Hollinder's hand flickered from the rush of air, then steadied. The single torch had been a matter of much debate. The refugees staying behind argued they'd need all the light and fuel they could get. One torch was all they'd allow. Cinq didn't protest. Far better to leave before things got violent. If worse came to worst, he could weave a spell—possibly. He'd expended all his magic to trap the first banshee, and that would take time to recover. If he needed to reach deeper, he risked permanent injury.

Nissa took a long look at the door before spinning to face Hollinder. "Your friends sure do hate us."

He grunted in reply. "Yeah, well, people are people. Bad day to be an outsider." He sniffed. "But not getting any better in the dark. So, who wants to lead? You know, in case we run into…"

Nissa strode past and plucked the torch from his hands. She stomped down the passage while the others trailed behind, staying close to remain in the torchlight. They trudged one after the other. Cinq kept one hand gripped on his staff and the other clutched to his side so he could feel the Tracer.

As his eyes adjusted, vague shadows gave way to stonework. Up ahead, the passageway descended into roughly hewn rock. More concerning was that the tunnel beyond was partially collapsed, perhaps from tremors of the Titan's footsteps. Chunks of the wall and ceiling had given way, while ominous cracks shot across the earthwork in others. Most of these cave-ins were minor, requiring no more than a sidestep, but others resulted in a massive jumble of rocks that had to be navigated.

Nissa looked over her shoulder. "Feel like home, Cinq?"

He grunted. "A little."

Yon looked back. "What's she mean?"

Cinq answered, "Back at Eastwind, when the tower got crowded, they discovered it was easier to dig down than build up. The junior mages lived underground. Rats, roaches, worms… and us." He gritted his teeth. The mages had a million and one ways to show who was at the top and who wasn't. Hierarchy infused where they lived, how they studied, what they ate. Leaving the tower had been liberating as well as terrifying. And now he was here, underground again.

Downward they traveled along the narrowing tunnel, until they reached the thing Cinq both suspected and feared. The path halted in a concave rock wall. Shovels and pickaxes leaned against the side as though about to be picked up again. Dust on the handles told a different story.

"Is this it?" Hollinder growled. "I mean, really? Did they just quit, or weren't able to dig farther, or what?"

Nissa ran a finger across the dusty tools and held it up to the light. "If they did quit, you could blame your grandparents, or maybe their grandparents." She turned back to the others. "Or maybe there's a door. Do you see any edges or handles or anything? Something cool and secret?"

Yon walked close to the wall. He knocked on the stone. "No door. Wait…" He pressed his ear against the wall. "I hear something. Wind, maybe? Or water?" He looked back and shrugged. "So… I guess we dig?"

Nissa put a hand on his shoulder. "Let me check first." She handed the torch to Hollinder and approached the wall, placing her palms on the surface. She remained motionless before turning to smile back at the monk. "Nobody out there. Either it's all clear, or just a lot more mountain."

Hollinder handed the torch to Cinq. He hefted a pickax himself, before glancing back. "So we dig. Mind giving me a little space. Or…" He trailed off. He cocked his head at Cinq. "If you can shatter the wall by wiggling your fingers, you speak up. I don't want to get all sweaty for nothing."

Cinq shook his head. "That would make things easier, but unfortunately no." He smiled. "But I'll dig beside you."

They worked in shifts, first Cinq paired with Hollinder, then Nissa with Yon. During Cinq's breaks, he studied the monk and wikken working alongside each other. They spoke low to one another, sometimes laughing, other times more subdued. He was glad they were able to relax, even if just a little. As for Cinq, he wasn't ready to let go. The Titan, the banshees, all of it only made him want to tighten down further and see this thing to the end— before the real end came. He'd hoped for some revelation with the three of them together, but his theories had been neither confirmed nor denied. He watched Yon, fascinated by the questions he raised. Though the boy swung the pickax with fervor—he used only his own muscles. Monks, at least those with training, could tap into their chi just as mages could channel magic. Did Yon refrain because he didn't know how? Did he lack the ability? Was he spiritually exhausted?

Cinq's focus snapped back to the wall when a ray of light emerged in the wake of Yon's blow. Nissa swooped between the two of them to wedge her face against the opening. She whistled. "Daylight! Nothing but sky."

Hollinder laughed. "South of town is Red Canyon. We must be coming out on one of the walls. It's almost straight up in spots."

Nissa said, "Ok, fine. But why is it daytime? Shouldn't it be night? How long have we been down here? It wasn't *that* long."

Cinq shrugged. This wasn't the time to speculate. He and Hollinder took over digging, attacking the wall with renewed vigor. With a few more swings, the rocks tumbled outward instead of in. Sunlight streamed into the tunnel, causing them to cover their eyes. When the hole widened to shoulder width, Nissa stepped forward. She twisted her body to wriggle through the opening and disappeared. Moments later, her feet reappeared and she crawled back inside.

Nissa slapped her hands together to knock loose the dust.

"What did you see?" Cinq asked.

She grinned back. "Oh, it's impressive. I'll have to give it that. And this tunnel was unfinished on purpose."

"What do you mean?" Yon asked.

"I mean, that this is as complete as the tunnel was supposed to be. No one finished it, because that would give the exit away to, oh, I don't know, whoever or whatever might want to come through."

"Like banshees?" Yon suggested.

"Or good old-fashioned thieves." Nissa patted the wall to the right of the opening. "Doesn't matter. There is a ladder running just outside the tunnel. Goes up and down for as far as I could see. Now either that means there are more escape tunnels, or the ladder was over-extended to hide the entrance. Either way, pretty clever."

Cinq nodded. "Do we go up or down?"

Hollinder replied, "There's nothing 'down' to go to. There is a river at the bottom of the canyon, but no one goes down because it's too much trouble to bring anything back up. Going up will take us outside the city walls."

Nissa stuck her head out of the hole for a moment before pulling it back in. "Well, we should get climbing. May be a ways. I'll be back later."

"No. We stick together," Cinq said. "In case something happens." He looked around. "Everyone ready?"

One by one they squeezed through the opening and scurried onto the ladder. As Cinq emerged into the outside air, the great weight of the underground lifted from his shoulders. He breathed deep of cool mountain air and felt the direct sun on his skin. He exhaled, then breathed in again. Even the sound was cleaner out here, not a mumble of endless reverberations. Looking out, the first thing he saw was a wall of cloudless blue sky, so complete and vivid in its nothingness that his mind struggled to adapt after the close quarters of the cave. Far below, the rock wall dropped to a small riverbed. The river was mostly dry save for a trickle of water in the center. On the other side of the canyon, scrub juniper and laurel scattered across the low hills in clusters, before giving way to a great, flat expanse.

Cinq grabbed the rungs of the ladder and pulled himself up. At Nissa's request, no one was to speak until they were safely up top, and so the only sound was the dull clink of boots on metal rungs and the slight breeze. The wikken might not have immediately sensed any banshees, but that didn't mean there weren't a few left behind. And the overlap may seem finished, but they might also have just passed out of it. This was an uncertainty. During an overlap, there wasn't a singular gate between this world and the otherplane. The two worlds existed in the same place and at the same time. Titans and banshees or other deimos crossed over as the barrier grew so thin as to become meaningless. Perhaps banshees were pulled in the wake of the Titan entering; perhaps they simply flocked to follow. But as to how the overlap happened in the first place, that secret—if ever known—was now lost. Cinq once studied under a professor, Master Ascertine, who chased overlaps. Even he had only speculations.

Rung after rung they ascended. The coarse, red sandstone was darkened with lichen in places and water stained in others. In areas where the rock curved inward, mud dauber nests had been built in the protected shelves. Cinq looked over the edge and his stomach tightened. What would happen if the rusted rungs were missing or came loose? He gritted his teeth, kept his head down, and continued upward.

A voice from above. "I see the top," Nissa called down in a stage whisper. "Everybody hanging in ok?" She paused. "Hold tight for a bit. I'll go look."

Nissa glided up the ladder and disappeared over the edge. Her steps were silent, a benefit of going barefoot. Since the day he'd he found her in the cage, she'd never once worn shoes. Cinq had even bought her a pair, which he carried around in case she ever needed them.

Cinq was shaken from his daydream when Nissa reappeared. "All right, come on up. Seems safe."

Cinq, Yon, and Hollinder scaled upward, one by one clambering over the edge to roll on the dusty ground.

"That's it," Hollinder panted. "No more stairs or ladders for me ever. And... holy smokes."

The view from over the cliff had been impressive, but nothing compared to the other side. The four of them turned to gape at the city, which lay below them at the end of a broad, open downslope. Or, more specifically, they saw what remained. The city wall had been ripped down so that only about half was left, which rose and fell in peaks and valleys to be more of an idea of a border than a barrier. The buildings ran the gamut from the obliterated to the partially crumbling. Still others had been swept away entirely. But most interesting of all, the whole town, once colored with the dull red of sandstone, bristled with green. Verdant moss crept on and over the walls, spreading through doorways and across the streets.

Vacant streets.

Yon skipped forward, only to stop abruptly. "Where is everyone? No wagons, no merchants, no goats, no—"

"No bodies," Hollinder finished.

Yon looked at his feet. "No bodies."

Nissa cocked her head. "And no tents. This place was tent city when we came through. Something is super wrong here. We should bail. Take the long way around if we have to, but let's not go down there."

"Because of banshees?" Cinq asked. He reached around to swing his staff from where he'd strapped it against his back.

"No. Time," Nissa replied.

Cinq nodded solemnly. He straightened his long coat, pausing for only a moment to pull the Tracer out for a glance before returning it to his pocket.

Yon looked back and forth between them in confusion. "What are you two talking about? No time for what? What happened here?"

Cinq set his jaw. "It's a lapse. Has to be."

"A what?"

Cinq turned to Yon. "A lapse, where time slips. It can happen during an overlap. You don't think those vines grew overnight, do you?"

Yon looked at the city for a long while before turning back to face them. "I have to get home. Master Shen will know what happened. And if anyone escaped, they must have gone to Open Eye." He dropped his voice low. "There's nowhere else to go."

5

~ Cinq ~

In Cinq's opinion, humanity preferred the familiar to the comfortable. Even during the time of the Pentarch, when the Titans targeted city after city, most people didn't flee. They rebuilt. There were always reasons, of course: access to a river, a harbor, mineral wealth, or favorable soils. Except for Ignaesdale.

The town had been founded at the edge of a desert wedged between an uncrossable canyon and impassable mountains. And why? To be close to a monastery that yearned for solitude. For hundreds of years, the monks of Open Eye lived apart, forging their minds and bodies in austerity. But after the end of the Titans' Age, pilgrims sought out this place as the birthplace of the Pentarch. Ignaesdale was born.

Therein lay the real problem: not the existence of visitors, but too many visitors. Over and over, the Titans proved their attraction to crowds, emotion, and magic. The more you had of one, the greater the chance of an attack. At its most basic, the larger the population, the greater the risk of Titans. A place like Ignaesdale shouldn't see a Titan for generations. But when crowds flocked together, they became a lightning rod. The festival was practically an invitation.

Cinq looked past the ruins to sandstone mountains carved by wind and water. Only yesterday, he had admired the delicate arches and twisted spires. But now, towers had been snapped, rocks lay everywhere, and mountainsides were torn down. Was this a preview of what was to come, or a recollection of centuries past?

The world was ending. Or would end in a few short years. All five of the disciplines agreed on that. The Titans—all the Titans—would return at the time of the Convergence, and not just for a few minutes here and there. No surprise, Cinq mused, that people flocked to these "Festivals of the Pentarch." They idolized the one man who had beaten the Titans back. Cinq patted the Tracer at his side. He needed to remember his own goals. He wasn't here to change minds or guide the masses. He had puzzles of his own before the end came.

Cinq hastened to catch up to the others as they picked through the collapsed buildings and ruined farms of Ignaesdale. Yon and Hollinder led the way, talking low amongst themselves. Occasionally, Yon would dart ahead to leap up and off ledges, or balance on the jumbled rocks. Then, as if remembering himself, he would fall back in line.

Over and over, Cinq's eyes drifted back to the moss-covered city. Part of him was fascinated and wanted to spend weeks studying the phenomenon. The other part wondered just how narrowly they'd escaped. How close had his grand adventure come to being stopped before it began? He shook his head.

When they finally reached the foot of the mountains, the four stopped where the winding road narrowed to a cobbled path. A stone archway crossed the trailhead, covered with runes of the monastic orders. Cinq had never learned to read the monks' writing. He likely never would.

"This is the entrance," Yon said. He grimaced. "We call it the long climb. Believe me, it seems longer the more you do it."

The warmth of sunset bathed the path. Despite the destruction around them, the flagstones were cleanly swept and glowing in the amber light. Had the overlap been only yesterday? Had any of them had a moment to even sleep? He didn't feel like he'd been up for twenty-four hours. Or had they been caught in the lapse as well?

Nissa spoke up. "Well, glad there's still a path. That's a good sign." She cocked her head and squinted at Yon. "How far to the monastery?"

"Not long," Yon replied. "Maybe an hour? My friends and I…" he trailed off, his smile wiped away.

Cinq didn't have to ask why. The events had been so sudden, so terrible, and ended so abruptly that he also found reality hard to absorb.

Nissa took a few steps forward and knelt. "Wait. Is this path… swept?"

Yon nodded. "Of course. Master Shen says we should take pride in our place."

Cinq shook his head. "So, you both built your home to be as far away from people as possible, and yet leave the foyer spotless. Interesting."

Hollinder patted Yon on the shoulder. "Don't listen to them, kid. I think it's a nice gesture."

"No, no, no." Nissa shook her head. "What I'm saying is that after a Titan crushed the town flat, and everyone is now—you know—*gone*, your brothers and sisters or whatevers thought the best use of time was to *tidy up?* Doesn't that seem odd?"

Yon brightened. "Well, maybe it's a good sign. Maybe the Titan didn't make it this far." His eyes lit up. "Maybe everyone's ok and waiting for us!"

Cinq tugged his hat down tighter on his head. "Maybe. Or the lapse wasn't confined to the city. Either way, we should keep moving. A clean path isn't an open door." He nodded at Yon. "And I'd like to hear what we should expect."

"What do you mean?"

Nissa said, "Tell us a bit about the homestead."

"Oh, sure. Of course." Yon started forward, passing through the arch with a nod of his head in deference. "I guess for starters, it's not that busy anymore. Open Eye—that's the real name—used to be packed. I hear only the lucky ones had a mat to sleep on. Master Shen said when the Titans started coming back, people quit showing up to train. There are only sixty of us now."

Hollinder asked, "And what do you do all day?" He made a face. "Don't look at me like that. I've never been up here."

Nissa said, "It's a fair question."

Yon laughed. "Well, we study, and we work, and we sleep. Townies probably think that's boring."

"Wait. *Townies?*" Hollinder nearly choked. "You call us townies?"

Nissa stepped between them. "That's what we called 'em too. Don't be so fragile. But, Yon, you left out 'eat.'"

The monk answered, "For the most part, we eat while we study. We rotate who serves, who speaks, and who listens. There's a lot to learn. You see, it's not really about you as a person."

Nissa let out a guffaw. "Now that's too much. What do you *mean* it's not all about you? I thought the whole point of monks was a lot of navel-gazing to find yourself in the world. You ignore anything that *isn't* about you."

Yon bowed his head. "We focus on ourselves and our spirit as a matter of humility. I mean, yes, we learn to focus and control our chi, but only because it is not ok to meddle in the spirits of others. We need to be able to understand how small we are."

Nissa nodded in mock-solemnity. "Ah, yes, young master Yon. I completely see how learning to punch through boulders is a matter of humility."

Yon's face reddened. He protested, "We don't really punch—"

Cinq cleared his throat. "Can you two focus? Yon, I want to know if there'll be trouble. Are they going to have a problem with me as a mage? Or Nissa as a wikken? Will we get the same reception the reavers showed us?"

Nissa interjected, "The stabby kind?"

"Exactly," Cinq said. "Will they even let us in? *Those* are the things we need to know." He paused. "Yon, are you ok?"

All frustration had drained from the monk's face, replaced by a blanched look of terror. "They… they didn't know I was in town. I snuck out! I'm going to be in so much trouble."

Hollinder rubbed his chin. "Well, the festival is a good time. Usually."

Yon shook his head. "No. You don't understand. That's not something they get over. I've gotten caught twice already and this will be my third time, and they could kick me out, or—"

Nissa put a hand on Yon's shoulder. "Easy, easy there, breathe. Perspective. Total destruction of town mean anything? I don't think kids sneaking out is a big deal anymore. Take it from an expert on getting in trouble, there are bigger things to worry about."

Yon bit his lip. "I don't know. I should go ahead and let them know you're coming. It's… it's better that way."

Before Cinq could protest, the young monk took off at a desperate run. He disappeared so quickly that the rest of them were left staring blankly at one another. With a shrug, Cinq followed. As he climbed, he thought about what he knew about the monks. They were both cousins and opposites of the mages. Mages used their knowledge of magic as an external force to manipulate the world around them. For monks, that control was internal. They focused their chi to sculpt the power within them. Skilled monks could do remarkable things, feats rivaling mages, if not different in execution. For mages, conversely, the chi was a distraction, an interference with their clinical observance of the world. The monks called mages arrogant; the mages thought monks narcissistic.

Cinq knew Open Eye tolerated the other disciplines out of respect for the Pentarch's legacy. Similarly, Eastwind Tower, where Cinq had studied, was amenable to visiting monks, wikken, scholars, and hermits. That had been before the reavers. Now, distrust of outsiders was the rule.

Up they went, along the immaculate path. No signs of rockfall, no signs that the Earth Titan had reached this stretch of mountain. And maybe it hadn't. Maybe the entity had only focused on the town. At the end of the path, Cinq saw another stone arch, a mirror of the first one. Seven kinds of stone, each brought from the foundations of other monasteries, interlocked with one another. The capstone bore the rune of the Open Eye. Cinq felt a twinge of excitement to see another facet of the Pentarch's history.

Beneath the archway, a great iron gate was closed across the path. Yon knelt motionless on the stone in front of it, his head bowed and hands clasped in front of him. Cinq did not disturb him. As a mage, he had only a cursory understanding of a monk's customs. But he recognized ritual when he saw it. Ten minutes passed. And though Yon did not flinch, the rest of them began to fidget. Nissa, oddly, was the exception. As mercurial as the wikken could be, she sat cross-legged, hands folded in her lap, and remained motionless.

When Cinq's patience had nearly expired, he heard footsteps from ahead. Three monks approached, their clean-shaven heads making age difficult to ascertain. The monks' faces remained impassive, betraying no hint of emotion at being reunited with Yon. Like Yon, they were dressed in chestnut brown mendicant's robes, though atop the robes were sculpted bronze plates threaded together as armor. Dressed for battle. Interesting. He watched as the welcome party came to a stop on the other side of the arch. The monk in the center spoke.

"State your business," he barked.

Yon's head snapped up, then he averted his gaze. The worlds tumbled from his mouth. "I am Initiate Yon. I apologize for my lateness. I was outside the cloister during the festival. These people and I made it to one of the shelters. We didn't dare return to the town, so I led them here. There are more people still in the shelter. We… we were sent ahead to make sure things were safe."

There was a long, long pause. The monks shifted and looked at each other. Finally, the middle monk replied, "And which festival is that, initiate? What is your temple?"

Yon raised his eyes once more. He glanced back at his companions. His eyes reflected confusion. "*The* festival. The Festival of the Pentarch." He hesitated. "I'm sorry, but who are you? Are you visiting?" Yon's voice became strained. "I… I need to speak to the abbot."

Another pause, this one stretching to the point of discomfort. The lead monk frowned deeply. "Yes. I believe that is for the best."

Yon, Nissa, Hollinder, and Cinq were led single file through the archway and up a series of staircases that were half outside of the temple and half-carved into the cliff walls. Cinq watched Yon carefully. An itch crept across his skin. The young monk was separated from the rest of them, following behind the elder, with the two other monks trailing behind. And though Yon stayed dutifully close to the leader, the long looks he took at cracked walls, ruined buildings, and empty pedestals showed his discomfort.

As they walked, they were watched. At every turn, Cinq saw another armed and armored monk standing just out of the way.

Some held spears, others nocked bows, and they all appeared on edge. What did they expect? That the four of them would turn into Titans themselves? Or perhaps they thought they were banshees, or some other deimos masquerading as men. Did they suspect them to be reaver spies? And if so, why the mistrust of Yon? He was one of them.

Nissa sidled up to Cinq. She whispered, "Is your weirdness alarm going off yet?"

"Loudly," he replied. "You ready to move if we need to?"

"Like a jackrabbit. But we'll need to all get out together. Yon too." She gritted her teeth. "So why are we going deeper?"

"We need answers—"

"And this isn't the *only* place to get them," Nissa finished. "I can see you mumbling, Cinq. Cooking up something magic?"

"I want to be ready," he said. "But I'm not fully recovered. Which means…"

Nissa nodded. "I got it. No magical bailout. We're on our own."

"Exactly. So if your friends can help, even with just a distraction, that would be welcome. If we need it."

The lead monk turned another stairway and led them into a domed chamber that had sunlight streaming in from high windows that cut over rows of lit, yellow candles. The light from both cast refracted patterns on the floor. The monks whispered to Yon, bowed, then pivoted to leave. The boy turned to face his companions; his face blanched.

"Spill it," Nissa urged.

Yon opened his mouth once, closed it again. The words tumbled out. "I don't recognize them. *None* of them. And I would, you know. There aren't that many of us. And they didn't know who I was either. Do you think this is another… what did you call it? A lapse? Like what happened in town? I thought we were far enough away?"

Cinq didn't have a chance to answer. The door opened and the three monks appeared again, this time trailed by an elder stooped with age. Unlike the others, he wasn't wearing armor, a hint of his importance. But most telling of all was that the man had a long wisp of a beard drifting from his chin. Only a monastery's abbot was allowed a beard, whereas for mages they were ubiquitous, practically mandatory. They had been given an audience to the man in charge.

The abbot spoke. "You are Yon? And you say you studied here?" The abbot settled into a lotus position and folded his hands into the opposite sleeves. "I must hear your tale."

Yon spoke quickly. And though Cinq could tell he was shaken, the boy recounted how he had gone into town for the festival, escaped when the Titan arrived, and later found the city abandoned. All this time the abbot said nothing. When Yon finished, he looked up expectantly.

"And your companions? I would hear their stories as well," the abbot said.

Cinq gripped his staff between his hands. "I think that's enough from our side. You know something we don't."

The abbot nodded. "Yes. And given our situation, I understand how etiquette and tradition are difficult to maintain, even for the esteemed mages. I'll be direct. You wish to know what happened after the Titan attacked Ignaesdale?"

Nissa interjected, "I want to know *when* it attacked."

The old monk said, "Five years ago, on the summer solstice. It is now the third week of November, in the year three-oh-five A.P."

Cinq stiffened. He'd been bracing for this. He'd guessed that the town had been caught in a lapse, a displacement of time—now he knew the bunker hadn't escaped unscathed. This, he mused, would seriously affect his plans. This meant the Convergence was less than three years away. The end of the world felt close indeed. He fought to control his expression.

Yon asked, "But what about the town? It looks like no one has been there for a lifetime. And where are my friends? Or Master Shen? Where is everyone?"

The abbot nodded solemnly. "The Earth Titan and the deimos left no survivors. The great masters sent runners when we heard of the event. From what we found, we believe the temple was overrun by banshees. My brothers and I were sent to investigate." The abbot's voice lowered. "We gave the fallen a proper burial, as was their due. And now we are honored with the task of restoring the Pentarch's home."

Yon crumpled where he stood. His knees dropped to the floor, splayed out to each side. His head dropped to his chest. Nissa darted forward to put her hands on his shoulders. She whispered something into his ear.

Cinq set his jaw. "And Ignaesdale? What happened there?"

"We aren't certain. But no one who enters returns. That is all. And all we dare to question." He turned to Cinq. "Some of your brethren came to us not long ago. They suggested letting the magic run its course."

Cinq said, "That *does* sound like them."

The abbot continued, "You must know, the mage's council wasn't only interested in the Titan, even when it came to the old home of the Pentarch. They were also quite concerned if a particular mage has been sighted within the town." The abbot tapped his fingers together. "The question was put to me very, very clearly. If I was to ever find this mage in the ruins, I was to alert them immediately."

Cinq shifted in place. "Did they give you a name? Perhaps I knew him."

The abbot pursed his lips in mild amusement. "I would say that you should, Cinq LeGarrec. At least I assume that's you?" The abbot turned. "And you must be Nissa al'Cedar. You are quite... as described."

Cinq's fingers tightened around his staff. If they knew his *and* Nissa's names, then they were being followed more closely than he thought. He exhaled slowly. "These men, they weren't just... concerned about us?"

The abbot kept his voice low. "They implied you had taken something—though they did not accuse outright. So perhaps it was something else." He smiled. "Since I don't know if you are criminals or heroes, etiquette dictates I treat you as guests." The old man rose to his feet. "And as you have had a very, very long day. Please eat, rest, and we will speak more in the morning. Much has happened while you've been away."

Nissa took a step forward. She'd shown restraint up to this point, but she wouldn't be dismissed so easily. "Ok, so let's just say that we got caught in a lapse. Five and a half years and— *fffflllipppt*—time flies when you're having fun. What're a few more minutes at this point? *So...* what did we miss? And I'm just going to throw this out there, a lot of you are wearing armor. Like, way more than I'd expect. You got a reaver problem, or something else?"

The abbot grimaced, causing Cinq's pulse to hasten.

"Well, my lady, suffice it to say, the world has changed. Our kind is no longer given their due. I will tell you everything, but first I must meditate on what you have said. We will speak again in the morning. You will need rest for what is ahead."

6

~ Yon ~

Yon stared at the smoldering coals. His soul had been ripped from his body and cast into pieces, not unlike the shambles left by the Earth Titan. For the monks—these new monks—time had healed the wound. But for him, he'd lost his friends and family only yesterday. He hated being in this guest room. He hated the luxury of couches, an open fireplace, and broad glass windows. He longed to return to his small, shared quarters and the straw pallet within. To be back with his friends. Now, he was a stranger. Homeless, within his own home.

Outside, the sky shone with cold stars cut by the silhouette of mountains. Cinq, Nissa, and Hollinder sat beside Yon, cross-legged or reclining. They didn't seem any more inclined to sleep than him. The monks had given them food, blankets, and shelter, but too much had happened to relax. And at least for Yon, he wasn't even sure what time his body thought it was. Had they lost time in complete years or months? What about hours? When was it, really? He sighed. It didn't matter.

Yon held out his hands. He studied the wrinkles of his knuckles and the flicker of the coals. His head swam. Open Eye was his home—had been his home—for as long as he could remember. He would wake to carry water, scrub the stairs, scour pots, play with his friends, and enact the rituals of meditation, training, and memorization. He'd been happy, he supposed. He'd never thought about being happy before, but now with everything stripped away but the walls and himself, he understood what he'd lost. The monks had been his family, even if he had never known his parents. Sometimes they fought, sometimes they grumbled, and they had their share of squabbles, but they always belonged.

And now what? In the space of a night, everyone was gone. Dead, all of them. The word tasted dry and bitter. Absence clawed at his belly. It pushed down the back of his neck and against his temples. His home was now a husk inhabited by dim reflections of the monks he'd known. Yon felt he'd been replaced too.

When they'd first arrived at the guest quarters, Yon had cried to exhaustion on the balcony. He knew monks weren't supposed to cry, but they all did from time to time. But no one ever spoke of it. Not during, not after. And when the decidedly un-monastic monk gathered himself together and returned to his work, those who had once been in the same place treated him with dignity. The tears were now gone, though the bitterness remained.

Cinq cleared his throat, eliciting looks from Yon, Nissa, and Hollinder. "All right, everyone, you've been patient. You should know that this has happened before. I'm hoping that will make it easier now. I'm talking about time."

Yon's mind focused, though the words didn't make sense. He looked over at Nissa, who winked back at him.

She said, "Brace yourselves, here comes Cinq with a scientific explanation—all designed to soothe in his clinical way." She shifted around. "Is there somewhere private we can go?"

Yon was confused. "More private than this?"

"I don't know, somewhere we weren't specifically told to go. In case someone is listening."

Yon said, "Yeah, I can think of a place. Follow me."

He led the others out of the guest quarters and up steps built into and carved from the mountainside. They encountered a patrol of two armored monks, who nodded as they passed. He climbed until they reached a flattened courtyard ringed on all sides by a low wall. Yon had spent hours here sparring with his brothers. And there was nowhere to hide if someone was trying to listen in. He lit one of the lanterns in the courtyard and turned to face Nissa. "Is this better?"

"Works for me. Open air is my friend." She winked. "I've been in a cave for five years."

Cinq murmured, "Ok, then. Where was I? Time and reality and everything in between. Abridged version. This will help with—as Nissa said—context." The mage drew a circle in the dirt with the base of his staff. "This is the world. Our world. The nearplane." He tapped with his staff, pointing at items unseen. "Trees, rocks, mountains, people, cities, everything." Cinq drew a second circle next to the first so that the edges just touched. "And this is the world of the fey, what we call the otherplane. It has its own trees, rocks, mountains, and whatevers. No one knows. I'm drawing two circles, but for all we know there could be more worlds as well."

Nissa huffed. "That's not the point though, is it?"

Cinq ignored her. "The position of our two worlds relative to one another is not fixed. Most of the time, they are apart. Wholly apart and ignorant of one another. Though there are areas," he tapped where the circles touched, "where they are *adjacent.*" He tightened his jaw. "Now all that changes during an overlap. Maybe it is *because of* the overlap, or maybe it is what *causes* the overlap. When that happens, the worlds are more like this." Cinq wiped the circles clean, then drew two more in their place. This time they overlapped one another slightly.

Nissa chirped, "Titans love diagrams."

"What?" Yon squinted over at her.

Cinq said, "Ignore her. Best to get in the habit. The important thing is that our planes of existence become close for a brief time, metaphysically speaking. And when that happens, aspects of one bleed into the other. Things pass through."

Hollinder nodded. "Banshees. Deimos. Titans. You don't have to convince me."

Cinq continued, "The creatures of the otherplane are a piece of that, but there's more to it. Our world merges into theirs, just as theirs does into ours. And during this *overlap,* not only do our spaces coexist, but our times do as well. One time can wash or flow into another. What's more, the closeness can allow for leaps in space and leaps in time. Crossing the lines of influence from here," Cinq pointed at one overlap of the circles, "to here, to here." He tapped his staff across the diagram. "Now this will become more frequent, and nearly complete, as we approach the Convergence."

"I think I've lost you," Yon confessed. "I don't think we are using the word 'time' in the same way."

Cinq sat down once more, laying his staff on the ground. "Ok. Let's try this a different way." He held his palm flat and, with two fingers, methodically tapped against his palm. "Consider these are passing days. One. Two. Three. Four. Now you do it."

Yon held his hand open. "One. Two. Three. Four."

"Keep counting. Don't stop. But let's say we aren't at the same pace. Maybe I go fast. One-two-three-four."

Nissa piped up, "And I go slow. One… two… three… four."

Cinq nodded. "Those are the passing days in the other worlds. And when the worlds overlap, who's to say what happens, and who wins, and who loses?"

Yon nodded dully. "Ok. I guess."

Cinq struck his staff down on the dirt. "Let's bring it back to here and now. We were caught in a lapse—thankfully temporarily—and lost *five years*. Now at some point, we crossed back into our world's normal time flow, even if we couldn't feel it. At first, I thought it was just the town that was caught in a lapse, but it was all of us."

Hollinder snorted. "Back up, Cinq. We were underground for five years?"

Nissa answered, "A bit more, according to the abbot. Or to be more specific, we were there for a few hours. It's just the rest of the world moved on without us. Think of it this way, you are now younger and prettier than your friends."

Hollinder cocked his head. "Sorry... remind me why you're an expert? I mean he's a mage. I saw that with my own eyes. But who are you? And how do you know about this stuff?"

Nissa locked eyes with Hollinder. "I'm a wikken. I know things."

"That's enough, Nissa."

"You're a *real* wikken?" Hollinder asked.

Nissa rolled her eyes. "Do I look like I'm faking it? You think they just give these runes out?" She gestured at the markings over her arms and legs. "Didn't you see me listening for banshees down in the bunker? I mean, come on."

"I assumed it was for the festival. That you were just dressing up."

"Ok. I'll make this simple." Nissa pointed to her chest, then Cinq then Yon. "Real wikken, real mage, real monk. Got it?"

Cinq muttered, "Nissa, are you done?"

"Am now. Were you getting to your point?"

Yon asked, "Are we safe here?"

Cinq replied, "Safe from the lapse? Probably. But that's not really what I wanted to talk about. I was just setting some context."

Nissa's eyes lit up. "Oh... this is 'the talk.' Why didn't you just say so? I'll help." She turned to Yon. "Long story short, time is squishier than you think. And as Cinq said, it's happened before. So, here's the big question, and this one's just for you. What's the first thing you remember? Not like, from this morning. I mean *ever*. And don't say you don't know. We're way past that."

Yon swallowed hard. The question might be meaningless for most people, but not for him. He remembered the day exactly. The angle of the shadows from the rocks, the dry, still air. The wisp of clouds above. He bowed his head. "I remember the steps. I remember the arch. I remember the monks yelling and pointing and asking questions. I was nine, I think. At least, that's what they guessed."

Nissa pressed, "And nothing before that? Absolutely nothing?"

"No—and I tried too. We used to do this thing where we'd try and remember stuff. Some of my friends could go a *long* way back. They could remember learning to walk, that sort of thing. But not me."

Cinq nodded. "My story is the same. I don't remember anything before arriving at Eastwind Tower. Five years ago for me, and about your age now."

Nissa chirped, "And I came to on the streets of Gorenheim when I was ten. No idea how I got there either. No memories, no nothing, complete blank."

Cinq continued, "We're riftborn, Yon. All three of us."

Yon was familiar with the term. Whenever a Titan manifested, people sometimes disappeared. Most were never seen again, but some of those people *re*appeared. Usually lost, confused, and a long way away—or a long time away. Days, months, and years had passed. Most couldn't remember anything, or maybe just the Titan. Yon had always wondered if maybe he was riftborn, or just had a poor memory. Since the monks never spoke of someone's life from before the monastery, it had been a moot point.

"I guess I knew…" Yon murmured.

Nissa smiled softly. "It's tough to know for sure if you were young. But sometimes that's better."

Yon pointed at Cinq's coat. "This comes back to the Tracer, doesn't it? That's what you're getting to."

Cinq retrieved the sphere and held it up to the starlight. "I've spent two years studying this. And if the archives at Eastwind were right, this relic is from the time of the Pentarch. You see, for hundreds of years there was only one light within, not five. And that light was so dim and inconsistent it couldn't be followed. Then, twenty-five years ago, a second light appeared. And on the *exact* day I showed up at Eastwind Tower, a third light appeared, and a fourth a few months later." Cinq studied the glow inside. "The fifth light appeared a year after the fourth." Cinq tucked the Tracer away. "I now know that each light was a person. I was number three, Nissa was number four, and you are number five."

Yon was too stunned to reply. Did that mean he was from the time of the Pentarch as well?

Hollinder clapped his hands, a smile wide on his face. "Hah! And I thought I was old. You telling me you three are hundreds of years old? That's a bit hard to believe."

Cinq frowned. "I don't see why. You just experienced it yourself. What's five years, or a decade, or a century when we are talking about the Titans and the otherplane? Maybe it was an overlap. Maybe it was something else. Remember that time is more like a river, curving and twisting, sometimes slow, and sometimes dropping fast." He straightened his coat. "There are many documented cases… even if not quite so lengthy."

Yon ventured, "But the Tracer? Why is that Tracer tracking *us*?"

Cinq sighed. "We went over this before."

"You… you don't know! Do you? No. No, you don't." He groaned. "I thought you were kidding!"

Nissa laughed. "Take it easy, monkey. Oh, I like that. Monk-ee."

"Do *not* call me monkey!"

Nissa raised her hands. "Ok, ok, I won't. Relax. Cinq, can you make this easier?"

Cinq nodded. "You said something back in the bunker, 'important lost things.' We know that much. That the mages of Eastwind are looking for me—or maybe just the Tracer—confirms we're important. We are gaining pieces of the puzzle—and it's a puzzle I intend to solve. It's why I took the Tracer in the first place."

Silence stretched between them. Yon felt Cinq and Nissa's eyes weigh heavy on him, though Hollinder's expression was more of bemused curiosity. Yon wasn't sure how to respond. He was from another time. So was Cinq, so was Nissa. He'd always been from nowhere. But so were most of the monks. He'd thrived, though. He had talent, more than his friends. But now, they were all gone.

Nissa raised her hand. "Hi. Um, not to interrupt, but, um, you know how you said people were looking for us?"

Cinq nodded. "The abbot said as much. And there were the posters back in Ignaesdale."

"Right." Nissa winced. "What if I told you that maybe we've been found. At least, that's what I heard."

Cinq asked, "Heard from who? Your friends? What do you know?"

Nissa turned and pointed across the mountainside. Cinq, Yon, and Hollinder hurried to look. Yon viewed past the edge of the cliff, past the ruined town, and out into the western desert. In the clear evening, the light of the stars painted a crystalline tapestry, only diminishing where the silhouettes of hills and mountains etched against the sky. But below, in the valley, the light shone dull and red. Yon's stomach knotted as he saw the long, thin procession of torches. A great many people were coming, and they were close, winding past Ignaesdale and moving to the doorstep of Open Eye.

"Yon, is that normal 'round here?" Nissa asked. "Maybe the kind of thing you see all the time that we shouldn't be *at all* worried about? And not, say, something creepy and ominous."

He tightened his jaw. "No. Other than the festival, no one ever comes here."

Hollinder said, "I recognize those lines from my military days. One, two, three across and spread out. That means reavers."

Yon swallowed hard. Hollinder was right. From an early age, they'd all been taught to watch for the signs. Armies worried about magical attacks didn't march in tight formation, to minimize the damage from a lightning bolt, explosion, or other unpleasantness. But there were too many of them. That wasn't a band of reavers, it was an army. Yon had never imagined such a thing here.

Cinq mused, "That *might* be reading a lot into some torches. But it begs the question, Yon."

"What question?"

The mage tapped the Tracer in his pocket. "We asked you once if you would come with us. So, what have you decided?" He paused. "Because I don't think it's safe for you here. For any of us."

Yon felt a rush of blood to his ears. His stomach knotted. Not long ago he'd thought about going with Cinq and Nissa because he had nowhere else to go. Now, it seemed he couldn't stay if he wanted.

Nissa pointed down at the procession of torches. "Yon, I don't think that's an accident. Whoever those people are, the fey don't think they're friendly."

Yon's head swam. "The fey?" He looked behind him.

Cinq tapped his chin. "Let's say for argument's sake they are reavers. How do they know we're here? We haven't seen anyone all day. And who could have told them? A spy among the monks? Or someone watching the city? They have to have known somehow."

Yon shouted, "But we don't even know why!"

Nissa said, "Yoo-hoo, guys? What's the plan? Do we run?"

Down the slope, in the main part of the monastery, a gong rang. Another answered it, then a third, until peals filled the air. Torches ignited along the walls and walkways. Monks appeared from every door. Yon felt a current run up his spine, spreading over his skin in a low, persistent buzz. There would be no hiding away, no hoping this would end. Coming here was a grasp at safety, normalcy. But that was only a passing hope.

Cinq kept his voice even. "Yon, I can't give you all the answers, because I don't have them. All I have are theories, but I'm *not* telling you anything a reaver might pry out of you later—if that's what they are. We'll likely fail without you, but it's still your decision to come or not." He exhaled deeply. "But if you're coming, we need to get out of here fast."

Yon closed his eyes. He opened them to look at Cinq and Nissa's sincere faces. "Ok, I'm in. And when we get away, no more secrets?"

The mage hesitated for a moment. "I'll tell you everything I know."

Hollinder cracked his knuckles. "That settles it, I'm coming too."

Cinq looked at the metal-toothed man. "You're not part of this. Not unless you want to be. You sure you want to get in the middle of all this?"

"I'm already in the middle of this. And I can't very well go home. Plus, you'll need someone to ground you fruity magic types."

Nissa smiled. "Peachy. A big, happy family. But how about step one: running away? Master monk, this is your home turf. Any great ideas to get us out of here? How did you sneak out last time?"

A slow grin crept across Yon's face. "Down the garbage chute. But first we have to see the abbot. He knows something… and I've got something better in mind."

The gong rang out, again, and again. And now the rousing monks were shouting to one another. Open Eye was awake.

The reavers were coming.

7

~ Yon ~

Yon led the way back down the maze of staircases. This time, they passed frantic monks scurrying up and down the stairs or pacing along the tiered walls of the monastery. All around was the buzz of energy as the monks focused their chi. After a stop at their quarters, they gathered their few possessions, waterskins, and some rope.

Once equipped, the four of them hurried to the abbot's quarters. Surrounding the entryway, a half dozen monks were busy securing armor, even as others raced off with urgency. Yon approached the main door, where a single guard stood in front. Her hair was drawn up over her head in a bun that cascaded thin tendrils across her face. Her taut arms were folded across her chest.

Yon lowered his eyes. "I need to see the abbot."

She did not break her gaze as she stepped aside. "Of course, initiate. He's expecting you."

Yon hurried through the door with his friends trailing him. After crossing the threshold, he skidded to a stop. He bowed his head and folded his hands behind his back. The abbot was already inside. He held a lamplighter in one hand which he used to ignite the candles lining the ledge below each window.

"Come in," the abbot said. "Time is short."

"Hi." Nissa smiled as she stepped past Yon. "I hope all this isn't because of us."

The abbot raised an eyebrow. "This is precisely because of you, but I am not surprised. The essence of the human spirit can anticipate action against it. To the chi, time is only a guide, not a master. Your young friend could tell you that. It is something I have spent these hours contemplating."

Nissa wrinkled her nose. "You *knew* an army was coming? Why didn't you tell us before?"

The abbot's eyes sharpened. "Possibility is not certainty. I felt conflict rising and swelling. But a tide that could fall just as quickly. And you needed rest, if only for a moment. Would sleep have come easier if you knew the reaver army was coming?"

Yon dropped to one knee. "Master, there's something I have to ask you. We need to escape. I thought perhaps," his stomach knotted, "we could use the waygates." The words spilled from his mouth. "Master Shen said they were there for an emergency. Maybe that's today."

The abbot became very still. "That is a very serious, and very dangerous request. But perhaps you're right." He turned to Cinq. "Mage LeGarrec, do you have it with you? I need to see it for myself." The abbot held out his wrinkled palm.

Cinq fidgeted for a moment before reaching into his long coat to extract the Tracer. He tapped the surface to set the lights in motion and handed it to the abbot.

Gingerly, the old monk took the Tracer in his hands. "It's true. One of the prime set, back again at Open Eye after its sister was lost." He turned the sphere in his hands to inspect it. "It's one of five, you know. One for each discipline—monk, mage, wikken, scholar, and hermit. The Tracers were given to five keepers so that no one sect would have all the power, for though we stood together, the Pentarch did not trust us apart. This one was all but forgotten, the others lost, or as ours was, kept a close secret."

Cinq spoke, his voice strained. "And you know what it follows? Why is it so important?"

The monk smiled. "*So* important? Such words do not suffice. I should say this is the *most* important. The five Tracers of the prime set lead to five keys, one key given to each discipline. The keys have been hidden since the time of the Pentarch, and only the Tracers can find them again. You unknowingly stole a compass to the greatest power the world has ever known. And now you must keep it safe. Safe from them." The abbot paused. He looked from Yon to Nissa to Cinq. "Ah, I see. You aren't thieves at all… *you* are the keys. Three of the five… together again." His face wrinkled in concern. "I can't let him get to you first."

A monk in battle-garb burst through the door. His brow shone with perspiration. As soon as he entered the chamber, he glared at the four of them before dropping to a knee.

"Your holiness, the reavers are at the arch. What are your orders?"

The abbot pressed the Tracer into Cinq's hands. He turned to face the warrior. "Take three men. Wait at the arch. Learn their demands, but do not let them enter. Delay them at all costs—and do not strike unless they do. There may still be a way to resolve this."

"Yes, master." The monk disappeared in a flurry of robes.

Nissa raised her hand. "I'm sorry. But could you back up just a moment? Keys to unspeakable power? Want to expand on that?"

The abbot whipped his head to stare at Nissa. "Not just keys, *the* keys. The legacy of the Pentarch and our last chance, not just against the reavers, but the Titans themselves. The reavers must not find you. They must not bring you to him." The abbot adjusted his belt. "Initiate Yon, I accept your request. All of you, follow me. Quickly. We must get you out."

Nissa protested, "Follow you where? What are you talking about? Did you hear me? I want to know what's going on."

Cinq tucked the Tracer back into his coat. "Nissa, for once, just listen."

The abbot turned and walked briskly to the far side of the chamber where a dark-blue tapestry hung against the wall. He brushed the cloth across to reveal a narrow opening, which disappeared into the dark below. "Hurry."

Yon's heart surged. Of all the legends and tales of the monastery, he wondered if he was going to see one of its secrets: an artifice built in the days of legend. He went through the entryway, nearly stumbling as the passage turned into a narrow stairway. They twisted lower and lower, dropping first into darkness before light from below grew up and crept across the staircase walls. They spilled into a perfectly round chamber with a low ceiling, about thirty feet across. Cinq, Nissa, and Hollinder arrived behind Yon, with the abbot last.

Cinq broke the silence. "A wayroom. I thought they'd been destroyed."

"They should have been," the abbot said. He flipped his beard and gestured around him. "The magics are too wild to be left unattended. It is a sin of my order that we left this one intact."

"Then why did you?" Cinq asked.

The abbot replied, "To destroy a wayroom is to mar the spirit of a place. Open Eye is sacred ground. We cannot desecrate the birthplace of the Pentarch. It is his memory that may one day unite us again. And it is in his memory, and to preserve his legacy, that I bring you here."

Nissa asked, "So what? We hide out down here?"

"No. The witchlord and his men would find you easily. But your journey must continue. I feel it in my spirit."

Nissa threw her hands in the air. "The *witchlord?* What the heck is a—?"

The abbot continued without responding. "Not now. I must leave so that I can't betray where you have gone. There is only one more thing I must tell you." His face grew dark. "The world *has* changed in the past five years. Don't assume that your kind will find welcome. Wikken, mages, and even monks are no longer shown the respect they once commanded. The reavers are no longer just an infection of thoughts, they have united. And they have their hooks everywhere. Don't assume your friends are still your friends."

Nissa asked, "But you are? We're supposed to just trust you?"

"That you must decide for yourself. But do not let that Tracer, or yourselves, fall into the wrong hands. Now… go!" The abbot strode to the center of the room. He reached upward, his fingers nearly scraping the top of the low ceiling. As he closed his fist, it ignited with ethereal blue light. In a single, vicious stroke, he struck down, hitting the floor with a muffled crack. The light sparked from the point of impact in all directions, streaking across the floor until it hit the walls. As it did, Yon saw that the walls were not the dull stone they appeared to be. Each was a mirror, oval-shaped, tall as a man, and as wide as their shoulders. When the light hit the mirrors, the rims glowed, and the surface rippled like water.

The abbot bowed once. Before anyone could speak, he had disappeared from the room and back up the stairs.

Yon spun around. "How does it work? Do we just pick one? How do we know which one to choose? Where do they go?"

Nissa paced the room, looking at each in turn. "You don't know? Isn't this a monk thing? Shouldn't you know?"

Cinq held up a finger. He walked to the center of the room. "Yon, Nissa, come close." Yon skipped forward, Nissa close behind, while Hollinder paced the room, studying the mirrors in turn. Cinq removed the Tracer; all five lights shone brightly. Three were predictably clustered around Nissa, Cinq, and himself, but the other two shone fiercely as well. Cinq walked forward, the Tracer outstretched as he followed the two points of light. "This one," he pointed ahead, "or that one. Nissa, which way?"

The wikken accepted the Tracer from Cinq. She held her palm in front of the first mirror. She repeated the action on the second mirror as well. She said, "This one is… quieter. Maybe not safer. But not as loud."

Yon was about to ask what she meant when he heard a shout coming from upstairs and the rumble of boots against the floor.

Hollinder said, "They're here."

"Pick, Nissa. We're running out of time."

She closed her eyes tight and shook her head. "This… this one. Join hands."

Together, they stepped into the mirror.

8

~ Cain ~

Mortimer Cain passed beneath the arch leading onto the monastery grounds. A twitch of memory nearly caused him to kneel but he pushed the feeling aside, and with it, the urge to vomit. He was disgusted with himself, but more so at what the arch represented. Tradition and habit were powerful, yet if the world was to survive, such relics must be discarded. Cain looked at the insignia of Open Eye. This was the home of the Pentarch centuries ago. And this was where the hermit predicted the keys would resurface. For as many lies as his old master told, he had been right about that one. The hermit had predicted it within a few days. And if Cain ever returned to the old man's prison, perhaps he would thank him.

Behind him, his men's torches lit up the muted sandstone, painting it dark red. The men making up the vanguard trailed behind him as ordered. The long tail of soldiers wound down the mountainside like a river caught in the light of the setting sun. This many of his reavers weren't necessary for this task. He hoped. Monks were dangerous, but they could be dealt with. The important thing was not to slaughter them too soon. At least, not until he got what he came for.

He pulled the crystal sphere from the pouch at his side. The lights of the Tracer had burned for only a day, and now they were dark once more. The keys had left, but these monks would know who they were. They could let him know what he was dealing with. Were the keys masters of their disciplines? Should they be feared and contained? Or were they doddering old men? Or infants? Or gods?

Cain drew his broad, curved sword and laid it on the ground. He placed his short dagger alongside it. Visibly disarmed, he walked forward toward the three monks, leaving his reavers behind. The monks, with fists raised and auras burning, glared at him.

"I'm here to see the abbot," Cain declared. He continued forward, and though one of the monks moved to block him, he sidestepped the man neatly. These fools were crippled by their traditions. If he had no weapons, and if he made no move to strike, they wouldn't touch him. He continued up the path, weaving through the monks until reaching the door to the abbot's chambers. Only one guard remained, a wiry woman with cold steel in her eyes.

"The abbot isn't receiving visitors."

Cain looked left, right, then back at his soldiers. "Of course he is. I know all about his visitors." He smiled. "And I know they've already gone. Ask again."

The guard shuffled in place. She gripped the spear in her hands. She wanted to attack. Oh, how she wanted it. But she was as crippled as the rest of them. The guard was rescued by a voice calling from beyond the door.

"Let him pass."

Cain smiled thinly as she stepped aside. He called back to his men on the steps below. "You hear that? We've been invited." He gestured with one hand, and the soldiers started filing in through the great arch. He didn't wait to make sure they were in position. He pushed through the door to enter the abbot's chambers. Despite how much had changed since his exile, he still felt the tug against his memories, triggering thoughts of deference and respect. He looked at the geometric tiles on the ground, the tall, thin windows, and the lit candles lining the walls. The last must be a shrine to those monks lost to the Titan. Good riddance. As much as he hated the Titans, as much as he sought to end them, they shared his hatred of witches.

Before him stood the abbot. The monk's hands were behind his back and his feet at shoulder width. The witch had the same look of superiority that all monks did. Cain spat on the floor. Monks were the worst. The mages were bad enough, they all thought they *knew* better than you. But the monks—they thought they *were* better than you. And in Cain's case, they were probably right. The price he paid to be an agent of change.

As one last double-check, Cain glanced at the Tracer again. As before, two lights shone dim and distant, the other three gone entirely.

"I expected a message," he stated. He walked to the side of the room and stood before the candles. He wet his fingers with his mouth and began snuffing them out, one by one. "That was our deal. When the keys arrived, you would let me know. In exchange, you keep your temple, and your lives."

The abbot shifted his feet. "I didn't know for certain. And when I did, I didn't have time."

Cain paused, his fingers poised. He toppled the candle on its side. The flame crept slowly around it. Cain turned back to the abbot. "Except that's a lie. I know you. I know you feel things *before* they happen. Which means you knew before it happened." He locked eyes with the abbot. "Tell the truth. Come now, old man. Leave the lies for those who are more practiced."

The abbot closed his eyes and puffed out his chest. "You are owed no respect, oath breaker. They were here. Now—"

Cain closed the gap between them in a moment. He wrapped his hand around the monk's throat, the concealed dagger in his other sleeve sprang into his palm and he pressed it against the man's neck. Cain could feel the abbot reaching for his chi, as did the other monks standing at the edges of the chamber.

"Ah, ah, ah. None of that. I'm just here to talk. Consider, what would happen to your brothers?" The surge of energies dropped away. "Show me where the keys went." The comment was directed not at the abbot, but at the surrounding guards. Behind them, his reavers filed in, weapons still sheathed.

The abbot said, "Wait. I'll show him."

Cain released the abbot, sending him stumbling for a moment before regathering his dignity. The old fool was too proud to lie, at least not for long.

The abbot crossed to the far side of the room and pulled aside a blue tapestry. On the other side, a dark opening led to a staircase below. Cain grabbed the abbot by his collar and dragged him to the passage, pushing him ahead as the two of them descended the steps. When he reached the bottom, understanding crept over him. Shattered mirrors littered the floors, not one left unbroken. Great energies swelled along the fragments of broken glass from the ruined waygates. A growl rose in Cain's throat. For all their cries of integrity, the monks were no saints. They would be brought to justice.

The abbot said, "You cannot harm them, oathbreaker."

Fury swept across Cain. He darted forward. "You call me oathbreaker, I call you witch. If not for your kind, we'd have no Titans. No crippled cities, no uncountable dead. It is *your* use of magic that drew them here. It is your…"

Cain looked down. He was surprised to find the abbot convulsing beneath him. The abbot gurgled as the last of the air escaped from both his mouth and the wound in his neck. Cain pulled his dagger loose. He watched as the blood ran from the wound, drawn to the glowing fragments of the waygates and disappearing within. He drew himself upright; his rage throbbed in his temples. This happened, sometimes. Sometimes the thoughts lurking in the back of his mind knew just what to do. Lucky for him. The abbot might have anticipated the attack otherwise. But Cain still felt a twinge of regret.

Cain cocked his head. Up above, he could hear the sounds of the massacre. Without a doubt, the monks would be overwhelmed. With luck, one would live long enough to be questioned, though monks could be stubborn. He knew that firsthand.

It didn't matter. The keys could run as far as they wanted. He'd find them.

PART TWO:

Keys

9

~ Nissa ~

The cold hit Nissa as she passed into the waygate. She gasped, but no air entered her lungs. Panic seized her. Her fingers instinctively tightened around the Tracer in one hand, and in the other—nothing. Yon was gone. Cinq was gone. Hollinder was gone. She whipped her head around but saw only deep black and the silver outlines of things that might or might not be real. The moment extended and twisted. Where a moment ago her skin felt the cold of the void, now it ached with new sensations. She tried to breathe again, and this time sucked in lungfuls of air. Still cold, but a different cold. Heavy, humid.

Her eyes snapped open. She lay face down on a stone floor covered with a thin layer of frost. In her right hand, she clutched the Tracer so tightly that her fingers ached. She scrambled to all fours. She gasped for air, and the cold sent her into a fit of coughing. She was inside a shadowed, circular chamber with walls extending up so far above her head that she couldn't tell if they ever joined at all. All around was gray. Gray walls, gray columns, bits of broken gray stone across the floor, and everything covered in frost. She had arrived in a wayroom, but one long since destroyed. Not a single mirror remained, nothing but broken glass, shattered frames, and splinters of bone. At first, she thought that the blanched and white objects were just debris. But while femurs could be mistaken, the skulls could not. And they weren't all human. Some were curiously elongated, or possessed sharpened canines, or eye sockets far too large.

As shock gave way to her new reality, the cold settled in. The creep began along her exposed legs and shoulders, scratching first at the surface before clawing deeper. Nissa tucked the Tracer away and pulled her knees to her chest for warmth. An idea took hold within her. Would this be her journey's end, to freeze to death in unknown ruins, alone, and with so many new questions left unanswered?

A hollow "thwock" echoed through the chamber, jarring Nissa from her thoughts. She spun to see first Yon appear, followed moments later by Cinq. Their bodies twisted into existence and promptly crumpled to the ground. She jumped up and hurried to their motionless shapes. After a moment, they began to stir. Cinq and Yon woke as slowly and groggily as she had, then lurched to awareness as they coughed and sputtered like someone dragged from a river.

Nissa reached Yon first. "Hey, you ok?" She turned around. "Cinq, grumble or something so I know it's you."

The mage opened his eyes. He sat up and held his head in his hands. He massaged his temples.

Nissa chided, "Come on, Cinq. Are you in there? Say something edgy."

He looked over at her, his eyes bloodshot. "I'm surprised you didn't say 'dance monkey, dance.'"

Relief washed over her. She forced her voice to be cheerful. "Oh good, you didn't lose your charm. Anyway… I already told the kid I wouldn't call him a monkey anymore, wouldn't be fair if I used that on you." She skipped back to where Yon lay. "Your turn. How about a thumbs-up?"

The young monk struggled upright and nodded sullenly. His eyes blinked open and shut slowly. He looked around at the shattered room. "Where are we?" He shuddered.

Cinq labored to his feet. He yawned and stretched. "Well, it was a wayroom once. But this appears to have been a one-way trip." He toed the broken glass. "If I had to guess, this was destroyed deliberately. Maybe the people were worried what might come through."

"We made it through." Yon looked around. "But *where* are we? Where's Hollinder?"

Dread washed over Nissa. The large, metal-toothed man was nowhere to be seen. She'd known—something inside of her had known—that they might not all pass through safely. And from the looks on Yon and Cinq's faces, they knew it too. She turned to Cinq. "Did you let go? I thought you had him."

The mage bristled. "I didn't let go. There was nothing to let go of. Once I entered the mirror, I was alone. Was it different for you?"

Nissa shook her head. "No." The weight of silence settled around the three of them. She waited, unmoving. She tried to be patient, tried to think about anything but the cold creeping deeper into her body. As she waited, she focused on her surroundings.

But all she heard was the breathing from Yon and Cinq, and the dull crunch of boots on debris as the monk paced the room. A faint odor tinged her nostrils. "Salt," she muttered.

Yon asked, "What's that?"

"I can smell it," she said. "Salt air. We're near the ocean. That doesn't exactly narrow it down. But it's a start." The words drifted away, a momentary distraction from the real problem. She shuddered. She clenched her fists to try and warm her fingers. "Holy hell, it's cold in here. I can barely think because of the cold."

Yon stood, pivoted, and walked to the far side of the room. He rummaged through broken mirrors, toppled bricks, and piles of bones. From beneath the rubble, he extracted a large swath of fabric, possibly a tapestry. He ripped it into sections. The first he handed to Nissa, who wrapped it around her shoulders like a cloak. He offered the second to Cinq, who tucked it under his arm, and took the last for himself.

Cinq frowned. "I'll say it. We're all thinking it."

Nissa braced herself. She'd been distracted, but she knew what was coming. Cinq was about to be Cinq.

The mage continued, "If Hollinder was coming, he'd be here by now. We all arrived together; he should have as well."

"And?" Nissa pressed.

"And if he's not here now. He's not coming," the mage finished. "We need to get out as soon as possible."

Yon protested, "But… we just got here."

"Right," Cinq replied. "And Nissa's already half-frozen. And what's to say who will come through the waygates next? It might be Hollinder, but I doubt it. What about those reavers?" He knelt to retrieve one of the inhuman bones from the floor. "Or maybe something a whole lot worse." He let the bone drop. "I can't even think in this place, let alone make sense of what happened back there. And we have a lot to think about."

Yon looked back at the mage. He bit his lip. "What the abbot said? About the keys?"

Cinq frowned. "Yes. And more than that. Keys. The prime set. The Pentarch. Power. He said a lot of things that I'm trying to sort out. And I do *not* want to die here before I can."

Nissa pulled the rug tight around her. She hated when Cinq was right. She hated when he spoke the dark, selfish thoughts she heard in the back of her head. She could tell herself it was for safety, or because of the reavers, or the cold, or to be practical. Cinq wasn't going to wait for Hollinder. And he wouldn't have waited for her either. She stood. No. He didn't get to just do this, even if he was right. Even if he would win out in the end. Not without an accounting.

"No," she snapped.

Cinq, who had been eyeing the exit, turned back to her. "No, what?"

She wrinkled her nose. "No, you don't get to just drop your friends and run. Do I need to spell it out for you, Cinq? Have you even taken a second to think about all the crap we've been through in the last two days? Or was it five years? Because that's a big difference when we're talking about people's lives. And my life, and Yon's, and all of us! A Titan! Can we start with the freaking Titan? A holy-hell monstrosity Titan just broke a town, cracked a hole in the world, and killed everyone in it but us. And when we got out? Boom! Reavers are trying to kill us. And don't forget that everyone in the world seems to know more about *this*," she brandished the Tracer, "than we ever did. And now we're something called keys—which has something to do with the Pentarch—and time is running out, because why not? So, I want to know…" she trailed off, breathing heavily as the burn of cold clawed at her throat.

Cinq looked back impassively. "Want to know what?"

She threw up her hands. "If you knew about all this. Did you, or didn't you?"

The mage's face darkened, his nose wrinkled, and his fingers tightened and retightened on his staff. "I… hoped."

Yon cocked his head. "Huh?"

Cinq continued, "I hoped that I was more than some poor sap who lost his memories. And yes, when I saw a Tracer with five lights, I fantasized about fives, the legacy of fives, and of course the Pentarch. And I wondered what that could mean for me. Then I thought about the world grinding toward the Convergence while I was stuck in the tower and told to mind my station. So yes, Nissa, I hoped for more. I wanted more. If I didn't, I'd have never left the tower. I hoped, but I didn't *know*."

Nissa kicked out, sending a skull skittering across the floor to smash against the wall. She fixed Cinq with a long stare, allowing the seconds to stretch on. She winked. "Ok, you're human. I needed to make sure."

Cinq's mouth opened, but he didn't speak.

She smiled. "I'm serious, I'm agreeing with you. Time to cut our losses. Get our bearings. Soldier on." She looked back at Yon. "You ok with that?"

"Hollinder…"

She hesitated. Then accepted. "We need to go. For now. At least until we know what's going on."

Yon nodded. The poor kid's head must be spinning.

Nissa clapped her hands. "I'll lead." She charged forward to the one visible exit at the far end of the narrow chamber. That had been cathartic. And now, there was the business of moving ahead. An intoxication of sorts she'd relished since she decided to leave the enclave. What's more, she had a knack for pathfinding. She and Cinq had worked out the arrangement naturally. For all of his knowledge of the great forces of magic, when it came to keeping an ear out for danger, the fey were always a step ahead. And if the fey knew, they'd tell any wikken who could listen. Then again, things here were quiet. The fey were quiet.

As they passed from the chamber, a leaning archway gave way to a corridor. This, too, was badly crumbled with the walls twisting at impossible angles and the ceiling collapsed in places. Nissa tiptoed through the debris, careful not to place a foot on any stone or rubble that would cause the pile to shift. She jerked her head back at Cinq and Yon. "Step where I step," she hissed. "And don't so much as whisper."

Nissa returned to her task. She had implied talking was dangerous. And perhaps too much sound could shift the walls, but mostly she wanted to think. The last few days had been a lot. And Cinq was right, they needed to consider what the abbot had said. They were keys to *something*. But this newfound knowledge felt distant. She had other questions first. In particular, why were the fey silent? Why couldn't she hear them? There had to be a reason, and she needed them. Now. She needed them *now*. Most people thought the wikken "talked to spirits" and left it at that. But the layers of complexity went much deeper. The more time a wikken spent with the fey, the more ingrained they became in the wikken's life. And whether the nature spirits—inhabiting plants and streams—or the bestial ones—concerning themselves with wild animals—they weren't just Nissa's friends, they were a part of her.

And yet, she understood how different humans and fey were from one another. She considered herself a friend to all the nearplane fey. That is, those who called this existence home. But no fey was native to this world. Even though some had lived here for centuries, at one time all fey had come from the otherplane. It was the fey who still lived in the otherplane—those labeled as the "deimos"—that were the dangerous ones. Banshees, haggards, tempests, and furies, all manifestations of the same wild essence. During an overlap, these creatures crossed over. Nissa shuddered to think of how many people were killed by the deimos during an overlap, and how many by the dread power of the Titans themselves.

But for now, she heard nothing. Not a whisper. They'd abandoned her.

Ahead, the light of the corridor grew brighter, pale, and silvery. With a few more steps, Nissa emerged into the open air with Cinq and Yon close behind. They stood on a ledge high above the streets on the edge of a building both massive and crumbling. This was one of the old cities of towering buildings, all boxy and angled as they reached for the sky. Many buildings were crumpled to the ground, no more than rubble, while others stood in defiance, still tall despite walls falling away to leave only a skeleton of wire and steel. In the light of the full moon, the ruined city looked deathly pale, mirroring the chalk and bone-white of the destroyed wayroom. What buildings remained stretched overhead, rising from frosted streets. The cold of open air clawed at her. Nissa tilted her head up. She watched the play of moonlight on the ruins.

"Look," Yon whispered. "The ground is ice."

Nissa leaned forward. Far below, the streets were caked in thick ice. It was wild, undulating, and upheaved, as though the entirety had been crystallized during a great storm or flood. She shuddered. "I didn't think it was possible, but it's even colder out here." She pulled her makeshift cloak tighter around her shoulders.

"Here, Nissa. Trade." Cinq slung his coat from his shoulders and handed it to her.

She exclaimed in mock-distress. "Not your coat, Cinq! That's like taking your soul. The alpha and omega of fashion." Nevertheless, she accepted the offer, replacing the crude tapestry with Cinq's coat. It was much warmer, she admitted. Cinq followed Yon's lead, wrapping the rug around his shoulders, and cinching the whole thing around his middle with his belt. He gripped his staff in both hands and pulled it close to his body.

Cinq turned to face the monk. "Yon, how are you holding up?"

The boy tugged the brown robe around his shoulders. "Don't worry about me. These things are warmer than they look. And, well, cold is one of those things we're taught to ignore. As they say, 'the snow bears no ill will.'"

Nissa squinted one eye. "Yeah, but it's still cold."

"It's just a saying."

Cinq nodded. "No need to apologize. We come from different places. We can compare backgrounds and philosophies later. And when we do find shelter—if we find shelter—I'll make sure we're warm."

She sighed. That was as close as Cinq got to promising to use magic. "Thanks for the optimism. I just have two questions: Where are we, and where are we going? There are a lot of dead cities out there, so which one is this?"

Yon squinted at the skyline. His eyes twinkled. "It's Alexandria, of course. City of the scholars. I've seen it in pictures. But never like this." He pointed at a tall, spired building in the distance. "See that? That's the great library. Back at Open Eye, there were pictures of this place. It's where the Pentarch trained in the sciences." The monk folded his hands and bowed his head.

Nissa whistled. "Uggh. The Pentarch again? I should have guessed it."

Yon looked up. "What do you mean?"

Cinq said, "The abbot said we were part of his legacy, or something. That remains to be seen, but we're certainly following in his footsteps. I woke up at Eastwind, where the Pentarch studied as a mage; Nissa in Gorenheim, where he trained with the wikken; and you woke up at Open Eye, where he studied under the monks. Without a doubt, we'll find the next of us here. And assuming we are chasing disciplines, that means a scholar. After that, a hermit. Five lights in the Tracer, five disciplines, five people—"

"Five keys," Yon completed.

Nissa clapped her hands. "But... we won't get anything done hanging around and freezing our butts off. So back to work. Catch." She tossed the Tracer into the air, which Cinq deftly snatched.

"Nissa, if this had dropped." He tightened his jaw.

She rolled her eyes. "But it didn't. Scholar hunt. Let's go."

Cinq studied the Tracer thoughtfully. "He's close by. Certainly in the city. But it's not quite as bright as on the other side of the waygate. The signal must have been amplified."

"Or he moved," Yon remarked.

"How far could she have moved in an hour?" Nissa asked.

Yon pointed up. "That's a full moon. Last night it was a crescent. Another lapse?"

Nissa replied, "Yeah. Probably. Six points for being observant. I should be nicer to you."

"There's a first," Cinq muttered.

Nissa sighed dramatically. "I'm *joking*, Cinq. Things are bad enough without you being so grim."

Cinq gripped his staff and started forward. "Anyway, if we're following the signal, we head toward the moon."

"West," Yon said. "It's setting."

"Very well. West."

Getting down to the ground level, or what Nissa thought of as sea level, proved slow and difficult. As they descended, she looked for signs of life with her eyes, her ears, and her mind. The silence of the fey weighed on her. Even if the city had been abandoned, there should be some hint of them. But not in the walls, not in the air, not even in the ground. So, when they reached the ice at the bottom of the building, her skin crawled with uneasiness.

"Ok, Cinq. We're down." She stomped on the ice, which looked so thick that no bottom could be seen. "Or at least as far down as we can get."

"Hooray," he echoed flatly.

Yon looked over in anticipation. "How about now?"

Nissa cocked her head. "How about now what?"

Yon's cheeks reddened. "How about you catch me up on things. I don't even really know who you are, much less what we're doing. So why don't we start there? Who *are* you two?"

Cinq remained impassive. "Do we have to do this now?"

Nissa shrugged. "What? You're hoping for someplace more private?" She gestured at the empty streets. "How much farther?"

The mage answered, "Only a few miles. We're quite close in the scheme of things." He looked at Nissa. "You want to go first? Assuming we really are exchanging life stories." He didn't roll his eyes, but Nissa knew he wanted to.

"Oh no, master mage. You are clearly in charge here. Plus, you're older, have more to tell."

"Very well. Let's get going."

10

~ Cinq ~

The frozen city lay before them. The street was maybe fifty yards wide, with hulking buildings rising on either side. Some of the structures extended hundreds of feet up, while others slumped in disrepair. The undulating ice beneath their feet formed a tenuous roadway as it swelled in waves, or broke under the pressure to create wide, jagged rifts. The intricate maze and massive ruins made Cinq feel insignificant.

This place, Alexandria, city of the scholars, had an echo of familiarity about it. Cinq had never been here before, though like Yon, he'd seen pictures and read descriptions in books. This was where the Pentarch, on his quest to master all five disciplines, had come to learn about science and the natural world. The Pentarch had been born as a monk, studied as a mage, traveled with the wikken, and abandoned society to become a hermit. When he emerged from the wilderness, he came to Alexandria to reconcile the mystical aspects with scientific ones. He learned of physics, biology, chemistry, gravity, electricity, and magnetism. In doing so—as the legend told—he was able to more perfectly wield magic in all its forms.

Cinq took a deep breath. Yes, this place resonated with the familiar. And he'd felt this way before. In fact, this feeling was his earliest memory.

He looked back and forth from Nissa to Yon. Their breaths rose around them in a frosty nimbus. Cinq brushed past Nissa to take the lead. "You want to know what I know? How I got here? From the beginning? Very well. My earliest memory was standing outside the gates of Eastwind Tower. And absolutely nothing before. My first thought was a question. I wondered how long I had been standing there, and where I was. That stuck."

Cinq walked as he spoke. His staff made a steady tapping against the surface of the ice, and yet the smooth, polished end slid ineffectually. He slung it over his shoulder. He kept his eyes ahead, but mostly down, concentrating on his footfalls as much as his memories.

"The mages," he continued, "knew exactly what I was. They'd seen other riftborn before me, and a few questions confirmed it. A junior mage took pity on me—I thought—but that was a lie. It was my first lesson in the motivations of mages. The 'generous soul' was a student writing a dissertation around the causes and behaviors of temporally displaced individuals. He was one of three mages with competing theories. I became a test subject and lab rat, but at least I had a place to call home.

"The three mages were only a few years older than me, or rather a few years older than I appeared to be. And without going into it, they asked a *lot* of questions. They had this idea of direct and indirect memories. Direct memories contained the events of my life and how I felt about them. All of that—and I do mean all of it—was gone. But my indirect memories were intact. Language was the big one. I didn't have to relearn how to speak. So, they studied my words, my phrases, my mannerisms. One mage recorded the things I recognized and the words and such I didn't. The next moved on to animals, plants, places, things, and locations. Together, they sought to date me. The towns proved the most useful. Given the Titans' habit of smashing things, they figured out I must have come from sometime around the end of the Titans' Age by the cities I recognized." He clenched his jaw. "They tried other things too. They taught me to control my dreams in case answers were there; they also tried hypnosis, and a few things bordering on torture. They tried it all."

Cinq came to a halt. In front of him, the path ended in a great split. A kind of mortar road ruptured the ice like a fractured bone through skin. They navigated first around, then up and over, before sliding down the ice to the other side. Cinq took another bearing with the Tracer and continued his story.

"I won't bore you with everything. Suffice it to say that after two months of observation, they deduced I'd once been a mage myself. And while their motives were not altruistic, they still spoke on my behalf. I was enrolled as a student and given the baseline curriculum. So I studied, and they watched me. And as I quickly progressed—I'd done this before, you realize—they finished their dissertations and their interest waned. By the time I was ready for advanced courses, I'd been left alone. And that's when things slowed down."

Cinq stopped again. The bright of the moon was starting to set behind the spired building at the end of the street. The corresponding shadow stretched in a perfect line across the ice and between the buildings on either side.

Yon prodded, "How did it slow down?"

"Hmmm?" Cinq clicked his tongue. "I guess it's more accurate to say I *was* slowed down. The higher-ups had tolerated me as a case study, but they didn't fully trust me. I don't know what they thought. Maybe I was a spy from a rival tower. Maybe I was a fey in disguise. Who knows? But they withheld training of any higher magic. I had to prove myself, but no one would take me as an understudy." He smiled. "And *that* is when I found the reliquary."

Nissa laughed. She took three quick steps and skidded across the ice, her boots sliding for several feet before she came to a halt. "And with the boring part out of the way, now things get interesting."

Cinq furrowed his brow. "You wanted to know everything. I was setting context."

Nissa rolled her eyes. "Whatever."

Yon mumbled, "I didn't think it was boring."

"So can I keep going?"

"Please," Nissa replied. "Continue with the epic of Cinq."

"Thanks. So, since no one would teach me, I started working my way through those archives open to an apprentice-level mage. The plan was to teach myself, and if I was lucky, remember things from before. Success was limited at best, but I did see a lot of the tower. One day, when I had been looking for a treatise on the otherplane, I found it." Cinq shut his eyes.

* * *

He pushed through the narrow oak door, the wood bowed and sagging on its hinges. On the other side, the room opened into a great archive. Shelves upon shelves, racks of iron and wood, some ornately carved, some no more than planks across boxes. The shelves were filled with an array of devices of every size and dimension. But one shape was repeated over and over again—the sphere. Crystal balls, ranging from no bigger than a pea to larger than a pumpkin. Most of the Tracers were dark, but many swirled with small, incandescent lights. And there, seated at a desk in the middle, sat the keeper. She had a Tracer in one hand and a pen in the other.

"Apprentice LeGarrec," she said, without looking up. "I've been following you."

* * *

Cinq shook his head. "To her credit, High Mage Aphrosis welcomed me when others wouldn't look at me. She even gave me a tour. Tracers, she explained, were her specialty. At first, I was furious she had preferred to follow me than let me know I was being traced. But I became more fascinated by the prospect of the devices. We talked, we discussed, and she took me as her apprentice. I spent my days working for her, and in my spare time, she let me study this." He reached into his pocket and removed the Tracer. He turned it back and forth in the moonlight.

"For two years under High Mage Aphrosis, I cataloged and measured. I evaluated light samples and material constitutions, indexed cross-references, filed letters of correspondence, and deconstructed packing materials. Most of what we did wasn't magic at all, though she did take some time to further my magical training. I practiced my spells, I researched, and I learned as much as there was to know about Tracers and magical artifacts.

Eventually, I found this." Cinq rotated the Tracer and pointed to a speck on the underside.

Nissa said, "It's night, Cinq. We can't see anything."

He said, "If it was a document, you'd call it a watermark. If it was a book, you'd call it a catalog number. It was the craftsman's signature. Once I found it, I was able to date the Tracer, the city of origin, and prove—just as was suspected—that it was from the time of the Pentarch. Just like me. Knowing this, truly knowing it, and knowing there were four others like me, somewhere in the world… it became too much."

Ahead, the wide street was blocked by a toppled building, though with walls remarkably intact. They climbed in through an open window on one side, traversed the building, and exited through a broken window on the other side. Cinq knocked a curtain of icicles aside with his staff, which chimed as they fell. Soon they were back in the open and on their way again.

Yon dusted the frost from his robe. "That's why you stole it?"

Cinq smirked. "I tried the proper channels. I applied for a grant to fund the scholarly endeavor to remove the Tracer from the reliquary and to locate and record the sources of the other lights. It was both my final dissertation, and my mission project if I was raised as a journeyman."

Yon said, "But they said no?"

"Well, they did raise me to journeyman status, but they weren't going to let me—a suspected spy and interloper—out of their sight with a three-hundred-year-old relic." He shook his head. "So, I filed an appeal and… didn't wait for their answer." He returned the Tracer to his pocket. "I walked out of Eastwind five years to the day of when I walked in. Wiser, I hope." He smiled slyly. "It took them a few months to know I had the Tracer. I guess my old teacher didn't bother to tell them. By the time they realized, I had met up with Nissa and we were on our way to find you." Cinq pointed down the street with his staff. "But hold that thought. What do you think of that?"

In front of them, a columned building lay slumped forward, collapsed to obstruct half the road on one side. On the opposite side, another crumbled structure, this one solid and angular, blocked the street. A gap of a few dozen feet lay between the two ruins, which was barricaded by a twisted web of iron fences, topped with sharpened spikes and razor wire. At the center hung a shut gate wrapped with a rusty chain.

They walked forward until the gate was a dozen yards away. Nissa stopped, holding out her arms to halt the others. "I think I could squeeze through the bars without any trouble. You could too, Cinq. Which raises questions."

Yon said, "Like if it's supposed to keep out big things? Bigger-than-us things?"

"That's not what I was thinking, but a good point. I was wondering if it is to keep things out, or keep things in." Nissa clicked her tongue. "Which side are we on? Seems important to know."

Yon bit his lip. "Or… it might not be meant to stop anyone. Just slow them down."

"How so?"

"Well, look at it," he answered. "You could go up and over if you put your mind to it. And there have to be other ways around."

Cinq pulled out the Tracer. The pinpoint of light shone strong, steady, and straight ahead. "One way or another, we need to get to the other side." He turned to Nissa. "How are you holding up?"

"Still cold as hell." She shuddered. "But the sun should be up soon. That'll help."

Cinq turned to look behind him. The eastern sky was now visibly lighter, and the stars above were fading into the pre-dawn gray. As if on cue, the first sliver of sun peeked through the forest of ruined buildings. As sunlight hit the ice, a sharp ripple and crack echoed throughout the city.

Nissa held up a finger. "Quiet. Did you hear that?"

Yon whispered, "Of course I did."

Nissa said, "Not the ice. The... the whine. Sounds like singing almost, or a..."

Another deafening crack as the ice shifted and expanded once more. The crack faded. A rumble followed.

Yon said, "Maybe this is normal for ice." He shook his head. "It's still making me nervous."

"I said be quiet." Nissa crouched low. She placed her ear near the ground. For a moment, she remained still before her eyes grew wide. She scrambled to her feet. "Run! Let's go, come on! To the gate!"

Cinq didn't question, only turned to race after the already sprinting wikken. And now he heard it too. A high, piercing keen layered across the cracking and shifting of ice. He slipped, his knees crashing against the surface before he scrambled up. As he did so, he darted his head to look behind him. In the distance, he could see movement. Hundreds of black and brown shapes flooded their way. He turned his eyes forward once more. He sprinted to the gate and skidded to a stop as an enormity of potential washed over him. The barricade thrummed with power.

Cinq shouted, "Stop! Nissa, Yon, don't touch the bars." He grabbed their shoulders. "It's a trap." He held his hand just above the wire. "I can feel it." But even as he said it, a different kind of rumble grew behind him. The things were moving quickly toward them.

"Follow me," Nissa snapped. She dropped to her belly and shimmied under a gap between the twisted metal and the thick ice of the street. Cinq watched with relief as she emerged on the other side. Yon went next, with Cinq wriggling through last. He had barely gotten halfway under before he felt the monk grab his shoulders and drag him through.

Yon asked, "Do you think—?"

Nissa yelled, "Don't stop!" She took off running, and Cinq scrambled to keep up with her. He made it a dozen yards before a great wail of sound reverberated behind him and a hot blast of air threw him forward. Cinq went skidding across the ice, the cold on his belly contrasted by a searing burn on his back. Yon and Nissa lay on the ground in front of him as well, their smaller frames thrown even farther. Cinq turned to look at the gate.

Hulking beasts filled the streets. They were a collection of hooves, teeth, claws, and thick, matted hair. No two were alike, except for being ice covered and filled with malice. The creatures raced toward them and threw themselves at the gate. With each collision, the gate replied with a blast of energy. Cinq assumed it was inverting the magical energy of the attackers. That wouldn't work on a normal animal. Which meant that those creatures were from the otherplane. Deimos.

Cinq sat upright.

Yon skipped to his side. "Are you ok?"

"I'm fine." He looked up. "Nissa, are they—?"

"God. Damned. Haggards."

The haggards looked like yaks, or bears, or bulls, or wolves. It was as though someone had taken the parts of each and thrust them together, patching and stitching fur, hooves, claws, and teeth. Drowned. That's what it was. They all looked like they'd been fished out of a river, frozen overnight, and raised from the dead. Cinq had always thought of fey and deimos as ethereal, but the haggards' hate and hunger were intensely primal.

The three of them moved as quickly as possible, keeping their bodies stooped and voices low. The haggards had lost interest in the fugitives and now concentrated their assault on the barricade. Cinq didn't want to consider what would happen if they broke through.

"There." He pointed to an open door of one of the adjacent buildings. The three of them entered to find a reception area. Inside, tables and chairs were overturned and mostly broken. Ice sheathed the walls on all sides, and icicles hung from the ceiling. In the center of the room, a grand spiral staircase hung suspended, though absent its railing. Cinq rushed to the stairs. After climbing the lower ice-covered steps, the remainder were clear. They climbed, only to find another set of stairs, and another. Flight after flight, they ascended until they reached a point where the steps were too damaged to go farther. Yon gestured to an open side room, and they entered.

As soon as they closed the door behind them, Nissa and Yon collapsed on the floor. Cinq wanted to join them but instead tried to clear his mind, to reach out with his spirit to feel the world around him. He had done the same thing the moment they had arrived in the wayroom, but he had felt nothing. Perhaps the waygates had disrupted him, but now he felt something else entirely: the nearplane and otherplane in close alignment. They were in an overlap. How had he not noticed before? What had changed?

"Nissa," Cinq kept his voice low, controlled, "how did we get surprised?" He paused. "I thought you had an ear out."

She jerked upright from where she lay. "Don't try and pin this on me. Nothing to hear until a few minutes ago. Plus, no fey around to warn me. Now I know why."

Yon said, "Well I don't. Why?"

Nissa shook her head. "When a Titan comes—you saw it— things change. The fey run away, or disappear, or something. That part I don't know."

Yon asked, "Which Titan was it?"

Cinq replied, "The haggards point toward the Fire Titan. Though the pairing isn't an absolute. Banshees with Earth, haggards with Fire, furies with Water, tempests with Wind."

Yon said, "But everything's frozen."

Cinq shook his head. "Heat and cold: two sides of the same coin. The Fire Titan can pull warmth from a place as easily as it can burn. The haggards would come on its heels either way. We're still in an overlap, otherwise, they wouldn't be here." He took a deep breath. "I want to know who made the fence. That took magic, and a lot of time. How long have things been like this?"

Yon said, "Could the Titan still be here?"

Nissa shook her head. "No. I'd know it if she was. Titans make a lot of noise, so to speak."

Cinq removed the Tracer from his pocket. Sometimes the object soothed him by providing purpose, even if he wasn't sure what that purpose was. "We're getting closer. We should press on."

Yon looked at Cinq in disbelief. "You can't be serious. I mean, maybe I'm just new to whatever we're doing here, but when does following those lights quit being important? There might be survivors out there. Shouldn't we try to help them? Something bigger is going on here."

Cinq leveled his gaze. "In my opinion, we need to keep following the Tracer *because* something bigger is going on. You heard the abbot. We're keys of some kind. To something important."

"But we don't know what that means! Why is that important now?"

"Yon," Cinq kept his voice even, "I don't know how much the masters share with you, but overlaps are becoming more frequent, and so are the Titans. Every year is more severe than the one before it. The otherplane is drifting closer and closer to our own world. This isn't just some rumor. I've seen the charts back at Eastwind. Time, location, severity, casualties. It all makes for some very interesting and very disturbing trends, leading to some very serious consequences. It was enough to make my teachers nervous."

"Nervous?"

Cinq bit his lip. "Back at the tower, we have a lot of rules. A *lot* of rules. There are more rules about what you can and can't, should and shouldn't do than you'd ever imagine. But a lot of mages are questioning if, given what's coming, we shouldn't be taking more drastic steps. Maybe some of the long-forbidden things wouldn't be that bad after all."

"And what *is* coming?"

Nissa cocked her head. "A poopstorm. Technical wikken term for the Convergence. My sisters are freaked out and aren't as shy to admit it. They know things are getting worse. What's more, the fey know it too. Of course, the fey are way less specific, and way *more* dramatic. Take the specifics with a grain of salt, but it's going to happen. The Convergence is a *complete* overlap between our world and the otherplane, a second Titans' Age. Titans wouldn't be an every-now-and-then thing. It would be all the time. Remember how Cinq and I were like 'oh fiddlesticks!' when the time slipped?"

"Fiddlesticks?" Cinq murmured.

"You know what I mean. Before Ignaesdale, the Convergence was eight years out. Now it's more like three and a half. That's coming up fast."

Cinq gripped his staff. "There's a part of me that wonders if maybe it already happened. What if we lost another five years when we went through the waygate? Maybe landing in a frozen city wasn't just bad luck. Maybe whatever it is has already started. And *that* makes what we are doing all the more important." Cinq exhaled slowly. "After all, it's at least important enough for people to try and chase us down and kill us. And as the abbot said, it's linked to the Pentarch. That makes us important too. And it makes finding the others crucial."

Yon's eyes widened. "So, what are we?"

"I don't know," Cinq admitted. "But assuming there is a connection, ask instead who the Pentarch was. He mastered five disciplines, certainly, but that was only a buildup. Somehow, *somehow*, he ended the Titan's Age. Now you can talk about cooperation and the power of teamwork, and all that feel-good garbage, but the truth is he still did it. And it took all the disciplines for him to do it. And what are we doing? Chasing five things, five types of knowledge, five people, five *keys*. I don't know the answer, but I see the pattern."

Yon paused for a few moments before venturing once again, "And you think if we find all of us, it'll make sense?"

"Maybe. Maybe not. Or maybe the abbot and the reavers are mistaken and we aren't important after all. Maybe after three hundred years, the Tracer finally broke and started latching onto people for no reason at all. Or maybe we were important when we were different people." Cinq paused. "Or maybe we'll be important in the future. Time doesn't have to be linear."

Nissa exhaled dramatically. "Boys, let's take a deep breath. Here's an idea. We are stuck in a broken-down building with uncountable nasty beasties crawling around in some kind of post-apocalyptic frozen hellscape."

Cinq asked, "That's supposed to make me feel better?"

"Yes! Because we have the Tracer thingee that is surprisingly good at finding living, breathing people. So maybe we should just see where it takes us, in case that happens to be somewhere warm and dry."

Cinq looked up. "Nissa, that is remarkably practical. I couldn't agree more. Any other strokes of brilliance?"

Nissa nodded. "Oh yeah. We need snacks."

"What?"

"Non sequitur," she explained. "The cold I'm getting used to, but water and food are going to be a problem before long. Staying still isn't going to help, and I'm nearing the end of my monastic goodies."

Yon asked, "But how can we go out with those haggards in the streets?"

Cinq smiled thinly. "We don't use the streets unless we have to. We stay inside as much as we can. We stay hidden."

"And what if one *does* find us?" Yon asked. "What if we can't always run?"

Cinq set his jaw. "Then we defend ourselves. We're not helpless."

11

~ Yon ~

Yon crept to the shattered window. He peered through broken panes down onto the streets below. He didn't dare stick his head out, but he didn't need to. The haggards were now clearly on both sides of the gate. A surge of panic ran up his spine and his head felt dizzy. Was the gate broken? Or was it only ever there to slow them down? Yon scanned the buildings from street level to the roofline. Something at the top caught his eye, but he didn't know what to think of it. He turned back to face the others.

"They broke through." His voice sounded small in his ears.

Nissa grinned. "Well, let's hope they aren't part bloodhound."

Yon was seized by the urge to either start running and never stop, or to cram into a dark hole.

Nissa's smirk changed to concern. "That was a joke. Mostly. And in bad taste. But still, you need to relax. Too hard to think if you're worked up." She tilted her head. "But that begs the question: what would you do if a haggard walked in? I mean, you've seen how stingy Cinq is with his magic, and I don't think my knives would do much against a hell-yak. Is that a thing? A hell-yak?"

Yon looked on in disbelief. His panic shifted to distraction. "Knives? What about your—I don't know—wikken black magic?"

"First off, that's just ignorant. And demeaning. There's no such thing as wikken magic, let alone black magic. I listen to the fey, and sure, I talk to those that bother with that kind of thing. Now those haggards and other deimos are different, they don't think and talk like the fey do. Maybe they could, but they're too focused on the whole, 'kill, kill, kill, eat, eat, eat' thing. So, yeah, I can listen out, which is kind of important, but I'm not a brawler."

Yon bowed his head and rubbed his temples. "Oh, ok." He looked over at Cinq. "Remind me why you don't use magic again?"

Cinq straightened up. "Being a mage isn't about the use of magic, it's the *study* of magic."

Nissa interrupted. "But it wasn't always that way."

Yon said, "Huh?"

Cinq grimaced. "She's right. When the world was full of magic, being a mage was more practice than study. But there isn't magic around like there used to be. So, I conserve. That way, if you have a 'we're getting chased by banshees' situation, then I'm not just decorative." He shrugged. "And like Nissa, I can listen out. I can feel the tides of magic around us." He looked out the window at the haggards below. "But I wouldn't last long against that."

Nissa tapped her fingers together. "Plus, magic draws attention. If Cinq does start casting spells, then every otherplane critter for ten miles is going to rush us."

Yon's shoulders sagged. Traveling with a mage and a wikken—though interesting—wasn't as advantageous as he'd hoped. He closed his eyes and considered this chaos of new ideas. The wikken worked through the fey, and the mages had their magic, but for the monks, it had never been about the outside world. A monk's powers centered in—and did not extend past—his own skin. Even now, he could feel his chi coursing through his veins. The spiritual energy had been building since he first saw the Titan.

"I… can fight," Yon stated.

"Beg your pardon?" Cinq looked away from the window.

"If it came to it, I could fight. If I had to."

"I knew it!" Nissa clapped her hands in delight. "I hope it's like in the stories. So, you can like what? Jump and kick and break bricks with your skull and stuff? If you were to say, get in a bar fight, what would happen?"

"We can't fight unless we're attacked." Yon paused. "Wait, what's a bar fight? Like with metal bars? Is that a kind of duel?"

Nissa cocked her head. "Right. You don't get out much, do you, kid? Try this one: Let's say we were walking down the road and a group of soldiers attacked you. What then?"

"I'd defend myself."

Nissa sighed. "Could you please be a little more specific? Or graphic. Could you be a little more graphic?"

Cinq said, "That's enough, Nissa. We aren't here to pick fights. Remember about keeping a low profile?"

Nissa shrugged. "So even if we *could* go blazing through the haggard-filled streets in broad daylight under the protection of Yon's righteous fists, we don't?"

"Correct."

Yon bit his lip. He realized what he'd seen. "We don't have to go through the streets at all."

Cinq folded his arms across his chest, staff crooked beneath his elbow. "Meaning?"

"Come look at this." Yon edged to the window and peered through. "See up high, near the skyline? Something's up there." He focused and there it was, a kind of line connecting the rooftops. "What do you think that is?"

Cinq said, "Might be a communication cable. Or old power line."

"A what?" Nissa asked.

"Or a bridge," Cinq continued. He turned back to Yon. "Let's go have a look."

After Nissa pressed her palm against the door to check if there were any haggards on the other side, the three of them passed through. Nissa took the lead. They hunted until they found some intact stairs going up. They continued their ascent, alternating from staircase to staircase until they emerged onto the roof.

By the time they reached the top of the building, the sun was high in the pale sky. They made their way to the edge, where a low barricade separated them from the overhang. From this height, Yon saw the skyscrapers arranged in a regular grid in all directions to where they ended at the ice-sheathed city wall.

"Hey kids," Nissa said. "Yon gets the prize. Come look at this."

Nissa stood next to an upright metal pole bolted to the corner of the rooftop. Two wires, one high and one low, stretched from the pole, across the gap between the buildings, and to a matching structure on the next roof.

"Whaddaya think?" She rapped her hand against the wire.

"I think," Cinq said, "that it would be hard to cross that if you had hooves. Too bad it takes us in the wrong direction."

Yon smiled. "But it's not the only one. Which way do we *want* to go?" He cast his hand out across the city. Now that he knew what to look for, the wires were unmistakable. Not all rooftops were connected, but the network of stabilizing poles and wires spiderwebbed around many of them.

Cinq frowned. "But do we trust them?"

Nissa pulled against the wire. "I'll go first, being the lightest and all. If it can't hold me, it can't hold anyone."

Cinq said, "But if I go first, being the heaviest, you two are probably safe." He shook his head. "This seems extraordinarily stupid." Another pause. "I'll do it. Nissa, you take the Tracer. If things go wrong, I don't want to lose that too."

They walked to the far side of the rooftop where another pole and set of wires stretched in two directions, one to the west, and another spanning an alleyway due south. Cinq took his staff and slung it into a holster on his back. He grabbed the upper wire and stepped onto the lower one. The cable flexed under his weight.

"Here I go."

Shuffle by shuffle, foot by foot, Cinq inched across the wire over the abyss. After the first ten feet, he moved more quickly. And though Yon was unable to see the mage's face, his entire body looked tense. When the mage stood on the far side, he waved back at them.

"I'm up, I guess," Yon said. He gripped the top wire and stepped up onto the bottom. The ice-cold metal sent a wave of pain through his hand, and he immediately stepped back down. "This isn't smart," he muttered.

"Oh, come on," Nissa chided. "If the bookworm can do it, we can do it."

Yon shook his head. "I'm not saying I can't, I'm saying it's dumb. I might make it across, but eventually one of us is going to slip." For a moment, he forgot about the ice and the haggards and the ruined city. He remembered a game at Open Eye. He and his friends would stretch ropes across the canyon above the river. They'd play at balancing and swinging. And it was all great fun, especially when they fell into the cool waters below. That's all it was: a game. He could see it as a game. He scrunched his face. "I've got an idea." Yon unwound the cords which wrapped around the top of one of his soft boots. He looped it under his arms and threw the other end over the top wire. He stepped back on the lower wire and cinched the rope tight. Not perfect, but better than nothing.

He started out. With every step his confidence increased, and in less than a minute, he had reached the far side. With a grin, he stepped onto the rooftop and untied the cord. He waved to Nissa on the other rooftop before looking back at Cinq.

Cinq pointed back across the gap. "What's she doing?" Yon watched as Nissa danced across the line. Where he had taken careful steps, she leaped and bounded. Yon realized she wasn't grabbing the wire at all. Instead she'd slung a piece of cord over the cable as she sashayed along. At the far end, she dismounted with a flourish.

Nissa grinned. "That's the way to go. Definitely saves the arms for the next one. What are you two looking at?"

Yon cleared his throat. "Can I see that rope?"

She handed it over. Yon spread it out in his hands to show where the center had been in contact with the wire. The hemp rope was worn almost in two. He handed it back to her.

"Oh… oh. Ok." Her cheeks flushed. "I didn't notice."

Cinq said, "Next time, we do it Yon's way. Quick, but not too quick. Come on."

From rooftop to rooftop, across cable after cable, they traversed the city. Both Yon and Cinq slipped more than once, the safety line pulling tight before they were able to regain their footing. But apart from one detour, they edged closer and closer, following the light of the Tracer. By the time the sun had faded to a dull red, Yon felt his arms at the edge of exhaustion. His stomach rumbled, and his throat called out for water. At Open Eye, he had worked and fasted, but it was different knowing hunger was a choice.

"Um, Cinq, Nissa, the sun's going down," Yon said. "Should we get inside?"

Nissa nodded dully. The tips of her hair were now solidly frozen as was the collar and back of her borrowed coat. Cinq pointed at one of the ubiquitous access doors. When they reached the opening, Nissa held up a hand to signal that they wait. She pressed her palms against the door, nodded an ok, and they all passed in.

The door opened into a nondescript stairway, gray, weathered, and constructed of the same solid mortar. They walked down one flight of stairs and opened the first door they saw. Inside, they encountered the first signs of humanity. Blankets lay stacked in the corner, as well as some small, chopped pieces of wood piled next to a metal stove.

Cinq walked over to the blankets and unceremoniously tossed one at Yon and another at Nissa before attending to the stove. His flint produced a small spark and soon the wooden pellets ignited. As the fire took hold of the room, Yon finally felt warm enough to shed his heavy makeshift coat.

Nissa paced the floor. "I don't think anyone lives here."

"No?"

"Nope," she said. "It's a shelter. They could be all over the place. Just in case people got caught outside."

Yon scrambled to his feet. "Then maybe there's food." He paused. "If we're lucky."

The three of them searched in earnest, and to their joy, found a small cache containing compressed foodstuff wrapped in waxy paper, as well as a ceramic jug that, while the surface was frozen, sloshed with water beneath. They tore into it before Cinq advised Yon and Nissa to slow down. In the end, compromise and discipline won out. Maybe there were more of these caches, or maybe they should conserve.

Utterly exhausted, his head swimming with thoughts of wires, keys, and haggards, Yon slept.

12

~ Nissa ~

Weariness consumed Nissa, but she couldn't sleep. As such, she volunteered to take first watch. She sat cross-legged on the floor near the stove in a nest of blankets until she felt not only cozy, but hot.

She occupied the time with two tasks. The first was converting the stockpile of blankets into clothing. She cut the cloth into long strips and wrapped them around her legs, torso, and arms by braiding them into one another. Not her best work, and not the most stylish, but better than spending another day in a coat far too big for her. Or a rug.

While she worked, she listened. The playful, sometimes demanding, and always capricious voices of the fey remained absent. Instead, all she heard on the winds were the low, hungry, and guttural mutterings of the haggards. She hadn't been able to hear them at all at first, but the sheer volume of them and the intensity of their emotions became clearer with each successive hour. Nissa didn't think the voices were getting clearer because they were getting closer. If anything, when she looked down at the streets, the haggards were scarcer. No, she was simply becoming attuned to them in the same way she had with the nearplane fey.

Nissa strained her ears—or rather her mind—to listen more closely. But the voices of the haggards were fading, fading, until they stopped altogether. The night was silent. Completely silent. No fey, no haggards, not even a breath of wind in the frigid sky. Then she heard something: a solitary jingle, the pealing of a bell. Over and over, the ringing filled the air. Nissa tiptoed to the sound. She found it in the corner, a brass bell hanging from a thread that disappeared into the ceiling above.

"What is it?"

She turned to see Yon looking at her. His eyes were noticeably sleepy, and his face was still scrunched and red from where he'd been curled on the floor. She whispered, "Not sure. What do you think?"

The boy took the offered candle and peered at the bell and the string. He turned back to look at her, his eyes wide. "It's an alarm. Probably hooked to the cable on the roof."

"Someone's crossing!" Nissa retrieved the candle from Yon and nudged Cinq awake with her toe. To the mage's credit, he took the news with his typical stoicism. Nissa asked, "So, what do we do?"

Cinq shrugged. "We either greet them, we stay put, or we hide. But if we think it's a person, and that people built those lines, maybe they're friendly."

Nissa nodded. "Well, it isn't a haggard, that's for sure." She saw Cinq's doubting look. "I'm getting better at hearing them, ok?"

"Good to know," Cinq replied. "Ok, we're all equal parties in this. What do you think?"

"Topside," Nissa said without hesitation.

Yon nodded. "Yeah. And we hope they're friendly. But it could just be a bird."

Cinq replied, "I haven't seen a lot of birds here. So be ready."

Pausing to wrap back up in blankets and coats, they moved through the door and up the stairs. Nissa took the lead, checking for the sounds of haggards at each door. She swung open the hatch leading to the roof. As the door opened, her breath caught in her throat, the cold sending her into a fit of coughs. The temperature had plummeted to the point that the smallest gulp of air chilled her from within.

Nissa heard a metallic whining and in the moonlight saw something speeding along the cable from the opposite building. The body seemed attached to the upper cable while using the lower cable to kick along as it glided. When the shape reached the other side, it disengaged from the wire in a sharp click, followed by the unmistakable slide of a blade leaving a scabbard, and the accompanying glint of moonlight on the sharpened knife edge.

"What are you doing up here?" the voice, though hushed, was full of condemnation.

"Easy there," Nissa called cheerfully. "We're just people. Nothing scary."

The voice dropped to a whisper. "Shut up, you idiots. You'll get us noticed."

As if in response, there was an ear-splitting shriek, as violent as it was inhuman. The person barreled past them. "To the shelter, now!"

Nissa turned on her heels and raced back to the door, nearly tripping over Cinq and Yon. The three of them, with the newcomer on their tails, retreated inside. The bulky shape slammed the door shut as soon as they entered. The newcomer grabbed a large iron crossbar and secured it in place across the door, then another, then another.

The shriek sounded again, louder and closer. It radiated through the shelter window, followed by a large thud as *something* landed on the roof. Nissa remained completely silent. She held her breath until her heart quit pounding. After an uneasy minute, the newcomer pulled down the thick scarf covering its face.

The "it" was not an "it" at all, but a "she," though any betrayal of male or female shape descended into meaninglessness under all the layers of fur. She pulled her mirrored goggles up to rest on the top of her head, revealing skin smudged with dark streaks of black. She almost looked like a haggard herself, albeit a non-hoofed, two-legged one. She was tough, weathered, but not much older than Cinq.

The newcomer spoke, for the first time not in a whisper. Her voice was thick and held a trace of a clipped accent. "So, who are you? Other than three barking idiots. And where the hell did you come from?"

Cinq, unperturbed as always, was the first to answer. "We came through the wayroom. Not much left there. Or here, for that matter."

The woman narrowed her eyes. "You're a long way from the wayroom." She paused. "Have you been traveling in daylight? You're even luckier and even stupider than I thought."

Nissa put her fists on her hips. "Well, we're new here. How would you have done it?"

The woman shook her head in disdain. "We wait until the sun drops and the land gets cold. It doesn't kill the haggards, of course, but they freeze like everything else. At least until morning when they thaw out and it all starts again. Night is safer."

Nissa replied, "Um… then what was that thing we heard? That's what passes for 'safe' around here?"

"Wyvern. Big bastard, too, and those don't freeze. This side of the city is her territory, but it's still a hell of a lot easier to avoid a few wyvern than a thousand haggards. Of course, you have to at least *try* to be inconspicuous."

Cinq raised an eyebrow. "Wyvern? This far south?"

The woman looked back at Cinq in disbelief. "You have to be kidding me. The wyvern came first. Everyone knows that."

Yon asked, "Came before what?"

Before the woman could answer, Cinq clarified. "Let me just set some expectations. We were in an overlap. We were caught in a lapse of at least five and a half years. We aren't up to date on things."

"Well, you missed some hard years." She paused, her posture relaxing. "And I suppose you can't be blamed. And since there are as many lies running around as there are truths, we need to get you to the doc. She knows the difference. And she'll know what to do. We should go now. Wyvern lose interest fast, but she'll be back."

Cinq nodded. "To confirm: This is Alexandria, right?"

"It was. But nothing is what it used to be." She folded her arms. "They call me Blue."

Nissa, Yon, and Cinq introduced themselves. Blue gave her a funny look, but by now Nissa was used to that. A wikken and a mage traveling together turned enough heads. Now that a monk had joined their ranks, the attention was inevitable. Blue didn't explain much more about who she was or what she was doing, other than an offhand remark about keeping up the patrol. Instead, she rummaged through cabinets to come up with a trio of metal devices consisting of a large metal loop attached to a wheel that trailed a leather strap. Blue handed one to each of them before pushing back through the shelter door and into the cold.

When they got to the roof, Blue crept out first, eyes scanning the horizon before waving them forward. She led them to the corner of the building where one of the pole and cable rigs was attached. She held up the wheel and strap device and showed them how to loop it around their wrist before hooking the wheel over the cable.

Blue whispered, "Make sure you keep your weight on it, so the wheel doesn't come off track. Other than that, just go as fast as you can without falling. Don't poke around. You'll be spotted if anything hungry looks up. Or down, for that matter."

By way of demonstration, she kicked off from the building and, with a low metallic squeal, shot across the gap between buildings. Her legs shuffled just enough to propel her along the wire, otherwise drawn up under her to keep them out of the way. When Blue reached the far side, she unhooked from the wire and crouched to wait. Nissa went next. She connected the wheel just as Blue had done and took off. The wheel whirred as she skated across the gap, and in a matter of seconds, she landed on the far side next to Blue. After the others crossed, they continued to the next wire. The travel was fast; much, much faster than their earlier crossings. In the space of an hour, they had covered twice the distance they had in daylight. At last, they found themselves across from a building that was so large it dwarfed their current rooftop. In the moonlight, she could see that the cable stretched to end directly in a wall, with no ledge or anything else to stand on. Not only that, but this cable was not paired like the others. There was nothing on which to stand or control their speed.

Nissa asked, "How do I kick off? And where do we land?"

"This cable slants down. You won't need to kick."

"And the landing?"

In response, Blue reached into her mess of furs to pull out and light a small candle. She waved it above her head three times before extinguishing the light and tucking it away. "Ok, they know we're coming—if the bastards aren't asleep. Wait until I'm through before you follow. I'll need to clear you."

Cinq asked, "And will we be cleared?"

"Trust me," Blue replied. "The doc will want to see you. And that's all I'll need to say."

Yon looked worried. "And what if she doesn't?"

Blue shrugged. "She will. That's her business." The woman hooked her wheel to the cable. She sped away as the trolly whirred along the wire. At the last moment, twin doors opened inward. After Blue passed through, the trapdoor shut once more.

Cinq exchanged a wary glance with each of them. "We sure about this?"

"Come on," Nissa said. "We're already committed. And if I don't get some answers soon, I'm going to throw myself off the building." She paused. "What's thingee say?"

Cinq looked at the Tracer before hiding it away. "We're extremely close. And I'm not going to check again until I know we're safe. I don't want to draw any more attention than needed."

Yon took a sharp breath. "I'll go first. In case things get out of hand."

Nissa grinned. "So now you're taking care of us?"

Yon shrugged, "I'll try."

He disappeared down the cable, hurtling toward the blank wall.

13

~ Yon ~

Yon held his breath and embraced his chi as he sped along the cable. With his vision sharpened, he saw the thin outline of the hinged door. The door snapped open just before he hit, and he was inside. The second he entered, the cable curved up and the angle of his descent slowed. A ramped floor sloped to meet him. Yon put down his feet to run along the ramp until he stopped. Just ahead, Blue stood off to the side. She waved him to join her. Yon unclipped himself from the wire and hustled over to meet her.

The heat overwhelmed him. Sweat formed across his skin. He'd been concentrating for so long on ignoring the cold that with actual warmth around, pins and needles rippled over his body. Yon looked back at the ramp leading to the outside. It was only a piece of extensive scaffolding that created gangways and levels in an otherwise open room. Unlike the city ruins, this place pulsed with voices and the sounds of industry. Torches lined the walls, giving the place a mine-like feeling. He noticed that the tinkering of hammers and bustle of people slowed. Dozens of workers in drab tunics turned to look at him. They were universally smudged with grease and wearing looks of suspicion. Their animated chatter turned to mumbles.

Yon snapped from his daze as a screech of metal heralded the arrival of Nissa, and almost immediately after, Cinq. Apparently, they had opted against spacing too far out. Yon was relieved to see them. What would happen if the people here were dangerous? Anyone who lived among haggards must be cautious indeed.

Ignoring the eyes of the onlookers, he rushed to help Nissa and Cinq unhook from the cable. Blue waved her hand to usher them up a ramp and through a door into a long, narrow room. Yon realized he was still clenching tightly to his chi. And why not? No reason to let down his guard. There were still lots of opportunities for these people to turn unfriendly. What if this was an ambush? Or what if this was a cult of reavers? Or cannibals? He shook the thoughts away.

They followed Blue into a corridor lined with wooden crates and shelves ascending the walls above them. Blue took the lead, removed her harness, and chucked it into one bin. Her gloves went into a second, her hat in another. She hung her thick fur coats on a peg against the wall. Cinq, Yon, and Nissa followed suit to remove their makeshift gear. Only Nissa kept covered. Yon realized this had nothing to do with temperature, and everything to do with not being easily identified as a wikken.

Out of her gear, Blue no longer looked like a shapeless mass. She was toned and fit, with defined muscles. She wasn't wiry, just solid. She wore scuffed leather pants with heavily reinforced knees, and a gray tunic belted around her middle by a broad piece of leather. Nothing here was either decorative or feminine. Functional to the last. It reminded Yon of the monks and their own utilitarian clothing. Maybe this place was a monastery in its own right.

Blue saw Yon studying her. "We're not monks, if that's what you're thinking. And this isn't an army."

"How did you—?"

"Everyone thinks that when they show up. We are here to survive. That means you need to check a lot of ideas about what belongs to who at the door. That's likely easy enough for you. Your mage friend might have to adjust. You'll all fall in line."

Nissa looked back at the entrance where interested faces peered in after them. "How many of you are there?"

"There are about a thousand of us here in the archive. And that includes the kids. A lot less go outside. It's too easy to get yourself killed if you aren't careful."

Cinq tapped his chin. "Archive? So, we *are* in the great library."

Blue nodded. "Once upon a time. Yeah. And it survived the Titan without much damage. The flood didn't reach this far. Among other things."

A soft voice called, "Blue, my friend. Welcome back."

Yon turned to look at the newcomer. She was a petite woman with stark white hair pulled back and gathered behind her head. She wore small, round glasses and behind them were steel-gray eyes, the left flecked with yellow, the right with green. Like Blue, she wore a simple gray hassock cinched with a thick leather belt replete with pouches and hooks. On one side of her belt, pliers, screwdrivers, calipers, and other instruments were neatly ordered. The other side held vials, pens, and a notebook buckled into place. Her hands were folded across the top of a polished wooden cane, which tapered to a silver-tipped point at the floor.

The woman crossed the room and cocked her head. "And who are your friends? We haven't had a new visitor in months." Her eyes brightened. "Why you're practically a delegation! A mage, a monk, and—somewhere under there—a wikken. And in equal proportions. You know, following the first Titans' Age, groups of equal membership of the three mystic orders traveled in just this manner. The goal was to show solidarity in a time of unrest, though some claimed that if balancing manners or loquaciousness, the distribution should be quite different." She laughed. "But I'm being incredibly rude. Welcome to the archive, and welcome to Alexandria. Doctor Elizabeth Yimini, at your service." She bowed her head. "And who might you be?"

"I'm Yon, of the Open Eye monastery." He returned the bow. "Well, at least until yesterday. I think it was yesterday."

"Mage Cinq, of Eastwind Tower."

"And I'm Nissa of the—not any of your god dammed business! And I haven't decided if I like you or not, *Doc*. Glad to hear you have a name though. After 'Blue' I assumed we'd all pick colors."

Elizabeth let out a peal of laughter. "Ah, I do miss the spirit of the wikken. And you are welcome to call me Liz if Doc isn't to your liking." Her lips pursed in concentration and her eyes focused. "But I must ask, how did you get here? The city is not easily entered."

Cinq answered, "We came through your wayroom. We didn't expect this."

Elizabeth's eyes lit up. "Fascinating and illuminating. Do you know that once there was great debate about whether destroying the mirrors of the wayroom would achieve anything at all? Certainly, there would no longer be a way out, but the way in was a function of the sending wayroom. To be sure, there was a link on this side but that receptor was not grounded in the physical world. One mystery is solved, and questions are raised to unveil another. I simply must make a trip to see for myself—once circumstances permit, of course."

Nissa blurted, "And we would just *love* to hear all about the unspecified nastiness. *Everybody* keeps saying they'll tell us what's going on, and next thing you know we're on the run again."

Elizabeth wrinkled her brow. "I'm not quite sure I follow. How is it possible that the world doesn't know what happened here? Or maybe I overestimate our importance. We are, of course, quite unable to communicate with the outside world."

Blue interjected, "Doc, these three were in a lapse. Lost a few years. Not really in touch with current events."

Elizabeth gasped. "My word. You aren't asking about Alexandria at all! You want to know about everything. I'm happy to explain. Follow me."

The old woman ushered them along a corridor lined with glowing torches. She talked low to Blue as they walked. The snippets Yon overheard related to the names of streets and locations, presumably updates from her patrol. And though he could probably have edged closer, he was too absorbed in his surroundings. While one side of the hallway held torches, the other was filled floor to ceiling with rows upon rows of books. The only breaks in the stacks were when a door opened to one side or the other, at which point the books arced up and over the doorway before leveling out on the other side.

At the end of the corridor, Elizabeth pushed into a medium-sized room with a low wooden table in the center and a series of comfortable-looking chairs surrounding it. Columns dotted the room in regular intervals.

"This is a study room, as you can see. But I like to use it when a private discussion is needed. The others in our refuge have offered it to me as a kindness where privacy is not otherwise easily found. Please have a seat. Blue, would you get our guests some food and, if possible, tea. The archive itself may be quite pleasant, but I find it takes a while to warm up." Elizabeth tapped her fingers together. "So where to begin? Or rather, what's the last thing you encountered? Before the lapse, that is."

Cinq and Nissa exchanged a glance. Cinq said, "We were in the town of Ignaesdale. It's the…"

Elizabeth interrupted, "The monastery where the Pentarch studied. Wonderful! Must have been fascinating to be at the site of his tutelage. From my understanding, the monks took special care to preserve the monastery in the same way—structure and practice—as during the time of the Pentarch. And in complete defiance of what other monasteries adapted over time. That would explain the wayroom remaining intact." She pulled the notebook from her belt and started writing in a tight script. "Pardon me, I must update my notes. Oh, dear me, on a tangent again." She closed her notebook and returned it to its pouch. "Please continue."

"*Anyway*," Cinq cleared his throat, "we took shelter when the Earth Titan manifested. And when we came out, we'd lost five years."

Elizabeth nodded. "Hmmm. You missed all but the beginning."

Nissa frowned. "The beginning of *what?* Spit it out, Doc, or I get grumpy."

"I'm sorry, I'm sorry. You see, the events at Ignaesdale—quite famous, actually—were largely regarded as the beginning of the Convergence. We are still a few years from complete Convergence, as you know. Just a second, I have all the dates." Elizabeth turned and scanned the shelves before retrieving a red leather-bound book. She opened it to reveal page after page of locations, dates, and Titans. Elizabeth tapped an entry. "Ok, yes. Ignaesdale, June 21st, 1201. The previous Titan was the Water Titan, May 19th in Hampshire. That one was quick, a handful of minutes with complete obliteration… and so not counted as the start, but just a fluke. That one was fascinating. Not even rubble was left, everything was reduced to salt. That's right, salt. So many questions raised. But what came after was even more illuminating."

Nissa turned to Cinq. "Ok, this has gone on long enough. Can I strangle her if she doesn't get to the point? Or does she get one more chance?"

Elizabeth tapped the page again. Her face darkened. "These aren't minor details. You know the Convergence, of course. It is the synchronization of nearplane and otherplane. Overlaps will become more common, and more lengthy, until…" she trailed off. "Is this making sense to you? I trust these are not new concepts."

Cinq nodded, Yon shook his head, and Nissa remained staunchly defiant.

Elizabeth pursed her lips. "Allow me to illustrate. For the monk." In a flash, the matron was on her feet. She pulled a spool of wire from her belt and wrapped it three times around a nearby column, around a second column, then back to the first. She grabbed a pair of wire cutters, then snipped and positioned the wire so that there were two lines side by side. Working with the wire again, she cut two lengths and secured them to the middle of the span, so that the long, loose ends hung to the ground. She returned to her desk, rummaging through drawers before coming up with two heavy metal seals, one bronze and one silver. She attached the weights to the wires so that both hung, though at different heights. Satisfied, she pointed at the bronze weight. "Let's consider this is our world, the nearplane." She pulled the weight back and let it go so that it swung back and forth like a pendulum. Next, she grabbed the silver weight. "And this is the otherplane." She let the second weight go and the two swung back and forth, crossing in the middle before starting up again.

Elizabeth stood back to admire her work. "Right now, the weights are quite out of sync. But as the lengths and weights are different, so too is the interval. So even if they started opposite," she paused to watch, "given enough time, the intervals will match on occasion. And that is the nature of the Convergence. It's all math. That's why we were able to predict this moment so long ago." She smiled kindly at Yon. "Does that help, my friend?"

Nissa cocked her head to one side. "She's leaving things out. I heard this Convergence will be permanent. Your weights are already drifting."

Elizabeth continued, "It's an imperfect model, only meant to illustrate. The real relationship is closer to that of the Earth and Moon, where each pulls on the other. Once full Convergence is met, a harmonization will occur. It's all quite measurable, as I said. And as we approach synchronization, overlaps will become more common. Or, as happened here, quite lengthy."

Yon rubbed his temples. Maybe Cinq and Nissa had this as part and parcel of their studies, but it was all new to him. This was the kind of metaphysics reserved for monks *after* they became masters. He asked, "But what about the Pentarch?"

Elizabeth's eyes lit up. "A fascinating start to what I assume is a fascinating question. What about him?"

Yon continued, "The Pentarch stopped the last Convergence. But how did he do that if it was inevitable?"

"I would say simply, but there was nothing simple about it. He knocked our worlds out of synch." She grabbed one of the weights, holding it for a moment before releasing it. "No small feat, but not permanent. And so here we are again. Granted, the reality is not so clinical. Haggards on the streets, wyvern on the rooftops, and the regrettable weather. But we will survive."

Yon looked around Elizabeth's study, taking in the books, the polished desk, and the plain-clothed woman in front of him. He considered what was beyond those walls. The frozen city, the haggards, winged terrors, and who knew what else? How could she be so… cheerful?

Cinq shifted where he stood. "Are there other places like this?"

Elizabeth grimaced. "I have to assume so, but we lost contact with the outside world. I have no idea how many, or to what extent. We are trapped here. The city walls are now triple their height, encased in ice, and guarded by wyvern. We are resigned to wait until the overlap passes, and our city is ours again."

Cinq continued, "And are there other dangers? Enemies within?"

A shadow passed over Elizabeth's face. "You mean reavers. Their numbers have… grown."

Nissa snapped her fingers. "Yes! That right there. *That's* what I want to hear about."

Elizabeth folded her hands together. She wore a look of smug satisfaction. "Did you mean, *please?*"

Cinq leaned forward, his voice low and polite. "Doctor, we encountered an army of reavers at Open Eye. I didn't think such a thing was possible. Now, would you *please* tell us about the people who want us dead?"

The matron nodded. "Yes, the world changed. As the Titans returned, the reavers grew bold. There is a man from the north, they call him the witchlord. He turned the reavers from a cult into an army. Their mantra is simple: destroy the witches and be saved from Titans." She tapped her cane with her index finger. "People are drawn to such a message. Clarity without nuance. So much easier to blame people than to measure the movement of nearplane and otherplane." A blanket of dread had settled across Elizabeth's face. She shuddered as though shaking it from her.

"The witchlord's real name is Mortimer Cain. He was a child from the mountain tribes, raised as a monk. And, depending on who you ask, was either thrown out of his order or righteously departed. He spent time in exile before returning to spread his message, preach, and recruit." Elizabeth shook her head. "It is something he does quite well. Fire and brimstone, doom and gloom, but with purpose. The frightened flock to him."

Cinq pursed his lips. "There have been prophets like this before."

"Oh no. Not like this. He's moved past prophet on his way to a warrior-messiah. And his army is growing."

Nissa said, "But… but does it work? Does the whole 'kill all the witches' thing work?"

"Certainly not. At least, not in the way he promises," Elizabeth replied. "Look at my precious Alexandria. Unregulated magic has been prohibited here since the time of the Pentarch. The Fire Titan didn't seem to notice." She smiled. "Don't worry, friends, the edicts against magic here were practical not prejudicial. Many researchers were concerned magic would disturb their instruments and corrupt their data." She tapped the top of her cane. "Forbidding magic *reduces* the chances of a Titan, but doesn't eliminate it. Conflict, war, and crowds are all factors."

Yon shook his head. "Then why do people believe it? If the Titans come without witches, wouldn't everyone see it's a lie?"

Elizabeth shook her head. "No. Because the reavers can always claim someone was using magic in secret. So hard to know—truly know—if all your friends are pure."

Nissa pouted. "So it's our fault, right? Mages, monks, and wikken. We're the enemy now."

Elizabeth nodded. "For many, yes. You may have done well to miss these past five years. When the reavers catch a witch—"

"They burn them," Nissa finished. "They always burn them. Unimaginative little boogers." She took a deep breath. "So, who is left? Of our kind, I mean."

Elizabeth held up her hands. "That's not easy for me to know, stuck here as we are."

"What about before you were trapped?" Cinq asked. "What happened to Eastwind, or the other mage towers?"

She shook her head. "They hadn't fallen before we were cut off from the world. I don't know if that remains true. Between the witchlord and Titans, much has been destroyed." Elizabeth drew herself up in her seat. "For the time being, we are isolated. Above all else, we must survive."

Cinq said, "That barricade in the streets, the one warded against the haggards. That was your work, wasn't it? You're a mage."

Elizabeth clapped her hands together. "Don't be ridiculous. I earned my degrees here. I studied ancient cultures, archaeology, and linguistics."

Cinq stared back in incomprehension. "But the gate was enchanted. Only a mage could do that."

Elizabeth tilted back her head and laughed. The chuckles turned to a high-pitched wheezing as tears rolled down her cheeks. Yon felt decidedly uncomfortable.

The scholar said, "Is *that* what they taught you at Eastwind? Do you think mages have a monopoly on magic? What about the things the fey do? Or even your friend monk when he focuses his chi?"

Cinq furrowed his brow. "That's different."

Elizabeth continued, "Only in application. Enchanting artifacts is a matter of science, not will. True, the art has been diminished of late, but that is only because there is so much less magic in the world to go around." She smiled. "My friends, this city is a closed system. We are besieged by haggards and wyvern. Many have learned to fight, but only to survive. We are not soldiers. I learned to use magic out of a lack of physical materials."

Cinq bit his lip. Yon could tell he was processing this information, not only in his assessment of Elizabeth, but how it impacted his worldview. Cinq asked, "Do you have a specialty?"

"Staying alive. So, I suppose I specialize in defense. Traps, glyphs, explosives. Outside of the arcane, I have studied medicine and human biology. They don't call me 'doctor' out of respect for academia. I act as the resident surgeon."

"And let me guess," Cinq paused a few moments before continuing, "that all came naturally? Almost as if you were born to it. More like remembering than learning?"

Elizabeth locked eyes with Cinq. For the first time, the matron's bubbling effervescence slowed. "Continue."

Cinq asked, "Tell me, what is your earliest memory?"

"Mage LeGarrec, you have my full attention. But you must first explain your question." Her eyes locked unblinking with Cinq's.

Nissa did not allow the moment to play itself out. She clapped her hands in delight. "Hot flaming Titans of terror! It's her, isn't it? It *is* her. And then there were four. Who says there's no such thing as fate?"

Elizabeth pointed at Cinq. "What do you know about me?"

In response, Cinq removed the Tracer from his coat. "Doctor, do you know what this is?"

Her eyes lit up in recognition. A mischievous smile spread her lips. To Yon's surprise, she reached into her tool belt and produced a small glass sphere of her own, five points of light, four of them bright. "Yes, I believe I do."

Elizabeth leaned forward, her Tracer in her hand as she held it next to Cinq's. The spheres were identical, with the slight difference of Cinq's being clear crystal, while Elizabeth's shone with a blue tint. She offered the Tracer to Cinq who examined them side by side.

Elizabeth said, "When I found that, there were only two lights in it, one strong and drawn to me. I assumed it was as I was the finder. Over time, other lights joined the first two. Then, about five and a half years ago, three lights vanished. I put the Tracer back on a shelf at that point, and it was dumb luck when I noticed it again yesterday. Back to full five lights with four burning the brightest I'd ever seen."

Cinq returned Elizabeth's Tracer. "Did you ever go looking for the last light? Do you know who it's attached to?"

Elizabeth shook her head. "Well… I always meant to. At one time, I had quite the plan. Here, I'll show you." The doctor walked to the stacks and removed a rolled map that contained a series of long, straight lines. "After there were only two lights left, and before the Fire Titan, I did a bit of traveling. I found that if I took measurements with the Tracer and a compass, I could get some idea of bearings. What I learned was that whoever—or whatever—the Tracer is attuned to was to the north." She tapped the map where the series of lines converged. "Then again, that's assuming that the whoever/whatever hasn't since moved. The bearing was the same when I repeated the exercise just yesterday, though I was more focused on the new lights, so bright and so near."

In a movement that surprised Yon, Cinq removed his long coat and spread it across the table. The interior, Yon saw, was not just a mess of cracks and threads, but a large-scale map of the continent. It, too, was crisscrossed with lines. The lines converged at Ignaesdale, Alexandria, and even the same northern location.

Cinq pointed to the map. "For me, Nissa was the challenge. She was always on the move, so I couldn't triangulate her. I had to chase her instead, following the one point of light that wouldn't stay put. The rest of you weren't quite so mobile, so I went after her first."

"Do you know the connection? What ties us together?" Elizabeth asked.

Yon blurted out, "We're keys."

The scholar replied, "I beg your pardon?"

Cinq looked warily at Yon. "The abbot at Open Eye, he said… just a moment, I want to get the words right."

Yon interrupted, "He said there were five Tracers just like that one. He called it the 'prime set.' And each of the Tracers led to the keys."

Nissa chimed in, "Don't forget 'unspeakable power.' He definitely said something about that."

Elizabeth looked at them. She had become still. "And those were his exact words? Who was he again?"

Yon shuffled forward. "The abbot at Open Eye. We only got a chance to speak with him for a minute before the reavers showed up."

Elizabeth shook from her daze and started pacing. She held one hand behind her back and kept her Tracer in the other. "The term 'prime set' is common in artificer circles. A prime set can never be duplicated, or more specifically, the underlying enchantment was inverted to stay hidden. To make a prime set of five Tracers, all with identical targets, and for those targets to be people… the chances of that happening more than once are infinitesimal."

Nissa rolled her eyes. "We already know they're rare. Remember? We almost got killed for them?"

Elizabeth shook her head. "That's not what I mean. I mean that there would be records of this sort of thing. One Tracer? Not noteworthy. But five Tracers, five targets, and a specific time period? That I can work with. After all, this is a library." She clapped her hands together. "Finally, some good scholarly work to be done!"

Nissa pouted. "We should have brought the abbot with us."

Elizabeth was distracted, back to scrawling in her notebook. "Scholar, mage, monk, wikken. Next would be hermit, don't you think?"

Cinq nodded. "If the pattern holds."

Yon said, "We guessed that maybe we were—in our own time—representatives."

Cinq muttered, "Maybe, but we have no proof. And we could be keys all day every day, but unless we know *to what* then it doesn't matter."

Nissa put her hands on her hips. "We don't have to figure this out, you know."

"Why not?" Yon asked.

She continued, "Well, with four of us, we just have to remember it. We've remembered other things, haven't we? Close your eyes and listen to your gut. No, no, no, don't answer right now, and don't say it out loud. We'll sleep on it. Tomorrow, make that the first question you ask yourself and remember the first thing that pops into your mind. We'll see if we have the same answer."

Yon said, "Will that work?"

Nissa said, "It does with the fey. Sometimes after you wake up that little line between the real and the unknown is a bit more blurred than usual. Trust me." Her eyes grew bright. "Or… we could all get royally drunk. We could have ourselves a vision quest! What's the wine situation here, Doc?"

"Let's try sleep first," Cinq said. He turned back to Elizabeth. "Back to the present. Is it going to be a problem for you, who we are? Will your fellows accept a monk, a wikken, and a mage here?"

Elizabeth pursed her lips. "They won't be excited about the prospect. The people here, they've been through a lot. A whole lot. Outsiders won't be accepted with open arms."

Nissa shrugged. "Fine. So, hook us up with one of those awesome gray smocks and we'll blend right in."

"I was going a different direction with my question." Cinq turned to Elizabeth. "Would you like to come with us? Only one of us left to find."

She leaned her head back and laughed. "What? And leave all this? If I wanted to run away from my problems, I'd have long been gone. But that doesn't mean I can't help you. And I'm not talking about just getting you warm, fed, and rested. That is simply a courtesy."

"Then what?" Yon asked.

"Why, you're surrounded by it. This is the great archive, and a whole lot more books were saved than were destroyed. I already know more about these Tracers than I did five minutes ago, including an important clue. That should get me started." She turned to Nissa. "We can try your way as well, but research is my specialty."

"I'll help," Cinq volunteered.

Nissa nodded. "You two have a good time. Yon and I will look around."

Cinq said, "But first we sleep."

"No. First we eat."

14

~ Nissa ~

Nissa woke tangled in a blanket in the corner of Elizabeth's reading room. A temporary arrangement, they were assured, until Blue had time to circulate the idea of their presence. The rumblings of haggards echoed in her ears. That must mean it was morning. According to Blue, the haggards froze each night, only to thaw and wake with the sun. And then it all started again. Nissa rolled to her feet and stretched, casting the blanket to the floor. Not far from her nest, Yon slept curled in a ball. Cinq, on the other hand, was entrenched at a table, surrounded by neatly arranged books on one side and a catastrophe of loose paper, unfurled scrolls, and scrawled notes on the other.

"Morning." Nissa yawned. "You sleep?"

"Enough," Cinq replied. "Finally warm, though." He looked down at his work. "Did your 'tapping of the unconscious' thing work? Any revelations?"

"Nah. That was kind of wishful thinking. How's the search on your side?"

"I'm making progress. Mostly trying to find where to look." He gestured to the piles. "Most of these are just catalogs. The real work won't start until Elizabeth gets back."

Nissa shrugged. "I'd ask what that is, but don't want to pass out from boredom. Did our host mention food?"

"Yes. Blue is in the hallway. I've eaten."

"I'll take the kid." Nissa crept over to Yon, leaned close, and said, "Hey Yon… good morning!"

Yon snapped upright. "What?" He looked around in confusion.

"Let's get some breakfast. I'm starving."

Nissa crossed to the far side of the room to three neatly folded piles of clothing. Elizabeth had agreed they dress like refugees to blend in. Fine by her. Clothes were just clothes. Nissa doubted Yon would care, either. Monks were supposed to be above all that, though it might feel weird anyway. Still, she waited for the moment when Cinq had to change. His long coat and broad hat didn't always scream "mage," but they certainly screamed "Cinq."

Yon dressed quickly and quietly. He looked at her with an uneasy smile. "How do I look?" he asked.

Nissa replied, "You'll need to grow hair to fit in. Or find a hat. Which would probably be faster."

"Nissa?" Cinq looked up from his books. "You should cover your runes. And put on some shoes."

She looked down at the tattoos spreading her arms and peeking from the tops of her bare feet. She wasn't trying to draw attention to herself. Admittedly, she hated having to hide, having to pretend she was something she wasn't. The reavers were the obvious threat, but a lot of people hated wikkens without trying to kill her. Forgetting to cover her runes wasn't an act of rebellion, just an oversight. When the voices of the fey picked up, her concentration divided, the natural world paled. The fey stood as bright bursts of color in a black and gray world.

"Sorry," she mumbled. Nissa pulled on a long-sleeved shirt and slipped her feet into leather moccasins fit for padding indoors and nothing else. Where did she put her boots? She definitely had some earlier. If she had to wear shoes, they might as well be sturdy enough to take outside.

She walked to the door only to find it locked. She rapped on it and the door immediately opened with Blue on the other side.

Nissa said, "Morning. I heard something about breakfast."

Blue nodded. Her expression made it look like she was just barely tolerating them. Was she here on Elizabeth's orders, or did she feel responsible for bringing in strays? Blue turned to lumber down the hall, with Yon and Nissa on her heels.

They ventured into the inner halls of the archive. And though marble tile lined the floor, the inhabitants in their gray smocks and soft shoes made no sound when they walked. The refugees' voices were loud at first, then died to whispers as Nissa and Yon passed by. Nissa kept her eyes low, sneaking a peek at the open doors they passed. She was surprised by how many rooms seemed intact. In some, books were neatly ordered and maintained. Other rooms resembled a military camp. Shelves were cleared and replaced by workbenches, cots, and crates. Blue wound them through the halls and down a flight of stairs to an open room. Marble columns and pewter busts contrasted tables made from overturned bookshelves. At a large table in the middle, a skinny man ladled soup from a tarnished copper pot to people waiting in line. Blue cut to the head of the queue, returning with three full bowls and a hunk of bread.

The three of them settled at a vacant table and immediately set into their meal. Yon was the first to sample the mystery dish. He started sneezing and snorting with the first taste.

Blue smirked. "Cook uses a lot of pepper. Distracts from the taste. You get used to it."

Yon heroically took another spoonful, this one he swallowed. "The pepper, or the taste?"

"The pepper," Blue said. "The taste is only as good as you are hungry. You do what you can."

Nissa took a bite. Awful, truly awful. But she was so hungry she didn't care.

After a few minutes of focused eating, Yon spoke. "Blue, who decides which rooms get used for what? And which books get to stay?"

"The doc, mostly. There's a give and take. Sometimes we need the space, and books get moved. Or maybe someone just takes over a place for their own. Doc doesn't mind so long as no one messes with the stacks." Blue slurped her soup. "She hasn't always been in charge. She rose to the occasion. In the beginning, the people hiding here were burning books for warmth. Until that happened, she was just another refugee. But she stopped the fires outright. She was so passionate that everyone else was a bit overawed. Doc eased off a bit, eventually. Some books were still burned, others are off-limits."

"Seems odd she'd burn anything," Yon said.

Blue shrugged. "The ones that get torched are what the doc calls 'the business.' Tax records, storehouse counts, that kind of thing. Those days are over. The doc fixed the furnace. There are so few of us, the city stores go a long way."

"But not forever," Nissa stated.

"No, not forever," Blue echoed. "But we don't think this is a forever situation. We buckle down, make do, and one day the overlap will end. And if not?" Blue shrugged. "Not much we can do about it, except pick off as many haggards as we can. Maybe one day we'll get them all."

Nissa raised an eyebrow. "I don't follow."

"They freeze at night."

"Right."

"Frozen haggards don't fight back. Ax to the noggin, and they don't wake up. But there are a *lot* of those hairy, stinking buggers. And for all we know, they just keep crossing over. On the plus side, we get this lovely stew."

Nissa snorted hard, soup shooting from her nose. "This is *haggard* stew?"

"You see any cows around here?"

Nissa stared at her bowl. Laughter welled inside of her. She dropped her spoon as she cackled, snorting and wheezing until her eyes ran with tears. "I'm sorry, I'm sorry. I just… It never occurred to me."

A metallic clang interrupted her mirth. Her eyes jerked upward to see a massive bell swinging back and forth. The room erupted in frenzy. Chairs were thrown back, and the nervous murmurs became panicked shouts.

Blue hopped up. "Time to move. Let's go."

"What's going on?" Yon said.

Blue barked, "We've got a breach. Something's in the archive."

"A breach in…" Nissa began, but Blue was already on the move. Nissa jerked Yon from his seat as she hurried to follow—in the opposite direction of everyone else. Blue didn't seem to notice. She bowled her way through the scrambling masses and back out the door they'd come in. As the crowd thinned, their pace increased. They ran down the hall, up a flight of stairs, and past rows of now-closed doors. Nissa followed as they turned onto the last corridor, a long, tiled hallway lined by windows looking out on the frozen city.

A high-pitched whine filled Nissa's ears, punctuated by a rapid thud. She turned her head away as the windows exploded inward. Glass pelted the far wall, stinging her exposed skin even as the frigid air burned it. Wind whipped into the hallway, howling as it snaked around pillars before exiting again through broken windows. The maroon drapes flapped and snapped before being ripped from the wall altogether. Nissa spun to look for Yon. The young monk had dropped into a three-point stance. He looked up to meet her stare. His cheeks were windburned and red, with a few trickles of blood where he'd been scoured by glass.

A second crash sounded behind her, followed by a heavy thud, and the excruciating sound of claws on marble. Nissa's heart leaped in her chest as she found herself staring at a large, black, and muscled creature. A serpentine neck connected its triangular head to a horned and ridged back. Skeletal legs stuck out at discordant angles. Translucent skin stretched its wings. A wyvern.

The creature opened its jaws and screeched. The cry drove Nissa to her knees, not just from the noise, but pain that assaulted her on a mental level. She clasped her hands over her ears, but it did nothing to diminish the cry.

Nissa tried to get her legs beneath her. God, but the pain. Her first thought was to escape, she had to throw herself from the now-shattered windows. If only she could make it across the hallways, she would be free. She could seek release.

Do it. Do it. Do it. DO IT. DO IT!

She snapped from her trance as Yon sped past in a gray blur. He wove through fallen chunks of plaster and broken glass until stopping between her and the wyvern. The creature drew its head back; jaws opened as it sucked air. Yon snapped forward, his body propelled like a crossbow bolt. Pale light flashed as his fist struck the creature.

The wyvern was thrown back, sent hurtling down the hallway. As it skidded across the tile, a series of intense red flashes reverberated through the hallway. With every explosion, flames surged across the creature. One, two, three, four, until the wyvern slid to a stop, nothing left but a smoldering pile of embers, black and sooty, on the marble floor.

Nissa clambered to her feet and limped over to Yon. The monk was panting, hands on his knees. The ethereal light which had consumed him no longer shone. "Yon! How did you… I mean… how?"

Yon shook his head in disbelief. "I didn't do that. I mean, I did the first part, but not, *that.*"

Nissa looked at the smoking remains of the wyvern. The intensity of the creature's attack—and its abrupt end—reduced the cold pouring through the windows to an afterthought.

Blue stumbled toward them in a drunken stagger. "What did you…?"

She was interrupted as one of the hallway doors opened, and Elizabeth walked out. Her face was taut with anger. Cinq trailed behind with his staff brandished in both hands. The scholar hitched up her skirts and knelt to study the scorch marks on the hallway floor. She looked at the pile of ash that had been the wyvern.

"Four," Elizabeth mumbled. "Can't believe it triggered four." She stood bolt upright. "All of you, out of here. Let's go." She held the door open until the others filed through. The howl of wind diminished as the door cracked against the frame. In the stillness, Nissa could feel the pounding of her heart in her chest. She looked over at Yon, his face blanched and breathing still heavy. She doubted either of them understood what had happened.

Elizabeth spun to face the monk. "I take it *you* triggered my traps. The first barrier would have killed the wyvern, but no, you had to throw it across four. This will take weeks to rebuild."

"I didn't do it on purpose…" Yon protested.

Nissa raised her hand. "Yeah! Give him a break. How were we supposed to know what secrets you didn't bother to tell us about? Maybe next time, you'll fill us in on your little plans. It was about to blast us with—you know, its screamy thing. We did what we had to. Where were you?"

"Waiting. Letting my traps do their job." Elizabeth sighed. "I suppose what's done is done." She tapped her chin. "The wyvern have never come this far before. People are going to notice that."

Cinq asked, "What do you mean? I assumed this was what passed for normal around here."

Elizabeth shook her head. "The haggards attack at every opportunity, but wyverns are quite canny. I've never seen one enter a building willingly."

Cinq replied, "Then it was after something. I haven't used any magic, so it wasn't drawn to that. What are you suggesting?"

She tilted her head to one side. "Perhaps it's us. The keys."

Cinq nodded. "It's possible."

Nissa threw up her hands. "Oh? You're all experts on keys now? Well, that's good news. You figure out what we're keys to exactly?" She squinted back and forth between Elizabeth and Cinq.

"No time to explain," Cinq said. "We—"

"Bullshit!" Nissa snapped. "I want to know *before* I die."

Cinq glared at her. "Everything, Nissa. We're the keys to everything. Now listen up. Because if we die now, that's not going to matter."

15

~ Cinq ~

Cinq was getting tired of things trying to eat him, murder him, or being impatient with him. This wasn't "good scholarly work," as Elizabeth called it. This was making snap decisions without enough information. He glared at the others, daring anyone to challenge him. When no one responded, he started shoving scrolls into the pockets of his coat. His stomach clenched.

Cinq said, "If we're drawing the fey's attention, we need to get out. Out of the city and out of the overlap. They won't just leave us alone."

Elizabeth nodded. "Getting out is probably for the best. But I can't take them all with me either. And they need protecting, nurturing. I can't abandon them."

Blue folded her arms. "Doc, it was rough at the beginning, but we've all learned to survive. They'll be all right without you."

The scholar looked up in surprise. "Dearest Blue, I wasn't worried about the people. I'm worried about my books!"

Nissa cocked her head. "Hmph. Well, at least I know you and Cinq would get along. Probably for the best you're staying here. Not sure how much of that I could take."

Elizabeth held up her finger. "Then again, I know I *should* go, out of obligation. And the promise of what we can learn. Blue, I'm putting you in charge."

Blue shook her head. "Not a chance. I'm going with you." She frowned at Nissa. "Someone needs to watch your back."

Nissa clapped her hands together. "Goody, goody, goody. Great. Wonderful. One big happy family. And I'd argue the point, but *it is terrible here.* So how do we get out?"

Blue picked at her teeth. "Skyways aren't an option. The wyvern will be looking for revenge. We've seen that before."

Cinq said, "Streets filled with haggards? Doesn't sound better."

Elizabeth pointed to the floor. "We go down."

Yon smiled. "Of course! You've got a bunker. I'm guessing it's a nice one."

"Not exactly," Elizabeth answered. "The water table is too high. But we do have alternatives."

Blue folded her arms. "What should we tell the others?"

"Nothing for now," the scholar said. "I'll leave a letter to explain. We can't all go together, and I certainly don't want anyone trying to stop me. I don't want them to think I've been misled."

Nissa snorted. "By who? Tricksy witches? That's fine. I'm used to it. I understand."

Elizabeth shook her head. "No, you don't. The people here deserve to be scared. They've earned that. It will be gentler if we go unannounced."

Cinq rapped his staff on the floor. "We've talked, we've decided. We'll argue later."

Blue walked to a bookshelf and grabbed a particularly large, red-bound tome. She removed it, only to stick the entirety of her arm into the stacks. With a metallic click, something released. Cinq whistled as a section of the bookshelf spun to reveal a slender opening. Blue disappeared within, with Elizabeth, Nissa, and Yon following. Cinq paused to check the table, retrieving one more scroll and sighing at leaving so much behind. Then he, too, ducked into the darkness.

Behind him, the passageway closed with a resolute thud, followed by murmurs as a rose-colored glow lit their feet, snaking down, down, down to reveal a staircase.

Yon asked, "Did you make this?"

Elizabeth answered, "Not the stairs, just the lighting. It uses magic, like the gate or the wards in the hallway, but it's not a trap. It creates light, nothing else. I have set the devices throughout the archive just in case."

Nissa said, "Ever hear of a good old-fashioned torch?"

"Ever hear of what fire could to a building housing the most complete record of worldly knowledge that is—unfortunately—quite flammable?"

"Point taken," Nissa mumbled. "So... down?"

"Down."

Blue led the way. As they descended, the sounds of hurried footsteps and the sharp barks of commands came muffled through the stone walls. The voices, urgent and panicked, soon diminished, until they heard nothing but the trudge of their boots. Cinq felt the isolation closing in once more.

"Everyone, hold a moment," he called. "Nissa, what do you hear?"

She titled her head. "A crap-ton of haggards. What do you think I hear?" She paused. "But I think they're up above. Pawing, snorting, hungry, grumpy."

Blue grunted. "If they're above us, we're almost there."

They continued down the spiral staircase until masoned steps became hewn ice. The red lighting ended.

With a strike of flint, Blue lit one torch, which she in turn used to ignite several others. In the dull, orange glow, the chamber stretched before them. They were in a cavern of sorts, broad and low-ceilinged. The torchlight reflected off ice-coated rock and glistening limestone. Not far from where the stairs ended, the cavern floor opened out into an underground sea that lapped gently against the ice and sandy shore.

Yon exclaimed, "It's warm in here. The water's not frozen."

Cinq watched the dull lap of waves. The water pulsed with heat which radiated above the surface. He approached the edge, crouched, and dipped in a finger. "Is this from the Fire Titan?"

Elizabeth shook her head. "No. Even before the Titan, hot springs were common. My colleagues surmised the city rests on a dormant volcano. Perhaps it's what drew the Fire Titan here."

Cinq shook himself back to the present. "We're still in the overlap. But it's less focused here. The energy is *diminished*. Maybe we are on the edge, or perhaps it's the effect of the water."

"Does it matter?" Nissa asked.

Cinq frowned back at her. Torchlight flickered across her skin. Was she deliberately messing with him? Likely yes. But that was beside the point. He cleared his throat. "If we don't understand the reasons, how can we predict the outcomes?"

Blue looked at them critically. "The important thing is we get out. We think the cave opens out past the sea. We haven't explored much farther."

Nissa asked, "Why not? You were stuck in the city and never tried to get out?" She paused. "There are things down here, aren't there?"

Blue's jaw tightened. But before she could reply, Elizabeth stepped between them. She held up one hand, her face unreadable. "There is a risk, Nissa. This place is an unknown. And as your friend said, we *are* in an overlap. So please, be patient." Elizabeth turned to Blue. "Which way? You know these caves best."

Blue stepped forward as the others followed. The torchlight played on the water and ice as they walked. Cinq cast his eyes at Nissa, who shrugged in response. He wasn't able to catch Yon's eye. The boy's face was scrunched in concentration, and his fists balled in readiness. Only Elizabeth looked at ease. She had taken out her leather notebook and, at intervals, would make a note.

Blue led them as they staggered along a narrow spit of land that followed the erratic shoreline of the underground sea. Her path meandered to stay on the crushed ice, avoiding the black and glossy patches of dangerously slick ground. Cinq followed her footsteps, though his eyes kept wandering to the frozen environment lit by torchlight. The ceiling's mixture of green-tinted rock, translucent ice, and pockets of darkness resonated with serenity and expanse. He shuddered. There didn't seem to be enough walls to hold the ceiling up, let alone an entire city. The feeling was different than in the tunnels below Ignaesdale. That had felt more like a rabbit hole in a mass of rock. This felt like Alexandria could shift and crush them at any moment.

The crunch of their footsteps on sand and ice reverberated throughout the cavern even as the drip of water contrasted the sound with its precise tones. They traveled without speaking, Blue leading and the rest of them staying close. Finally, they reached a point where the path ended in a spit of land with a long wooden boat dragged up on the shore. The sea stretched out beyond.

Yon turned to Blue. He whispered, "Are we going across? What's out there?"

Blue pulled a compass from her pocket and rotated as she found her bearing. "We're not sure. The first party never came back. I like to think they got lucky." She added, "There used to be two boats."

Cinq looked at the narrow vessel. A pair of long oars extended from the sides like the legs of a water bug. Had it been carried down the steps? Was it built here? Or leftover from long ago?

Nissa scowled. "After considering the options.... Yep, I don't like this."

Now it was Cinq's turn to smile. "Of course not. You're effectively a cat."

She wheeled to face him. "Did you hear me complain about landing in the water after we went down the well in Ignaesdale?"

"Yes."

"Well, I could've said more," she pouted. "And I care less about getting wet than getting lost. Am I the only one who was told not to play in caves when I was a kid?"

Cinq cleared his throat. "You used to live in a cave."

Yon said, "Can you two stop for a moment?" He turned to face Nissa. "Do you hear anything now?"

Nissa cocked her head. "Almost nothing. The haggards and wyvern are far away."

"Anything… in the water?" Yon's eyes were wide.

Nissa replied, "If there is, it's being quiet."

Cinq said, "You keep listening and I'll row. Probably better if we move before we're noticed. Blue, which way?"

"In theory, going north will take us toward open water. I'm going on stories, though. That's all we have." Blue gripped the boat. "Give me a hand here."

They pushed the rowboat into the black waters, and everyone piled in. Cinq and Yon sat facing one another as they grasped the oar handles. Blue took a position on the bow, while Nissa and Elizabeth climbed into the back. Nissa wrapped her arms tightly around herself and hunched down. Elizabeth withdrew her journal, made a few notes, and returned it once more. Cinq watched her closely. Just because they were connected by the Tracer, didn't mean they were all equally trusted.

Cinq and Yon pulled on the oars. With each stroke, water swirled around the blades to echo throughout the cavern, followed by the drip-drip of falling water. At first, working in concert with Yon occupied his thoughts. He turned his curiosity to the scholar.

"What is that?" Cinq asked Elizabeth, still scrawling in her notebook.

Elizabeth looked at him in surprise, as if just now realizing that she shared the boat with others. "Thoughts, observations. I can't help but wonder what carved this cavern or even how it exists."

"What do you mean?"

"By my math, we are below sea level. So why do pockets of air remain at all? Or is this a new phenomenon? Perhaps the caves were always dry, or perhaps the water was expunged when the Fire Titan came."

Cinq murmured assent.

Elizabeth clasped her hands below her chin. "What did you say to the wikken? 'You must understand something to predict it.' I think these questions are important. Sooner or later the ice will recede, and life will return to normal, or adapt to a new normal. At that point, knowing what lies beneath can be of immense value."

Nissa interrupted. "Quiet, you two."

Cinq and Yon stopped rowing. In the following silence, solitude closed around them. The light from the torches extended a dozen yards in all directions, but other than that, they were surrounded by a formless void. Even the roof of the cavern was no longer visible.

Nissa whispered, "I can *hear* her."

"Hear who?" Yon asked.

Nissa ignored him. "Go that way." She pointed off the starboard side. Cinq and Yon adjusted the angle of the boat. "Now pull."

Cinq leaned against the oars once more, harder than before. They guided the boat through the waters. Occasionally, Nissa would stop them to listen and suggest changes in their course. Cinq didn't ask for details; this was Nissa's territory. He remained patient.

"Is that it?" Elizabeth pointed off the rail.

There, in the center of the endless pools of black, a glimmer disturbed the surface of the water. Just a ripple and hint of light. Then it was gone. Cinq held his breath as he listened. Another shimmer echoed the first, this time closer. Cinq saw the water riffle and glide as something edged closer. He thought he could almost make a shape out by the torchlight, but something wasn't quite right.

He watched as a hand extended from the water to grasp the stern of the boat. The rowboat tilted as something climbed from the water and glided aboard. It crouched on the stern, legs to the side and hands between them. While Cinq watched in dull fascination, Blue scrambled for her weapon. Nissa held up a hand to calm them. The creature—or whatever it was—did not drip with water. Instead, its feminine shape was made from water. What kept it together? The spirit looked at each of them in turn before fixating on Nissa.

Nissa repositioned into a crouch mimicking the—Cinq searched for the technical term—the naiad? Nereid? A water spirit. A fey. Nissa watched it closely, occasionally nodding, occasionally shaking her head as they communed in silence.

Months ago, when Cinq had asked Nissa about her talent, she described speaking to the fey as being less of a conversation of questions and answers, and more akin to what passed between people and their pets. Understanding was shared emotion, feelings, anxieties, and impulses, but no words. To Cinq's mind, this meant that the conversation could be as much about what the listener wanted to hear as what was said. Nonetheless, she produced amazing results.

Nissa turned to her friends. "It's all right. She's mostly curious. Wants to know if we're fishing."

Cinq didn't reply.

"She says that the black-fire-monkey-tooth-fur are gone now. No idea what those are supposed to be… haggards maybe? Wants to know if we fished for them. It… doesn't really translate."

Elizabeth cleared her throat. "Ask her if she knows—"

"Hold that thought." Nissa tilted her head forward. She held out her hands, palms up. The naiad leaned forward to place her own liquid hands atop Nissa's. "She says we're close to the edge. She wants to know if we'll melt. Again, sorry this is rough."

Understanding washed over Cinq. "Ask her if she would melt past the edge. See what she says."

Nissa kept her hands flat. The naiad's form rippled as it moved.

"She says no. She says she was here before the big-party-meeting-hate-defense, that it's her homeplace."

The hint of a smile tweaked Cinq's lips. "She means the overlap. She was here before it happened. She's not tied to it like the haggards. She's a nearplane fey."

"Of course she is. She's too cultured to be anything else."

Elizabeth scrawled in her notebook. "Does she know the way out?"

Nissa said, "Sheez, I'm working my way to that. Thought I'd ask if anything was coming to eat us first. But… yes… she does. But she wants butt-slide-over-perch. She wants a ride."

"By all means," Cinq deadpanned. "Happy to give a butt-slide-over-perch to a new friend."

Cinq returned to his seat and grabbed the oars. He pulled slowly against them while Yon followed his lead. Nissa's focus remained on the naiad. The creature leaned back against the stern with legs crossed over one another. She looked back at him with impassive translucent eyes. He felt a tickle at the edge of his awareness, the same feeling he got when someone used magic. Not precise, not concrete, but a whisper of an idea.

You have many heads. The thought drifted over Cinq like a daydream.

More than most, Cinq thought. Whether this could be picked up or not, he didn't know. *We share history.*

Sisters-mothers?

That time, the words and thoughts had been clearer. *We share purpose. Like family,* Cinq answered. *Do you have a family?*

The naiad shook her head. Had she picked that up from Nissa? *Family into big-party-meeting-hate-defense. Lonely-notfriend-onlyfish now.*

Cinq nodded, hoping that would hold meaning for her. And at the same time, he noticed that Nissa was nodding, or shaking her head in turn. Was the naiad communicating with all of them at once?

Nissa turned to Cinq. "Turn a little more left. She thinks she can find us a dry way out. Which sure beats swimming."

Cinq looked back at the naiad. Whatever strand of communication he had picked up was now gone. In a swift, soundless movement, she stood. Her slender form lit up in the torchlight. She was beautiful, in an otherplane water-fey kind of way. She turned and slid back into the water. Her shape gave way as she reentered—not in a splash—but as a merging with the underground sea.

"Nissa," Cinq said, "what happened?"

"She doesn't want to go shallow. Too many people, too much dirt. Her feelings, not mine."

Cinq rowed for several more yards before the boat lurched to a stop. He looked over the side. In the darkness, the water had an inky quality, and yet he could see a hint of sandy bottom in the torchlight. He pivoted in his seat to look in front. Up ahead, the cavern's ceiling sloped down to hang several feet above the water, though not dropping to touch it. The taper became a tunnel farther ahead.

"Nissa, Yon, your eyes are sharper than mine. Do we have a way out?"

Yon breathed deep. "I don't see it, but I can smell it. You can feel that, can't you?"

Cinq closed his eyes and slowly inhaled. A salty, organic scent rode a warm current of air, contrasting the sulfuric smell around them. Fresh air was coming from somewhere; they just had to find it.

Blue rose to her feet and pulled one of the torches from its holder. "I guess you lot haven't spent much time underground."

Nissa snorted, "Um, at least five years. Plus, Cinq says I used to live in a cave."

"Then follow the flame." Blue nodded at the torch, and now Cinq saw what she meant. The flame flickered slowly in one direction, then another. The flame moved in the air of the cavern as though caught in the breath of an enormous creature. "Come on, time to get our feet wet." Blue stepped from the boat into the shallow water, which rose just above her knee. Yon and Cinq grabbed the other torches and disembarked. The lessened weight freed the boat from the sand. They pulled it along for another dozen yards before Nissa and Elizabeth climbed out as well.

The ocean floor consisted of sand and gravel over stone, slick in spots from patches of algae. Cinq was grateful to have his staff for balance and considered—though dismissed—loaning it to Elizabeth. He assessed the magic he'd accumulated since coming to this place. Power surged through him, revitalized by the overlap. It comforted him.

They trudged through the shallows. At times, the water only covered the tops of their boots, while in other places they were soaked to the waist. The tunnel had tapered now, snaking back and forth as it narrowed. Cinq had to duck his head to avoid banging the ceiling. As the tunnel twisted one last time, they came to the end.

The passage terminated in a pile of fallen rocks, the water chest-high at the terminus. Blue held her torch up to the boulders. They watched the same breath of wind, in and out, as it passed through. She pressed her face to the cracks.

Blue said, "For what it's worth, I see daylight. That's a kick in the teeth. I'd start digging, but I don't want to pull the whole thing down on us."

Yon handed Blue his torch as he waded to the front. After a series of deep breaths, he ducked below the surface. Cinq expected the boy to come up immediately, but time stretched on.

A minute later, Yon burst through the surface, grinning widely. "It's clear! Not far either. Maybe twenty feet. Tight at the end, but not bad."

Blue asked, "Tight for you or tight for us?"

Yon shrugged. "You won't get stuck. But I can follow you if you want. The only thing is…"

"What?" Nissa asked. "The only thing is what?"

"Well, it's dark. You don't want to take a wrong turn."

Cinq unslung his backpack and fished out his rope. "We'll make a guide. Yon, swim this through and secure it on the other side. If you get turned around, follow the rope back and we'll do it again until we get it right. Tug three times once you're through. Sound good?"

Yon nodded vigorously. He grabbed one end of the rope and disappeared once more. After a minute, Cinq felt three sharp tugs on the rope. Before he could ask for volunteers, Nissa disappeared underwater. Blue followed a minute later, leaving Elizabeth and Cinq behind.

The scholar looked at Cinq with wary eyes. "I'm not as young as the rest of you."

"Nonsense, we're all centuries old."

"That's not what I meant."

"Look. You have two options. You can go next, and you've got friendlies on either side, or you can go last and, worse comes to worst, we pull you through. Personally, I'd rather swim myself." He placed a hand on her shoulder. This was where that whole empathy thing came in. "You can do it because you need to."

Elizabeth nodded. "And because this is just the beginning."

"Something like that."

Elizabeth took a deep breath before ducking underwater. Cinq waited behind, now realizing that between the rope, his staff, and the torch, something must be left behind. When he felt three sharp tugs on the rope, he took a deep breath, dropped the torch, and dove under.

As the torch extinguished, the water blinked into darkness. He resisted the urge to call forth a light out of fear of drawing the wrong kind of attention. They'd seen one fey, no reason there couldn't be others. Cinq held the staff in one hand and pulled against the rope with the other. His long coat impeded his strokes and threatened to tangle him. He pulled along. The coarse fibers of the rope dug into his skin. The rope became taut. Cinq held on as he was dragged along the tunnel, shoulders brushing against rocks, until he saw a glimmer of daylight above. It grew brighter and brighter until he burst through the surface.

He gasped and spluttered. The daylight hurt his eyes as he took deep breaths of warm air. In front of him, Nissa's face was grim. She opened her mouth to speak and shut it promptly.

"What? What is it?" he asked.

"I'm sorry, Cinq. But there's nothing we can do. It's just not worth going back. I'm afraid she's lost."

Cinq darted his eyes around. Elizabeth, Nissa, Blue, and Yon, they were all there. This didn't make sense.

Nissa placed her hand on his shoulder. "It was a good hat, Cinq. The best. I'll always cherish her memory."

Cinq smiled a wicked smile as he reached into his waistband. He pulled out his folded and sodden hat before shoving it down on his head. "For what it's worth, Nissa, I wouldn't leave you behind, either."

He stood upright, the water dripping off him as he faced away from the tunnel and into the daylight beyond. They were out of the city, out of the water, out of the tunnel, above ground—and at least for the moment—safe.

Most importantly, they were out of the overlap.

16

~ Nissa ~

Nissa hummed as she warmed her hands on the driftwood fire. Strips of cloth, a fur blanket, Alexandrian tunics, socks, shoes, and the holster for her knives were hanging to dry on a nearby bush. Being warm, rested, and out of immediate danger went a long way to making her feel human.

Funny, she thought, how the loss of five and a half years didn't bother her. Then again, she'd left no family behind. She shook off the pain of memory. Had her old enclave escaped the reavers? Were wikken, mages, and monks really being hunted down by this witchlord? Nissa knew that anyone looking for trouble with the wikken would find them slipperier than expected. But still, angry men with swords had a way of getting what they wanted.

She exhaled. The dark thoughts kept creeping in, but she needed to focus on the positives. She was warm, she was dry, nothing was trying to eat her. Nissa felt like a weary prisoner finally crawling into daylight. Blue, on the other hand, had whooped and danced at finally, *finally,* being out of the overlap.

She'd cursed, laughed, cried, and then… nothing. Her stoic demeanor returned, and she tromped off to go fishing. She was good at that too.

Nissa saw a pair of bare feet step up beside her. Cinq held his palms to the fire. He looked comical not wearing his long coat and hat, all skin and bones and scowl with only his smallclothes to maintain decency.

"Drying out, Nissa?"

"Slowly." She smirked. "Why does this remind me of Tronhelm?"

"That was entirely different. I still don't know why you picked a fight with fishermen. Or why they threw me in the river and not you." He sat beside her and held his palms to the fire. Blue and Yon were in conversation on the far side of the fire ring.

Nissa pouted. "They would have backed down if you didn't try to save me."

"Believe it or not, if you held your tongue, you wouldn't always need saving."

"I don't *need* saving. That's the point. Ok, there was that one time, but that wasn't even my fault."

"Ah-hem." A polite clearing of the throat and heavy stomp of boots heralded the arrival of Elizabeth. Unlike the rest of them, she had opted for wet clothes and modesty. Her tools, however, she had meticulously cleaned, oiled, and laid to dry on a nearby boulder. While Elizabeth's tunic had looked scholarly at the archive, out here she resembled a soldier. She faced the fire, hands folded behind her back.

Elizabeth drew herself upright. "All right, my companions, as we have now left the city, are we ready for next steps?"

Cinq turned to regard Nissa. His serenity vanished. He said, "I was waiting for you before I explained. Now's the time."

Nissa grinned. "Oh, goody. Are you done being dramatic? What was it? Keys, something-something, super important, something-something, and… go."

Cinq bit his lip. "I don't want to oversell this."

Nissa sighed. "Really? Earlier we were the keys to everything." She covered her mouth as Cinq fixed her with a glare.

He straightened. Cinqsplanation incoming. "Elizabeth enlightened me as to what I'll call a gap in my knowledge. I was taught that the Pentarch came to Alexandria to learn about the natural world. Science, physics, and chemistry would make him a greater magician. This was only half true."

Elizabeth picked up. "The scholars in the Pentarch's time aren't the same as today. They studied all those things, but not only those things. Magic was seen as a natural force, like the others. And at the intersection of the physical and the arcane, they created things. Devices, artifacts, machines. Some ran on steam power, others by magic. The outcome, not the method, was what mattered."

Cinq looked around the circle. "The Pentarch didn't master the five disciplines just for the challenge, and not just to strengthen his magic. He meant to combine all the knowledge together. Magic from mages and monks, knowledge of the fey from the wikken, and the workings of the mind from the hermits. With all of that together, he constructed a great machine. He called it the 'Black Gate,' and it could tap into an unfathomable amount of power. He could use that power to break a world, or save it."

Nissa clapped her hands together. "And I thought it was the power of friendship. So why keep it a secret?"

Cinq stood up. He tossed a chunk of driftwood into the flames. Sparks burst out. They twirled as they ascended.

"Why? Because it was all too much. That much power posed absolute temptation. Imagine, a device that could deliver anything you desired. Anything. Certainly, the objective was to stop the Titans, but what about after that? No one could be trusted with that much power. And he couldn't build the machine by himself. He needed all five disciplines working together. The longer they worked, the more the disciplines distrusted each other."

Elizabeth tapped the top of her cane. "They made a compromise. The Pentarch would build a safeguard into the machine, a lock with five tumblers, a *lockspell*. Mage, monk, wikken, scholar, hermit: Each discipline would nominate a representative to serve as one of the keys."

"Keys! She said 'keys,'" Nissa exclaimed. "Finally."

The scholar continued, "Five disciplines, five representatives, five keys. All were needed to activate the machine. And the Pentarch, representing the hermits, would be the pilot."

Cinq returned to his seat beside Nissa. He held his palms up to the fire, rubbed them together, and returned them to his knees. "Jump forward a bit. The machine worked; nearplane and otherplane were separated. The Convergence ended."

Nissa tapped her foot. "And the Tracers?"

Cinq said, "They were linked to the keys. Each discipline got one so that no matter what happened, and no matter how much time passed, they could find each other. And if the responsibility of being a key was passed on, they could be found." He pulled the orb from his pocket. He held it and watched the fire through the crystal. "Only it didn't happen that way. After the Convergence ended, the keys—and the Pentarch—disappeared. The Tracers went dark. Eventually, the disciplines quit looking."

Nissa put her hands on her hips. "Except the keys were just tossed forward in time, without our memories. Does that sum it up?"

Cinq held up a finger. "That's one theory. Or maybe we inherited the burden *because* we lost our memories. Maybe the machine is waking up on its own. I have a hard time thinking that kids were first choice for unlimited power. Yon was nine when he showed up at Open Eye. I was maybe thirteen. Believe me, you would *not* have chosen thirteen-year-old me for the job."

"Hey. I'm thirteen," Yon said.

"But you get the point," Cinq replied.

"I guess so."

Nissa said, "This is… kind of a lot. How did you find all this in an afternoon, Cinq?"

"Before, I was looking for the wrong things, and in the wrong place. Between the date, knowing there were five Tracers, and the signatures on them, Elizabeth tracked the scholars' diaries. We found one who wasn't as good at keeping secrets."

Blue, quiet until this point, said, "I suppose something's still missing."

Nissa said, "Let me guess. We don't know where the machine is. Because keys or no keys, Tracers or no Tracers, if people knew where it was, there'd be a line of pilgrims ten miles long waiting to see it."

Elizabeth tapped her fingertips together. "Correct. The location remains a secret. But even if it wasn't, we have a conundrum. If we are these keys, and if we can use a machine of unlimited power, what do we do with that knowledge? Do we try to find the fifth one of us?" She folded her arms across her chest. "Or do we go our separate ways? Perhaps such a device should remain asleep."

Blue looked up. "Excuse me? I may not be in the special club, but aren't we in the *exact same situation* as before? It worked once, let's do it again."

Nissa grinned. "Thank you, voice of reason. Let's say—big 'if' here—that you're right and things go according to plan. We find key five, turn on the Big Machine, stop the Convergence, and kick some Titan butt in the meantime. Elizabeth might be right, maybe unlimited power is too tempting. I mean, sure, Titans can smash a city flat, and haggards and banshees are nasty business. But let's not forget people. People suck. Reavers lead the charge, but people suck in general. Imagine if a reaver had the machine?"

Yon said, "Good thing we're the keys and not them."

Nissa hopped to her feet. "We are for now. What if they could take that away? And even if they can't, you're assuming *we* know what's right. We basically just met. For all you know, I could be a psychopath. Or Cinq, or *yourself*. Stay with me a moment. What if it turns out Yon hates the color yellow? Just *hates* it. All yellow has to go, no questions. Now we wouldn't know that as there isn't much yellow around here except sand and stuff, but once Yon gets the keys to limitless power, he's off on a yellow destruction spree."

"You're taking this a little far," Cinq said.

"Which is the point. Or maybe we're all everything we think we are. And if we use that machine, we'll be the best thing to ever happen to the world. Peace, prosperity, love, and kisses all around. And much later, when we get tired of saving the world, we pass the torch. Lucky us, our successors are better at it than we were. Then *their* successors get the keys and they've been trained from birth to be wise and restrained and they are *even better* than the last. And so on and so on for ten generations until BAM! The   great-great-great-great-great-great-great-great-great-great grandheir? Yellow-hating psycho."

Blue cleared her throat. "Well. Nissa is pro-Titan."

"I didn't say that. I just want us to think before we turn on a machine that could clearly become a weapon. Let's remember that, ahem, the guy who built it took a lot of steps to keep it turned off. That's all I'm saying."

Blue said, "So don't decide now. Assuming you are these keys, there are only four of you. Doesn't Number Five get a vote? Maybe he or she hates yellow, or whatever, and that makes the decision for you."

Cinq exchanged a look with Elizabeth. "Plus, we still don't know how to use the machine. Even if we can find it."

"But you'll figure that out?" Nissa prodded.

"We've come a long way already…"

"That's beside the point," she said. "The more rocks we turn over, the harder it will be to change our minds. And the easier it would be for some yellow-hating bastard to pick up the trail even if we do."

Elizabeth snapped her fingers. "No more 'yellow.' This is serious."

Yon fidgeted. "Do we have to talk about this now?"

"Yes!" Cinq, Nissa, and Elizabeth said together.

Yon said, "Ok, ok. So what? We vote? Elizabeth said something about voting. I'm not sure I know how to do that."

Nissa sighed. "It's times like these I wish I never agreed not to call you names. Let me explain democracy: We all say our piece—which we've done—then we all say what our choice would be, then we count up both sides. Works better if we agree, but we don't have to. This should be all or nothing. The word for that, Mr. Monk, is unanimous. What do you think?"

Elizabeth was the first to reply. "The Fire Titan destroyed my city, came close to destroying the archive and the record of human history. I've seen haggards kill people in the thousands. And if we are headed to a second Titans' Age, that'll be the fate of the world. If there is a chance to stop it, I'll do whatever it takes. But yes… when it's over, we can take steps to make sure the machine isn't misused."

Cinq said, "This may sound selfish, but maybe I'm selfish. My whole life has been dedicated to this puzzle. I need to know."

Nissa grinned. "Ok. Well, I'm in too."

"Unbelievable," Elizabeth muttered.

Nissa rolled her eyes. "It's called being the devil's advocate. I thought you were a scholar. How else are we going to test the argument? *But* if I smell one hint of yellow-hating on any of you, you will never see this sneaky witch again."

"Count me in too," Blue said.

Nissa shook her head. "Sorry, not a key. No vote."

Blue growled, "I live in the world too. As do a lot of other people."

Nissa smiled. "That actually makes sense. Vote accepted. That leaves you, Yon. As the representative for the brotherhood of righteous dragon-punching monks the world over, do we find the machine? Or do we let the color of cowards live for another day?"

"What?"

"What's your vote?"

Yon nodded. "I think we should do it."

Nissa danced a hornpipe. "Ok! We're doing this, everybody's in. Mage LeGarrec—hand-picked representative for all magekind—if you will please: the map."

Cinq retrieved his long coat from the nearby bush. He spread it out flat along the ground to reveal the map etched on the inside. "Blue, may I borrow your compass?"

Blue handed the compass to Cinq who used the needle to rearrange his coat so that it faced north.

"Now we are here, in the coastal midlands." He placed the Tracer on the mark signifying Alexandria. He leaned down to sight the dimmest light. "The bearing has been unchanged since I found Nissa, which means our hermit doesn't move much. That puts Number Five at a north-northwest line. Somewhere between us and here." Cinq gathered a few stones from the ground. He placed the first one on the edge of his coat in line with the Tracer. "Now, using the bearing I took at Ignaesdale, we can triangulate. Number Five must be somewhere *here*." With this, Cinq placed the last stone where the two lay lines intersected. "And so that's where we're going."

Yon wrinkled his brow. "But that's nowhere. That's the middle of a desert."

Elizabeth nodded. "But we expected that. The fifth aspect of the Pentarch was the hermit. Of course he'd be away from people. Though that is deep within the witchlord's territory. And hostile, to say the least."

Nissa frowned. "Or Number Five *is* the witchlord." She looked around at the horrified eyes. "Oh, come on, everyone else was thinking it."

Elizabeth said, "Well, technically it could be anyone. And given the location, I'd say it's unlikely that our number five has remained unaffected by reavers. Perhaps he's in hiding. Perhaps he's a soldier in the army."

"Perhaps he's a she, and she's communing with nature and stuff," Nissa said. "Or the reavers already caught her."

Yon said, "So we just keep following the light? That's simple."

"Moth-like, even," Nissa said.

Now it was Blue's turn to grunt. "It'll take months to walk. We need a ship. We should head up the coast to the next town. From there we can charter to anywhere we want."

Nissa leaned forward over the map. "Or we go back to Open Eye."

"What?" Yon asked.

She continued, "Think about it. We go back to the monastery and do our little mirror trick again. That would throw everyone off."

Cinq's brow wrinkled. "Except reavers might still be swarming the place. But it's a creative idea, nonetheless."

Nissa threw up her hands. "Fine. Just thought I'd bring it up before we start marching *into* danger. But fine, let's catch a boat." She tapped her chin. "Where to start? Blue, Elizabeth? Any towns around here not—how to put this—not resembling the frozen armpits of hell?"

"Laurel's Hollow," Blue answered. "Home."

17

~ Yon ~

The afternoon sun raked across the coast. The rays snuck under the branches of twisted scrub trees motionless in the still air. Yon, who had only experienced dry heat, worked for every breath. He wanted to get moving, to set out on their path before second thoughts crawled back in. Blue, however, wouldn't allow it. They didn't have enough water to travel in the heat of the day. Like it or not, they had to rest. And so, Yon was forced to be alone with his thoughts. The past few days felt like a nightmare. But all he had to do was turn around and see Alexandria hulking in the distance, sheathed in ice and shrouded in fog, to remind him of how real it had been.

His companions distracted themselves in their own way. Cinq was head down comparing the two Tracers. Nissa had gone looking for fey. And Elizabeth was busy assembling a device from springs, wires, and oddly shaped mechanical bits. Blue was more practical. She had wandered off alone, only to return with a newly crafted spear in one hand and a string of five fish in the other. Finally, once they had eaten and packed their few meager belongings, she gave the ok.

Blue led them north across the wetlands. Before the Fire Titan came to Alexandria, she had traveled up and down the coast. Much of that had been by boat, but she was familiar with the overland routes as well. Alexandria rested at the end of a long peninsula, and most travel by land would have been back to the city to reconnect with the great highway. However, there were a few towns nearby that might have escaped Alexandria's fate. Laurel's Hollow, Blue's hometown, should be reachable before nightfall. From there, they could charter a boat. Provided, of course, it was still standing.

They trudged over sandy ground as they navigated through squat and prickly vegetation. After a while, Nissa drifted back to walk alongside Yon. She smiled at him.

"You seem quiet."

He sighed. "It's kind of a lot to take in."

"That's true. Plus, we're making guesses as we go. I've been meaning to ask you, did the monks ever mention the whole key thing to you?"

He shook his head. "No. I don't know how that abbot knew." He bit his lip. "No special treatment, that's for sure." Yon tilted his head to glance across the sea. Seagulls made lazy circles around a cluster of terns diving at a disturbance on the water. "Nissa, have you always been able to hear the fey?"

"As far as I remember. And after the wikken took me in, they encouraged it."

Yon hopped up and over a piece of sun-bleached driftwood. "Do you miss them?"

"The fey?"

"The wikken. Your enclave."

"No." Nissa spat the word. "I left them, not the other way around. And I don't want to go into it."

"Oh, ok." Yon let the words trail off as they trudged along, still side by side, but now with a dark cloud that hung between them. Yon stretched his mind and found the questions once more. "Are there fey here now?"

Nissa shook her head. "No. Which isn't surprising. After a Titan comes, the nearplane fey just… disappear. It could take years before they'll come back."

"Why?"

She wrinkled her nose. "I… don't know. Some people think they get pulled back into the otherplane. Or maybe it just scatters them. After a Titan comes, places get scarred. The fey stay away."

"Oh." Yon thought he understood. Even if he could go back to Open Eye, would he want to? He'd been unable to sleep without thinking of the Earth Titan coming across the desert, or remembering the ones he'd lost.

Nissa patted him on the shoulder. "Buck up, kid. It's been a wild few days. And you punched a dragon. How many people can say that? Points for modesty, though, Mr. 'I'd fight if I had to.'" She cocked her head. "Can all monks do that stuff?"

Yon took a deep breath. "Not like that. I think it was the overlap. My chi was just… easier to find."

Nissa nodded. "Cinq mentioned something similar. But as you saw, he's as stingy with his magic as ever."

Yon looked over his shoulder to see Cinq and Elizabeth walking side by side. They were in a fierce debate. And though they were both animated, the conversation looked friendly.

He said, "Yeah, I guess I was expecting to see a bit more magic around him."

"Well, it's a long road. I've been traveling with him long enough to know that if there is any other way, and I mean *any* other way to do things, that's the way he goes. I don't think he's nervous, he's just, um, conservative. Mages will be mages, as the wikken say."

Yon bit his lip. "What about me? What do the wikken say about us? Will monks be monks?"

Nissa smiled. "You really want to know? The word narcissistic comes up. Sitting in your little retreats, shut off from the world, thinking only about yourselves. Reminds me of a joke. What do you call a monk with—?"

Yon interrupted. "And the wikken are any better? You care more about the fey than people."

"Oh no, no, no, no, no. We are not having this argument, so I'll say it once. The wikken don't care *just* about the fey. They *also* care about the fey. And all life, for that matter. That means that if it thinks and if it feels, then it has importance. Just because the rest of you think the fey are a plague doesn't make it true. Of course, people also hate people that look different, or talk different, or think different, so I shouldn't be surprised."

Silence stretched between them, filled only by the sound of boots through sand and the occasional cry of a gull. Yon cast a glance over his shoulder to make sure Elizabeth and Cinq hadn't fallen too far behind. He cleared his throat.

"I'm sorry, Nissa. I haven't seen much of the world."

"I'm not mad at you, Yon. I'm mad at how opinions matter more than reality. But hey, once this is all over, we'll go find an enclave and you can make up your own mind."

Blue came to an abrupt stop in front of them, and Yon nearly stumbled into her. She held up her hand to signal them to stop moving, then pointed to the north where a column of smoke rose in the distance, transforming the sky into haze. After the others had caught up, they wove through the dunes to where the smoke coalesced to distinct black plumes. The smell closed in around them, heavy and thick. When they reached the top of a sandy ridge scattered with yucca and knifegrass, they could see the flames.

The town ahead looked as large as Ignaesdale, though instead of confined by walls, it wrapped the shoreline of a crescent lagoon. Cottages stood atop stilts along crooked streets which did not end at the water but morphed into docks as they stretched into the sea. And everything, from houses to docks to bushes and even ships in the harbor, was blackened, smoldering, or still burning.

Yon exchanged a nervous glance with the others. There was no movement in the streets. Whoever or whatever had done this was long gone. He closed his eyes. He breathed deep. Distance was an illusion, size an illusion. When he opened his eyes once more, his vision had sharpened. Now he saw the details missing earlier. Broken window glass along the ground, shattered wagons, abandoned goods. Bodies slumped in the streets and floating in the water. Many of the fallen wore the shapeless gray of the Alexandrians, but others were in soldiers' uniforms, with a recurring pattern of red, white, and black. He blinked; his vision returned to normal.

Cinq scrunched up his face. He hung onto his staff with both hands and narrowed his eyes. "Think it's another Titan?"

Yon said, "It looks like—"

"Not a Titan," Nissa interrupted. "Definitely not. I'd feel it if it were. And there are fey down there. Smoke dancers. Now be quiet. I'm trying to listen."

Elizabeth wrinkled her nose. "I suspect reavers."

"Shhh," Nissa urged. "I said I'm trying to listen."

Yon remained silent. He'd heard of smoke dancers before. They were fey that relished fire and yet couldn't start it alone. They haunted bakeries and smithies where the flames rarely went out. Mostly, they followed soldiers. Especially the kinds of soldiers that liked to burn things. And if the rumors were true, the smoke dancers encouraged it. Never directly, only through whispers.

Cinq asked, "What are the fey saying?"

Nissa sighed. "It's more what they're not saying. Outside of the usual burn, burn, burn, fire, fire, fire, there's no talk of people."

Blue pointed to the harbor. "There are people. Look. There's a ship."

Yon twisted to look out at the harbor. Among the bristling forest of charred masts was one ship that looked intact. The sails were lowered and bound, but undamaged. He didn't see any nets, so maybe not a fishing boat. Then again, Yon had never seen a ship outside of books. Shouldn't he be more impressed? Shouldn't this be fascinating? Or had the long-lost him—the forgotten him—gotten used to ships? He was shaken from his daydream as he saw movement on the deck.

"I see people," he said. "And they're not soldiers."

Blue frowned. "We'll check for survivors in the town first. Or food, or anything. Then we make for the ship."

Cinq said, "Why even bother with…" but Blue had already started tromping down the hill.

Yon hurried to catch up with her. His boots skidded along the sandy slope as he descended. At the bottom of the hill, Blue picked up her pace to just shy of a run. Yon remembered what she'd said earlier: Laurel's Hollow was her hometown. That meant she'd seen the destruction of Alexandria, and now this. A feeling flitted across the back of his mind, not pity, but sympathy. The memory of his friends and those whom he'd called family flooded over him. But like Blue, he pressed on.

By the time they reached the outskirts of town, the sky had shifted to an angry orange as the smoke in the air amplified the setting sun. The stench of smoke was everywhere, saturating the land, and drifting upward where the coals had not completely gone out. It rose in thick plumes from those buildings still aflame. The ground crunched as they walked; the once-stiff marsh grass reduced to blackened char that crumbled with each step.

He saw the gallows.

In the husk of a building where only the frame remained, corpses hung in the still air. Some bodies were blackened and burned, but many more were not. At first, Yon only saw a handful, then more, then more. The streets were lined by the burned and hanging dead. Blue took several steps. She drew her knife from its sheath and held it loosely in one hand. She looked both ready to fight, and yet aware there was no one to fight. She staggered to one of the fallen soldiers and tipped the body over with her foot.

Elizabeth pointed. "That's the witchlord's insignia. This is his work."

Nissa's arms clenched around her body. "A town, a whole town. Why would they do this?"

Cinq asked, "This wasn't a wikken enclave, was it? Or a school of magic?"

Blue's voice was tight and low. "No. Just fisherman, dockworkers, lobstermen. None of 'em nice, but you shouldn't be burned for that."

Elizabeth had her back to the group. She looked at the makeshift gallows with her hands behind her back. "It's not just about magic anymore."

Yon asked, "What do you mean?"

Elizabeth's fists clenched. "This was either a show of control, or possibly spite. First off, they came for a specific purpose. That is undeniable. You can't get to this town by accident, and there's no military reason to be here. They must have been looking for something specific. And if they'd found it, they would have left. Probably without all this. But they failed."

Cinq cleared his throat. "I hate to think it's always about us… but I think it was about us. This is too much like Ignaesdale, they turned up too fast. I don't think that's just bad luck."

Elizabeth turned to face him, her eyes cold. "They must have their own Tracer. Or whoever sent them here does. I suspect they came to Alexandria looking for me. They couldn't get into the city, so they occupied this town instead. When the three of you appeared, they got orders to—how shall we say—try a little harder. This was the result."

Blue's eyes were wide. She clenched the knife in her hand so tightly that the veins stood out on her forearm. "That's it, huh? Not about witches at all. Or let me guess, they'll say they were witches. Or helping witches. Doesn't matter. If they can't cure the world of witches, they'll cure the world of people."

Yon looked around. "Where'd Nissa go? She said there were fey here. Maybe they'll tell us. Nissa?" he called. "Nissa, where are you?" His stomach lurched in a flash of panic. What if the reavers were still here? What if this was a trap?

Cinq pulled the Tracer from his pocket. He glanced at the lights and started down the street, only to turn into a narrow alleyway. Yon and the others followed as it let out onto a wide-open area, perhaps a marketplace, perhaps a wharf. Nissa stood in the middle of the square. Three reptilian creatures, the size of horses, milled around her. Each greenish-brown beast was like an alligator, though with stumped noses and long, storklike legs. The creatures would step carefully forward, then crouch, the knees sticking in all directions. They scooped up mouthfuls of ash in their powerful jaws, methodically crunched, and swallowed. Occasionally one would take a few steps, dip for another bite, and resume chomping.

Nissa drifted from creature to creature, resting a hand on their sides before moving to the next. She scowled as she saw her companions and pointed back the way they'd come. Cinq backpedaled, bringing Blue and Elizabeth with him, but Yon stood transfixed. He watched the creatures crouch and chew and grunt. All three smoke dancers raised their heads at once. They looked first at Yon, then to the sky. In a burst of light, the smoke dancers were engulfed in fire. Then they were gone, as though the flame had completely incinerated them. For a moment, Yon and Nissa looked at one another without speaking.

Nissa dusted the ash from her hands. "Well, that was interesting. For what it's worth, Elizabeth is a good guesser. The reavers left yesterday. The smoke dancers are pretty happy about the fires they set."

"And the reavers are here for us?"

"Not sure, but it makes sense. That point goes to Cinq. They must have been too busy with… this." She glanced around at the scorched buildings and the endless gallows.

Yon hesitated. Nissa's eyes were red, her cheeks streaked with tears. He wanted to comfort her, but he couldn't. Or maybe he shouldn't. There was no reason for comfort. The monks would say now was the time to sit, to meditate, to find his center. But he didn't want to find his center. This was unthinkable, all of it. A Titan was one thing. A Titan was a force, not a human. And that made a difference. The reavers had done this. He wanted to find them and make them pay. He wanted to make *them* burn. To line them up, to get the fire hot, and push them in. That was the only thing to do. The only way to get even.

Yon stopped himself; the violent thoughts snapped away. He pivoted to see a smoke dancer standing behind him. It looked at him with ink-black eyes that reflected his own surprised face. The smoke dancer ground its teeth, shards of coal dropping from its jaws. In a flare of light, it disappeared like the others. Yon shut his eyes. The green-blue afterimage danced behind his eyelids.

He snapped his eyes open to the sound of angry shouts coming from the other end of the alley. He pivoted and dashed toward Blue's voice, dragging Nissa along with him. He burst onto the street to see Cinq, Elizabeth, and Blue surrounded by five large men. Their skin was deeply tanned and awash with tattoos and brands. In contrast to the runes on Nissa, these gave off a raw, messy, and unapologetically human vibe. The men held weapons, from hatchets to cudgels to a double-bladed ax with a blackened blade and charred handle. Not reavers. Pirates.

The man in the front, with a shaved head and scars covering his scalp, turned his eyes to Yon and Nissa. "And now we've got two more." He grinned. "I guess it's a fair fight."

Another of the men wrinkled his nose. He spoke in a serious tone. "Except, of course, that we're bigger than they are. And three of them are ladies. I'm not so sure that's completely fair at—"

Blue cursed. "Call me a lady again, and I'll cut off your tackle." She tightened her grip on her knife.

The bald pirate's eyes lit up. "Wait. Is that Blue? Blue! Blue my girl! Come here. We thought you were dead! Well, we thought everyone was dead, because mostly everyone is." He lowered his ax and held his arms wide.

Slowly, Blue sheathed her knife and took a step toward the man, where she was swept into a bear hug before he leaned back to put his hands on her shoulders.

Blue said, "Gully, what happened to all your hair? You look… terrible."

"This? Oh, I lost a bet. Don't worry, I won the next one."

"And these scars? I didn't recognize you."

"A disagreement among gentlemen. And a shark. Gentleman shark. Now, who are your friends?"

Blue pointed to each of them in turn. Her eyes were alight, and she wore a faint smile. "This is Elizabeth, Cinq, Yon, and Nissa. Everyone, this is Gully. He got me out of this place when I was a kid. Saved my life."

Gully spread his hands. "Well, that's probably a little bit true. But you earned your keep." He looked at the rest of them. "Blue was the hardest working stowaway I've ever met. And a genius with rope."

Elizabeth cleared her throat. "Well, if she learned ropework from you, sir, then I am in your debt." She winked. "You would love to see the skyways."

Blue said, "We all owe each other." She paused. "We'll swap stories later. We should get out of here."

Gully frowned. "Because of the reavers? They're long gone." He nodded at the surrounding buildings. "Nothing left here anyway."

Blue asked, "Then why are you here?"

"In case they missed something." He tapped the ax to illustrate.

Cinq stepped forward. "We… have reason to believe they'll come back. They're looking for us."

Gully squinted. "'Cause you're a bunch of witches, or something else?"

"Something else."

Blue said, "Gully, was that your boat I saw in the harbor?"

"You mean the one that wasn't floating ash? Yes, that's her." He cocked his head. "I get the feeling you want a favor. Now for you, Blue, you always have a place on my crew. But your friends? They'll have to negotiate."

Nissa said, "Do we look rich? Do we look like we have anything at all?"

Elizabeth interrupted. "Ahem. I have something you may like." She opened the pouch on her belt and removed a silver cylinder as big as her fist and covered with an array of screws, wires, and a mechanical turnkey. "I was saving it for the haggards but didn't need it." She held the cylinder up to the waning light. "This, sir, is a level six incendiary device with a hand-activated armament. It can deliver an explosive charge capable of reducing a small building to ash, or boat, or anything you might want. Consider it a cannonball in your hand. It could be useful for a… man of the sea."

Gully grinned. "Well, Miss Elizabeth."

"Doctor."

"Well, Dr. Elizabeth. You've got yourself a ship. Where to?"

She turned to Cinq and smiled. "Have you decided?"

Cinq nodded. "We need to find the Rendezvous."

18

~ Cain ~

The wind howled across the mountaintop, blowing wave after wave of snow across Mortimer Cain's path. The Tannisong Stronghold lay just ahead, both built on and carved into the mountain. A long time had passed since he had returned to this place. This had been his home before his exile. At least, for a time. He left as a disgraced monk, and now they called him witchlord.

Cain looked at the band of soldiers that had accompanied him out of the Expanse and into the mountains. They were two dozen of his most loyal warriors, the elite of his personal vanguard. Each of them had earned a life of luxury and ease— but they may never see it. Unless the Convergence could be stopped, and those responsible destroyed, he wouldn't rest. Nor would those around him. But perhaps they were getting closer. With each day, his message spread farther. With every day, they found more believers.

The oaken doors of the stronghold emerged from the blizzard. Cain dug his heels into the side of his horse to harry her forward. When the door did not immediately part on his approach, a trace of concern swept over him. He had returned to this place after the Fire Titan had come. Anything not carved from stone had been burned, including his old masters. He had searched the halls, but only found their corpses. They had received their punishment, though it left him unsatisfied. Cain and his reavers drove out the haggards and claimed Tannisong as their own. Five years later, smoke, magic, and evil still lingered.

He strode forward, crossing through the great doors and into the torchlit corridor beyond. The fortress's small garrison stood at attention. Most of the soldiers had already been sent to the front line, only enough men remained behind to hold the position. He knew these men should be treated with honor. They were, after all, believers.

Wasting no time, Cain passed through the great hall and into the side wing. More soldiers were here, bearing the marks of three different clans. They knuckled their foreheads as they parted to let him through. On the other side of the door, in front of an enormous open hearth, the remnants of a feast lay on a solid wooden table. Empty tankards and clean-picked bones lay beside half racks of mutton, piles of beef, and mountains of rolls.

Cain looked at the faces of his council: Yanamadra, Isil, and Golloth. They led the tribes of the north, west, and central mountains, and met him with expressions of annoyance, fear, and boredom in turn. The fourth seat was occupied not by a man, so much as a shape. It was wrapped in a burlap cloth and bound from head to toe.

Cain took his seat. "Untie him."

Golloth, a hulking man covered in a patchwork of furs, removed a curved knife from within his coat and sliced the ropes as though skinning a rabbit. Within the husk, sat a spluttering, red-faced, and disheveled man dressed in once-fine clothing. He squirmed to get free of his bindings, freezing when his eyes met Cain's.

"Lord Devan, welcome to the highlands."

The captive fought to regain some composure. He darted his head left, flinching when he saw Golloth. "I suppose you're the witchlord. I wondered if you were real."

Cain poured a drought of wine into a carved cup. He kept his face stern. "A ridiculous name, perhaps. My enemies are not without a sense of irony. If I had put to death a thousand cattle would they have called me the cowlord? They used to call me the witch doctor. I preferred it. I intend to cure the world of witches, not rule them. And this is where you have failed me. Isil, explain to our guest why he's here."

An overweight man with balding pate turned to face Devan. He had a series of brands covering the right side of his face, and others visible along his right arm. Isil said, "The Titans are moving to the south and the west. That's where the witches are strongest."

Golloth, equal parts muscled, tattooed, and scarred, leaned forward. "They're coming your way. That means you're falling behind."

Devon fought to keep his voice steady, but strain reverberated through it. "That means nothing. The Convergence is coming, that's all. Everyone knows that. You said it yourself. Of course, there will be Titans."

Cain set down his cup. "Yes, but not in proportion. The more witches, the more Titans." He started to pick apart a leg of lamb. "I've brought you here to explain."

Devon straightened. "There's nothing to explain. I'm carrying out your orders. Or I was, until I was brought here. Why drag me this far?"

Cain motioned with his finger. "Hold him down."

Golloth darted forward. In a moment he had grabbed Devon by the chest to throw him atop the table. A reaver came from each side to hold arms and legs fast. The rich man squirmed, but received a clout to the head, then another, until too terrified to move again.

Cain pulled a curved knife from his belt. "This isn't difficult to understand. Magic draws the Titans. Mages, monks, and wikken use magic. Remove the witches, remove the draw."

Devon's eyes had gone wild. He followed the blade. "The witches... they're too powerful. The monks are advisers, influential. And the mages? They have money. They own half the cities. I can't just order them out."

Golloth grinned to show metal-capped teeth. "We're not asking you write them a nice letter. We want them dead."

Devon squirmed. His forehead glistened with sweat. "But if they're dead—the witches, that is—the Titans will come for us. Can't they just... act as bait?"

Cain thrust the knife down through Devon's hand, pinning it to the table. Cain's eyes flooded with a haze of red. When his vision returned, he found himself standing on the table, one foot on the man's chest. "This isn't about buying time! This is about the world! We must be complete, absolute! They must all die, magic must be ended!" He forced himself to regain his composure. He dropped his voice low. "All must be pure before the Convergence, or it will be too late."

Cain stared down at the cretin. Devon cried and sniveled, snot running down his nose just as blood dripped from his hand. Cain jumped down from the table. "I expect a decree. You will strip the monks of their positions and the mages of their wealth. As for the wikken," he snorted in disgust, "exterminate them." Cain grabbed the hilt of the knife and wrenched it free. "Of course, I would hate for you to forget our talk. We should write this down."

Isil mumbled, "I've got some parchment. Just a moment."

Cain said, "I had a different idea." He tapped the point of his bloody knife against his chin. "Golloth?"

The large man sliced open Devon's shirt. Cain leaned over, the knife held tight. With careful, even strokes, he began to carve.

* * *

Lord Devon had passed out long before Cain finished etching the decree. Once the man lost consciousness, Cain felt the passion run out of him. He motioned for the soldiers to remove the man, adding a request to make sure he lived. Cain sank into a melancholy haze. He slouched in his chair and picked at the food in front of him. His three lieutenants watched.

Yanamadra was the first to speak. As always. "That was... theatrical."

Golloth added, "I still don't see why I had to lug him all this way. I would have happily carved him up down south."

Cain waved his hand. "That was a minor matter, an example." He wiped his hands on a napkin, paying no mind to the blood soaking the front of his shirt. "We won't rise or fall from one nobleman. We must fight this war on all fronts."

Yanamadra tapped one long fingernail on the table. "Then why are we here?"

Cain pointed to Isil. "Tell them what you've learned. What you told me."

Isil cleared his throat. "The keys have returned. They survived the waygates."

Golloth and Yanamadra shifted in their seats. Their disaffected expressions replaced by ones of keen interest.

"Where?" Yanamadra asked.

Cain replied, "They were in Alexandria. The first three have joined with the fourth. They are moving again." He frowned. "As for the gaps, perhaps time is slipping. Or perhaps they have a magic we haven't seen."

Yanamadra asked, "What does Ezekiel say about this?"

Cain's face flushed. "Do *not*, I repeat, do not speak his name to me. He is not an all-seeing god, and you should never, ever take his words as truth. Do you understand?" He forced himself to calm down, to relax the grip on his mug. "Leave the hermit to me. The matter remains. We need all five keys, or the machine will be useless. We must find them."

Yanamadra twirled her finger. "Why? They'll come to us eventually."

Cain shook his head. "I don't want them arriving as unknowns. And I will not underestimate their strength. You've seen what one key can do. We should expect the same from the others." He picked at his beard with one hand. "We must be in control. Given time, perhaps we can make them see reason. That would be so much easier. If we succeed, there won't be a need for blockades, treaties, or… negotiations." He gestured at the drying blood on the table. "We can exterminate the witches and stop the Convergence at once."

Golloth scowled. "How do we find them? Are you ready to loan out your Tracers?"

Yanamadra hissed. "Are we really talking about this again? The Tracers are too precious to be trusted to soldiers."

Cain said, "We have an alternative. Isil?"

Isil picked up a polished wooden box and set it on the table. He removed a greenish-tinged Tracer from his robe and placed it to the side. Cain removed his own Tracer from his coat pocket, this one a faint red, and set it beside the first.

Isil said, "The Tracers, according to the hermit, are attuned to the keys. With two, we can pinpoint their locations. Triangulation. It's how we know where they are. But the Tracers are unique, irreplaceable. We cannot duplicate them."

Golloth grunted. "Get to the point."

"But…" Isil continued, "what if we didn't need to? The Tracers aren't unique. In fact, they aren't different things at all, but *one.*"

The three shifted to watch Isil more closely.

"From all my tests, from all my research, I can find no difference in the two Tracers aside from the faint discoloration. And then I understood: They are the same object, but perhaps displaced from different times."

Golloth hammered on the table. "The point, Isil! The point. Get. To. The. Point."

"The point is that we don't need to know who the Tracers are tracing. Because if we can trace one Tracer, then we can trace them all. The keys have a Tracer of their own. Are you following me so far?"

Isil opened the box in front of him. Within the polished interior was a velvet lining with two large, empty indentations and rows upon rows of spheres the size of robin's eggs. Isil placed the two Tracers in each of the large indentations. As he did so, lights appeared in the smaller ones, facsimiles of their parents.

Yanamadra smiled thinly. "You made Tracers… to trace the Tracers. Clever."

Cain rose to his feet and slid the box in front of him. He plucked the first of the small Tracers and threw one at Golloth, who grabbed it with both hands. He tossed another to Yanamadra.

The witchlord bared his teeth. "Find the keys. Convince them to join us, or else become them. Time is short."

PART THREE:

Otherplane

19

~ Nissa ~

The ship's bow cut through the blue-green waves, sending a spray of water which shot up to tickle the soles of Nissa's feet. The smile on her face grew wider as she guessed which of the waves would part cleanly, and which would result in a harder slap and the inevitable spray. In two weeks aboard the ship, she had learned her way around the decks, the names of the ropes, cleats, and equipment, but the sea remained a mystery. The water was as wild and capricious as the fey. And that's why she loved it.

Nissa's smile dropped. She may not have spent her life by the ocean, but she knew the fey here were not as abundant as they should have been. In her time since the enclave, she marveled at the ubiquity of the fey. Every river, every stream, every mountain, the forests, the swamps, the deserts, and the badlands: all were populated by the otherplane creatures. Now, their presence was diminished.

Not gone, of course, just lessened. She would still catch the passing ear of the nereids and merfolk, the zephyrs, and those who made their homes along the coves and beaches. And though she always asked, the responses were the same as what she had heard in the undersea cavern. Their brothers and sisters were missing, but they didn't know why. The things the fey did speak of were men. People were on the move. Unfortunately, fey didn't pay attention to the details. The people could be refugees, pilgrims, or soldiers. In the end, what all the fey agreed on was that something big was happening.

Nissa unwrapped herself from the bow rail and scurried across the deck to where the others sat in vigil. As she moved across the planks, the sailors gave her a wide berth. She no longer wore clothing that covered up who she was. Here on the open seas, she had seen no need. She allowed her skin to feel the wind, and the runes which stretched across her arms, legs, and the bare part of her back were exposed to the salt air. She had floated the idea to Blue that wearing a shirt at all was unnecessary. The more grounded guide persuaded her that while a wikken was unnerving to the crew, that would be a bit too distracting.

Nissa sat down on the deck where Cinq and Blue huddled in conference. Elizabeth was out of sight, likely belowdecks assembling one of her devices. Yon was high above in the riggings. The monk had taken naturally to the ropework. The sailors had, in turn, adopted him as one of their own and had been actively trying to recruit him as a crewmate.

Nissa said, "I think when this is done, I'm going to become a pirate."

Blue raised her eyebrows. In a way, she almost rivaled Cinq for her expressions of skepticism. "They aren't pirates. They just have unusual cargo. In this case, us."

"Ok. So not smugglers, they just smuggle. Crystal clear to me."

Blue huffed and turned away. Nissa snickered. Pushing the guide's buttons was her new hobby. Nissa might not have said it out loud, but over the past weeks, Blue had gained their respect many times over. In the days before the Fire Titan, she had worked the docks to load and unload the large merchant ships. She had been part of the muscle until she showed her talent with ropes and pulleys. Blue had risen to become head rigsman, unusual for both her age and gender. And after the Fire Titan showed up, she used her talents to build and maintain the sky cables over the rooftops of Alexandria.

As promised, Blue's friend Gully agreed to sail them to what Cinq called the Rendezvous, some kind of raft-up or outpost for unsavory sailors. In exchange for transport, Blue worked alongside the sailors while Elizabeth put her engineering mind to improving the ship. The rest of them worked as well, or at least, they were tolerated when they tried to help. Something about the arrangement was unspoken. Blue and Gully had a history. Blue was tough, tough as the boards and rigging of this ship, yet Gully treated her like a daughter. Would they have gotten the same treatment otherwise? Perhaps. In a Titans' Age, some people shunned outsiders. Others opened their arms wide.

"So," Nissa chirped. She looked where Cinq hunched over a scroll covered in annotations. "You work anything out?"

Cinq patted the inside of his coat. "I've been studying these letters. He spends a lot of time on the *why* of the keys. What's missing is where the machine is or how it works."

She cocked her head. "Does the how even matter?"

Cinq tightened his lips. He did that when he was irritated, or maybe when he knew Nissa was trying to irritate him. "Imagine the machine is like this ship—more complex, of course, but just imagine. Think we'd make it very far if we didn't know about wind?"

A burst of sea spray covered her skin and sent Cinq into curses as he dried the texts. He dabbed them with his shirt in exasperation.

Nissa said, "Point taken. We need to know where the machine is, how it works, how to use it—you left that out—and of course all five keys, or all the knowing in the world won't help." She smiled. "It's just so simple. And your friend at the, uh, Rendezvous can help?"

"Teacher. And I hope so. Ascertine is a leading scholar of magical devices and overlaps. In hindsight, I suppose that meant these machines. Which kind of irritates me. No, not kind of. It makes me furious."

Nissa waited.

"I mean, they *knew* I was studying Tracers. They knew I was specifically looking for things from the time of the Pentarch. But I had to come to Alexandria to even hear about the machines? It took meeting Elizabeth to tell me scholars built them? The mages knew the whole time. They were just covering it up."

Nissa looked out at the waves. "It probably wasn't about you, Cinq. Maybe the mages were just, like, embarrassed machines could do what they did. Maybe they wanted to be special."

Cinq went back to rolling and storing his papers. "Well, maybe Ascertine will know. He follows the Rendezvous, which means he's not afraid to leave the tower. And he's not like most of the mages. He probably won't turn us in."

She nudged him on the shoulder. "Aww, Cinq. Price on your head got you down?"

He turned to the side. "Now if you don't mind, I've got work to do."

Before Nissa could prod him further, she heard Yon shout from his place in the crow's nest above. "I see it! Rendezvous City ahead. We're almost there!"

Nissa scrambled back along the rail, scurrying around the winches and rigging to reclaim her place on the bowsprit. She held onto the forestay with one hand and closed her eyes; the spray tickled against her cheeks as she listened. Whispers, then murmurs, then voices rose in her ears. Even if the presence of the fey was diminished on the sea, at Rendezvous City, they should thrive. She opened her eyes.

At first, the shape in front of her was engulfed in fog. But as they grew closer, the spires became visible, bristling through the tops of clouds. The rest of the island appeared, a dichotomy of white and green. The island wasn't made of rock at all, but of ice covered in great swaths of green as vines climbed across icy crags, simultaneously reaching to the sun, while their roots crawled to the sea water below.

Amidst the contrast of jungle and ice stood the two faces of Rendezvous. Bristling across the iceberg, windowless spires jutted skyward, each coming to a stark point, and with no doors or windows with which to enter. Hundreds of these towers covered the island, some in clusters, others alone. Below the monoliths, down by the water's edge, sat Rendezvous City.

Where the towers spoke of ancient times, the city was constructed anew each year from an accumulation of wrecked ships and floating debris.

The makeshift roofs rested across walls hewn from ice as a temporary refuge for those seeking solid ground. From what Nissa had heard, few people lived on the island, favoring instead the floating city, one formed from the boats and ships which had been moored together and crisscrossed with gangplanks and rope bridges.

Yon descended from the mast and scurried over to the others. Elizabeth joined them as well, emerging from belowdecks with a notebook in one hand and a mechanical contraption under her arm.

The scholar said, "According to Captain Gully, this Rendezvous has been in place for eight months. That's the longest in over twenty years."

Yon asked, "So it's just a bunch of ships?"

Cinq shook his head. "That's half right. Rendezvous City is the ships, but it's always on the same iceberg. And it moves. One day the iceberg is there, maybe for days, maybe for months. And the next… gone. Until someone finds it again."

"And the towers?"

Elizabeth said, "No one knows. But they're always there."

Cinq looked out over the water. "Master Ascertine may know. He's an expert in these things. He'll know about the Pentarch's machine if anyone does."

Elizabeth asked, "And if he's gone?"

"We'll go to Northwind Tower. That, or head straight for the fifth key."

Nissa looked at the iceberg rising from the sea. On the near side, dozens of ships bristled in an enormous raft-up. Despite everything they had seen so far, the place radiated the ethereal.

Captain Gully's voice called from behind them, low and gruff. "You five, that's enough chicken-necking. Either make yourselves useful or get out of the way."

Nissa skipped aside. Soon, the great ship swarmed with activity as sailors dropped sails and coiled lines. As the sails came down, the oars emerged, holding for just a moment until the ship's momentum slowed. With a steady pull, pull, pull they moved through the water. One of the crew raised a dark-green pennant to the top of the mast, the flag of the visitor. Later, it might be replaced with other colors if the captain decided to trade, or needed more crew, or was ready to leave.

The ship coasted to the outer edge of the raft-up. The sailors retracted the oars as they cast woven bumpers out to protect their ship from bumping against the others. Nissa moved to where Blue and Captain Gully held their final negotiations. The two spoke low, with a lot of muttering and protesting on both sides. When they ultimately parted, Blue shouldered her pack and crossed over the rail. Nissa followed, swinging over the side to land beside her on the deck of a long, thin boat acting as gangplank between the larger ships.

"What was that all about?" she asked, stomping along behind Blue.

Blue grunted the reply, "Payment."

"I thought Elizabeth paid?"

"Don't worry about it. It's done." Blue didn't slow; she plodded along until the planks on the longboat ended and she crossed over to the next.

Nissa scurried to follow. She seethed, but also knew when to let things go. She had glimpsed into Blue's world and her past, but that was all. She knew how to defer when out of her element. But it still hurt to be left out.

Blue, Elizabeth, Yon, Nissa, and Cinq wove into the heart of Rendezvous City. At first, Nissa felt a surge of panic as she realized that she would be helpless to navigate back through the maze of gangplanks, longboats, ship decks, and smaller dinghies. But maybe they wouldn't go back. Which raised a bigger question: Where were they headed?

"Blue," Nissa asked, "what's the plan?"

The guide shrugged. "There is a bazaar out on the ice. That will be the best place to start looking."

After crossing three more planks, two longboats, and a set of stairs, they reached a place where ships gave way to ice. Cinq bent to press his hand against the dirtied white surface and looked up at the others in delight. "The ice… is pulsing with magic. I'd heard of this."

Nissa laughed. "And who knows what's up ahead?"

Yon bounced forward. He turned a circle, his eyes lingering on the sights and smells. "Forget the magic, this place is amazing! I've never seen so many things. I thought the festival was cool, but this… this is completely different." He bounded to a stall where a series of paper fans danced in the wind. The shopkeeper grinned at him.

Cinq grumbled, "Yon, we've got a job to do. Come with me. We'll ask around about Ascertine."

Blue cracked her knuckles. "I'll look for our next charter. And all of you, keep a low profile."

"Huh, why?" Nissa asked. "I'm around people again, thank god. I'm going to have some fun."

Cinq shook his head. "Nissa, we don't know if we're welcome. So—"

"Right, right, don't be too witchy. I get it." She sighed dramatically.

"And take Elizabeth with you."

"Why?"

Cinq stepped back as three women in armor brushed between them. "Because no one goes off alone."

"What about Blue? She'll be alone."

"And she fits in. Let's not overcomplicate this. We meet back here in an hour."

Blue pointed to a stall where a woman was hawking meat on a stick. "Sounds good to me."

Nissa grinned. "Cinq, do you have any money? I need stuff."

After taking a few coins from Cinq, she grabbed Elizabeth by her shirtsleeve and forged into the market. The eclectic crowd milled about in the half-aimless and half-purposeful way of any bazaar in the world. The fact that they stood upon a magical iceberg didn't seem to bother them. Nissa pushed through, one hand resting on her coin purse by habit. Elizabeth tottered behind. Every time Nissa glanced back, the scholar wore an expression that combined bewilderment with clinical study.

"Nissa, wait," Elizabeth said.

"Yes?"

"What are you looking for? Or do you know?"

"I'm looking for another wikken. There's bound to be someone hanging around and…" Nissa stopped. "Her."

Elizabeth beamed. "Excellent. By all means, you must introduce me."

"What?" Nissa shook her head. "I don't think that's a good idea. You're an outsider. Technically, we're both outsiders, but I don't want to scare her off. Just, stay close—but keep your distance. You know what I mean."

Elizabeth gestured for Nissa to go ahead.

Nissa elbowed through the crowd to where a small woman sat at a table made from stacked crates covered by a blanket. She wasn't just small, she was tiny. The woman had feathers and beads woven into long hair streaked with black, white and storm gray. She wore a brown shift which stopped just above her knees, and on her arms, wikken runes peeked through. The woman arranged and rearranged beads and necklaces atop her table.

Nissa curtsied. "Lady."

The woman glanced up, her blue eyes bright and alive. "Lady? You've been away for a while." She paused. "You *have* been gone. You've lost some time, haven't you?"

Her stomach tingled. She blurted the truth without hesitation. "Five years, give or take. There was a lapse." She shrugged. "Everybody's doing it."

The woman cocked her head. "Five? Hmmm. No need to explain to me. Time is a funny thing. A lot has happened in those five years. That's why I came here. I was trying *not* to be bothered. But here you are anyway."

Nissa rolled her eyes. "Oh, well sorry about that. Guess I'll get to the point. The fey. What's happening to them?" She cocked her head. "I mean, I've seen a *few* since I was back, but their answers were…"

"Sideways?" The woman straightened her wares.

"More than usual."

The woman raised her eyes. "You are a speaker. A valuable gift. Maybe I'll tell you."

"Ok."

"I said 'maybe.' Why should I trust you? The wikken have fractured, as you may know. And I can't ask your name, there's danger in that. Can't see your motive, as your spirit is shrouded, and not… whole. Nope. No way I could trust you."

Fine. I get it, Nissa thought. "How much for this one?" She pointed at a cord necklace with six beads, alternating between silver and turquoise.

"That one… not for you. This one would be better." The old woman tapped a necklace beside the first, a smaller choker style with three black cords threading through a disk two inches wide.

Nissa reached into her pocket and dumped out her coins. "That's all I have. Everything. Serious enough for you?" Her voice caught in her throat as she saw a glimmer of gold in the pile of copper. Crap. Where did Cinq get that? Too late now.

"Deal." With a swipe of her hand the coins disappeared, and Nissa found the choker in her own open palm. She put it on. "Trust me now?"

"It's not the amount, as you said. But that you gave it all. That is always… enough." The old woman leaned back. "Let's start simple. You know of the Convergence, of course. And you know the fey are getting restless. They are returning to their primal state."

"Well, they certainly… aren't normal."

The old wikken continued, "The border between nearplane and otherplane grows weaker. When that happens, fey and deimos grow akin to one another. The benign become awakened, aroused, disturbed. Some flee, some return to the otherplane, some are changed. Have you seen it?"

"Maybe. I came through Alexandria. In the whole city, nothing but haggards. All the fey must have run off when the Titan came."

The old woman smiled. "If you say so."

Nissa's eyes went wide. "Wait. I'm not saying so. Are you saying so? Or are you saying the fey became deimos?"

"A ridiculous question. Fey and deimos are the same thing. The difference is intention."

Nissa snorted. "Ok. That's enough aura of mystery for me. Spit it out, granny. What's up?"

The old woman cracked a broad smile. "Ah, I miss the young ones. You must have been a joy to teach. Very well, little wikken, I will tell you what I know. The Convergence is changing the fey. It *will* change the fey. But others are changing them as well. People are changing them."

"How could a person change a fey? Why would they?"

The woman's face turned dark. "I said be patient. Wait and listen, witch."

"Oh, I'm a witch now?"

"If you act as a witch, you will be called a witch. Now be still so you can learn. And you have *much* to learn. But I see where your heart is. The fey are being called, changed, and used by your sisters. The wikken are turning the fey into weapons."

Nissa recoiled. "What?! No. That's impossible. We wouldn't. That's against everything—*everything*—we stand for. We're here to protect them. And—"

The old woman cocked her head. "Who are you trying to convince, little girl? You want to know why things are different, I'm telling you. The fey flee, because they are afraid. Or they stay, and they change."

Blood rushed to Nissa's face. "And this is what? Common knowledge?"

"Common enough. Some wikken cling to the old ethos, but many embrace the new. They find justification in survival." The woman picked up a piece of leather cord and started stringing it with beads. She looked at her work, deliberately ignoring her.

"Anything else?" Nissa asked.

The old wikken murmured, "My last advice, don't trust them."

Nissa snorted. "Who really *trusts* the fey?"

"Not them, fool, your sisters. Beware the wikken."

"You're a wikken."

"No. Not anymore. Now I'm just an old woman who listens, waits, and watches." She looked down at her table. "Now run along. I have other customers."

Nissa saw no one waiting nearby, but she understood a dismissal. The blood was running too hot in her veins to argue. She'd left the enclave for a lesser reason than corrupting fey. But this, this was anathema. She stomped several yards away. She saw Elizabeth next to a rack adorned with copper fishing lures. Nissa tapped on her shoulder.

The scholar turned back. Her smile fell. "You look upset."

"Yes, I'm upset!" she snapped. She lowered her voice. "I mean, I just heard some crazy things. That old lady said some of the wikken are using the fey. It's unthinkable. Fey aren't playthings. They aren't slaves. They're living, thinking, feeling, understanding creatures. Wikken don't swear oaths, but if we did, this would be number one." She closed her eyes and exhaled. "Look, I'm still processing all this. I just need time to think. The whole thing is getting tangled. Let's hope Cinq and Yon got better news."

20

~ Cinq ~

Cinq pushed across the bustling Rendezvous market. Even after the time spent on the boat, and its strange normalcy, he was unsettled by the noises and smells of humanity. The people haggled and laughed and pushed and shouted, as though Titans and reavers and the Convergence were a dream. Not to mention they were standing on an iceberg whose existence was tenuous at best. Beside him, Yon gawked at the combination of merchants, pirates, and fishermen. Cinq watched closely as well, but mostly to see if any reavers lurked in the ranks. But he saw neither the livery of the witchlord nor the clothing of northerners.

After they passed from one end of the market and back again, Cinq considered his options. Why not announce his intentions? Would the witchlord bother to come all this way? Master Ascertine had been welcomed here, after all, and he hardly fit a sailor's profile. Perhaps Ascertine was welcome as the town eccentric, or perhaps—Cinq's smile dropped—his welcome had worn out.

And so, Cinq opted for discretion. He didn't speak to every vendor in sight; he picked his targets. Cinq and Yon waded through tightly packed stalls filled with hawkers of every ilk looking for someone who fit the bill. A vellum seller? Rare whiskey? Silks? Perfumes? But before Cinq had made the first inquiry, he felt Yon tugging on his coat. Cinq turned to see a concerned look on the young monk's face.

"What is it?"

Yon nodded to the right. "Someone's watching us. That girl."

Cinq turned his head to see a dirty face peering at them with wide blue eyes. The child appeared to be six or seven years old, though between the tattered rags, the dirt-caked skin, and the hunched posture, any real assessment was impossible. More importantly, he wasn't sure that was a child at all.

"I think it's just curious."

Yon wrinkled his nose. "Except we're not that interesting. At least not as interesting as everyone else. I mean, look at this place. Everything's amazing. Well, everything except for us. Why would the kid pick us?"

"It's not a kid," Cinq muttered. He turned to face it. "Can I help you?" He took a long look at the fey and its mostly human form to examine its *in*-human eyes. The peculiarity wasn't in the shape, but rather the reversed color: white pupil, black iris, blue orbital.

The fey made a chirping sound and skipped a few paces away, traveling in a crouched gait of feet and knuckles. It peered over its shoulder.

Yon said, "What does she want?"

Cinq sighed. "It's not a she or a he. It's a fey."

"Oh. Ok. Are there a lot of fey here?"

Cinq didn't answer. He peered closer and saw something that he'd missed before. The fey had a metallic band on its right arm. Even from this distance he recognized the marker; the reliquary had contained thousands.

"It wants us to follow." He took a step forward.

Yon grabbed the back of Cinq's coat. "Is that a good idea? What about your friend?"

A wave of annoyance swept over Cinq. He hated explaining himself all the time. "You see that bracelet? That's a mage's catalog tag. I'll bet the fey leads us straight to Ascertine."

As he said the name, the childlike fey scuttled away. Cinq quickened his pace while Yon dogged behind. They weaved through merchants hawking everything from jewelry, to tools, to weapons, to live chickens. And every time he thought the fey had disappeared, he would see it again, waiting just long enough to make eye contact.

Cinq and Yon came to a halt as they passed the last of the vendor stalls at the edge of the shantytown. Beyond it, the expanse of the glacier stretched up and out of sight toward the distant towers. Cinq studied the combination of blue-white ice and the emerald vines wrapped in knotted cords. The market of Rendezvous might rest on the shore, but the area beyond, ice and vines, was a different kind of foreign.

Yon tugged at Cinq's sleeve. "Uh, Cinq? What about the others? We're supposed to meet them soon."

The mage looked at the young monk and then back at the ice. "They'll understand. Elizabeth has a Tracer. They can find us if they need to." He paused. Anxiousness clawed at his belly. He wanted to move ahead. "Here, take my Tracer and go back. You can find me later." He held out the orb to Yon.

Yon didn't move. He shook his head. "I… I don't think I should. You said it yourself, no one goes alone. We stay together."

Cinq hesitated. The boy made sense, but… no. He couldn't go back. "Follow me." He took the first step onto the ice. While there wasn't a road, he saw traces of grime, hints that others had passed this way. But while that trail snaked throughout the glacier, the fey's path was more direct. They scaled over the icy crags, climbed across vines, and navigated treacherous ice slicks.

"Can I ask you a question?" Yon whispered.

Cinq replied, "Huh, sure. About what?" The impact of boot against the ground made a dull sound between a squeak and a crunch.

"About anything. Being on the boat was weird. It's like we weren't running away the whole time, but we couldn't exactly chat either. Did that bother you?"

Cinq scrambled over a log-sized root. "I've gotten used to it. Nissa and I had to be careful even before we found you. I don't think I've gotten to let my guard down since. It's not like back at Eastwind, though."

"Do you miss it?" Yon asked.

"What, the tower?" Cinq shrugged. He hopped over a chunk of ice. He watched as the fey scurried out of sight once more. "I miss my colleagues."

"Not your friends?"

Cinq winced. "The tower is… different. Competition hangs over everything. Ranks in class, pressure to succeed, to publish results." He paused. "No winners without losers. No one wants to be a loser." He cast a sidelong look at Yon. "What?"

"Is that why you started looking?"

Cinq exhaled. "Perhaps. I feel like I've missed out on a past." He shook his head. "At first, I felt special to be a riftborn. I thought, I could be anyone. But the novelty wore off. One reason I left Eastwind was to be special again. Maybe get some closure."

Yon said, "But now you know. We are special."

"Maybe. Or maybe we have to do something about it."

They climbed up and over the next hill. Yon kept opening his mouth to speak and then shut it again. Cinq didn't prod him. He concentrated on scaling the ice and roots and trying to keep his footing on the sometimes rough and sometimes slick surfaces.

Yon spouted, "It's just… it's weird to be part of a machine."

Annoyance swept over Cinq again. "Look. You wanted purpose. I wanted purpose. Now we have one."

"Is that why we're chasing a fey over an iceberg?"

"We're seizing an opportunity," Cinq replied.

They continued on and up, until they passed the first of the towers. The most striking aspect to Cinq was that, up close, the structures didn't appear to be built at all. The blue-gray surface was as polished and smooth as marble. No openings, no patterns, no hints at the construction. Even the vines which crawled across the ice didn't touch them. Either the towers contained a repelling force, or more likely, the vines couldn't find purchase. Around the base of the towers, the blue-white tendrils of ice stretched up as though trying to pull them into the ground. How far down did the towers reach?

In truth, the greatest distraction was neither visible nor tangible, but oppressively present. The iceberg hummed with a low throb of magic that did not so much radiate across the surface as it pulled like the suck of a retreating tide. All that power, wave after wave. He had no doubt that they were heading to its source.

"I suppose you can feel it," Cinq said. "The draw."

The young monk nodded. "Yeah. Something's... pulling. It's pulling hard. It's not... it's not too late to get the others. We know where it's going."

The comment jarred him. Yon was absolutely right. They didn't need the fey as a guide, not with the current of magic. The pull called him. "A little farther," Cinq said. Instead of slowing, he quickened his pace. He saw ahead that the slope of the iceberg was changing, cresting. Though the fey had disappeared, the draw called him forward. Farther, farther, until he jogged along the ice. Over and over, he would stumble, only to scramble upright once more. He was almost there, he could feel it, and...

"Wait!"

The shriek snapped Cinq from his daze. He turned to see Yon clambering behind.

"You need to stop! Look!"

Cinq forced himself to look; the landscape had changed. He stood at the edge of a crater, a caldera of ice where one more step would have sent him down a slope of polished ice and through a dark hole in the center. The lure of power had not lessened, but he had regained control. He turned back to Yon, aware of the shortness of his breath and the bruises and scrapes covering his hands and legs.

"I…" Cinq began. He shook his head. "I couldn't stop myself."

Yon trotted to Cinq's side. He looked pained. "You're not going to jump, are you?"

"I can still hear it," Cinq mused. His gaze returned to the hole at the bottom of the caldera.

"Well?"

He shook his head. "No, no, I'm not going to jump. But… maybe keep an eye on me."

From inside the hole, a fey scrambled out, gestured for them to follow, and disappeared within.

"What's down there?" Yon asked.

"I think it's a gate. A thin place between here and the otherplane." He closed his eyes. "I should have felt it before. This iceberg, the whole thing is like an overlap. But down there, that's the opening. That's the way through."

A high, lisping voice called from behind them. "Well, well, well. Anyone can see that, silly. But it's the science and the proof that's the hard part."

Cinq turned to see a tall man with a brown beard so long that he tucked it through his belt then threw it over his shoulder. He wore a short lavender coat and leather pants tipped with reinforced copper kneepads. He held a staff of carved wood in one hand. Spiked metal cages encased his high leather boots. A pair of round reflective glasses sat in front of his eyes, which he flipped up on top of his head as they approached.

"Master Ascertine," Cinq tipped his hat in greeting. "You probably don't remember me. I was in your class back—"

"Cinq LeGarrec? Of course I remember you! The riftborn boy." He looked down at the caldera. "I thought you were going in. Wouldn't be the first. I almost dove in myself the first time." The man giggled, a high-pitched, childish cry. "I slid halfway down and caught myself. But I at least had equipment. Hah! You're barely dressed to be outdoors."

"The fey…" Cinq began.

Ascertine leaned back and laughed. "Oh! So, the tricky little bastards brought you here, did they? It's a game to them. And the little stinkers—whom I love dearly—think it's hilarious."

Cinq turned to the monk. "Master Ascertine, this is Yon of the Open Eye temple. Yon, this is my old teacher."

The eccentric mage bowed low, removing his hat in a flourish before returning it to the top of his head. "I am humbly at your service." He grinned broadly. "So, Journeyman LeGarrec, you must be here about the machine."

21

~ Nissa ~

Nissa and Elizabeth hurried back through Rendezvous City to the meeting place. Nissa's mind reeled with the knowledge she'd received—ok, bought—from the old wikken. Even the stalls with fresh fruit didn't lift her spirits. The wikken, or perhaps better to say *some* wikken, were breaking the oldest rules. The idea of the fey as weapons made Nissa's skin crawl.

They filtered through the crowds, working together to pry out rumors, gossip, and news. In this, they complemented each other perfectly. Those merchants too stuffy and disgruntled to tolerate Nissa's questions were charmed by Elizabeth's air of grace and scholarly inquiry. And those too guarded to speak with the silver-haired matron had no problem gossiping with a young wikken. Certainly, many rumors were exaggerated, but still, themes emerged. The witchlord's armies and influence had spread across the continent. And while some of the city-states fought, most preferred to give in to the reavers' conditions.

Nissa was most interested in the stories of resistance. The most impressive display was at Eastwind Tower. There, the besieged mages retaliated with summoned lightning, fireballs, and tornadoes, all under cover of unnatural darkness. Each time the reavers attacked, they were beaten back by some novel calamity. Finally, the troops were called back, and the siege began. Occasionally the reavers would fire arrows or siege engines, and occasionally the mages would answer. But for now, each side was content to both contain and be contained.

The wikken assaulted less directly. And because most of the enclaves were not permanent establishments, the reavers had more difficulty tracking them down. The wikken waged a guerrilla war. Food was spoiled, wagon wheels spun off, supply depots caught fire, and crows would attack the sleeping. The wikken were never caught in the act, so it was unclear if it was them or the fey at the heart of any mischief. Nissa wondered if the fey helped willingly, or if they were forced by her sisters.

Lastly, were the monks. Their resistance tended to be much more, well, monk-like. They protested with words and nonviolent resistance. And if the reavers were wise, they left it at that. They would capture or restrain the monks, or simply take them away. For those soldiers foolish enough to attack, they faced righteous retribution. But after time, the reavers learned from their mistakes. They used crossbows, spears, and siege engines, and eventually the monasteries would fall. The rumor was that the witchlord, having been a monk once himself, bore a special grudge against them.

When the two of them returned to their meeting spot, Blue was already there. She had acquired a new weapon, a thick-bladed cleaver as wide as her palm and strapped to her bicep. Apparently, she'd decided her knives weren't enough. Blue wore a half-smirk, which surfaced for only a moment before fading to her usual stony expression. "What do you ladies think of the Rendezvous?"

"This place? It's awesome." Nissa let her smile drop. "Except for what we heard." She stuck out her lower lip. "The world went to crap."

Blue sniffed. "I heard a few rumors myself. For what it's worth, I found us a way to the northlands. There are a few arms runners that will take passengers. All depends on how long we're staying. We need to lay low, though. Apparently, you witches—no offense—have been disappearing."

Elizabeth asked, "What do you mean 'disappearing'?"

"The reavers have a bounty on witches. We're a long way from the mainland, but some people here still look for opportunities."

Nissa darted her eyes around the crowd, tugging at her sleeves to make sure her runes were covered. "Now I'm worried," she said. "Where are Cinq and Yon? They don't blend in like you."

Elizabeth said, "Either Cinq can't find his friend or he's been distracted by the reunion. Just a moment." She retreated beneath her shawl like a turtle to study her Tracer. "Oh no…"

"What? What!?" Nissa asked. "Are their lights out?"

"No, but they are no longer nearby."

Blue's eyes narrowed. "Out to sea, or what?"

"Inland."

Blue muttered under her breath. "And the sun is going down. Idiots."

Nissa looked to the west. The sun had dropped low, just a few degrees above the horizon, and turning a dull orange. "Why does it matter? Blue? Does it matter?" Nissa folded her arms to give a long look at their guide.

"The Rendezvous ends at dark."

"Define 'ends.' You mean every night? Like this whole place is going to poof? Or like it starts crawling with haggards? I've done that once already. Although I guess that was daytime. But lots of nasty stuff in the world, I'm told."

"Not 'poof,' but it gets unfriendly. See for yourself." Blue pointed.

Minutes earlier, the marketplace had been bustling. Now shopkeepers were rolling up their blankets, tucking their wares into boxes, and securing everything away. Some of the merchants would take their entire display and roll it up. They strapped the bundle to their shoulders and returned to the ships. Others would work together to stack their boxes, constructing a palanquin with the poles they used to hold their canopies aloft. A few stayed, tucking their tables away before crouching near the ice, bread, and dried fare appearing from pockets as they hastily ate their dinner.

"What about them?" Elizabeth nodded to those who remained.

"They have nowhere else to go," Blue muttered. "We should consider getting back. Gully will let us stay aboard for at least tonight."

Nissa bit her lip. "How dangerous would it be to stay?"

"In town? Safer than most places. Leaving town would be something else. There are rumors of things on the ice at night."

Blue turned to Elizabeth. "Can you tell if Cinq and Yon are still moving?"

Elizabeth pulled the Tracer from her pocket and returned it just as quickly. "It's difficult to be sure. They aren't close enough for that."

Nissa said, "Well. Clear enough to me. Let's go get them. Cinq probably needs saving. Again."

22

~ Cinq ~

Master Ascertine led Cinq and Yon into a low tunnel carved into the glacier. Grooves spiraled the length, channeling the waning light from outside to refract across the walls. The tunnel snaked hard left, then right, then opened up. In the center of the room, a firepit smoldered with coals. The smoke trickled up and out through a vent at the top of the room. Furs and patterned blankets covered the floor, while the outer walls were ringed by shelves containing scrolls, books, and assorted tools.

Ascertine kicked off his boots, flinging them and his mage's staff against the far wall before flopping onto a shaggy bear pelt. He propped himself on one arm. "Sit, sit! I never have human visitors." He winked. "I heard you went missing, heard you were dead."

While Yon politely removed his shoes and lined them against the wall, Cinq stared down at the old mage.

Cinq said, "The Black Gate. You knew about it. Why didn't you tell me?"

Ascertine cocked his head. "That's a terrible way to start a conversation. Try this instead: How are you, dear teacher? Looking well, sir. Tell me about your presumably fascinating research. Everyone misses you *soooo* much back at the tower. Hear about the price on my head? Such a misunderstanding." He smiled. "Now you try."

"Did you know or didn't you?" Cinq pressed.

The old man rolled up to sit cross-legged. His face split into a wide grin. He leaned back his head and laughed. "Yes! Yes, of course. Magic machines are my specialty. But it's not a topic for students. Just because we don't tell apprentices everything, it doesn't mean there isn't more to know. The tower is built on secrets."

Heat crept up Cinq's neck and covered his face. He reached into his pocket and brandished the Tracer in front of him. "And this? Did you know about this?"

"Oh? Why there it is. It'd be so sad if you lost it." He winked. "Find anything interesting?"

Yon looked from Cinq to Ascertine and back to Cinq again. He opened his mouth, and Cinq silenced him with a finger.

Cinq demanded, "Is this another game? Do you know what this is or don't you?"

Ascertine rolled onto his stomach and rested his chin on his hands. "You're the one who came to see me. You presume to know things. So, what do you think it is? Or do you need to stomp around a bit more first?"

Cinq closed his eyes. He concentrated on his breathing. He concentrated on how little he knew, and how many people wanted him locked up, dead, or worse. He couldn't lose another ally. "Sir, I've been told this Tracer was one of five just like it, built to track the keys to the Pentarch's machine, the Black Gate."

"And?" Ascertine asked.

"And? What do you mean, 'and'?" Cinq huffed. The calm slipped through his fingers. "And you study relics. The bigger the better, right? If anyone knows, it's supposed to be you. I want to know things like," Cinq ticked them off on his fingers, "where the machine is, how to use it, and how it can even do the things that it does."

Ascertine rolled onto his knees and clapped his hands. "Well, now that wasn't so hard, was it? Amusing, but not hard."

Cinq asked, "Why is that so funny?"

"Why, it's the dumb luck of it all. You think I study relics? No, Cinq my boy, I study machines. You fell backward, and you made it here, but for all the wrong reasons. You've the devil's own luck." He narrowed his eyes. "Or maybe you're not telling me something. And maybe you remember more than you let on, which is why you landed here. Anyway, I'll play along. Machines, machines, machines. You want to know about machines. It's easier just to show you." Ascertine hopped to his feet. He tilted his head. "What are you waiting for? Boots back on, boy. It's right outside." The mage stood and shuffled over to a rack containing pots and pans and removed a kettle. He dipped it into a bucket of water and set it on a tripod atop the smoldering coals. "For when we come back."

They crawled back out of the snaking passageway and onto the ice. The sun had disappeared below the horizon, leaving the island in the purple-gray of twilight. As Cinq straightened, he saw humanlike fey skirting around the ice fields, occasionally disappearing over the edge of the nearby caldera.

Ascertine hummed as he walked to the edge. He held his tall, carved staff in one hand and a lantern in the other. They crossed to a platform built of scraps of wood at the top of the slope. The old mage gestured to the pit below.

"You wanted a machine. Well, there you go."

Yon leaned out. "It's a hole."

Ascertine shook his head. "The pit is just the focus. The machine is *everything*. The iceberg, the towers, the seawater below, and even those roots. Everything is placed just exactly to create what is at the bottom of that crater. And do you know what that is?"

Cinq said, "A gate?"

Ascertine smiled. "Technically, yes. And why do you think that is?" He drummed his fingers against his staff as he bounced in anticipation. "Oh, I just can't wait! I'll tell you. The machine creates a siphon, a kind of wellspring. It pulls magic from the otherplane and to this point here." He patted the balcony lovingly.

Yon screwed up his face. "But why?"

The old mage winked. "What a strange question. Since when have humans needed a reason to seek power?"

Cinq dropped to one knee. He reached out with his hand to feel the tide of magic as it flowed throughout the land and into the nexus. The pulse breathed, then lulled, then breathed again. "It's going the wrong way."

Ascertine giggled. "I know! Clearly, it's broken. Ask the people down in Rendezvous City. Ask them why they have to relocate when the glacier vanishes. It's been broken for centuries."

Yon whispered, "Wait. Are you saying this is it? *This* is the Pentarch's machine?"

"It was *one* of his machines. This was a first and failed attempt, yet unstable. But it's not the one you're looking for. The Black Gate came later."

Cinq held his staff in both hands. He hadn't come all this way for so little. Master Ascertine had to know more. "So where is it? Is that another thing everyone knows but me?"

The old mage folded his hands across his chest, his carved wooden staff crooked in one elbow. "Why should I tell you?"

The irritation returned. "You saw the Tracer. I'm a key, the Convergence is on its way, and anyone who uses magic—and thus could solve the problem—is being hunted. What other reasons do you need?"

Ascertine picked at his beard. "Hmmm. Those are good, lucid, and time-sensitive reasons. I suppose it's either that or keep hiding here until the reavers come calling." He nodded his head. "All right, I'll do it."

Yon asked, "You'll do what?"

"I'm coming with you. I've been hiding out from the reavers just long enough that I can probably stomach talking to those elitists at Northwind Tower. They consider the Black Gate to be their exclusive domain. So, we'll just have to convince them."

23

~ Yanamadra ~

The double-masted sloop glided across the ocean on a reach. Its bow cut through the waves as it bore down on its destination. The woman on the foredeck smiled as the shadow of the iceberg came into view. She closed her eyes and reached out to the fey dancing upon the ice. She sensed others as well, great leviathans swimming in the deeps, and imps playing around the edges of a vortex. The fey here were wild, raw, not softened by years living in the nearplane, and very different from those that used to haunt her enclave. Then again, it had been a long time since Yanamadra called herself a wikken.

Yanamadra reached to her neck and retrieved the small sphere fashioned into a pendant. The lights within pointed clearly and brightly to the shadow in the distance. The mountain of ice was faint in the moonlight, and yet vividly apparent in her mind. She slipped the Tracer beneath into her blouse. She looked back up at the tanned and tattooed man watching her.

She ordered, "Take us in."

The sailor grunted in reply and left to carry the message back to the captain. Yanamadra felt no slight at the lack of civility. These men had shown remarkable competence, rivaled only by their lack of curiosity. She imagined that taking a few passengers into the middle of the ocean might not have been the most illicit activity they'd undertaken.

She studied the reavers making up her escort. They were all dressed as mariners, though one look at their queasy expressions meant the illusion was thin. Subterfuge was beneficial, as she didn't intend to conquer, only to collect. And if they drew attention, she hoped that it was "noblewoman on a rampage" attention, and not "the witchlord is coming for us all" attention. Though that sometimes had its uses.

Patience. One did not become lord of the northern tribes without degrees of patience and discipline unheard of in the southern and weaker regions. Compared to the northern tribes, everyone was weaker. Cain would have made a good northerner. The central wastes had adequately sculpted his character. But his passion… his passion was his strength. He was perhaps the only man in the world she respected. The other lieutenants were dangerous. But so were moose. And you could be wary of a moose and not respect it. Despite all her other talents, Yanamadra knew her strength was her patience, her discipline, and her fortitude—not her charisma. Lucky for her, Cain hadn't been looking for diplomats.

She considered the paradox. Cain was a fanatic of fanatics. His divine mandate was to exterminate the witches: mages, monks, and wikken. So why were his lieutenants born of the same? Yanamadra had once been a wikken. Isil had studied in the towers as a mage. And in the strictest technical sense, Golloth was a scholar—although his research was indistinguishable from torture. Perhaps the answer was that Cain was himself trained as a monk. Maybe he saw those who abandoned their disciplines as the most willing to destroy them. Or maybe it was something else. Eventually, once the other "witches" were exterminated, Cain would likely turn on her.

She wondered if Golloth and Isil were on their way. In theory, all of Cain's lieutenants set out on equal footing, each with a mini-Tracer to guide them. But Golloth had an unhealthy suspicion of ships and water. Isil, on the other hand, was probably going for the "let them come to us" option, which Cain was so against. Each to their own. She preferred to overtake her prey than trap them. Ideally, before they knew they were hunted.

Yanamadra closed her eyes. She felt the mist of the sea on her face. Even more than the iceberg rising in the distance, she could feel the Rendezvous in the air, and the murmurs of the fey on the wind. In the wikken enclave, Yanamadra had never listened to the fey. She could direct them, bend them, order them, so why bother to understand them? As far as she was concerned, if you had enough will, anything else was a distraction. Her enclave tried to expel her for that.

If any were still alive, she could've asked why.

She heard footsteps on the deck and opened her eyes. The captain stood waiting. "Madam, we make landfall shortly."

"Keep your crew aboard the ship in case they run. If you must send someone ashore, allow only one or two, nothing that would impact our ability to set sail."

"Of course," the captain gruffed. "Anything else?"

"Information. Have you been here before?"

The captain cocked his head. "I've been to a Rendezvous. Not this one. Years ago. Different part of the ocean. Different folks, more or less."

"And the island? Is that different?"

"Not… exactly an island. But it's never the same, though it draws the same people. The same types of people. Different faces. But the same."

"You're skirting the question, Captain. Do you have contacts? Are there those that would be aware of the comings and goings of anyone out of the ordinary?"

A thin smile graced the captain's face. "I think you are giving the Rendezvous a whole lot more credit than it deserves. It's not an organization, it's a happening." He cleared his throat, and his face became somber once more. "No one at the top, but the biggest fish will have their lackeys. Coins tend to talk."

"Even from someone like me?"

The captain shrugged and scratched his neck. She read a twinkling of mirth in his eyes. "As long as you don't start torching ships and burning witches, people won't care. Or at least not in public. These people aren't here for the scenery, just the opportunity."

Yanamadra looked over the rail at the iceberg growing in the distance. She saw the towers bristling from the surface, though they were little more than silhouettes. "I understand."

The captain cleared his throat. His calm demeanor had shifted. He fidgeted, shifting his weight from foot to foot. "One more thing, a warning. Maybe superstition, but you asked to know what I know."

"Speak."

"The locals, they stay off the ice after dark. There are things out there."

She nodded. "I'm aware."

The captain continued, "So you might not find anyone off their ships. You sure you don't want to wait until tomorrow?"

"Quite."

The captain plodded back to the cockpit where his presence incited a flurry of activity from the crew who, although never truly idle, worked at a different pace when unobserved. As they approached, the sails were dropped. After a few moments of coasting through the water, the oars were extended to guide the ship in. To Yanamadra's surprise, nearby boats assisted with the landing. The greetings were universally good-natured, though at the same time not betraying familiarity. Perhaps this was the way of things. Comrades of the sea.

Yanamadra motioned for her soldiers to wait, while the captain clapped his hands and commanded the crew to stay aboard. This was met by a medley of complaints, which were placated as the captain ordered that rum be brought up from the hold. Yanamadra tightened her lips. If this crew became too drunk to sail, there would be consequences. She met the captain's eyes, who barely tilted his head in acknowledgment. The message was clear: if his crew had to stay, they would stay on his terms. Very well.

She checked the Tracer again. The keys were either ashore or moving to the opposite side of the island. This was the flaw in the artifact—only direction, not distance. She crooked her finger and her reavers came to her side. She whispered a word to Eiger, her commander, and one by one they disembarked onto the gangplanks. Eiger led, followed by five of his men, and lastly Yanamadra. As she stepped onto the first of the planks, the wood shifted and sprang under her step. The salt water sloshed through the cracks around her feet. The next plank, round and massive, barely moved, while the third was a series of small hand width boards they had to shuffle back and forth from one side to the other. Yanamadra turned her nose up in disgust. She'd spent time in military camps, but this place was held together by a string, nothing more than loosely bound garbage. The sooner she was free of this place, the better.

She picked across the decks of smaller boats and the impromptu gangplanks until they reached a wider boardwalk lashed to floating barrels. Most of the people were traveling in the opposite direction, their arms and backs laden with goods. Within a few minutes, they had passed through the crowds to stand in a vacant shantytown populated with empty stalls. Yanamadra stepped past her men. She walked through the abandoned market, across a pile of strewn garbage, and onto the expanse beyond.

She knelt to place her palm on the glacier. The island pulsed beneath her. She recoiled. The wikken—or in her case ex-wikken—may concentrate their studies on the fey, but they weren't ignorant of magic. Here, the drifting currents of power were a raging river, pulling her and everything to the center of the island. No wonder this place swarmed with fey.

"Madam," Eiger spoke, "your orders?"

Yanamadra held the artifact at arm's length, swinging it back and forth to gain the bearing. She pointed at the towers silhouetted in the distance. "The tallest tower. The one in the middle. I'll know when we're close."

Eiger nodded. He spoke low to two of his men and they took the lead as he and the rest trailed behind. Yanamadra approved. A good commander knew who had the best eyes and ears. On they went across the barrens. In a matter of minutes, the terrain was consumed by the ice fields. Moonlight lit up the expanse. At first, the tundra felt familiar, at least compared to the ocean. The northern mountains had snow at the peaks year-round. But this was no northlands. The air held a midsummer's warmth, which turned to thick fog as it swept across the ice.

Eiger bent down, he retrieved a fist-sized chunk of ice and tossed it aside. He faced Yanamadra. "Are we in a hurry?"

"Do you have something better to do?"

He shook his head. "I can't make out a path—if there even is one. My men are no strangers to walking on ice, but we're asking for a broken leg if we go carelessly. And that'll either slow us down or," he hesitated, "leave us short-handed."

Yanamadra seethed. Not at Eiger—the man was practical—but at herself. She couldn't afford to lose any strength. Their quarry was likely dangerous. Isil had cautioned about the power of the people who served as keys. And there were four of them. If they were together, they weren't clueless. She couldn't afford anything that would weaken her hand.

"Madam?" Eiger said, but Yanamadra now looked past him. "Quiet."

Yanamadra narrowed her eyes. Something was coming their way, small, noiseless, cutting through fog like a fish swimming upstream. It surfaced to perch on a chunk of ice that protruded from the landscape. The fey resembled a child, crouched with hands flat on the ground in front of it. It regarded her with wide eyes. It recognized her for what she was.

The fey motioned to her and scampered away. But Yanamadra had no intention of playing chase. She whipped off her glove and thrust her hand up and out, fingers crooked as if snatching a moth, not to crush, only to contain.

The fey stopped short, writhing in her grasp. Holding her hand steady, Yanamadra strode past her soldiers to come within a few feet of the ensnared fey. She looked down as its facsimile eyes shone with terror. And though its mouth opened and closed, no sound emerged. Its pathetic heart fluttered between her fingers.

"You will obey. Or you will suffer."

24

~ Nissa ~

"Uggh," Nissa groaned. "This fog is up to my tits." She darted a glance at the grandmotherly Elizabeth. "Um, I mean my mid-chestular area."

Blue chuckled. "We're on a magic chunk of ice, chased by reavers, and the world is trying to kill us. Call 'em what you want." She turned to the scholar. "Is this fog natural?"

The scholar turned to face them. Her eyes lit up. "Actually, yes. You see, the higher moisture-content air is cooled and condensates as it passes over the ice. During the daytime, the solar output keeps the air warm so that this becomes most likely only a nocturnal phenomenon. I'm thinking of using the same principle to build a device that generates fog. Maybe not a boon in Alexandria now, but perhaps after the thaw."

Blue raised an eyebrow at Nissa. "You get all that?"

"Natural. Natural-ish, given the circumstance. I still can't see the ground." Nissa looked down at where her feet disappeared beneath her. At first, they had followed a clear trodden path. But as night set in, the fog grew from a light haze to the soup that nearly consumed them. By holding their torches low to the ground, they could see just enough to prevent stumbling, but their progress was slow.

"This isn't really so bad," Nissa mused. "Kind of peaceful, actually. I'm still not sure where the watchers went."

Blue glanced over her shoulder. "What watchers?"

"Oh, sorry. I just assumed you noticed them. This place is crawling with fey. They're really shy."

Blue plodded ahead. "They saying anything?" She cleared her throat. "Anything useful?"

"Nope. They seem content to follow us. All gone now, though. I guess we're not that interest—"

A shrill keening ripped through the air. The screech caused Nissa to drop to her knees and cover her ears.

Blue darted to her side. "What's the matter?"

Nissa drew herself upright. The shriek, initially piercing, lessened and faded to the high-pitched buzz of a mosquito. "It's a fey. Something's hurting her. A lot. She's very upset. But it was so quick. I don't even know where it came from."

"Quick? Quick how?" Blue asked.

Nissa exclaimed, "I mean it was quick! Short and nasty and painful, and now it's quiet." Her voice dropped low. "I think something killed her. Or worse."

"Worse? What are you talking about?" Blue persisted.

"It's not a science," Nissa pleaded. "It's an emotion. She was scared, and now she's—not dead—but trapped." She looked back down the slope. "Maybe it…" She pursed her lips. "I think it's back near town. We need to go back and help her."

Blue shook her head. "Or actually, we don't, because that's not why we're here." She turned back to the path. "Elizabeth, lead on."

"But she's in pain," Nissa protested.

Elizabeth spoke softly. "Nissa, I can't pretend to know the fey like you do. That's never been my strength. I build things, I study things. And maybe it's more unfeeling, but that's not to say I don't care." She gestured around her at the swirling fog, the crawling vines, and the shadowed towers. "But this place, this whole place isn't natural. I think we are taking that for granted. Cinq and Yon are out there. And if the fey are in danger…"

Nissa exhaled. "We are too."

She strained her ears. The absence of sound unnerved her more than the shriek. But though the cry was gone, murmurs rose in the void. This time, the direction was clear, evident. And in the exact direction they had been traveling. As much as she hated it, Elizabeth was right. They should keep going. They had to keep going.

"You're right. No time to waste."

Elizabeth passed the Tracer to Nissa. With torch held low, Nissa paced up the slope. She gripped the sphere in one hand and kept her eyes on the ground, trying to make out objects through the fog. She navigated the chunks of ice and the occasional swath of messy vines. She no longer climbed with the air of exploration, but instead, with relentless drive, not for herself, not for Cinq and Yon, but so she could turn around as soon as possible. The fey needed help. She knew that. And the memory of what the old wikken said about the fey being turned into weapons weighed heavily on her mind. Was that happening here as well?

Up and up they climbed, moving through the fog to emerge on the upper reaches of the glacier. Turning around, the clouds wreathed the island, obscuring Rendezvous City and the ships below. Only the great towers rose above the mist. They protruded like broken pilings from a shipwreck. Up here the terrain had shifted. The roots had become far less prevalent. And the ice looked as smooth and unblemished as a polished sphere.

At the top, Nissa saw Cinq and Yon. Her heart leaped in her chest. She was surprised at the relief that washed over her. Cinq was a mage, sure. He was self-centered, stodgy, too serious, and grumbled too much, but he was also the brother and best friend she'd never had. And he was perfectly safe. Of course he was.

"Hey, Cinq!" Nissa waved her arms. "We made it!"

Oddly, he did not turn around. He did not call back. He remained standing with his back to her. She started toward him, and soon she was in a dead run. "Cinq! Cinq!" Faster and faster, she scrambled over the ice. But not only did her friends not turn, they were drifting farther away. "Cinq!"

A solid weight hit Nissa from behind, sending her sprawling onto the ice.

"Hey!" Blue shouted. She pinned Nissa down with her knees. "What the hell is wrong with you?"

Nissa struggled and rolled over to see the stern face of Blue. "Wrong with me? Get off me! I think you mean what's wrong with Cinq? And you. What's wrong with you?"

"Nissa, I'm right here," Cinq's habitually calm voice called from *behind* her. She pushed Blue off and sat upright. Sure enough, both Cinq and Yon were walking to meet them. But that was impossible. They were just... Nissa looked behind her. The landscape had decidedly changed. No longer an open ice field, the glacier caved in on itself, descending with slick, sloped walls into a darkened pit below.

When Cinq reached her, he helped her up. "They nearly got me too. You better now?"

Nissa stood. "Yeah. Yeah, I am." She paused. There was a message, something important she needed to say. "It's... not safe out here. I heard something on the ice. The fey are scared."

Cinq nodded. "Master Ascertine heard it too." He turned to where an old man stood. He had a long beard that was cast over his shoulder. The man's eyes walked a line between mocking and deeply inquiring. A mage. Obviously, a mage. From tip to tail. So how had he heard the fey?

Ascertine nodded. "I've been living beside them for a long time. We talk, but they don't always listen to me."

"Did you read my mind?" Nissa asked.

"Didn't need to." The old mage winked. "It's the first thing a wikken would ask." He bowed, flinging his arms out, his staff swooped to one side as his head nearly touched the ground. "Julius Ascertine, at your service."

"I'm Nissa. Don't mind Cinq, he sometimes forgets to introduce his friends because of, you know, social skills and stuff. This is Blue, and that's Elizabeth."

Elizabeth nodded at Ascertine and paced over to the rim of the caldera. She peered over the edge. "A gate, I presume?"

"Very astute, madam." Ascertine asked, "Are you a mage?"

Elizabeth shook her head. "Oh no. Just a student of things. I am currently the curator of the library at Alexandria. On sabbatical."

Ascertine's eyes twinkled. "Of course. You're the scholar. Cinq is the mage, Yon as monk, and Nissa the wikken." His eyes lingered on Blue. "You're not the hermit. You look closer to being…"

"I'm the chaperone."

Ascertine shrugged. "Four out of five. You're practically there."

Nissa said, "Right. Well, we've kind of got a quest thing going on. Did Cinq tell you why we're here?"

Master Ascertine nodded. "He did. You're looking for the Pentarch's machine. I'll repeat my answer: There is a vault at Northwind Tower. It contains all records of the construction, though the mages of Northwind are quite guarded when it comes to—"

Cinq interrupted, "He's agreed to convince them."

Nissa said, "He's coming with us? We came all this way… just to turn back around?"

Ascertine bristled. "Knowledge isn't nothing. I've spent twenty years studying the machine on Rendezvous. I daresay I know a thing or two. You're not going to just stroll up to the Black Gate and flip it on."

"And what if I do?" Nissa challenged.

Ascertine shrugged.

Nissa wrinkled her nose. Cinq had been bad enough. At least he didn't treat her like a child; at least he acknowledged they had different strengths. But this mage was just like all the rest. The world was on the brink of the Convergence, and he'd rather lord over her than try to help. What a piece of garbage. No wonder the witchlord had such an easy time convincing people they were the enemy.

A scream pierced the night. Nissa jerked her head to the far side of the crater to see an armored man rocketing down the face. He flailed as he grasped frantically for purchase, only to disappear into the black orifice at the bottom of the pit. She heard shouts from the top of the caldera. The soldier wasn't alone. Several armored men and a severe-looking woman were storming across the ice. Dogging behind was the hunched form of a creature scurrying on all fours. It was a fey, and it cried out in pain. Pity seized her heart.

"Cinq," Nissa's voice cracked as she spoke. "Hostile witch, large men, pointy metal things. This is not ok."

Blue scowled. "They found us."

Nissa loosened her daggers in their sheaths. She crouched to tighten her boots, not breaking her gaze from the approaching men. The soldiers, too, drew their weapons. Cinq, Yon, Blue, and Elizabeth prepared in their own way. A subtle glow gathered at the tip of Cinq's staff. Yon's eyes narrowed as he focused. Even Elizabeth removed one of the dread cylinders from her tool belt. Blue forwent subtlety. She unsheathed the mutant meat cleaver strapped to her bicep and hefted it. As for Ascertine, the old mage bit his lip; he started to sweat. His mouth and jaw worked nervously, as though he was either trying to form words, or else just gasping for breath.

As the woman and her guards crossed to meet them, Cinq raised one hand. "That's close enough."

The woman's face betrayed no emotion. She spoke in an accent that suggested the northern mountains, though highly refined. "I've been looking for you. I would have never guessed this time and this place. And I can't decide if I am intrigued, or simply annoyed."

Elizabeth spoke. "May I ask, madam, who you are?"

Nissa did a double take. She'd spent so much time thinking of Elizabeth as a fascinated grandmother that she'd forgotten she was the leader of Alexandria. She may look weather-beaten, but she spoke like an empress. And if her devices did what she claimed, she was a dangerous one at that.

Elizabeth continued, "For I'm afraid, my child, that we do not seek you."

"Don't call me child, southerner. I've endured more winter than you've imagined. I am Yanamadra, of the northern clans. And I've found you." The woman retrieved a pendant from her neck and held it aloft, a glass bauble that had both the size and appearance of an eye. Lights swirled within.

Nissa clicked her tongue. "You've got a Tracer. A teeny-tiny little cute one."

Yanamadra smiled. "And you have two yourselves, which led me to you." She looked down at the caldera and back to them. "You should know, I don't need you alive. But I don't prefer that path. Now, which of you are the keys?"

Elizabeth drew herself further upright. "We don't know you. And your entourage hasn't the look of hospitality. We'll tell you nothing."

Yanamadra snickered. "You don't know me? Of course you know me. We both stand at the top of a mountain of ice as ephemeral as the gate at its heart. This is not a place people happen to appear. You are here for a purpose, as am I. And like as not, that purpose is the same. The Black Gate sleeps, but it is time to awaken." She exhaled slowly. "I suggest you come willingly."

"And if not?" Nissa asked. "I mean, I'm guessing you didn't bring all those soldiers up here for the company. It's like you aren't even a proper witch."

Yanamadra's eyes narrowed. "Well, well, the little wikken speaks. You should know what is offered. My master, Mortimer Cain, will control the Black Gate. When that happens, the age of witches will end. He will rip the magic from your souls; he will stop the Convergence. And this time, it will be forever. But if you help, he will permit the four of you to live. Imagine, the world as your plaything. No rivals, no superiors."

Nissa's stomach knotted. There was no clean way out of this. Before the thought had completely formed in her mind, she acted. The dagger flew from her hand.

Someone muttered a gasp, but Yanamadra didn't flinch. Instead, the fey sniveling at her feet leaped into the air to intercept the dagger with its body. It cried out as it fell to the ground. The soldiers readied their weapons. They moved around Yanamadra in a protective arc.

Yanamadra glanced at the fey. "Your fate is sealed. But you don't *all* have to die. Last chance, come forward and live."

Nissa looked at her friends. She would kill herself before she was captured. She wouldn't be a tool for that devil. There was no *way* that was happening.

Yanamadra snapped her fingers. "Get them."

Five reavers advanced at a run, one holding back to guard their mistress. As they approached, an arc of light coursed from Cinq's staff, throwing two men into the air. One landed motionless on the ice, while the other dropped into the open crater. He skidded down the slope into the caldera. The other three did not slow, their shields raised.

The second attack came from Elizabeth. She threw her cylinder at the reavers. It detonated in a flash of blue light, accompanied by a shockwave, which flung soldiers and friends alike to the ground. Nissa and the others struggled to regain their footing. But the soldiers, who had received the brunt of the blast, were much slower to rise. Nissa had barely gotten to her feet when she saw Blue and Yon colliding with the soldiers. Blue was the strongest of them, but she wasn't a professional soldier. Even so, she struck with such ferocity that one of the soldiers now struggled to challenge her. Their exchanged blows rang out across the ice.

If Blue looked unmatched versus the reavers, Yon was an insect. And yet the force of his summoned chi struck like a tornado. He sent one soldier skidding back twenty feet across the ice. Yon closed the gap to attack and struck again. He raised his fist for a third strike, then stopped as his victim was incapacitated. He turned to the last guard between him and Yanamadra.

Nissa, now recovered, gripped her remaining dagger. She and Cinq stood side by side, with Elizabeth and Ascertine behind them. Cinq held his staff level. Why had he not lashed out with magic again? What was he waiting for?

A reaver lunged forward, sword arcing toward them. Cinq met the soldier with a parry of his staff. When the sword's edge connected, there was a metallic ring. The sword disintegrated into sand. The soldier scrambled back in surprise. He dropped the remnants of his sword and drew a knife. He drove his shoulder into Cinq, knocking him to the ground. The soldier raised his arm to strike when Elizabeth lunged between them. She struck ineffectively at the soldier's chain mail. The man flung her to one side, her tiny form falling motionless as she impacted the ice. A moment later, the soldier advanced on Ascertine. The reaver swung his ax, the head burrowing into the mage's side with a sickening thud. Ascertine crumpled.

Nissa charged at the soldier's back. She struck up, finding the soft gap between helmet and cuirass to plunge her knife into the soldier's throat. He folded, desperately clawing at her knife, and lay still. Nissa wrenched her dagger free.

She stood, chest heaving and sweat dripping along her arms. She was numbly aware of Elizabeth motionless on the ground, and Ascertine bleeding where he lay. But more than that, her senses were filled with the screams of the fey. She struggled to pull herself to the here and now. She watched another soldier swing at Yon, who parried with one open hand. He pivoted, flipping the guard over and onto the ground.

Now, only Yanamadra was left. Yon crept closer to her. He stood in a wide stance, one palm outstretched and the other held open and tight to his shoulder. Nissa looked at the others. Cinq, still shaken, had maneuvered to stand in front of where Elizabeth and Ascertine lay. Blue jogged forward to join Yon. She pointed her cleaver at Yanamadra.

She said, "Start talking. Maybe you'll live."

Yanamadra seethed with fury. "This is not finished. Last chance. Drop your weapons, and I'll make your deaths quick. Not you, little witch." She glared at Nissa and spat on the ground. "Maybe none of you."

The cries of the fey rose again, louder than a tornado. The mist, which had hung just beyond the crest of the mountain, swelled up, rising and taking shape. Nissa felt that the mist was not just vapor, but the wretched souls of hundreds of fey. As they coalesced, fey became banshees, haggards, furies, and tempests. Others took a different form altogether, that of their master. In a matter of seconds, they stood across from hordes of Yanamadra doppelgangers shoulder to shoulder with the deimos. Their real adversary was lost in the tide. Cinq and Blue backed away to rejoin the others.

"Cinq…" Nissa said. She wanted to close her eyes and drown out the screams. "Looking for ideas."

Cinq caught her with a sidelong glance. "Can you convince the fey that—?"

"No. I. Can. Not. That is Yanamadra the Dread. She has murdered thousands of my sisters. I'm nothing to her. I'm nothing to *them*."

With a heavy groan and wet, rasping cough, Ascertine dragged himself to his feet. The right half of his body was drenched in blood. He hunched over with one arm clutching the wound. His cheeks were sallow, his eyes wild. Blood dripped from his nose and the corners of his mouth. He lurched forward, step by step, leaning heavily on his staff to brush past the others. With a shake, his long beard dropped free. "Yanamadra. You are unwelcome at my *Rendezvous!*"

Ascertine spread his arms, staff in one hand. His cloak shone a brilliant blue. For Nissa, her awareness of magic existed on the side, an appreciation and occasional glimpse when a spell was cast. This time was different. Every fiber, every element of Ascertine, from the threads of his coat to the wisps of his beard, throbbed with potential. The glow was not physical, not light, but power. Energy crackled between his fingers. He turned to the others, his eyes pulsing with electricity. "You must escape. You must finish it."

Cinq said, "He's closing the gate." He pointed frantically to the caldera. "I said he's closing the gate! Let's go, follow me."

"Go where…?" Nissa's voice trailed off as Cinq took several steps and leaped into the caldera. He clutched his staff to his body as he skidded down the ice. Blue followed next, Elizabeth gathered in her arms. But this was insanity. They didn't know what was on the other side. Was it anything at all? What if the hole was just a hole?

Nissa looked back at Ascertine, his body had been replaced by a silhouette of power. Arcs of lightning lashed out to disintegrate fey as they charged with fangs bared and claws outstretched.

Yon clasped Nissa's shoulder. "Go. I'm right behind you."

Sheathing her dagger, she balled her fists, turned, and leaped into the open maw.

25

~ Yon ~

Yon watched as Nissa disappeared into the gate. He felt the energy of Ascertine behind him. What had once been a man was now a flare of energy collapsing on itself. The gate at the bottom of the caldera was almost closed—with his friends on the other side. Yon focused his chi in the core of his stomach; his senses heightened. Salt air brushed against his skin; magic breathed in and out of the gate. Ascertine's magic swirled in fury, and the fey screamed with murderous intent.

Yon leaped onto the slope of the caldera. He sat back, skidding across the ice while he scrambled to keep his feet in front of him. Down, down he fell, as the power from Ascertine and the fey filled the sky. Stars disappeared in the maelstrom of energy. The pitch of the slope steepened. He dropped into a freefall through a disk where light ceased. As he crossed the plane, sensation blinked away. Yellow light consumed him. He fell for several seconds before something collided with him, knocking him from his descent and sending him sprawling across a cool, mossy floor. Yon tried to wriggle free, only to find himself looking at—himself.

"What the—?" he began.

"It's ok. Stay calm. Just get back there and catch yourself, or none of this will work out again. Now go!"

Dazed, Yon scrambled to his feet, only barely registering the words of his doppelganger. He stumbled to the edge of the tunnel where a black pit disappeared below him. High above, something appeared and dropped through the hole. He sprang to intercept the object, slamming into it hard as he and it collided to land in a heap on the far side of the pit. Yon looked into his own surprised face.

"What the–?" it began.

The words spilled from Yon's mouth, "It's ok. Stay calm. Just get back there and catch yourself, or none of this will work out again. Now go!"

Yon rolled off his twin as it in turn charged back to the pit. White-hot flame surged from the pit below, throwing him backward and onto the ground. When the afterimage faded, Yon saw no trace of either the him that he'd caught, or the him that had caught him.

At the back of his awareness, like words echoed off a mountain, he heard Cinq's voice. *We should move on,* Cinq said. *"Things are a bit sideways here."*

Yon, still dazed, turned to his friend. But no one was there. His head reeled from the chaos of the battle, Yanamadra, Ascertine, the soldiers, Elizabeth, the…

Blue's voice called in the exact same cadence as Cinq's, *"We should move on. Things are a bit sideways here."* Then Nissa, soft as a whisper: *"We should move on. Things are a bit…"*

Yon lurched forward. He stumbled down the mossy hall, using one hand to steady himself against the cool, damp walls. Where were Cinq and Blue? Where was everyone? As he walked, the light moved with him. The walls lit up ahead and dimmed behind. Too overwhelmed to continue, he sank to his knees. But as he quit moving, the surrounding glow faded, leaving him in absolute darkness. Another surge of panic, and Yon bolted upright. In response, the light shone once again.

"Ok, so don't stop moving," he said aloud. "Easy enough."

"…easy enough," something echoed from around him.

Yon continued, his steps becoming more measured. The feeling of uneasiness remained just at arm's length. He tried to gather his chi, but it remained slippery, elusive. This wasn't just exhaustion. Still, he tried to relax. He didn't want to upset the strange magic around him.

"Which is a good idea."

Yon snapped around to face the sound of a voice, clearly his own, but that he didn't speak himself.

"Definitely getting weird, monkey."

This time it was Nissa's voice. Or at least it started as Nissa, before subtly changing to the formal cadence of Elizabeth.

A panic grew in his chest. He swallowed hard. "If you can talk, I can talk," he said.

"And no one's stopping you."

That time was Blue. Or something like Blue, or maybe a memory of Blue. He shook his head. Perhaps *not* thinking about this was for the best.

"You've got that right," his own voice whispered.

Yon lowered his head and gritted his teeth, picking up the pace as he snaked farther through the broad tunnel. As he moved, the world around him flitted from one thing to something entirely different. He ran along the tunnel where the vine-covered (moss?) walls and the dripping icicles (bats?) that clung to the ceiling as the floor oozed downhill (uphill?) as his bare (booted?) feet crunched (squished?) as he crawled (ran?) down the corridor. Yon had a thought, sudden and clear when all else was muddled. Instead of seeking his chi, he turned his mind inward. He severed himself from the magic entirely.

The corridor snapped to darkness. The moist air evaporated from his lungs, replaced by a clammy miasma.

"Got you!" A hand snapped onto Yon's shoulder, and he squeaked in dismay, only to see the sudden and clear face of Cinq, his staff wrapped in a bit of burning cloth.

Yon blinked. He was—in an instant—in surroundings as solid as they had been surreal. He stood in a tunnel of polished wood. The light from the torch reflected from the walls to cast faint images all around. He slowed his breathing. Cinq watched him with weary eyes.

"Where is everyone?" Yon asked. "Are we... under the iceberg?"

"That's one way to put it. We're in the otherplane. And be careful, things here react poorly to magic. Or maybe I should say they feed off it. The magic here is... not healthy."

"Where are the others?" Yon took a step and stumbled. "I may need a minute."

Cinq took the lead by sitting down on the smooth wooden floor. "I haven't found anyone else yet. Did they follow you? How about the soldiers?"

Yon shook his head. "I was the last through the gate—I'm not sure about after that."

"Time might not matter as much here." Cinq sighed. "I suspect it might not matter at all. Now take a breath and have some water." He reached into his coat and removed a small flask. He studied the monk closely.

"What are you doing?" Yon asked.

"Just seeing how intact you are. How do you feel? Are you wounded?"

"No. Just scraped up. Who *was* that woman?"

Cinq shook his head. "I'm not sure, but Nissa seemed to know her. But if she works for the witchlord, you can bet he knows about us." Cinq's brow wrinkled as though trying to order words before he spoke them.

Yon ran his finger across the polished wood of the tunnel floor. "What happened to Master Ascertine?"

"He used his magic. All of it. Then he used more. It's something you don't survive. I suspect it's why the witchlord doesn't attack more mages directly. Lucky for him, few of us are willing martyrs."

"Do you think that woman survived?"

Cinq shook his head. "I don't know. I just hope we weren't followed."

The words hung in the air for a moment. Yon tried to clear his mind without reaching for his chi. He looked at Cinq. "Do you still have the Tracer?"

"Yes, but there's a problem." He held the Tracer in one hand. Instead of five lights within, there were thousands, a swarm of fireflies trapped in the crystal. "I can only guess. It could be tracing different versions of you, me, or the others. Different times, things that haven't even happened, or maybe only might happen. Who knows? But it's not going to bring us back together."

"So, we wait?"

Cinq shook his head. He stood back up. "No. That doesn't feel right either."

"Then how do we find everyone?"

The mage did not answer for a long moment. "Well, I have no direct magic, and I assume you can't channel your chi. The Tracer is useless, and at its most basic," he stomped the polished wooden floor, "no footprints."

"But…"

Cinq scowled. "I don't know. This is my first time here. Maybe we should be happy we can breathe the air. Do you have any ideas?"

Yon chose his words carefully. "We're the outsiders here. We're the thing that's strange. And the place… reacts to us. Maybe it's doing the same to the others. Maybe we look for that reaction?"

Cinq looked pleased. "You're a natural, Yon. So, are you ready?"

"Yeah… if you think it's a good idea. Aren't you supposed to stay put when you're lost?"

"You think Nissa is staying put? Or Blue? Come on. If our friends are causing a 'disturbance' the better for us."

Cinq and Yon set off down the corridor, though the idea still picked at Yon if any of this was real. The polished wood didn't feel real, except that when studied closely, or knocked against, it felt as solid as anything else. They hadn't gone a hundred yards before Yon paused. He felt a presence in the air, as though the walls called out with yearning, as though they lacked something just out of reach.

"Cinq, can you feel it? There's something here, something in the air. It feels…"

"Hungry."

With a low rumble, the corridor shifted. The walls rearranged like a snake constricting its coils. Yon stumbled, before steadying himself.

He said, "Hungry feels right. Something's out here."

Cinq put his open hand on the wall. "The same energy from the Rendezvous, it's all around us." He bowed his head and shut his eyes. "We can follow the flow."

Frustration overwhelmed him. Yon said, "We're not looking for the magic, Cinq. We're looking for our friends."

"Well, I can sense the magic, but I can't sense them."

"What about me?" Yon asked.

"What do you mean?"

"I'm right here, can you sense me at all?"

Cinq furrowed his brow. "I can… but it's all wrong. When I try to sense you, I can't distinguish you from myself. It's like I'm looking at my reflection."

Yon's eyes widened. "That's… that's good." He spoke more quickly. "Maybe everything here is so different from us that we all seem the same. What else is the same? If you were to look for more of that same 'Cinqness' would it help?"

The mage gripped his staff in both hands. His eyes remained closed for a long time, to the point that Yon felt compelled to shake him. Cinq said, "You might be on to something. I can feel traces of myself. It's like footprints in the air, or trails of smoke. I can see where we've been, but I can also see other paths. Maybe it's where we will go, or maybe where we *should* go. But one is different. It has no start, no end."

"I don't know what—" Yon started.

"Follow me."

Cinq darted forward. With head ducked and the staff trailing in one hand, he wove through the branching corridors. Left and right, they climbed into passages that splintered overhead and dropped through gaps in the floor. As they moved, Yon felt it too. Following Cinq felt like following himself.

A horrifying scream filled his ears.

26

~ Blue ~

Blue landed hard on the debris-covered floor of the archive's observatory. All around her, toppled bookshelves had disgorged leather-bound tomes across the tile. A layer of frost, dust, and light ash covered everything. Blue was caught in both realization and horror that she had returned to Alexandria. Familiar, yes, but also back where the nightmare began. She struggled to her feet, her bruised muscles protesting the effort. Her palms throbbed with pain where they had been gashed in the fall. Her mind felt muddled, as though each thought was like wading through deep waters. Where was everyone? Had the haggards broken through? What was she doing here? And…

Elizabeth.

The name jolted through Blue's mind, and with it the cascade of events. At the fight above the caldera, she had taken Elizabeth in her arms. Together they had slid into the darkness. And now she was here.

"Doc!" she cried. She paced through the stacks, her feet crunching against fallen bits of stone and plaster. At first, she was in a panic. She threw aside tables, upset piles of books, and lifted debris, hoping for some glimpse of her friend. She strained her ears for any sounds of movement or faint breathing. Nothing.

"Doc? Where are you?" This time she whispered, both so she could listen for a response, but also out of concern for what might be lurking in the shadows. The seconds passed along, and with each tick, apprehension welled once more.

"Doc! Doc, can you hear me? Cinq? Nissa? Yon? Where are you?"

She heard a shout, followed by the thud of boots and clank of armor. A moment later, a soldier appeared below one of the arches leading to the hallway. He had a short-handled ax in one hand. Blue recognized him immediately. This was the same soldier that Cinq had thrown into the caldera. He had lived after all. Blue drew her cleaver from its sheath. She locked eyes with the man. He was a trained warrior, but perhaps he'd been injured in the fall.

A second soldier stepped through the doorway, this one with a short sword. A third appeared, a fourth, a fifth, and more, until reavers lined the walls. Were there fifty of them? A hundred? The men flickered and overlapped with one another, their shoulders passing through like mist. Blue took a step back and bumped into someone behind her. She spun in panic, only to see…. herself. This was not a reflection, not a discarded mirror. The person looked in every way like her, from clothes to the broad cleaver in her hands. The doppelganger turned to face the soldiers on the far side. Blue did the same, only to see herself multiplied once more. With every turn of her head, there were more of her. Now, there were at least as many of herself as there were the soldiers.

As one, the reavers unleashed a battle cry and charged at her. Blue and her facets screamed back. They closed the gap, cleavers held high. As she collided with the reavers, sights, sounds, and smells muddled together. She swung and stabbed and connected in a fury of grunts and cries. The reavers, in turn, attacked her. She could feel the blades of the ax, the thrust of swords, the tips of spears. She heard the clang of steel parried, and the wet squish as they connected. Her blade made contact, or was parried, or missed entirely. She was both herself and the others. She swung and chopped and screamed and died.

Blue felt a hand on her shoulder and swung hard behind her. The cleaver angled up and from the side to cut into Elizabeth's unprotected ribs. The world dropped into a sudden, horrible focus. Gone were the hordes of reavers, gone were the infinite reflections of Blue, gone was the Alexandrian observatory with its fallen bookshelves, crumbling debris, and pale non-light. She watched as Elizabeth crumpled to a polished wooden floor.

Blue dropped her cleaver and rushed to her friend. The scholar's side turned dark with welling blood. She went still.

"No, no, no!" Blue's frantic cries shifted to sobs. She tore off her coat and tried to use it to staunch the bleeding. "Doc? Doc, say something. What should I do? Tell me what to do. What should I...?"

Blue kept her coat pressed against the wound. Her mind buzzed with adrenaline, even as her new reality crept around. She knelt in an oval chamber with a smooth wooden floor and ridged walls emitting a pale, yellow light. While her multiples were gone, three reaver soldiers lay crumpled around the room. Their bodies wounded, bleeding, and still. Blue looked back at Elizabeth. The scholar's chest no longer moved, there were no longer sounds of any pained or labored breathing. Elizabeth was dead. And Blue had killed her.

Her strength drained away. Blue crawled backward a few feet and sat down hard. She couldn't make sense of it. The glacier, the battle, and now this. All of it had been real while also a frenetic dream. She stared at Elizabeth's body and down at herself. Other than the scratches on her palms, she had no wounds. The blood on her clothes was not her own. The cleaver she'd dropped only moments ago was once again clutched in her hand.

This isn't real, it isn't real, it isn't real, it isn't—

A light appeared from one of the three tunnels snaking away from the main chamber. *More of them*, she thought. Rage surged in her veins. She tightened her grip on her weapon and lumbered to her feet. The sticky blood on the handle oozed between her fingers. She kept her eyes fixed on the tunnel opening. Two shapes stumbled into view. They looked like Cinq and Yon, or was this another trick?

"Stop," Blue ordered. She tried hard to sound commanding though she could hear the weariness in her voice. "Are you real?"

Cinq—assuming it was Cinq—looked at the fallen bodies, his eyes lingering on Elizabeth. "What happened here? Are you hurt? Is…" He trailed off.

Yon cried out, "Elizabeth!" He pushed around Cinq as he dashed to the fallen scholar.

Blue tried to protest, but the words died in her throat. As thoughts of danger ebbed, the realization of what she'd done— and how she'd be judged—crept in. She let her sword arm drop; the blade clattered to the floor. Yon crouched over Elizabeth's body as he checked for signs of life. Darkness gathered at the corners of her vision, as though watching through a tunnel. Yon stopped. He looked up at Blue.

Elizabeth was dead. Blue came to the realization again and again as her mind fought to decipher dream from reality. She wrenched her eyes from the body to look at Cinq. The mage had not shifted from the entryway. His jaw clenched and unclenched; his emotions were unreadable. He circled the room, passing by each of the three soldiers before stopping over Elizabeth. Cinq knelt. He unclasped the pouch on the scholar's belt and removed her Tracer.

Blue tried to speak, her voice cracked. "I didn't know what was real. There were hundreds of them, hundreds of me, and… I couldn't tell. I," she sucked in her breath, "I killed her."

Cinq stood. He held out Elizabeth's Tracer to Blue. "She'd want you to have it."

Blue nearly started sobbing once more. But it was different around other people. She had to be strong. She took the Tracer and put it in her pocket. But that wouldn't be enough. She knelt to remove Elizabeth's tool belt and cinched it around her own waist. When she looked up again, Yon's eyes were welled with tears; Cinq's expression was blank. He was probably trying to figure out what it meant to lose a key. Of course, unless they could get out of here, it wouldn't matter.

"All right," Blue said. "Where's Nissa?"

27

~ Nissa ~

Nissa tumbled through the black.

Just when she thought she was reaching the bottom, just when she thought she could glimpse something real, she drifted back up. If not for the wind whipping against her, she would have doubted she was falling so much as floating. But from the moment she dropped through the gate, she had thought about the fall. And now, that thought was stuck.

She tried to cry out. But the roar of the wind was so deafening that she couldn't hear her voice. And so she waited, playing with the twists of the air against her body, the whip against her hair, and squinting as her eyes watered. The novelty wore off. Nissa was bored.

With no point of reference, no direction, and no light except her own illuminated body, she reached out in other ways. She closed her eyes and wrapped her arms around her knees. She ignored the howl of the wind. She listened, and just beyond the black, she heard a murmuring. The voice was quiet at first, no more than a hint of imagination. The murmur grew into a whisper. It was joined by others until she was engulfed in the screams of millions of fey.

Nissa opened her eyes.

She was no longer falling, no longer in darkness, no longer alone. She sat atop iridescent black sand. The grains stretched out across the ground in all directions to disappear out of sight. Above the sand, a jungle rose, or rather hung suspended. At first, she only saw the vines, but as she followed the tendrils, they connected to branches which in turn joined to the trunks of trees of impossible size. The trees spanned the width of buildings as they grew not up from the ground, but down from the sky. The roots formed a lattice ceiling, a living dome shrouded in viridescent, ethereal haze.

She wanted to run across the sands to leap into the hanging vines. She wanted to feel the bark of the trees and breathe deep of the scent of flowers. And yet she remained motionless. The voices, once deafening, became whispers.

A fey appeared. Nissa saw the aura first, a hint of pale white light. But as it moved, the vines filled and twisted around it. The spirit solidified and took shape in mimicry of Nissa. She appeared to be a young girl, though with brown skin and wearing clothes of twisting green vines. The fey dangled above the sands, a single tendril connecting it to the leafy world above.

"Hello?" Nissa ventured. The words weren't important, only the feeling.

The fey flinched. She crouched, then sprang into the air, flitting upward, shifting to become light as she joined the other lights swarming above. Nissa watched, mesmerized by both the fog and the luminescence. The lights were certainly fey, though most were only hints of awareness. These fey had no form, were between forms, or didn't see the point of them. But the fog, the mist surrounding the roots—that was something else entirely. Stranger still, it felt familiar.

Cinq would know, Nissa thought. *He'd know or at least guess at it.* Her cheeks flushed. She had been so caught in the surrealism of the otherplane she hadn't thought about her friends. She cursed herself. Then she cursed Cinq and Elizabeth for hogging the Tracers that would have brought them together. Where were they?

She looked at the inverted trees, the roots, the flowers, the vines, and the buzzing of the formless fey. This place was more dreamlike than her actual dreams. And of course, there was the matter of escape. Crap. Crap, crap, crap, crap, crap. She needed to find her friends—and an exit—before the dream became a nightmare.

Nissa dropped to one knee and placed her hand atop the sand. The grains were rough, dry, and subtly reflective. They reminded her of the scorched earth of Laurel's Hollow. She scooped up a handful and allowed the sand to sift through her fingers. Compared to the fetid air, the sand was cool. She dusted off her hands. A shiver crawled up her spine as she realized that not one plant, not one flower, not a single root or leaf touched the sands. And neither had the fey.

Uneasiness crept over her. She became aware that somewhere in her descent she had lost both boots. And now the ground grew colder. She dashed madly across the sands, but the loose grains were difficult to navigate. The farther she went, the more she began to sink. Closer, closer, almost there. Nissa's hand grasped a dangling vine just as she sank to her waist. She struggled to pull herself up, using hands and feet together until she was safely above the sand. The grains fell from her bare toes. Nissa looked down, her heart racing. There was no trace of her footsteps, not even the tiniest impression.

I need to get out of here, she thought. Nissa climbed up through the hanging vines until reaching a branch thick enough to support her. She gripped the branch with her thighs as she considered the sands below. The sand had felt—if only briefly—parasitic. In turn, the inverted trees made some sort of twisted sense. The ground was dangerous, and so the trees had found another way.

She shuddered. This time, not from the cold, but the memory of seeing Yanamadra in person. Back in the enclave, Nissa had heard tales of the renegade wikken. Of course, a lot of those stories could have been exaggerated. Or maybe they weren't. Nissa had never seen anyone exert such power. Not even the strongest of the elders back at the enclave came close. Of course, the elders wouldn't have used the fey as weapons. She paused. That wasn't true. The old wikken in Rendezvous City claimed that the wikken *were* using the fey to fight. Or maybe Yanamadra was a new breed of reaver. She had controlled hundreds of fey. *Hundreds.*

The awe fell away as Nissa remembered the rest of the legend. Yanamadra had been raised in an enclave, a prodigy. She had mastered all the wikken disciplines and created more of her own. But that made the rest of the wikken nervous. As much as wikken like to scoff at the traditions of mages, they had their own unshakable rules. Above all, they sought harmony with the fey. Yanamadra saw the fey as interlopers. Foreigners. Aliens. The price of that transgression was to be used as tools. She was cast out. But she found a new home within the northern clans.

Nissa was nudged from her daydream by rustling in the branches above her. Something crept her way. The aura of the creature marked it as the same fey that had approached earlier. She slithered headfirst down the roots to stop, inverted, to stare at Nissa with amber, questioning eyes.

"You know," Nissa said, "you could have warned me back there. Maybe just a head shake and a point or something? You know, finger across the throat in a 'get it moving, girl. You gonna die.'"

The fey cocked her head. Nissa decided to try again. She was a speaker, after all. Talking to the fey, understanding their feelings, that was her whole talent. Fat lot of good it did in a fight, but at least she was in one piece. And if she was lucky, maybe Ascertine had been able to fight back.

Nissa reached out with her emotions. She tried to hear with all her senses together. She didn't ask any questions, only projected a feeling of warmth, kinship, and kindness.

The fey remained motionless; its expression not changing. And why should it? This could be the first time it had ever even seen a human. Maybe they could learn together.

Emotion cascaded over Nissa. It buzzed in her ears like the lap of ocean waves. The sentiments shone through: curiosity, caution, foliage. Nissa shook her head; that last part didn't make sense. The feelings became thoughts. The creature wanted to know why she—whatever she was—had come from the sands to get onto her tree.

"Oh no, no, no, no." Nissa projected the emotion as she spoke words. "I didn't come from the sands; I just fell in them. I come from—" she pointed at the swirling green of the sky— "you know, up. The upperplane. That's not a word. The nearplane. But I guess you don't call it near. You know what I mean."

An outpouring of relief flowed to Nissa, accompanied by revulsion of the sands (black, dark, cold, hungry, hurting, pain, avoid.) This relief was followed by emotions, hints, waves, and energy. Nissa suffered a bombardment of questions without understanding them. But it wasn't hostile, just back to being curious. In Nissa's experience, that was where most fey spent their time—banshees and haggards notwithstanding.

Nissa leaned forward, eyebrows raised. "Listen. I'm happy to chat until we figure each other out. And I'm sure we will. But maybe we could kind of walk and talk? I'm looking for my friends. They're like me." She snorted a laugh. "At least compared to you, they are. That's not the point. They're my friends. And knowing them, they're probably in danger." She beamed at her new acquaintance. "So, can you help me out?"

The feelings returned to Nissa, with a few thoughts forming clearly: *Friends. Danger. Help.*

She smiled. "Yeah, that's right. But you may need to go slow. I'm not exactly a dryad, you know. That's what we'd call you back home. A tree spirit."

The fey issued a wave of confusion.

"It's just a name. We'll get to your real one later. I'm Nissa, by the way. Nice to meet you."

28

~ Cinq ~

There had to be a way out. That assumed, Cinq mused, that there was an out. Perhaps the otherplane was nothing more than a knotted mass of snaking tunnels with polished walls and an overreaction to anything and everything magic. The combination of chaos and uniformity infuriated him. At first, the idea of the otherplane had offered infinite questions and answers—a place of fey and magic and possibility. It was out there; he knew it was out there. But first he had to escape. Was this another well-kept secret the archmages had withheld?

"Yon, Blue, hold a moment."

Cinq cupped his hand around the end of his staff where the light from his makeshift torch had begun to dim. He reached for another strip of cloth and stopped. Whenever he moved, the walls glowed. Before, he hadn't trusted the phenomenon enough to let the torch go out completely. But he also didn't want to waste his supplies. In theory, as long as they kept moving, the tunnel would stay lit. He watched the embers on his torch fade. No. He couldn't risk it. He prepared the torch once more.

Illumination was the least of his problems. Firstly, Cinq needed to find Nissa. Unfortunately, he didn't have the same intuition of her whereabouts that he had with Blue. Either she was blending in, or something bad had happened. If any of them would survive this place, it would be Nissa. Plus, he missed her.

The real problem was Elizabeth.

Cinq had lost a friend in the scholar. They'd had kindred minds and grown close in their short time together. But the problem was larger than that. He had to put his personal feelings aside. A key, one of five keys thrown forward in time over centuries, was dead. Did that mean this project, this quest, this *everything*, was doomed? Uniting the lights of the Tracer had consumed him long before he knew about the keys. But now his goal had grown. Could they really unlock the Black Gate? Could they really end the Convergence just as the Pentarch had done? What would that mean for his own legacy? Such fame, such prestige, would open all the doors ever closed to him. And not only in the short term, but forever. He could be the next Pentarch.

Was that dream lost?

Five people. Five keys. That had been the goal, but now one was lost. Cinq had no doubt that if they found the Black Gate, they would also find five locks. Four keys wouldn't be enough.

But death had to be accounted for, right? No one was immortal. Was there a way to pass being a key to another? Would Elizabeth reincarnate in Alexandria once more, memories of her past life gone? Cinq thought about Yanamadra. She hadn't just tried to capture them. What would have happened if she'd killed them? She wanted the machine for herself, not just to make sure it remained unused. For the hundredth time, Cinq wished the Tracer worked in the otherplane. It would solve his problems— or at least get him closer to answers.

Cinq glanced back at Yon and Blue. No one spoke; it didn't seem appropriate. Yon hadn't bonded with Elizabeth in the same way Cinq had. But for Blue, everything had changed. Elizabeth had been more than just Blue's friend. She had also been mother, mentor, and savior. She had united the refugees of Alexandria, she had given them all hope, and she had opened Blue's mind to learning. And now, Blue considered herself a murderer.

And worst of all, they'd lost a key.

Yon tugged on Cinq's coat. "Stop a second. Can you feel that?"

Cinq strained both his ears and his spiritual awareness of the world. The surging of magic in and out, in and out, overshadowed the energy buzzing all around. He couldn't look past the yearning of the otherplane. The entire world thirsted for magic. Had the otherplane always been this way? Was this yet another secret, or something else?

Yon placed one hand against the wall. "Something's moving. I can feel the footsteps. You think we're being followed?"

Cinq mimicked Yon's action, but he felt nothing. Where are you, Nissa?

Blue put a hand on Cinq's shoulder. "For the sake of argument, let's just *assume* there are some haggards in these tunnels, or something just as bad. I'd feel better if you had these." Blue pulled the rolled bundle from her back. She had collected the reavers' weapons—along with their supplies—just in case.

She picked up a short sword in one hand and a scimitar in the other. She held them out to Cinq and Yon.

Yon shook his head. "I swore to never use a weapon."

Blue snorted. "Don't be so dramatic. If you think your chi is less of a weapon than this, you're lying to yourself. No chi here, so the rules have changed. That goes for all of us."

Yon hesitated, then accepted the sword.

"How about you, oh wizened mage? Any moral objections?"

Cinq shrugged as he grasped the hilt. "I can be practical. Don't tell anyone."

A hint of a smile graced Blue's lips. "Your secret is safe with me." She patted the handle of her cleaver. "And I don't want to fight alone. Not again."

The mood darkened once more, but only for a moment as a faint skitching sounded down the corridor behind them. The noise grew to a piercing staccato. Something was coming their way.

"Follow me."

Ahead, the tunnel converged with another offshoot. Cinq turned onto the side path and waved for the others to join him. He snuffed out his torch and crouched low. As they remained still, the light from the walls faded, the clattering grew louder. *Something* dashed past them, moving so quickly that it remained ahead of the light.

When the last skittering abated, Cinq, Yon, and Blue returned to the main passage, the walls now shining brightly. The floor and walls bore heavy scars. Whatever had passed through had left deep gashes behind.

Cinq fingered the scratch marks. "Maybe it knows the way out."

Blue wrinkled her nose. "Or we're walking into its hive."

Cinq straightened his shoulders. "Well, it seems to know where it's going. Which is more than we can say."

Yon said, "But we don't really want to *catch* it, do we? It sounded big."

"Yes. Yes, it did. And no. No, we don't."

29

~ Nissa ~

Nissa scaled the enormous tree. She wasn't sure if the tree was upside down and she was climbing up, or since she was moving from the upper branches and toward to the roots, that she was technically descending. The situation was confused further since while something pulled her *down* to the ground, another force drew her onto the tree itself. She could walk vertically up the trunk and limbs of the tree without holding on, and as long as she didn't think too much about it, it seemed to work. Perhaps this was how spiders did it. They just didn't let it bother them.

Her fey guide scurried around the tree, pausing on one branch then leaping to land on another. The fey's movements were quick, frantic, and *decidedly* squirrel-like. Once the thought entered her head, Nissa couldn't shake it. Her giggles kept slipping out—to the fey's great annoyance.

The fey—the dryad—didn't speak in words, phrases, and certainly not sentences. Instead, the thoughts migrated to Nissa through scents, colors, and emotions. But the longer the dryad chattered, the more easily the picture formed. There was the black/hungry (below), the green/hungry (nearby), the blue/running (above), and the yellow/angry (within). From these building blocks, a tapestry wove in her mind. The black/hungry—Nissa decided—was the ground itself. The ground was hungry, consuming anything that it touched.

The green/hungry was a different level of need. This wasn't a hunger for everything, but rather the pangs of someone without enough to eat. More importantly, the dryad had a kinship and affection for the green/hungry. This must be the trees. At some point, when the ground became hungry, the trees stretched up for their food, to what Nissa assumed was the blue/running. This confused her. For one, the glowing above her was most notably purple and not blue. And more importantly, what was it? Food of some sort? Or magic? Or the magic was their food?

As for the yellow/angry, Nissa guessed these were the other fey. Or maybe some of the fey. Or a specific fey. Or some type of fey. Or how the fey were feeling at that moment. Now she was just guessing. Right or wrong, spoken or unspoken, she was learning a language in a place without words. And she was trying her best, thank you very much.

The twist of the enormous tree grew close to a junction, where a branch grew out, twisting to point down at the sands. Nissa followed the dryad as she flipped from walking on the sheer vertical of the trunk to navigating around to the underside of the branch. They had done a similar maneuver twice before to cross from one tree to an adjacent one. The first tree, which Nissa had coined "Big Oak," had given her a calm, relaxed feeling.

Perhaps it was the dryad's home tree, or at least a favorite. But the new tree, rising into view, felt different.

For starters, it wasn't even a tree at all, so she decided to call it "Big Weed." Certainly, it had a trunk, branches, roots, and such, but in all the wrong places. The trunk wasn't a solid chunk of wood replete with bark. It was a knotted twisting of tangled wood. On its surface, the tree had a series of thorns, ranging from three times Nissa's height to as small as the hairs on her hand. The limbs were similar twists of wood, and in place of leaves, Big Weed bloomed with parasitic mushrooms. The organism radiated sickness in a way that Nissa could not fully describe, much less pinpoint. And the bleed of emotions made distinguishing her thoughts from the dryad's impossible.

"Well, if you hate it so much, can't we go somewhere else?" Nissa asked.

The dryad shuddered. It jumped ahead, the sentiment of *Danger-Friends-Help* replaying again and again. Nissa made another connection. The "friends" here weren't her friends. These were the dryad's friends. What's more, the "danger" was clearly not coming from the black/hungry, but from the blue/running. Nope, didn't make sense. She'd try again later.

Nissa came to the edge where the branch from Big Oak crossed within a dozen yards of Big Weed. The fey scurried forward and sailed through the air, bridging the gap to land on the tree. It turned and looked back with impatience. Was this seriously it? Was this the punchline to a drawn-out and malicious joke? Nissa would jump, the arboreal stickitude would give out, and all the fey would have a great big laugh at the little wikken that dared come to the otherplane. Nissa looked around. Was there a wisp of vine, some fallen limb, *anything,* that could get her out of a jump?

She looked back at the dryad. "Ok, before I do this—and let's be honest, I'm probably going to do this—why are you angry? Or yellow/angry or whatever?"

The response came in colors, smells, and no small amount of impatience: first the blue/flowing, then the black/hungry, and lastly the green/hungry. The ideas floated in a maelstrom of fury. Things hadn't always been this way. The ground hadn't always tried to suck the life out of everything; the trees hadn't always needed to drink the sky. And somehow, the blue/flowing was the cause *and* the solution.

Nissa turned the emotions around. An interpretation, to be sure, but it felt like the right interpretation: At one time the otherplane had had more than enough magic. Something had stolen it. Now everything from the trees to the sands to the fey themselves were fighting for what little remained. And now the black hungry sand threatened to consume the last of a distorted, inverted world, all while the fey watched the last of the magic trickle away to the nearplane. They both resented and lusted after it.

Nissa took a few steps back, sprinted forward, and jumped. For a moment, direction became meaningless as gravity shifted from Big Oak behind her, to the ground, and then to Big Weed. She collided with the trunk, grateful she hadn't fallen to her death. Above her, the dryad watched. She loped along the branch until it reached the mass of twisted wood forming the trunk. The dryad pressed against the bark, and it opened to reveal a darkened passage within. The fey glanced at Nissa, chirped, and disappeared into the shadows.

Nissa bit her lip. This was a trap. Clearly, it was a trap. But what other options did she have?

She felt a tug at the back of her mind. Something called from within the tree, a great many somethings. Calling, calling, calling. She heard the voices of the fey as they gathered within. Yellow and angry? Absolutely. Nissa had to know why. Why was this all her fault?

30

~ Yon ~

Yon raced along the twisting, polished tunnel in pursuit of the creature. He chased not only the sound of its passing and the light left in its wake, but also the urgency screaming from the walls themselves. Whatever called to the fey also called to him. To all of them. As he ran, he tried to imagine the creature. An insect perhaps? All legs and spines and angles—or did it have a form at all?

He nearly stumbled as a new awareness blossomed in his mind. He felt a connection to Nissa, as though her energy reverberated through the wood around him. Had she finally arrived in this Gordian maze? Should they retrace their steps to find her? Yon stopped short; he looked back at the others.

"You ok?" Blue asked as she and Cinq stopped beside him.

"It's Nissa. She's here."

Cinq looked around. "Where? Which way?"

Yon shook his head. "I don't know. It's just a hunch. She's alive though. I'm sure of that much."

"So why did you stop?"

Yon looked up. "Huh?"

Cinq pressed. "We're… we're losing the trail. Let's go. We'll find her later."

Yon didn't answer. Frustration and anger rose within him. How could Cinq be so unfair? Did the mage even care about them or only that they were his precious keys? He'd barely shed a tear for Elizabeth. Yon wondered if they did find the machine, if he wanted Cinq to be a part of it. Or was this place just affecting him? All of them.

He started off down the corridor once more. The light left behind from the creature's passing had nearly faded away. He had to get closer, closer, closer.

Yon skidded to a halt as the corridor came to a dead end. The ceiling curved down to stop just above the floor, leaving a gap only a foot high. Light shone through the opening, growing and waning arrhythmically. He wanted to be in that light, to follow it to the end. Then he stopped. He breathed. He turned.

Blue and Cinq came skidding around the corner after him.

Cinq asked, "What is it?"

Yon pointed. "We need to go through there. But…"

"But what?"

Yon fought to remain calm. "The tree is talking to me. It's angry."

"Angry?" Cinq repeated.

Blue nodded. "He's right. I've got all these weird thoughts pushing in on me. It's like I'm drunk, or drugged, or something. I'm seeing things that I'm not *seeing*, you know?"

Cinq pressed his lips together. He rapped on the wall, then laid his palm against it. "I hear the tree too."

Yon's face lit up. "So, it *is* a tree?"

"Of *course*, it's a tree," Cinq rumbled. "It's Big Weed, and we all know it." He sighed. "Just don't listen to it."

Blue brushed past the two of them. She dropped to her belly and army-crawled through the gap. Several seconds later, she whispered for them to follow.

Yon pushed away the smells, feelings, and colors drifting into his mind. He dropped flat against the floor and wriggled under the low hanging wall. After about ten feet, the ceiling opened up into a vast chamber. In front of him, a kind of wooden ridge protruded from the ground. Blue sat flat on the floor, her back against the ridge. She pointed to the space beside her. She didn't speak, so Yon remained silent as well. He crawled out to join her, and a few moments later Cinq sat beside them as well.

Blue held her finger to her lips and pointed at her eyes. Yon rotated so that he faced the low wall on his knees. He peeked over.

On the other side of the balcony, the corridor opened into a massive amphitheater. The walls, floor, and domed ceiling were of multi-hued wood. The warps and whorls repeated in colossal iterations and refractions: pale yellow, white pine, deep ebony. Every grain of wood glowed with ethereal light. And below, circling the base of the sphere and perched on the surrounding walls, were the creatures.

The arena was filled with hundreds upon hundreds of fey. They filled the chamber, from spindly and insectoid, to hulking and shaggy, to winged and leathery, to squat and humanoid. Each and every fey stood, twitched, shifted, and buzzed with a common orientation. At the center of the room, an obsidian monolith hung suspended, wrapped in a vine which stretched from ceiling to floor. The rock pulsed with negative energy that counterbalanced the light of the walls. Yon peered at the monolith, the creatures, the patterns on the walls, and lastly back at Blue.

Cinq spoke in a low whisper. "They're all there. Furies, haggards, banshees, and tempests, and more I don't recognize. What are they doing?"

Blue said, "Either it's a ritual, or they were called, same as us. It looks almost religious."

"Hold on," Yon said. "Something's happening."

The swarm of fey below stood rapt. Their eyes, necks, antennae, and heads craned up to where glowing purple mist effused from the top of the chamber. A tendril snaked down, drifting along the vines, until it touched the monolith. The mist grew smaller, smaller until it disappeared entirely. The rock quit spinning.

Silence enveloped the room. The light flowing along the walls faded and died. In the darkness, the negative pulse of the monolith continued, though slower. Once, then a second time, then a third before the energy gave way. Darkness mired the chamber, disturbed only by the ambient noise of a thousand otherplane creatures. Yon slowed his breathing. He focused on the rhythm of his heartbeats.

White light arced from the monolith. It twisted to strike the far side of the room, flooding the chamber with light. A strobe image, no more. But where the lightning had struck the side of the chamber, the light persisted. The illumination spread out from the grain of wood, following the pattern of light and dark.

It spider-webbed out to trace the grain of the wood. As the energy spread, the glow advanced not only along the floor but also to the top of the chamber, where the ceiling crackled with energy.

The fey screeched in delight. And even as they shrieked, roared, clicked, and trumpeted, their bodies lost substance. One by one the fey became energy. They piled atop one another, their flesh melding into one. The blob morphed into a shape: a head, arms, feet. The entity hulked larger and larger as more fey sacrificed themselves, until a colossus hunched within the chamber.

A flash of light filled the chamber, followed by a pulse of thunder that knocked the air from his lungs. Yon shut his eyes, the afterimage seared into his vision. When he reopened his eyes, the entity and the fey had vanished. The only thing remaining in the chamber—aside from themselves—was the cruel black monolith.

Cinq cleared his throat. He spoke without whispering, which made his words sound too loud in the still of the room.

"Well, well, well," he mused. "That, my friends, is how Titans are born."

31

~ Nissa ~

Nissa dropped to her knees. Tears ran down her cheeks to drip on the wooden floor. She didn't cry from awe at the Titan, but at the eradication of the fey as thousands gave themselves up willingly. When the fey joined together, their individual voices had been silenced. What's more, they hadn't cared about her. They knew she had been watching. Every one of them knew, but in the presence of the monolith, not one of them cared. They wanted more, a hunger for the magic now lost in this world, and the hopes that together they could pull it from the nearplane.

She crawled from her hiding space to venture into the chamber. The cavernous room now felt eerily vacant. The only thing remaining was the obelisk. She walked half the distance from the outer wall and stopped to observe it. The jet-black rock hung from a vine just above the ground. She felt a draw of energy from the obsidian. She looked closer. It wasn't a monolith at all. It moved, it pulsed, it shifted. That wasn't rock; it was sand. The same sand that hungered and devoured and drove the forests into the sky. And yet the sand was held here, captive as it were, harnessed by the fey. The unholy energy of the sand, combined with the strength of the united fey, was enough to open a gate and create a Titan.

Nissa felt the monolith reaching for her. Her skin crawled in revulsion. She was consumed by just how much she wanted to get away. She turned to leave; then looked down in horror. Her bare feet slid down the face of the polished wood.

Panic seized her. She turned to sprint up the slope, but her feet found no purchase. She dropped to her belly and scrambled to draw her knives. She tried to dig into the floor, but the blades skittered away harmlessly.

"Nissa, hold on!"

The familiar call came from the corner of the dome. Nissa saw Yon vault over a ridge to land on the sloped floor. He held a coil of rope in his hands, while Blue stood planted behind the ridge at the other end. The monk went into a slide along the surface until near enough to throw Nissa the end of the rope. She snatched it from the air and looped it around her wrists.

The obelisk reacted by tugging harder. And at the same time Yon, Blue, and Cinq pulled back. Nissa felt as though she would be torn in two. The tide shifted. Inch by inch, she crept up from the edge of the pit and toward the wall.

When the four of them were safely on the other side, Nissa unwrapped the rope from her wrists. Raw, red welts covered palms and forearms. She smiled at her friends.

Cinq tapped his chin with one finger. "Nissa, were you being dramatic? Or does Yon have perfect timing?"

She first scowled and then grinned. "Hey, it's a mystical, magical, messed-up place. What's a little coincidence among friends?" She looked around. "Where's Elizabeth?"

They looked away.

"Oh no…" Nissa whispered.

Cinq cleared his throat. "She didn't make it."

Nissa's voice quickened. "So, is that it? Is this whole thing over? What does that mean for the keys, and the machine and everything? Wait, why is *that* the first thing I'm thinking of? That's more of a heartless Cinq thing to say."

Blue snatched the front of Nissa's shirt. She held the much smaller girl within inches of her. "And if you *ever* start thinking that way again, you can keep it to yourself. Am I clear?" The veins in her neck pulsed.

Cinq snapped his fingers. "Blue, Nissa, this is *not* the time. We need to get out. Now, does anyone have any ideas?"

Blue let go of Nissa, giving her a little push in the process. Blue asked, "Can't we follow the fey?"

Cinq shook his head. "The gate is already closed."

"So? We'll make our own with that thing."

Nissa said, "If by 'that thing,' you mean the evil black rock that tried to eat me then I have to ask, *are you nuts?* I mean look, even the tree won't touch it."

Yon looked up, "Did you say tree? You call it that too?"

"Of course, I do. We're inside a massive, thousand-foot tall twisted, knotted—terrifying—tree. Haven't you been outside?"

Yon shook his head.

Nissa brightened. "Oh-ho! You are missing out on some premium weirdness. This tree is just one of a forest of them.

They're all huge, and they're all upside down in this weird mist, and…" she trailed off. "You know what. It'd be easier to show you."

Cinq closed his eyes. "We're not here to sightsee."

Nissa asked, "Why *are* we here? Oh, right. We followed you into a hole in the universe. Smart move, team."

The mage peaked his fingers. "That was just to survive. But at least now we know where Titans come from. This is far beyond theory."

Nissa folded her arms. "And it's not important."

The three of them looked at her in disbelief.

She continued, "This world is ruined. I mean *ruined*. You heard what Ascertine said, the mages used to open gates to draw magic out. Well, there's none left. Whatever happened here, things are not ok."

Yon bit his lip. "How do you know that, Nissa?"

"Looking outside was part of it, but you hear a few thousand fey in a room all screaming for more magic, and you kind of get the point. If we just knew what happened here, then—"

Blue cleared her throat. "Kids, this is all fascinating. Just fascinating stuff. But can we talk about getting out? Titans don't stay in the nearplane forever. And that means it'll come back. I do *not* want to be here for that."

Nissa smiled. "No problem. We brought a mage with us, so come on Cinq. Get magicking. I know you like to save for a rainy day. Well, it's pouring." She paused. "What? Why are you looking at me?"

Yon spoke first. "Because you're right about the magic. It doesn't work here. I can't even focus my chi."

Nissa stuck out her lower lip. *Crap. Crap, crap, crap, crap, crap.*

Silence spread out between them. Nissa concentrated hard on the grain of wood on the floor, hoping for inspiration. If they went back outside, maybe there would be some fey that knew of a gentler crossing. Some fey walked back and forth easily. Or maybe they could find another gate like the one that took them here.

Nissa looked up. "Ok, I've got an idea and… what's so funny?" Across from her, Cinq's eyes were alight. "Oh, dear. Cinq has an idea too. What was your last idea, Cinq? Something along the lines of 'jump into the otherplane gate without looking, I'm sure it will all be fine'? It was *something* like that. I am having such a hard time remembering."

"You made your point. And yes, I have an idea. Why don't you go first?"

"Oh no. You think I can follow that kind of buildup? Let's hear what Journeyman LeGarrec of Eastwind Tower has to say. After all, he's learned *sooooo* much since he got here."

Cinq quite deliberately looked at Blue and Yon. "Like I said, a regular spell won't work. That's because a regular spell involves storing energy, weighing the quantity of magic, focusing, and directing it. There's nothing controlled here."

Blue coughed. "Yes, Cinq, being a mage is *tough.*"

Cinq looked back and forth from Nissa to Blue. "Not helping, Blue. My thought is that I just shape the magic. We'll let the fey do the rest."

Nissa said, "That doesn't make any—"

Cinq held up a hand. "If it doesn't work, we'll try something else." He paused. "But not close to that thing."

Nissa followed Cinq as he led them out of the main chamber and into one of the snaking tunnels that made up the interior of Big Weed. When they reached an open area, Cinq stopped and produced a piece of charcoal from his coat pocket. Using his staff and a piece of twine as guides, he worked on his design.

As Cinq worked, Nissa closed her eyes and took slow, measured breaths, trying to expel the memory of the Titan, the lost fey, and the monolith. Maybe she'd be better at this if Yon taught her how. She listened to the mark of the chalk moving across the wood and tried not to think of the newfound silence of the fey. When she opened her eyes again, Cinq's diagram or runes, or self-portrait, or whatever was finished. It was a glyph, not unlike the runes tattooed across her body. The concepts of a glyph were shared among mages and wikken. They gave magic and energy a defined flow path to obtain specific results.

Yon asked, "Is it a spell?"

"Not by itself," Cinq replied. "This is more of a framework. It's like what we saw on the ceiling of that big chamber with the rock. The pattern in the wood reacted to the energy, just like a glyph captures and shapes magic."

Nissa commented, "You ever made one before?"

"Not in a long time, not since my first years at Eastwind."

She continued, "And can it open a gate?"

Cinq shook his head. "Not by itself. This is a replica of a similar glyph on the floor of Northwind Tower. A long time ago, there were mages there capable of opening gates themselves. They'd use the glyph as a focus. What I'm hoping for is that with a spark of energy I can create a tone, a ringing a—"

Blue completed, "A harmonic symbiosis." She looked around at the others staring back at her. "What? Elizabeth used to talk about those. Was I the only one listening?"

Cinq said, "She's right. I'm surprised, but she's right. It may not open the gate, but it might help us find one. Or at least get us closer."

Confusion passed over Nissa. She'd been noticing these kind of "just in time" revelations more and more. Cinq had been having them for a while. And now Blue? Yon hadn't been acting like a kid monk for a while, and even she was getting way better at talking with the fey than she'd been before. Something was going on.

Yon said, "You'll need a spark."

Cinq nodded. "Yes. A little one."

The monk asked, "Where?"

Cinq pointed to the topmost part of the diagram and backed away. Yon stood and exhaled. He made two fists and pressed them together. His jaw clenched as he steadied his breathing. He stood with feet spread over the topmost part of Cinq's rune. He mimed his strike once, twice, three times. In a sharp exhalation, Yon's hand blurred down toward the glyph.

As Yon struck, he was thrown back across the floor. His body convulsed. Blue was there in a moment, her strong arms holding him still while she wedged a knife sheath between his teeth. "Cinq," she barked, "help me."

Cinq did not budge, and now Nissa felt it too. Emotion filled the room, a hunger much like that in the coliseum. But this time the emotion was formless: desire without substance. The glyph lit up, first pale blue, then green, then an unearthly white that traced along the outer rim of the glyph. Once the entirety of the rune glowed, luminescent dust drifted above it. The swirl became a shape, then a skeleton. Bones, skull, teeth. The apparition thickened, gaining mass and texture as the bones wrapped with veins, muscle, and sinew. The creature shifted from a vision to a reality. The entity morphed. The fingers stretched into claws; knees jutted above its head. The spine curved to hunch, while a serpentine tail snapped behind. The arms shrunk until they were no more than stubs with hooks. Lastly, the face turned to regard its creator with a single liquid eye, dark and black as a midnight pool.

The creature's mouth split and uttered a shriek between glee and rage. It snapped forward, and Nissa jerked back. The creature took off down the corridor, oversized limbs plodding in enormous, awkward strides.

"Help me!" Cinq barked. He and Blue lifted Yon from the ground. "Nissa, go!"

Nissa raced after the creature, and within a few turns found herself on familiar ground—the way out of Big Weed. Even though she only caught the creature in glimpses, the sheer force of its hunger permeated everywhere, a palpable stench. Faster and faster, she ran until she stood at the exit, a circular aperture bristled with jutting thorns. The creature leaped through the center and into the mist.

She hesitated. Before, the inverted forest had been surreal, now it felt hellish. The luminous fog descended from the canopy of roots, stretching and curling in slow-motion tornadoes. The energy reached from the sky to lap against the black sands below. The ground pulsed with hunger, while ground and trees alike fed.

Cinq's creation flew through the air. It sailed up and up to a sphere of suspended yellow light. The fey disappeared, passing through to somewhere unseen. Footsteps came from behind her. Blue and Cinq approached, carrying the unconscious Yon between them.

Nissa pointed. "That globe. It went in there. Is it a gate? A little one?"

Cinq held his staff in front of him. "I think so. It feels—it feels right."

She bit her lip. "It's closing. I know it's closing, because *it* knew it was closing. But we can jump."

Blue said, "I can't jump fifty feet up."

"Otherplane rules. Trust 'em. Trust me."

Nissa reached to grab Cinq's staff. In doing so, energy flowed between the four of them; they had become one body with four minds. Without a count, without a word of "go" they leaped. They didn't fall. They continued on an unerring course as the sphere grew larger and larger in their vision until so impossibly large that it contained the world. All things, all places, all times. Nissa felt their collective bodies fill with white-hot energy.

Their minds folded into each other.

PART FOUR:

Legacy

32

~ Cinq ~

Cinq opened his eyes to a beam of sunlight across his chest. He followed the ray, studying the slow rotation of dust and motes dancing up through the light at the same pace they floated down. The sunbeam entered through a tall, narrow window fifty feet up, one of four across the wall. His body ached. His head ached. His *teeth* ached. A realization crept over him: where there should have been four walls, there only stood one. The others had crumbled and fallen.

He snapped upright. Around him, scattered in lumpy piles of clothes and bodies, slept Yon, Nissa, Blue, and a slender woman with grayish skin and long dark hair. The woman's glossy mane wrapped half around her, serving as both bed and protection for her modesty. A fey.

Cinq shook his head to clear it. He tried to absorb his new surroundings, but was distracted by memories of the otherplane, the obelisk, and their final leap into the gate. He had other memories as well. He remembered landing in black sands, climbing an enormous tree, fighting reavers, and even catching himself. Those last memories were a blur. They persisted like dreams—but not his dreams. He looked at the gray-skinned woman. Was this the same fey they had followed into the gate? She looked harmless now. So, which was real? The form in the otherplane? This? Did she have a true shape?

He struggled to his feet. He straightened his wide-brimmed hat and picked up his staff. The shaft thrummed with energy. That was a surprise. Whatever had transpired in the otherplane, Cinq's store of magic bubbled to capacity. Given the hunger for magic in the otherplane, he'd expected the opposite. Worth considering later, but he wouldn't curse a stroke of fortune. He studied his friends to ensure everyone's chest moved up and down. They needed their sleep. And he needed a moment to himself.

Cinq scanned the room, or rather, what had once been a room. Angular columns circled the great dais in the center. Each column had a polished copper base etched with runes depicting magical disciplines. Beyond the ring and the intact columns, the walls lay in collapsed chunks. In some places the stone was pristine and white, while in other areas blackened by fire. He examined the blue-flecked etching beneath his feet. Even hidden by his sleeping friends, he recognized the mark.

It had worked. They had survived.

Cinq knelt to nudge Nissa. She didn't wake with a start, but a sleepy rousing and blinking eyes. He placed a finger to his lips, then pointed at the sleeping fey. *Is this ok?* he mouthed. Nissa shrugged. She rolled back over and closed her eyes.

Different priorities, he thought. As noiselessly as possible, he stepped past the dais to a round—and surprisingly intact—

window on the remaining wall. It stretched ten feet across, an aperture with a rose center pane and eight glass petals on each side. Through the window he saw emerald hills in all directions. Blue lakes rested in the valleys, perfectly reflecting the sapphire sky. Down the hill from where he stood, a town nestled in a long valley. A road wound from where he stood to a blackened scar halfway between the town and the ruins. Cinq's eyes lingered on the burned remains, his mind slow to accept what he saw. That should have been Northwind, but the only thing remaining was a hole in the earth.

His stomach clenched. Ascertine had urged him to come here, but there was nothing left. He should be grateful just to be alive, but his mouth tasted bitter. He turned back to the others. Nissa was now—inexplicably—fully awake. She was conversing with the fey, who mimicked her posture of sitting back on her heels with hands folded in front of her. They both waved at him before the fey evaporated in a swirl of dust. Nissa rose and skipped over to join him by the window.

"She forgives you," Nissa said. "For forcing her into that thing."

Cinq nodded. "I didn't entirely anticipate that."

"You just described the history of magekind."

"Is that really what you wanted to talk about? We've got bigger problems."

"Right. First things first." Nissa's face scrunched up. "What happened to Elizabeth?"

Cinq's stomach dropped. He'd been so focused on the tower ruins he'd pushed away his other concerns. He sucked in his breath. "I'm not sure about you, but for me, things there weren't *normal.* Yon and I found each other, but the reavers found Blue." He closed his eyes. The images flashed across as though they had been his own memories. "There was a fight. She survived, the others didn't. Elizabeth didn't." He paused. "Blue thinks she killed her."

Nissa didn't reply. The seconds stretched out. Cinq wanted the conversation to end, to turn back to something external, something not so... human. He'd rather deal with fallen towers and the collision of worlds.

She put her hand on his shoulder and squeezed. A minute passed as they both looked through the window at the charred pit beyond. Nissa released his shoulder and cleared her throat. "Did you check the Tracer?" she asked.

"I couldn't. The otherplane scrambled it."

"Well, what does it say *now?*"

Alarm surged within Cinq's veins. He reached into his coat, fumbling until he found the pocket where the Tracer was still intact. Removing the sphere, he saw—as usual—four points of light shining brightly, and a fifth dimmer and distant. Five points of light. Not four. Five.

Cinq turned back to the seal. He moved the Tracer around, confirming that the two brightest points of light were drawn to him and Nissa. He walked to the source of the other two lights. One, as anticipated, was locked on Yon. But the other fixed on Blue. The key wasn't gone. It hadn't gone dormant for another three hundred years. The burden had passed from Elizabeth to Blue; she had taken the scholar's place. He turned to Nissa, who peeked around to look as well.

She nodded. "Guess we're all replaceable."

"Yes." He thought for a moment. "Should we tell her?"

"What?!" Nissa shrieked. She lowered her voice. "How could you not tell her?"

"I mean should we tell her right away. She's been through a lot. We all have."

Nissa folded her arms. "Look. You want to give her the day off, fine. But that's it." She stuck out her lower lip. "It's not like the machine will even work."

"Why not?"

"You saw the otherplane; you *felt* it. That place is *not* ok. Very, very, very not ok. I mean, maybe there was magic there once, but not anymore. The fey, the trees, heck, even the sand was starving for magic."

"What's your point?"

"My point is that the Black Gate, or whatever it's called, can't pull magic from the otherplane if there's no magic to pull."

Cinq clenched his jaw. "So, it's all for nothing? Doomed from the start? And this isn't helping." He gestured to the ruins.

"To be fair, we didn't know what we were doing 'from the start.' Nothing's changed."

Cinq rubbed his temples. "Maybe. Or maybe—"

A thump of footsteps and rattle of metal interrupted them. Cinq gripped his staff as he deftly returned the Tracer into his coat. Three men appeared through the remnants of an archway on the far side of the room. They were… jarring. Their hands and faces were blackened with soot, and they brandished pickaxes, hoes, and shovels like weapons. They appeared to be mountain climbers, yet gold glittered on their fingers, and talismans hung from their necks. One wore a thin layer of ceremonial chain mail, while another had armbands that could have been a thousand years old.

"What are you doing up here?" the man in chain mail barked. "Guildies only."

"Hello," Cinq called. This was less for the benefit of the men stalking toward them and more to rouse Blue and Yon. Blue rolled to a crouch, cleaver drawn. Yon stood so quickly that Cinq barely saw him move. Relief swept Cinq; he was glad the boy was ok.

Cinq spoke clearly and formally. "I'm an emissary from Eastwind Tower, and these are my companions. We arrived via the gateway rune." He gestured to the seal. "Where are the mages?"

"What mages?" the chain-mail-clad man said.

A voice shouted from beyond the archway. "Wait! Wait for me. I told you to wait for..."

A red-faced man appeared at the top of the steps and bustled past the three men. He wore the sapphire and gold-flecked robe of an archmage, yet neither his long blond hair, nor his drooping mustache, showed any gray. Cinq placed the man in his mid-thirties—far too young for his vestments. The copper scepter tucked in his corded belt added to Cinq's confusion. That was the instrument of the tower precept, a role never combined with the acting archmage.

"Well, well, well, and welcome," the mage bubbled. He wiped the sweat from his brow. "I tried to get here first, but... you know, steps and robes." He bowed low, one hand on his scepter. "Archmage Calladius, precept of Northwind," he winked. "Or what's left of it." He tapped the dais with his foot.

"Did you come through the rune? Lucky for you this whole thing is warded." He stomped the ground. "Practically indestructible. Can you open gates?"

Cinq kept his voice level. "Under specific circumstances."

Calladius clicked his tongue in appreciation. "Because you are...?"

"Journeyman LeGarrec, of Eastwind."

The archmage snapped his fingers. "Ah... the infamous Cinq. You're the thief."

Cinq gritted his teeth. "Is that important? Now? Here?"

Calladius forced a laugh. "No. No, not at all. We're all thieves here. Well, everyone but me."

The two mages stared at one another until Cinq broke the silence. "What happened to the tower? Was it a Titan?"

"Worse, reavers." He tilted his head. "You... didn't hear about this? How has this been a secret?"

Cinq chose his words. "We—encountered a Titan a while back. Time has been tricky since then. It slipped. What's the date now?"

"May 25th, 307. Only a month to go, if you know what I mean."

Cinq's legs buckled. The bravado of having survived the otherplane was yanked from under him. "We lost a year." The words fell from his lips. His head swam. How much more had the world degraded? How many more cities and towers were lost to Titans and reavers? The Convergence was almost here.

Calladius clicked his tongue. "Can't be blamed for that. Though I am curious what you've been chasing—or should I say tracing. Come along. I'll show you what's left. Bring your friends, ignore mine."

Before Cinq could respond, the archmage retreated through the entryway. Nissa skipped ahead of her friends, leaving the rough-looking men behind. They descended a few dozen yards from the backside of the ruins when the broken pathway turned to the great, scorched remnants of Northwind. As they walked, Cinq saw what he had missed before. Canvas tents were scattered around the blackened rim of the pit. All around, people milled about. Some haggled with tables covered in objects, not unlike a market. Others busied themselves around a set of scaffolding anchored at the top, with ropes threaded through pulleys. Occasionally, men would surface from the pit with laden baskets, or disappear over the edge holding empty ones.

Calladius traipsed down the path. He gestured over the site. "The problem with Northwind was that there was always more of it underground than there was above. Easier to dig down than build up. So, when the reavers torched it, the whole thing collapsed inward."

Cinq caught up to the archmage. "How many survived?"

Calladius replied, "Mages or reavers? Most of them, not many of us."

"You didn't fight back?"

The man stopped walking and drummed his fingers on the scepter. "Some did. But we've never been warriors. I wasn't here when it happened, so I can't say for sure. A few others were lucky to be traveling, and I know at least some of us escaped." He winced. "I'm the only one who came back." He started forward again.

Nissa nodded. "Which makes you the archmage."

Calladius winked. "Exactly. What was your name?"

"Nissa. Also, that's Yon, and that's Blue. Cinq sometimes forgets we're worth introducing."

A cheer rose from the scavengers as a man climbed up and over the edge of the pit. He dumped a canvas bag on the ground amid laughs, backslapping, and congratulations.

Cinq asked, "What are your duties here… as archmage?"

"You mean with them? The pickers and I worked things out. I help identify what they haul up, and they keep the valuable stuff. In exchange I get the books, records, and artifacts they don't care about. It works for now."

"What survived?" Cinq asked.

"The fire got most of it, of course. Luckily some of the rooms were enchanted against heat. There were also a few caches and chests that escaped by luck. And a lot more was buried, though intact." He cast a sidelong glance at Cinq and winked. "But let's talk about you. I doubt Eastwind chose you as ambassador." He glanced at Yon, Nissa, and Blue. "And you don't look to be on official tower business."

Blue pushed forward. "We're here about the Black Gate. We're looking for anything and everything on the Pentarch's machine. Blueprints, journals, primary sources if possible, but secondary as needed. I'm hoping that counts among the things you kept."

Calladius raised his eyebrows. "And you are?"

Cinq answered, "She's our scholar. From the library at Alexandria."

The archmage cocked his head. "And I thought the city had fallen." He shrugged. "Well, you're in luck, somewhat. The writings of the Pentarch are here. They are one of the most well-protected stores we have. Normally, I wouldn't admit they exist. They are kind of a secret. But given current events, I'll show you the way."

Nissa asked, "What's the matter? Is it all burned up? Under a million pounds of rock? What are you going to do, hand us a shovel?"

"Easy there, easy there. As far as I know, it's all quite intact. Hard to tell for sure, though." He sighed. "Follow me, just a bit farther."

Calladius led them away from the pit where the pickers dug through the ruins. They wound around the backside of a hillock burned on one half and green on the far side. Just beyond, a small five-sided building rested atop a marble slab. A layer of thick dust and caked mud ran along the walls, though it was free from moss, vines, and weeds. Cinq walked around it once, noticing the carved insignia on each side: Monk, mage, wikken, scholar, and hermit. A set of double doors had been cut into the corner between the scholar and hermit walls.

Yon asked, "Is it a tomb?"

"Only by design," Calladius replied. "They say the only person who could enter was the Pentarch himself. Of course, they never found a body to bury."

Cinq asked, "So it's warded?"

"Oh, yes. The Pentarch set the wards himself. And the door would only open by his hand. Or by someone carrying his corpse."

Cinq weighed the statement. Words could twist after three centuries. Ascertine must have thought so. And with the Convergence coming, perhaps—

Nissa piped up. "Well, it's obviously meant for us. I mean, of course it is." She threw up her hands. "What? It's not a secret. Blue already gave us away." She put her fists on her hips. "Aren't we all in this together? We're all witches, aren't we?"

Yon replied, "He never said that."

"It's still true."

Calladius smirked. "If you think you can open it, go ahead. But... be careful."

"Here we go!" Nissa sprang up to the double doors and grabbed the handle. At the first touch, the smile dropped from the archmage's face. She twisted the brass ring and hefted against it. The door shifted in the frame. She turned to the others. "Can I get a hand with this?"

Blue reached out. As she touched the handle, the door exploded with light. The blast threw both her and the archmage ten feet from the vault to skid onto the grass. She lay on her back in pain, eyes clenched shut, and head pounding.

Yon ran to her side. "Blue! Are you ok? What was that?"

Blue sat up with difficulty. She rubbed her shoulder. "Chosen ones only, I guess." She looked back at Nissa. "You're on your own."

Nissa pulled at the door once more. And this time, Yon joined her. He touched the handle, but there was no reaction. The two of them worked together to pull. Mud cracked around the frame, dust fell, and the ancient stone pivoted open. Cinq walked up the steps to stand beside Yon and Nissa. Inside, the vault was less of a crypt than a study. A stone table with a marble top was set into the back wall, and surrounding it were bookshelves filled with parchment, books, and loose reams of paper. Two of the shelves stood intact, while the other three had rotted away, spilling their contents on the floor of the chamber.

Blue shouted from behind them. "Don't touch anything, not unless you have to. That paper's going to be brittle as ash. If we're lucky, at least some of it will be on parchment and will have stood a better chance." She looked back indignantly.

Cinq turned to Calladius, still sitting on the ground. "Anything else you forgot to mention?"

"N-no," the man stammered. "No one's gotten this far before."

"I'm going in," Nissa called. She stepped through the door. "I'm still alive!" she declared. "Smells funny, though."

Calladius stood and picked up his scepter. He stepped forward just enough to peer inside. "Opened... by a wikken." He shook his head in disbelief.

Nissa pointed to Cinq. "Get in here. Time to get to work. Or should we get some snacks first? Let's find ourselves a Black Gate!"

Calladius fidgeted. "Oh... that's what you're looking for?" He clenched his jaw. "The witchlord already found it."

33

~ Blue ~

Blue lay flat on her cot and stared at the tent's canvas ceiling. She felt like a different person after a bath—albeit a cold one—and a change of clothes. After having eaten a meal neither dried nor dragged across realities, she felt mostly repaired. Calladius had been hospitable, though he reminded her of a used-goods salesman. She should be thankful, so why did she feel so awful?

She swung her feet over the edge of the cot and massaged her temples. Her head felt ready to explode. Was this a backlash from the vault explosion? Thin air? An otherplane hangover? She suspected the last. Where else were these memories coming from? The clawing dread returned. For all the wonders and horrors of the otherplane, she kept coming back to that terrible event: hundreds of reavers, hundreds of her, and Elizabeth.

"Blue, are you in there?" Cinq called from outside the tent.

"Come in," she said.

The mage pushed aside the flap and stepped inside. He looked like a different man. Clean, beard trimmed, and eyes—still sunken, but less weary. "How are you feeling?"

"Fine. You find anything worthwhile?"

"Maybe. I could use some help."

Blue rolled to her feet and strapped on her cleaver. She'd resolved to stay armed for the rest of her life—not that that would be much longer. Cinq led her out of the tent and along the rim of the ruins.

"How are you feeling?" he asked.

"Still fine. Same as a minute ago."

Cinq didn't press further. Together, they wove past the excavation site and onto the path leading to the Pentarch's vault. The door to the building was again closed, but much of its contents had been moved outside. Books, scrolls, and loose parchment had been laid atop sheets of canvas in ordered rows.

Blue asked, "What if it rains?"

Cinq fidgeted. "Then we scramble. Staying inside makes me nervous. Plus, Calladius wanted a look."

"Why do you put up with him? I don't trust him. And call it what you will, he's looting the place."

Cinq shrugged. "Normally I'd agree, but there is the matter of perspective. If we survive, we can talk ethics."

Blue bit her lip. Part of her had a twinge of respect for old things, perhaps from hanging around Elizabeth. And while she was appalled at Calladius, she was more disturbed that Cinq wasn't.

Cinq pointed to the array of knowledge. "I've got a few piles going so far." He gestured to the first stack. "These are all about the construction. Pillars, struts, materials, even accounting. Nothing but architecture. Either the Black Gate was built in a temple—or, more accurately—the temple is part of the machine. It's hard to believe something so huge could be lost."

Blue said, "But it's not lost. Not anymore. You heard Calladius. The witchlord found it."

"In the Expanse. Yes, I know. All the more reason we need to know as much as possible *before* we go ourselves." Cinq stared down at the piles. He was obviously distracted.

When the silence stretched, Blue said, "What's that other pile?"

Cinq gathered himself. "Those are the ones I can't read."

"Why not?"

"The Pentarch—I'm assuming he wrote these—didn't always write in plain language. This was common among mages. They'd use dead languages for privacy. Not foolproof, but much less likely to have someone steal your work."

"Even when it's in a vault no one can open?"

"Even then."

Blue folded her arms. She felt the itch of impatience. "Why am I here, Cinq? You need me to sort books for you? Move some things around? Take notes? Make you tea?"

Cinq locked eyes with her. "Not exactly. I need your help with the Genjish script. Recognizing the characters is about as far as I can go. But that's not going to be enough for the technical details."

"You have got to be kidding me." A pause. "You woke me up from a deep, deep sleep after the evil jungle adventure... to ask me to read a dead language? You are delusional."

"I want you to try."

Blue rolled her eyes. "I may have lived in a library, but I wasn't trying for a degree."

He bit his lip. "And… we need to talk about Elizabeth."

There it was. Emotion washed over her, welling up from her chest to flood her vision, momentarily turning it white. When she had regained her senses, she turned to the mage. "So *that's* why you brought me here? Listen to me. Elizabeth was like my mother. You knew her for what, a few weeks? I do *not* want to talk about her right now. I'd rather read Genjish."

Cinq threw up his hands. "So much for the subtle way." He set his Tracer on the table. "Pick it up."

Blue did as requested. She gripped the sphere in three fingers. "Now what?"

"Look at it."

Blue examined the points of light within the globe. Two were particularly intense, one on the edge of the glass in line with Cinq, and the other… oh no. "Cinq, why is this thing fixed on me?" A pause. "Unbelievable."

Cinq gently retrieved the Tracer from her. "I think that after Elizabeth died, you took her role as key. That woman, Yanamadra, said the bond could be passed. Maybe it was because you and Elizabeth were so close. Or maybe because you were nearby when she died."

Blue said, "Or maybe you dropped your Tracer too many times."

Cinq nodded to the books in front of him. "Would you give it a try?"

"What would that prove?"

When Cinq didn't answer, she knelt and grabbed a book from the pile. She scanned the symbols on the page. Nonsense, obviously. Then the shape of one character looked familiar, and then another. A pattern shifted itself to the surface, first letters, then sounds, then words, then sentences. She let the book fall. "This is impossible."

Cinq didn't reply.

"I'm not a key like you, ok? I didn't wake up fully grown with no memories. And I certainly wasn't born centuries ago." She winced. "I was a little girl once. I lived with my uncle. I had a brother named Rufus, and a black-and-white dog." Her voice wavered. "And I have *no* reason to read Genjish."

Cinq unfolded his arms. He knelt beside Blue. "I have a theory."

"Go ahead."

"Being a key is an honor, as well as a means of control. The Pentarch made five keys and gave the responsibility to five disciplines. In theory, they could control who took the burden when the previous key passed away. I imagine it was supposed to be the best, the brightest, and the most trusted of their ranks. But maybe it's not *just* an honor. Maybe a little bit of the last key is passed as well. Maybe that's why I had memories of magic before I reached Eastwind. Maybe it's why Yon remembered monastic forms he'd never been taught."

Blue's skin crawled. Cinq was trying to make her feel better, but the thought of inheriting Elizabeth's memories was horrifying. Would she remember dying at her own hands?

Blue shook her head. "Wait. What about the vault? When I touched the handle, I got thrown a dozen yards. Not you, or Yon, or Nissa. Just me. How do you explain that?"

Cinq frowned. "I can't. Not yet. Maybe being a key is still settling in. Or maybe something different. Nissa was raised a wikken, Yon an ordained monk, and I am ranked as a journeyman. Maybe it's both being a key, but also passing a test. Perhaps you need a doctorate." He shook his head. "It's a better theory than what Calladius said."

"That only the Pentarch could enter?"

Cinq said, "Well, it didn't stop Nissa."

Blue swallowed. "You think that means something?"

"Maybe. Or maybe it's just another rumor. Not everything is grounded in truth" He grabbed another book from the pile. "Maybe the answer is in here. And even if it isn't, we have a job to do. Now, how's your Eidilogian?"

Blue gritted her teeth. The letters were already reshuffling into words. "Improving."

Cinq smiled. He wasn't doing a good job of it.

"One more question," Blue said.

"Yes?"

"Do trust him? Calladius? He took us in pretty quickly."

Cinq's smile dropped. "He knows what we are, but I don't think he cares. He has," he tossed his head in the direction of the pit, "other distractions. But let's not stay longer than necessary."

34

~ Nissa ~

Nissa wandered the camp, gathering rumors. The pickers, as Calladius called them, were akin to the prospectors she'd known in Gorenheim. As such, their mood depended on their luck more than the questions she asked. The pickers spoke about two main subjects. Those who had been here from the start talked of the reaver's siege. They spoke of thunder, flame, and lightning as the mages fought back, and then the collapse of the tower once the fire took hold. The reavers had exterminated all who survived. They lingered a few days, picking through the ruins, and left.

Other pickers talked about the dig. Most of these had come later. They described the things they'd found, and those who'd discovered the hard way which relics shouldn't be touched. Still others succumbed to the dangers of working in a ruin that hadn't time to settle into stability. As for their opinions on world events, many pickers thought the mages deserved what they got. Others were sympathetic to the mages' plight, though not going so far as to surrender their treasures. After all, there were fortunes to be made.

No one mentioned the Convergence. Either they knew about it and avoided the subject or had managed to remain willfully ignorant. More likely, Nissa considered, they were hedging their bets. If the world was to end, so be it. But if it didn't, might as well be rich. She smiled. No matter what happened, people would continue to be people.

Nissa peered into the blackened pit. All that remained of Northwind Tower was a mesh of ash, scaffolding, ruined stonework, and debris. According to the pickers, the aboveground floors had been where the mages slept and ate. But the belowground—the understory—contained everything else. The rooms had been filled with arcane devices, collected artifacts, and chambers where the mages would run their experiments. Nissa wasn't looking for things at all. She hoped instead to find pickers with less-guarded tongues who would be more honest without Calladius nearby.

Nissa turned to the fey standing beside her, a spindly creature ten feet tall, with slender arms and spidery fingers. She knew that the pickers probably saw only a cloud of hanging dust. "Must have been a big fire," Nissa said. "Did you lose anyone when it fell?"

The fey said "no" by flooding Nissa's mind with smells of orange petals, cedar, and morning dew. On the heels of these came danger sensations of peril and foolishness: burning hair, rust, acrid smoke. Mages dabbled with dangerous things, the fey said. So, the fey avoided the tower. The foolish could wind up as an experiment.

Nissa breathed deep. She radiated thoughts back at the fey. "Sure you don't want to come?"

The fey vanished. The dusty form became nothing at all.

"Suit yourself."

Nissa scanned the perimeter, looking to see if anyone was watching. With a skip, she dropped over the edge of the pit to a beam slanted at an angle. She scrambled down from support to support, sometimes on the ruins, and other times on makeshift ladders or ropes from the pickers. Occasionally, amidst the debris, she'd find an intact staircase that lasted a flight or two before falling away. Other times, she would press her body against the wall as she heard pickers making their way back up, mumbling to themselves or whistling as they carried their haul.

Part of Nissa was relieved the Northwind mages were gone. She'd been dreading coming here for exactly that reason. A year ago, after leaving the enclave, she had run into a group of six mages traveling together. She felt invincible with her newfound independence, ready to pursue truth unfettered by tradition. She had approached the mages and challenged them to exchange ideas. In return, they had drugged her, thrown her in a cage, and tried to use her to lure the fey. An experiment, they claimed.

The mages kept her caged for six days before concluding no fey would come. They also discussed what would happen if Nissa escaped, and in no small part because of her incessant threatening. One day, they left her alone at their camp while they went away to discuss. Thanks to an eavesdropping fey, Nissa learned they were torn between murdering her, selling her, or just renting her to anyone who would pay.

She spent the next several hours in panic. She'd resolved that she'd escape that night, even if she had to gnaw through the cage to do so. But when the time came to try, she was overcome by weariness and fell asleep. When she finally awoke, she was in the back of a straw-filled wagon as it bumped along the road. A tall mage, only a few years older than she, was at the reins. He wore a traveling coat and a wide-brimmed hat. He introduced himself as Cinq, a journeyman mage, and explained he was on a mission. He never said what happened to her captors.

The pickers might be rough and self-serving, but she could deal with them, understand them. Mages made her skin crawl—except Cinq.

Down, down she climbed. She counted the distance not by the number of floors, but by the long line of oil lamps hanging from a cable down the shaft. Most of the pickers had small lamps with them, so she was able to know when someone approached by the glow preceding them. Nissa continued down. And as she dropped, she noticed a change in the ruins. Charred timbers gave way to metal reinforcing girders that had been twisted and smelted by the heat.

Nissa's foot slipped as one of the beams crumbled under her weight. Fragments fell to the ground, sending a cloud of ash up, and immersing her in fog. She wrapped a scarf around her nose and mouth. She closed her eyes and forced herself to take slow, measured breaths. The dust would settle. She just had to wait. She would be fine. But why the *hell* was she even down here? What could she learn that the cost of a few drinks wouldn't have wriggled out of the pickers?

As if on cue, Nissa heard footsteps and murmurs from below. She opened her eyes and saw outlines of fallen beams and a fire-blackened staircase. She padded down the stairs in near darkness. She lay flat on the floor so that looking over she could see two pickers wearing climbing harnesses over mage's robes. One of the men held a pendant that glowed with pale blue light, while the other raked through debris with a hoe. The man with the pendant wore a cylindrical canister on his back. He would occasionally take something from the other man and place it inside.

As she waited, their words became clear. "So, there wasn't anything in there?" His voice was clear, husky, and with a highlands accent.

"Just a lot of books," a second voice spoke. This one sounded younger. "The mage and the scholar have been there all day."

"What about the other two? The kid monk and the wikken?"

The younger man grunted. "Just hanging around. The archmage says to ignore them."

For a minute, she listened to the hoe moving against the rubble and the occasional clink of a found object. After a few minutes, the men switched jobs. The man with the husky voice took the backpack and lantern, handing the hoe to his younger counterpart.

The younger man said, "So what's Calladius going to do?"

"Huh? It's already done. He's sent word to the reavers. Now, all we have to do is wait."

More digging.

"I don't know. Just seems wrong. They're just kids. More or less."

"Yeah, but that's the deal. We follow the rules, they let us be."

"I suppose." The younger man stopped digging again. He cleared his throat. "If we're lucky, they'll leave on their own. Then maybe they'd have a chance."

The younger man looked up. He locked eyes with Nissa. She froze. The air seemed to close around her. She waited in terror, but the picker looked away first. He clapped his companion on the shoulder. "That's enough for this load. The bag's full anyway."

35

~ Yon ~

Yon held his chi bundled in his chest. In his heightened state, he could feel the movement of each hair on his arms. He sensed the wriggle of fish in the stream, the wingbeats of birds in the air, and the unsuspecting breathing of his quarry. Daring a look, Yon crept forward, bare feet and fingers gripping the rock as he watched the path below.

There she was. Proud. Wary. Perhaps a bit too sure of herself compared to her slower companions. Certainly not the most likely to be targeted by a predator. But Yon wasn't looking for the weak, he wanted the strongest, the queen of the hill. He leaped into the air, diving headfirst. The white-furred mountain goat bleated in surprise. Yon wrapped his legs around the goat's body. He tied the leather pouch around her neck, then released her. The goat bounded up the hillside, the Tracer bouncing in the pouch as she fled.

Yon stood and dusted the gravel from his palms. He grinned. What would Master Shen say now? The months disciplining himself to be silent, to be unseen, to move without detection. This, the culmination of all his training, to catch a goat.

Nissa ambled up to stand beside him. She clasped her hands behind her back. The sky was still dark, though the fading of the stars signaled the sun was soon to rise over the rolling hills. Even though in the shadows, Yon saw that Nissa's face, arms, and clothing were still smeared in soot from exploring the tower ruins.

She said, "You sure there wasn't an easier way?"

"Maybe," Yon replied. "But she won't let herself get surprised twice. Next time, she'll run. The reavers won't get close." He brushed his hands together to knock loose the traces of goat hair and grass, both damp from accumulated dew.

Nissa giggled. "You know that vein in Cinq's forehead is going to explode when he finds out."

Yon shrugged. "He told me to hide it. Plus, it's Elizabeth's Tracer, not his. Or I guess it was Blue's." He watched as the last of the herd disappeared over the hill. "Too bad *we* can still be traced."

Nissa cocked her head. "Wait. What? I thought that was the whole point of this."

"Huh? No. The mini-Tracers trace the Tracers. The real Tracers trace the keys. This'll just—I don't know—make things harder."

The wikken threw up her hands. "You know what? I don't care. Let's catch up with the others. They're probably waiting for us."

The two of them made their way back over the hills. They followed the narrow goat path which traversed the hillside where the animals had taken the same route, day after day. They crossed three open knolls, scrambling at times down the rocky outcrops, until reaching the meetup point. Hunched between two mossy boulders, Blue and Cinq sat cross-legged. They had a candle between them, and each held a book from the Pentarch's vault. A scraggly mule stood tethered to a rock beside them. Its saddlebags bulged with water, provisions, blankets, and cookware, but absolutely no books. Those, Cinq and Blue carried themselves. When they drew close, Cinq blew out the candle. He tucked the book into one of the large pockets of his coat and shouldered his pack.

"Good, you're here," Cinq said. "It's just a matter of time before my *colleague* goes looking for us."

Blue pointed at a far hilltop where the first rays of sun lit the top of the knoll. The grass glistened from the sheen of dew, an emerald atop a field of shadow. She tucked her compass into her shirt. "That's our waymark. No farms, no people. No road, but it should still be passable."

Yon took the mule's halter and urged it forward. The four of them set off across the hill. They didn't speak, just put one foot in front of the other. Yon felt exposed on these hills in a vastly different way than the hills near Ignaesdale. There, rocks created crags and endless caves and shadows. Here, with the smooth, rolling green, there was nowhere to hide. He longed to put as much distance between themselves and Northwind as possible.

After the sun had reached a mid-morning height, Nissa broke the silence. "Can Calladius follow us with—not a Tracer, don't think he has one—but other magic?"

Cinq snorted with disdain. "I doubt he cares enough to try. If the reavers press him, maybe. We should be long gone by then."

Nissa paused to consider, and Blue pushed past her to take the lead. They wove snaking paths through heather and thistle, circumventing the occasional jumbles of boulders. They encountered no shepherds, no hunters, no buildings, no roads, and no other signs of humanity. They even avoided the fey. After the encounter with Yanamadra, they couldn't count on their discretion.

When the sun reached its zenith, they stopped by a creek running along a thick grove of elephant-head bushes. Blue and Yon unburdened the mule of its saddlebags, while Cinq handed out cheese and bread.

Nissa stood over them, arms folded as she glared. "All right, Blue, Cinq. Spill it. What have you learned?"

Cinq glanced over. "Blue? This is your work."

Blue nodded in resignation. Yon wondered just how much she'd accepted her new role as key and the newfound talents accompanying it. Blue extracted a leather book inlaid with silver. Scraps of paper were lodged between the pages at intervals.

She said, "Ok. Most of what we thought we knew has been confirmed. The machine needs all five keys to operate. But it's not a democracy. At any point, only one key is in control of the machine. At the last Convergence, the Pentarch was to take the lead. Again, nothing we didn't suspect."

Cinq bumped in. "We also don't know if the other keys have to be willing participants, or just physically present."

Blue glared at him. "Am I explaining this, or are you?" She flipped to a marked page. "Now here's something we didn't expect. We assumed the Black Gate siphoned magic from the otherplane."

Nissa chirped, "Not much left there."

"True, but that's not how the Black Gate works. It can pull magic from anything and anyone. That means the nearplane, otherplane, people, and the fey. But—and this is the important bit—it works through the Titans. All four Titans. Together."

Nissa laughed. "So what? We need to round 'em up and ask 'em nicely? And I thought finding keys was hard. So where does that leave us?"

Cinq tugged at his beard. "Well, now we know the Titans are the fey."

"So?"

"So, we need to talk to them."

Yon asked, "Aren't we avoiding the fey?"

Cinq continued, "I'm not talking about nymphs and naiads and smoke dancers. I mean the old fey. Ones old enough to remember the last Convergence. Maybe they know how the Pentarch brought the Titans together."

Yon turned to look at Nissa. She plucked grass from between her legs where she sat. "Nissa, can you do that?"

She said, "Talking to ancient fey is more 'high priestess' stuff than 'little Nissa' stuff."

Cinq smiled. "Then it's settled. Nissa, take us to your enclave."

36

~ Cain ~

Mortimer Cain, the witchlord, regarded the stumps on his left hand with a low, burning disdain. Losing two fingers was unfortunate, but no real impediment to a general. In some circles, an unblemished officer may lack credibility. But Cain had no problem with that. His problem was witches. They were getting creative. A blizzard of razors? He hadn't expected it. No one had. The event had been more surprising than damaging, but eventually, they might get lucky. A lucky witch—clever, powerful, or both—could derail his plans. None could be spared.

The crimson flaps of his tent pulled aside, and Yanamadra glided in. Her wounds had long since closed, but they were still disturbing. Half her face was blackened and burned. One eye was completely gone, while the other was glazed with a milky white film. Despite her injuries, she still bore herself like an empress.

His guards followed Yanamadra and stood at the tent's entrance, hands on their weapons. She sent a withering look at them before turning to Cain. Perhaps she thought that if she decided to attack, mortal weapons wouldn't protect him. He disagreed with that point. He might be down a few fingers, but the witches hadn't gotten him yet. She wouldn't either.

"You summoned me?" Her voice sounded polite, though riding on a current of disdain. Cain valued that. Yanamadra was mean as a cobra and she was, ultimately, a witch herself. But he knew where he stood with her.

Cain said, "I received a message from Isil."

"About time. Is the excavation complete?"

He shook his head. "Not yet, but close." He tapped the missive in front of him. "This concerns your friends. The keys have resurfaced at Northwind Tower. All four live."

Yanamadra bristled. "I never said they were killed, only that they were gone. I even sent my soldiers into the otherplane after them."

"Nevertheless, they're back." He picked at the bandages on his hand. "The keys, tell me about them."

"We've been through this," she replied.

"Then it should be easy for you."

Yanamadra exhaled. "There were six of them at the Rendezvous. The old mage I killed—I pulled the head from his shoulders myself—he wasn't a key."

"And the others?"

She recounted the names they knew from interrogating the monks: Cinq LeGarrec, Nissa al'Cedar, and Yon of Open Eye. She described the newcomers: an old woman wielding bombs and a younger mercenary. Yanamadra added nothing new, nothing he hadn't heard before.

He said, "These keys present complications. Without them, the Black Gate is useless. But if they gain control, my armies mean nothing."

Yanamadra looked at him impassively. "They'll come to us. Nothing is more certain."

A flash of anger welled inside him. He slammed his fist down on the table, breaking open his wound. When he lifted his hand, a blood spot remained. "You know that, do you?" He felt the red rising behind his eyes. "You're certain? But you know nothing else. How are they moving? Why do they disappear? What are they capable of? Too many unknowns. They are not harmless." He glared at her missing eye.

"The past is behind." She folded her hands atop the table. "And their movements are expected. They pass into the otherplane or through gates, seemingly without concern. It's not a miracle, just risky. They are resourceful."

Cain lowered his voice. "That is beside the point. Until we have them, our work can be undone. Though *if* we have them, victory is assured." He inhaled deeply. "Until then, treat them with the same caution as Ezekiel."

Yanamadra turned her head to one side. "You spoke his name. You must be upset."

Cain reached for a flagon and let his hand drop. "I can't ignore him forever. He's part of this too." Cain paused. "He's toying with Isil, feeding him lies."

"Of course he is. He hates Isil."

"Everyone hates Isil. I hate Isil. He's still useful."

"I am not one to lecture…"

"But you will."

Yanamadra straightened. "Ezekiel has spent lifetimes avoiding people. Despite your humble beginning, you are a conqueror. He sees you as tainted by the world."

Cain reached past the flagon to a piece of hardtack. He tore off a chunk. "What do you recommend?"

"About the keys, or the old man?"

"Both."

Yanamadra said, "We use Isil's toys to intercept the keys before they reach the Expanse. We treat them with caution. And for the hermit…" she trailed off.

"Yes?"

Her eyes narrowed. "He is not to be underestimated, and certainly not trusted. His only purpose is to survive to unlock the machine. After that, kill him immediately. Don't give him an ear in which to whisper. No matter how much he claims he knows, nor how tempting the knowledge is."

Cain rose, giving a nod that suggested she do the same. "I hear your council. But I must choose another path."

"Of course. But remember, he will say anything to achieve his ends. He will do anything to take your place."

"Of course he will. I know my own teacher. One more thing."

"Yes?"

"Find Golloth. I need both of you at the Expanse before the solstice. We must be ready."

37

~ Nissa ~

Nissa looked at the valley stretched below them. After a week crossing the hill country, the great rivers of Cox and Osum joined below. The city of Gorenheim, with its storied buildings and high, peaked roofs, nestled in the confluence. For some, the city marked the beginning of the highlands, either a final chance to provision, or to abandon plans to venture farther. For those coming from the highlands, Gorenheim welcomed trappers and prospectors back to civilization. The result was a place of wealth where the riches of the north met the goods of the south. She knew the history—almost too well—and yet what amazed her was not the city, but that it looked just the way she left it.

Cinq took a place beside Nissa. He gripped his staff with both hands. "It must feel like a long time."

"Since what? We go somewhere not busted to hell?"

"I meant since you've been home." He paused. "We could still go around."

Nissa turned to the mule and scratched his ears. He had taken to his new name of Bookwagon with the enthusiasm that a mule took to anything. She thought the name was just this side of hilarious, as books were about the only thing the mule didn't carry. "You don't have to baby me. I'll do things the Cinq way."

He raised an eyebrow. "And what way is that?"

"The forget your feelings and get it done way. I mean, for all I know, the enclave isn't here anymore. I guess the oracle would probably still be there regardless. I'm kind of hoping that's the case."

Cinq turned to face her. "Nissa, come clean. Is this about coming home or something else?"

Her face screwed up in distaste. She held up her arms. She felt a tingling across her skin, not unlike the static and charge before a thunderstorm. "Cinq, there's potential in the air. Maybe because we're coming here, or maybe it would happen anyway. *Something's* going to happen. I mean, maybe it's just been a few days since anyone tried to murder us, but Gorenheim feels a whole lot like Ignaesdale."

"An overlap? I don't feel it."

She grimaced. "No, not yet. But the fey are jumpy. And they tend to know when something big is going down. Way before people do."

Cinq called to Blue and Yon who were re-securing Bookwagon's pack. "Everyone come over here for a second. Nissa, want to repeat that?"

She rolled her eyes and sighed. "Ok, all I told Cinq was that it *kind of* feels like something is about to happen. The fey are twitchy."

Blue asked, "Well, what bothers them?"

"A million things. When people are upset, or there is fighting, or just general bad blood. They pick up on things. For all I know it's just a wedding, or the weather, or just fey being fey."

Yon asked, "Ok, but isn't the Convergence almost here? Is it that?"

"Yes. But… I don't know. I'm just saying we need to be ready."

Blue said, "We're not going around."

Nissa threw up her hands. "I'm not saying we go around. No one's saying that. So, let's just go already."

Yon looked down at the city and back at her. "How far to the enclave? Is it in the city?"

Nissa said, "Sometimes. But it moves around. We'll need to get invited, or we might never find the way in. Maybe it's down there, maybe it's in the hills. Lots of caves and hidden places out there. I'll need to find a wikken and hope she won't remember me. They probably assume I'd be older by now."

Before anyone could protest—including herself—Nissa bounded down the path towing Bookwagon behind her. As she walked, she considered what Yon had said. The Convergence was in less than a month, and even on horseback and running full speed, they wouldn't make it to the fifth key before the solstice. Cinq claimed that wouldn't matter, that the Convergence was more of an era than an event. Still, she didn't like the idea of being in the mountains once it started. The wilds had enough fey as it was; who knew how they'd react?

Down they went, traversing the hillside populated with flocks of sheep and the occasional narrowed eye of a shepherd.

They continued to the main road where they met the slow migration of others: prospectors, farmers, and far fewer soldiers than Nissa would have expected. Then again, Gorenheim was removed from the fighting. The reavers here were likely just enough of a militia to remind people who was in charge.

As they crossed the great bridge spanning the Cox River, nervousness crept up Nissa's spine. Years ago, on a crisp fall morning, she had awakened on that bridge to the sound of feet and rumbling wagon wheels. She hadn't known who she was, not her name, not how she had gotten there. She had spent the first night shivering, huddled amongst the refuse outside a tavern. Some men had seen her. They'd been kind when they could have so easily been cruel to a ten-year-old girl. Nixon, a beggar missing one leg and half his arm in a mining accident, gave her some of his day's collection. The next day, she worked alongside him.

The stray cats of Gorenheim had pegged Nissa as an easy target. They sought her out, hung around. And Nissa, delighting at the companionship, encouraged them with scraps. After three months on the street, she had gained a bit of a following, but in a city like Gorenheim little went unnoticed. Nixon was confronted that his "daughter" was a witch. And when one night a drunk tripped on the cobblestones, he came up seething and looking for someone to blame. The man saw the strange little girl with her cats and advanced on her with a hatchet.

The next moment, the man lay dead on the street with his own weapon buried in the back of his head. Nissa hadn't even seen the woman, her cloak a swirl of browns, greens, and grays. She had taken Nissa by the hand and led her through the streets, across the Osum River bridge, and into the hills.

The next day, Nissa's life in the wikken enclave began, and it was where she'd remained for five years. Now she was back.

They passed through the gateway and onto the streets of Gorenheim. The scent of fresh-cooked bread wafted out of windows; the thud of hooves on cobblestone clacked in her ears. The smell of grass drifted from beyond the walls, mixing with the shadowed scent of the river and the tangy aroma of farmers, miners, and prospectors. Storied buildings leaned out over the streets, bracing against one another.

Yon tapped on Nissa's shoulder. "Look. Just like at Laurel's Hollow."

Nissa's stomach knotted at the sight of the banners, the same as they'd seen in the burned town. While the witchlord's banners flew proudly on some establishments, the same symbol had been hastily scrawled on others. These had smashed doors or broken windows, displays reduced to splinters, and interiors with nothing left intact except fragments. No explanation was required. Those who supported the witchlord thrived. Those who didn't were punished.

"Town seems clean enough," Blue stated. "Orderly."

Nissa agreed. No rubbish lined the crooked alleyways, no bodies of witches hung from the eves, and no people were in the stockades. The signs lurked beneath. Guards traveled in pairs. Voices were subdued. The occasional burst of laughter sounded forced. Nissa studied the people watching the guards. Here and there, shopkeepers looked wary: a woman selling rolls. Her customer, holding one but not looking at it. A young girl pushing a cart of potatoes and not noticing them tumbling over the edge.

A craftswoman arranging the wares in front of her over and over again.

Nissa cleared her throat. "Dearest family, can we move a little faster? I'm getting hungry. And there is nothing here I want to eat. Not. At. All." She tugged on Bookwagon's halter to move it along. They made it a dozen yards when a guard called out to them.

"Ho there. Where are you headed?"

Cinq turned to the soldier. He replied in his patented weary voice. "To the Ulinean hills. And from there, north."

The guard spat on the ground. "I mean, where are you headed now? You look to be in a hurry."

Cinq leaned toward Blue who gave a scowl and a murmur in his ear. He came up confused, and Nissa had to fight back a chuckle. They looked like an old married couple. Bravo, you two. Good show.

Cinq replied, "Uh, now? To the Osum bridge. It's not far, is it?"

The guard opened his mouth to say something, likely nasty, and then muttered and shuffled away.

Nissa leaned close to Cinq. "What was that all about? Did you, you know, do anything magicky?"

A smile tinged his lips. "We've been in the hills for a week. I assure you, if we smell of anything, it's not money. I guess—"

A high-pitched whine filled the air; Nissa dropped to her knees. She threw her hands over her ears. The keening reduced all other sound to nothing. Then it stopped.

"Nissa, are you all right?" Yon rushed to her side.

She darted her eyes around. She wasn't the only one who heard it. The baker, the shopper, the girl with her cart, the craftswoman. All of them now hurried about their business, packing their goods with a speed one hair behind panic.

Nissa looked at the others. "We need to get out of here right—"

Ka-boom. Ka-boom. KA-BOOOOOM.

A shriek went up from the streets as thunder echoed around them. With each explosion, water erupted from the river on each side, rocketing a hundred feet in the air, only to hang suspended at its apex.

Ka-booom. Ka-boom. KA-BOOOOOM.

Three more bursts, and the water began to twist, each of the plumes wrapped around each other. Some of the plumes turned white as they hardened to ice, others expanded to become dark as storm clouds. The initial cacophonous explosions were replaced by a continuous rumble as water, ice, and thunderheads coalesced, all the while cracking with a now-continuous pulse of deep amber electricity that ricocheted around the burgeoning, chaotic form.

Bookwagon bolted, ripping the halter from Nissa's hand as he disappeared into the streets, their belongings in tow. White-hot panic seared through Nissa, even as the screams of the fey filled her ears. Back in Ignaesdale when she had heard the screaming, she'd assumed they were the cries of the nearplane fey. Now she knew better. Those frenzied shrieks of rage, pain, lust, and desire emanated from the thousands of fey joined into the entity before them: the Water Titan.

"Go! Go! Go!" Nissa yelled. She grabbed hold of Blue and Cinq's arms to usher them forward. Yon jumped to help her, catching Blue's other arm to snap her from shock. In Ignaesdale, when the Earth Titan arrived, the streets had been so packed that the crowds became a slow crushing stampede. Here in Gorenheim, with streets occupied but not crowded, people didn't move, they *sprinted*.

Nissa stumbled, and Cinq quickly caught her. Something wrong was happening here. Why wasn't everyone running? The women Nissa had found suspicious were all turned toward the Water Titan. Each of them had knuckles pressed to their heads, mouths chanting. Nissa saw runes visible as skin showed from the ends of sleeves and collars. Some of those now glowed with pale, amber light.

They were wikken. They weren't running from the Titan because they were trying to *control* it.

A colossal leg, ice and fog and lightning, slammed into the street, reducing one of the wikken to a smear. So much for control. As the Water Titan walked, it shifted, taking only a semblance of human shape. Rather, it was a person embodied as thunderstorm. First, it struck with a defined fist to annihilate a three-story building. A moment later, a starburst of lightning struck out, dancing between towers, buildings, and churches, setting each afire as it did. Compared to this, the Earth Titan's plodding destruction seemed quaint.

The Osum River bridge stood just ahead of them. Soldiers wearing reaver colors lined the rails in a display of either shock or bravery. But as their spears were leveled, Nissa came to a grim realization. The reavers were stopping people from fleeing the city. The four of them slowed for a moment, watching as the citizens either tried to break through the barrier, or else cast themselves from the bridge to fall into the swift-running waters. Blue pointed at the side of the bridge.

"Let's do it. Let's swim."

She started forward but was held back by Cinq. The Water Titan leaped into the air, arms outstretched that distorted to become bat-like wings, which hooked and crackled with lightning. The Titan gave a single flap and landed with both feet on the Cox bridge on the other side of town. The bridge exploded in stone and splinters as the Titan crashed through and into the current.

The corpus of the Water Titan drained into the river; it spread in all directions. The Cox and Osum rivers churned with ice, clouds, and lightning as all those who chose to jump were drowned and crushed in turn. Moments later, the waters boiled, steam billowed from the river.

"Stay together!" Yon called. He grabbed Nissa and Cinq's hands while Blue held onto Nissa's shoulder. They watched in horror as clouds rose from the water, consuming the city in viscous fog. Nissa listened, straining her ears. The screams and cries continued, along with the shouts of soldiers issuing commands, and the shriek of women's voices in the language of the wikken. A soldier charged them, appearing from the mist, only to be struck by three arrows in brief succession. A woman in loose black clothing darted forward, retrieving and firing her arrows before disappearing again.

Blue had her cleaver out, standing with her back to the others. Yon adopted a defensive posture with fists raised. His body radiated with the surging power of his chi. The screams continued, but now they were the sounds of men and women fighting one another, not of the divine carnage of the Titan.

"What the hell is happening!?" Blue yelled as another soldier appeared, this one she attacked herself, her cleaver finding the gap between his helmet and breastplate.

Nissa felt first a surge of potential, and then a draining of energy as the presence of the Titan snapped away. It had faded back across realities to return to the otherplane. But something remained behind, a flurry of energy previously unnoticeable.

A shriek ripped through the air, half the roar of a tiger and half the roar of an inferno. Meteors plummeted from the sky, streaking to the earth in a cascade of sparks. Nissa let go of her friends' hands to draw her dagger. She neared the smoldering mass, then jumped back as it stood from the wreckage. The creature looked like a bull with the head and jaws of a hyena, and small back legs relative to its hulking front. Its eyes smoldered, and its soot-colored skin radiated flame. A fury.

The creature leaped, jaws wide and dripping flame. It was intercepted by a flash from the top of Cinq's staff. Ice encased the creature in mid-air. The creature dropped, shattering on the cobblestones like crystal.

Yon yelled, "Together! Stay together." He darted forward, deflecting a charging fury with a chi-fueled elbow strike that sent the creature over the edge of the bridge and into the mist below. He spun again, and in a few short steps had crossed the distance to the next fury. He struck, the blow crumbling it like burning coals dashed on the ground. Yon kept fighting, and the blue bolts of ice shrieked from Cinq's staff one after another. Blue, cleaver held high, tried to attack as well, but her strikes did nothing. One of the furies bowled her over, sending her across the stones, her clothes in flames. Cinq stopped it with a flash of light, repelling it. But even as one fury was sent reeling, another advanced. This one charged Nissa. She could feel the heat as it barreled closer, and the searing burn as it sent her to the ground. She heard something crack as its hoofed foot came down on her arm.

A flash of green light knocked the fury asunder before it could finish the job. The light collapsed to a singularity. A tall, sinewy woman stood where the light had been. Her arms and legs were covered with runes; streaks of black war paint ran across her cheeks. The wikken warrior had an ornately carved rod tucked into her belt, and held a longbow knocked with an arrow in her hands. She spun to face where reavers and furies clashed with one another. The warrior aimed and released the first arrow. She drew again and again and again, targeting the reavers and ignoring the furies. As she fought, other green flashes burst around the bridge and around the city. And with each burst, a wikken would appear—or sometimes disappear as quickly as they had come.

Nissa struggled to stand, but her body flooded with pain. She was numbly aware of her friends gathered around her. She saw the tall wikken stomping toward the four of them. The wikken removed the carved rod from her side and held it to the sky. Piercing green light flooded the object, so bright that the wikken was reduced to a silhouette. The wikken leaped into the air. As she descended, she brought the rod to strike the ground beneath her.

A wave of energy radiated outward to engulf Nissa and her friends. Nissa's vision was filled with green. Then black.

38

~ Nissa ~

Falling water echoed through the cave. It dripped and moved in tiny rivulets and still pools cradled among the rocks. The air was as damp as the dark green moss spreading across the floor. Damp as the rivulets trickling down the walls. Damp as her skin from the ever-present heat. Nissa sat up. She watched a stream of water that fell from the darkness overhead to land in the pool just in front of her. The stones of the pool bloomed with thick, spongy algae, budded with red flowers. She reached out to interrupt the flow until her palm filled up and the water poured over and through her fingers.

Though she was alone in the alcove, someone had applied fresh bandages to the burns on her arms and legs. Nissa stood, her legs protesting at first. She splashed some water on her face and stepped out from the alcove and into the cavern. Her head surged with familiarity and strangeness all at once. She knew this place, and yet it had been transformed. This had once been a holy site for the wikken of Gorenheim, a place of spiritual retreat. Not anymore.

Nissa placed one hand on her tender side and leaned against the wall. Before her, the sanctuary had become a war camp. In every twist and nook of the cavern, the wikken were hard at work. Many tended wounds or sharpened blades, while others prepared foodstuffs or assembled supply kits. The women paid no mind to the water that streamed from heights unknown to fill the pools and create little rivers that continued before disappearing beneath rocks.

Years ago, Nissa had been sent here alone with only a small torch to guide her way. This was a ritual of all new wikken when they left their old lives behind to embrace their place alongside the fey. At the time, she feared the waterfalls would extinguish her torch. She learned later that was expected. She had become lost, until finally she made contact with one of the resident fey. They had fallen into conversation, staying for almost three days before the other wikken went looking for her. The wikken had expected to find her body or locate her lost within the catacombs. Instead, they found Nissa, giggling and swimming in the pools, a retinue of fey keeping her company, lighting the walls with a happy, internal phosphorescence. She began her training the next day.

The fey were now gone from the cavern. Perhaps the existence of so many people had driven them from their home. Or perhaps the Titan had swept the fey up. Maybe they had been powerless to resist and consumed by rage. If so, what happened to them afterward? Did they return to the otherplane, or did they lose their identity forever? Nissa felt a tickle at the back of her neck, something in the quiet of her mind. Excitement swept over her. One fey remained—the one that mattered.

Forgetting her injuries, Nissa stepped forward, her mind now focused and her determination set. She descended into the main cavern. She passed women as they pounded wind chimes into spear points, sliced and stitched leather armor, or worked to dye colorful feather cloaks and animal skins with earth tones meant for camouflage. Nissa kept her eyes straight ahead. What should have felt like a half year of separation felt like lifetimes. Some of the faces she recognized, though the subtle aging of everyone but her widened the gulf between them. She didn't need to talk to these wikken. Why bother? They had chosen war, to turn the fey into weapons. She knew the wikken didn't swear oaths—but they had broken them all the same. A sour taste rose in her mouth. These people wouldn't have her answers. But the oracle might.

"Welcome home, Nissa," a soft voice called.

Nissa jumped. She whipped her head around to see a muscular woman with loose blonde hair standing just behind her. Alora. She and Nissa had been playmates since Nissa's earliest days with the wikken. Alora had been born into the enclave. She had been asked to help Nissa learn the wikken way. Like all the wikken, she'd never been assigned the task. Instead, it had been a suggestion by the elders. Most of these suggestions—but not all—were followed.

Nissa looked in astonishment. "Alora, how have you been? It's been—" She stopped short. "You look *amazing!* So grown-up." She reached out to embrace her childhood friend who now—through the benefit of Nissa's time in the lapse—was in her early twenties.

Alora took a step back. "Tarra wants to speak with you. She's been waiting for you to wake up." Her old friend smiled. "We can catch up later. But for now, don't keep her waiting." The blonde wikken sighed. "She gets such terrible moods these days."

"Where are my friends?" Nissa blurted. "Cinq and Yon and Blue?"

"They're here; they're safe. And I will take you to them as soon as you speak with Tarra."

Nissa shook her head vehemently. "Nope. Uh-uh. You know that as soon as Ms. Important sees me, she's going to chew me up and spit me out. Metaphorically, if I'm lucky."

"You don't know—"

"Yes, I do." Nissa stared intensely at her friend. "Look. I need to see the oracle. It's kind of why I'm here." She held up her finger to stall any protest. "This is my one chance, and you know if I ask Tarra she'll say no out of—I don't know— to teach me a lesson or something. Listen, Alora, I *need* to talk to the oracle. It's the last and only favor I will ever ask you. *Please*. You don't need to come with me; you don't need to go in. Just give me a little time. I wouldn't ask if this wasn't the most important thing I have ever, ever, *ever* asked you, and…"

Alora cleared her throat and spoke loud enough that the wikken all around turned to look. "Nissa, as I said, Tarra has requested your presence. Follow me." She wheeled and walked away, with Nissa hobbling behind. She fought to keep the smile from spreading on her face as they turned not to the center of the cavern where the wikken leader received visitors, but through a low tunnel, passing through the veil of a waterfall and into an adjacent chamber. Thank goodness for good friends.

On the other side of the cascade, a cavern opened up. Here the water dripped as well, but in a series of pools that dumped water from one to the other in succession. The drops and falls emitted wafts of steam as hot water from the spring mixed with the cool of glacier melt diverted from outside. Bathing wikken occupied the pools, conversing with one another and ignoring Nissa. Some spoke in grave tones while others laughed, though the drip of water muted their words. Nissa and Alora ascended the cascade until they reached the top where glacier melt and hot springs merged together. Between them was a perfectly round opening curtained by verdant moss. Alora stopped at the entrance, leaving Nissa to continue on her own.

The tunnel through the rock was low, round, and smooth, with a slick stone floor covered in algae. Nissa dropped to a crawl. She passed through and into the next room. The passage ended at a round pool populated by floating, moss-covered boulders. A fey, small, brown, and shaggy, sat atop a rock in the center of the pool. She chewed on a root held within her tiny, clawed hands. Matted hair framed her face like the drooping branches of a willow. The fey looked at Nissa with liquid eyes set in light fur accented by a black stub nose. She caught and held Nissa's gaze.

Nissa said, "I need your help…" The worlds trickled and died as she said them. All around, the cavern, the moss, the boulders, and the fey dripped and faded. The forms slid down like an image shift in a dream. Nissa found her feet no longer on the stone floor, but atop a smooth, glasslike surface which dropped to infinity below. Above her, the ceiling had given way to glittering stars on a cloudless night.

Welcome home, Nissa.

The voice came without sound. This was a direct link of consciousness with none of the double-talk, confusion, or blend of senses she experienced with some fey. The voice rang cool and articulate. Either the oracle was practiced at speaking with humans, or simply had a purity of thought. This was the oracle, an ancient fey. She had been here generations before the wikken came as fleeting visitors.

Nissa's skin tingled in nervousness and anticipation. "Thanks. I… I never really thought I'd come back." The words tumbled from her mouth. "Place has changed a lot, hasn't it? I really don't think it's just me. I… I miss the others." She bit her lip. "The other fey."

No response. Only the slightest feeling of annoyance accompanied by the rapid movement of the stars overhead. Seasons passed in a few moments before slowing to the almost imperceptible speed of the normal night sky.

"Ok, I get it," Nissa fumbled. "You're a busy lady. Chit-chat isn't really a thing anymore, I guess. I'll get straight to it. My name is Nissa—which you already knew since you said my name. Long story short, my friends and I are keys to this machine… The Black Gate, it's called."

Nissa let go. She continued to speak, but that was only a formality. Emotions, thoughts, and memories flowed through her as they passed to the oracle. She told of her friends, their travels, their challenges, and their struggles. When she reached the end of the narrative, she opened her eyes once more. "And so, we're on our way to find Number Five, and then the machine, I guess. But the problem is," she sucked in her breath "we need the Titans. Like, all four Titans. But I don't even know where to start with that. I mean, I saw what the other wikken did in Gorenheim. You probably already know about that, too, but they kind of fought with the Titan, not against it. Maybe if we could…"

She stopped. The oracle looked back at her. A deepness of thought reflected at her. Nissa felt a tightening at the base of her neck. She wasn't sure if the fey was mad at her, the wikken in general, or maybe just the audacity of Nissa's request. What was she even *doing* here? It was too much for her to come. To bring her problems to—

You've forgotten. After so much effort to learn?

"Learn what? I'm pretty sure I never knew…" the words trailed off as Nissa realized the fey was not speaking to her as a runaway wikken, but as the person she had been in another life. A residual memory bubbled in her mind. She'd had this discussion before. And the oracle knew it. Nissa winced. "You're right. If you put it that way, I guess I've forgotten everything. I know I was once another person, or maybe better to say I was once a different person. Or that different person is now me. But I'm not really them. And if I am, I can't remember it. So can you help?"

First, you must understand.

The imagined sky filled with green light which coalesced into a translucent, viridescent sphere. The textures and shapes on the surface were reminiscent of the maps she'd seen aboard the ship, an enormous, curved depiction of the heavens.

This is your home, the nearplane, in circuit of your sun.

The sphere spun as it turned, then another overtook it.

And this is my birthplace, the otherplane.

The second sphere was a mirror of the first, but with its own texture and topography. It emitted a dull purple aura. The two spheres, nearplane and otherplane, traveled the imagined sky, two separate but intersecting routes, one the afterimage of its twin as they chased, and passed, and crossed, and lagged. Occasionally they would brush against one another, heralded by a spark of intense white light which lasted for a moment before the worlds drifted apart again.

Our worlds circle the same star, though in different planes. Yet we have a common need. We are sustained by energy emanating from the life in our realms. This is what you call magic. Magic comes from life. It is life. It sustains life.

The spheres filled her vision, this time tinged with swirls of amber which drifted across the surface, occasionally wisping from one world to the other.

Magic is natural to both our worlds. It builds and grows, and just as easily can be caught and ridden. As life creates magic, it in turn needs magic. This attraction tugs at strings across realities to bring our worlds closer so that the threads become entwined. We drifted together.

Nissa started to twitch. These lessons of worlds and magic felt too distant. This was mage stuff, right? She wanted to interrupt, but her words wouldn't come. The spheres shifted. The collisions became more frequent, the bursts of white-hot light were no longer isolated. A staccato spark rippled across the spheres of nearplane and otherplane.

During the first Convergence, my kind rejoiced. We hoped for happy coexistence, where we could pass from nearplane to otherplane freely. The magic of our worlds would thrive, flourishing off the other. But in your world, humans coveted our magic. They ripped away the living energy. And for the first time, our kind was left hungry. For us, magic wasn't a means, it sustained us. But humans created machines to take that power. We couldn't simply wait for the overlap to end. So, we learned to open portals of our own. We joined together. We became Titans to take back what we had lost.

The surface of the spheres, now in near-constant overlap, boiled with amber storms and white-hot light ripping from nearplane to otherplane and back again.

As Titans, we reclaimed our lost power. But the more we fought, the deeper the humans drank. It was a war of power and for power. We fought, we died, as did you. We wanted only to survive, but the people of the nearplane thought we meant to destroy. All the while they took, and took, and took.

Nissa lay captivated, both by the words but also the celestial display. The spheres of nearplane and otherplane were no longer distinguishable from one another. Light filled the room, so intense that she shielded her eyes. When she looked out, the spheres were on opposite ends of their orbit, though with one difference. The otherplane shone so dimly that the sphere looked to be only a shadow.

"What happened?" Nissa asked. "Just then, what happened?"

The voice of the fey spoke in her mind once more, echoing with loss and regret. *You happened, Nissa. Your former self, before you split. You built the Black Gate. You used the Titans to open a portal between our worlds. With the machine to control, and the Titans as conduit, you pushed our worlds apart. But you drank so deeply that our world was left dying. Some survived, but not many. And it was not to last forever.*

The stars above shifted and turned. The spheres of nearplane and otherplane sped up once more as the years melted away like seconds. And over time, the two orbits came closer and closer together, until the turning of days came to a jarring halt. Nissa didn't need to be told. This was the second Convergence. This was now. Nissa watched the healthy glow of the nearplane, and the diminished sphere of the otherplane, black and cold.

Nissa bowed her head. "It was the Pentarch. He killed your world. We all thought he was a hero, but he traded you for us." Her temples throbbed. At every turn this stupid quest got harder. First it was finding the keys, then a machine, then came the stupid reavers. And now what? Even if they did make it, and even if she did manage to summon the Titans, then what? She'd kill another world? No. She couldn't take it. There had to be another way.

The night sky faded to black, so that only she and the oracle remained, alone in the dark. Nissa scowled. "So, I guess we just quit."

The oracle looked back at her. The room was so perfectly dark and perfectly silent, Nissa could feel the individual beats of her heart.

If you quit, there will be others. Others who would make a different choice. Others who do not care. You created this problem. You must fix it.

Nissa wanted to scream. Whoever the oracle thought she used to be, she wasn't that anymore. "I don't get it. There's nothing I can do. What about the Titans, huh? Maybe old me used to whistle and the Titans would come running. But new me? Little Nissa can't do that stuff."

The oracle stared back.

Unless…

"Unless what?"

"Nissa!"

The shout cut through the black. The illusion was ripped away, replaced by the dank of the cave. She jerked her head up, gasping and coughing. She was on hands and knees in the pool of the fey's room.

A voice called. "Get out of there!"

Nissa whirled to see a tall wikken with white dreadlocks storming her way. The woman grabbed her by the neck and lifted her from the pool. Nissa fought against the woman's iron grip until released. She dropped, gasping, into the water. She looked up at the furious woman, the white of her hair contrasting skin so covered in runes that the actual tone was impossible to divine. Tarra, the wikken high chief.

Nissa turned to look for the oracle. "Wait! I still don't know what you—" The fey slid from the rock to dive beneath the water.

"Get her out of there," Tarra ordered.

Two wikken in leather armor seized Nissa's arms. They dragged her to a patch of sand on the edge of the chamber where they set her down roughly.

Tarra spoke. Her voice was a layer of calm over a sea of fury. "You have violated this sanctuary."

The awe and reverence Nissa had felt from speaking with the oracle was ripped away. "What?! You're lecturing *me*? I'm not the one using the fey as weapons. How *could* you?" Nissa shook with fury. "It's against everything we were ever taught, against everything *you* ever taught. The fey aren't our slaves. It's what we've fought to keep the mages from doing for centuries, to keep them from being tools."

Tarra said, "That's enough of a lecture from you."

Nissa narrowed her eyes. "Don't pretend you didn't do it, Tarra. I've seen Titans before. What happened in Gorenheim wasn't normal. That wasn't a slow build, that was a push. You *forced* them. Why make one fey do your dirty work when you can have a thousand?"

"You're mistaken, Nissa. I'm not forcing the fey to become Titans. That is inevitable. The gate between nearplane and otherplane *will* open somewhere in the world. All I do is pick the place."

Nissa scowled. "So, you admit it."

"I'm not using them. I enticed them." Tarra let the words sink in. "Better a Titan amongst our enemies than our friends. And we don't control them any more than we control the fey. They remain free."

"Free? They barely exist once a Titan comes. You know that as well as I do. Or maybe you don't see, because you are busy running away. I shouldn't have to tell you those weren't just soldiers in that town. Men and women, kids and cats and dogs. You set the city on fire. You're a murderer!"

"Wrong." Tarra shook her head. "There are no innocents. *You* are the one who left. *You* are the one who abandoned your sisters. Do you know what the witchlord does when he takes an enclave? He burns, of course, the old fallback. But when you have to burn hundreds, you can't be bothered to stake them one by one. No, he's far too busy for that. You dig a trench and throw the women in. Cover them with pitch and light it. Don't talk to me about innocents. We do what must be done."

Nissa stood with arms crossed as she assessed her old teacher, a woman she had admired for her passion and charisma from the first moment she'd seen her. "Sure, Tarra, you're a real hero. Where do I sign up?" She turned to stalk away, only to be stopped by the warriors.

"Oh no," Tarra said. "That's not how this works. You had questions, now it's my turn. Where have you been these past five years? You haven't aged—much. Did you sell every secret to that mage friend of yours? And what did you want with the oracle?"

"Sorry, Tarra, all I heard was 'blah-blah-blah, I'm a self-righteous wench. Blah-blah-blah, nothing matters but me.'"

One of the guards struck Nissa hard on the back of her head. Her vision went white as she stumbled. She wheeled around and lunged at her, only to be struck once more and thrown to the ground. Nissa focused her most intense look of disdain before turning back to Tarra. She lunged forward again, only to be caught, and this time held tight. She kicked and squirmed, but the much stronger women just shoved her back.

Tarra looked on impassively. "You were saying?"

Nissa, cowed, rubbed her arms. "First off, you are incredibly rude and none of this is necessary. Secondly, I was in a lapse, obviously. At least two of them. Maybe more. I've been busy."

"But why are you here, Nissa? Are you a spy for the mages? I don't think you just decided to come home."

Another insult leaped to Nissa's mind, but maybe her point had been made. And there was still an infinitesimal chance she could walk back from this one. Honesty then. "Ok Tarra, you win. I found out that I'm one of five keys used to unlock a machine of unspeakable power built by the Pentarch. You know the one. Black Gate? My friends, they're the other three keys. There's only one of us left to find, but oh, the fifth is basically up the witchlord's butt. So, I thought I'd come here first and make sure I knew the whole story so we didn't screw anything up. But I'm guessing you tortured as much out of them."

Tarra scoffed. "You're lying."

"I'm not… I'm not lying!" Nissa screamed.

Tarra's sneering resolve diminished. "I don't believe you. What's more, it doesn't matter. We're doing just fine here by ourselves, Nissa. We don't need you, we don't need your little friends, and we certainly don't need you spreading tales about something that can't possibly be true."

Nissa threw up her hands. "You know what? Don't believe me. Why would you, I'm just a little girl that ran away. So why don't you ask her?" Nissa nodded at the pool where the oracle swam, her small, shaggy form gliding around in lazy circles like an otter. "Show her what you showed me," Nissa demanded. "Maybe it'll make more sense."

The oracle flipped around to float on her back, peering back at Tarra.

Tarra sneered at Nissa. She walked to the edge of the water. The oracle dove down once more. As she did, the pool changed from a primordial green to a milky, luminescent color. Tarra dropped to one knee and placed her palm flat against the surface of the water. A long, grayish tendril, not unlike a tree root, extended from the pool to wrap around Tarra's forearm. The tentacle jerked the wikken into the pool where she disappeared.

The guards sprang to attention, but none dared go closer to the water. Nearly a minute passed until Tarra burst through the surface, wide-eyed and gasping. As she emerged, the water became clear. She crawled from the pool, head drooped low.

Nissa darted forward. She tried not to sound too smug. "So… am I still lying?"

Tarra's eyes radiated contempt. "I don't know. She wouldn't listen to me."

"I can't imagine why not," Nissa stated.

"Shut up, Nissa, and listen. She didn't say anything. Not about who you were or what you claimed. But she said I had to help you." Tarra scowled. "She also promised to bring you the Titans, but said this time you have to fix it."

39

~ Cain ~

Cain watched sand twist across the desert in eddies and zephyrs made visible. The Expanse filled him with both dread and regret. His soldiers, however, considered this a holy land, the cradle of their leader. The cracked and featureless flats radiated in all directions, interrupted by the occasional mound of white/gray sands and the fissures that coursed through them. In other places, twisted rock sprouted from the land, or the ground fell away into chasms lacking order or design. His eyes drifted to the small building standing alone at a distance from the camp. The squat, rectangular edifice consisted of five stone slabs: four walls and a roof. Cain had spent three years in that hovel after arriving as an exile from the monastery. He had planned to use the building as a shelter for only one night. Ezekiel had taken him as first refugee then pupil.

For the first two years, Cain had no idea what lay beneath him. The hovel had been the center of his universe even before he learned it was the center of so much more: the graveyard of the Black Gate.

Cain let his eyes drift from the building to the encampments surrounding the excavation. At least that looked more familiar. The canvas tents, soldiers, and livestock had all the appearance of a long-term outpost. That served him well. As far as his armies were concerned, he kept his troops here out of nostalgia. Even those who worked to dig thought they were looking for a temple. He never explained more.

The wind rose in gusts, throwing waves of dust and sand against his body. He raised a cloth to cover his face, including a strip of translucent fabric over his eyes. He trudged away from the camp and toward the hovel. Behind him, he heard the footsteps and grumblings of his escort. He no longer tried to dissuade the men from following him, even in a matter as personal as this. Witches could come from anywhere.

Cain tensed as he placed a hand on the canvas covering the door. He stepped inside and out of the elements. The room was empty, which was almost worse. A straw mat was in one corner, a blackened firepit in the other. In the opposing corner, Cain imagined the indentation still formed from where he'd slept. No mat, no blanket, no comfort. But, ah, the wisdom. The things he learned, the stories he was told. Ezekiel had been so stingy with knowledge at times, and other times so generous.

A voice called from behind him. "My lord?"

Cain turned to see Isil, his lieutenant, push into the hovel. He turned back to the room without greeting him.

"Why did you come here of all places?" Isil batted at the sand layered on his clothes.

"Presumably to reflect. And yet I find myself disturbed." The conversation irritated him. Isil had that effect on people.

Isil didn't reply.

Cain turned to his lieutenant, hands still in his pockets. "Your legions thrive, even in your absence. Do you miss the front lines?"

"My lord..." Isil paused before continuing, his serpentine voice managing to be both infuriating and groveling at the same time, "this is a front as well. Albeit a different kind."

"Of course. Which is why I put you here. Have you found the entrance?"

Isil said, "I believe we're close. We reached a new room just last week. Any moment we will break through."

"You don't need to remove every grain of sand. What did Ezekiel say?"

Isil bit his lip. "That's what concerns me. He has become... cooperative. Clear in his direction. I assume the Convergence, but he likes his games."

Cain nodded. Ezekiel wasn't generous without reason. That wasn't how the old man operated. "What about Yanamadra's idea? Will the fey dig?"

Isil shook his head. "No. They won't—can't—go near the place. The void hasn't wavered. *He* says it's good luck. Less chance of a Titan."

"You can drop the pronouns, Isil. Call him by name if you need. He's not the devil. Unless he lied about that too."

Isil's face scrunched up. "You're not going to free him, are you? Don't be insane."

In a flash of rage, Cain spun to seize Isil by the throat. He picked him up and slammed his lieutenant against the ground. Cain drew a curved dagger and held the edge to Isil's throat. He kept his voice even. "Insane? No, not insane. Insane would be to cut the tongue out of a sniveling mage for his insolence." He released Isil and calmly returned to his feet. "Then who would keep this place on schedule? As for Ezekiel, I need him as I always did."

Isil rolled over onto his knees. He rubbed his neck. "What if he escapes?"

"He won't. He wants to be here when it happens. And when the time comes, I'm going to need a mage, a wikken, a monk, a scholar, *and* a hermit." Cain hauled Isil back to his feet. He patted the man's shoulder. "And some of you are harder to find than others."

Isil pursed his lips. "But not yet?"

"Not yet."

The uneasy silence continued. Isil straightened his clothes. He glanced around the room and back at the door. "Would you care for dinner? Refreshments? It's a long journey to—"

"Where is Ezekiel now?"

"At the dig. We put him in a storeroom… for safety. He was disturbing the workers."

"That, I suspect, is an understatement."

Cain pulled his mask back into place. He followed Isil on the slow traverse to the encampment. With the sand whipping sideways, Cain knew they were but shadows against the storm, and yet, word had spread of his arrival. Men lined the entrance to the camp. Some were armored, but most held tools of labor: shovels, pickaxes, buckets. All of them wore wrappings so that they looked like an army of the faceless. And with the roar of the wind, they were also voiceless. Cain did his best to provide approving nods and the occasional salute as he marched to the large white tent in the center of camp.

Passing through the flaps behind Isil, Cain removed his coverings. The wind made the canvas walls reverberate, but at least the sand no longer scoured his skin. With another nod to the guards, he walked to the dead center of the tent where ladders protruded from the ground next to a system of ropes, buckets, and pulleys. A great belt turned the gears, retrieving bucket after bucket of loose, dry sand, which was in turn ferried into wheelbarrows and dumped outside. To Cain's amusement, the sand didn't have to be hauled away. Load after load was seized by the gale and scattered.

Cain followed Isil down the ladder, dropping forty feet into the antechamber. The underground room was square, with large hewn stones on all sides. Next to him, a noisy apparatus hauled sand to the surface. The device had been transferred from the mines in the hills to the north, and the miners who ran it did so with great reluctance. Cain ensured they were paid, but perhaps they had hopes of finding riches elsewhere. The contraption occupied most of the room. Away from the sand and wind, they toiled, dripping with sweat from the labor. The men gave Cain a nod of respect, then returned to their duties. He took no offense. The machine only worked if all moved in concert.

"He's in there." Isil pointed to one of several doors leading from the room. "No way out." He shifted nervously. "We wanted him in the void. Yanamadra suggested it, but I had been thinking the same thing. Though he pretends to be powerless, he may be hiding something."

"Well, he's definitely hiding something." Cain toed the sandy floor. "It's interesting the Tracer can find him within the void."

"But it is not a normal artifact."

Cain walked past Isil and into the adjacent room. An armored guard stood in front of the opening, stepping aside to let him pass. On the other side lay a chamber, the same length as the first, but only eight or so feet wide. Cubbyholes had been carved into both sides, though most were vacant except for a few bags right near the entrance. Cain turned and continued down, stopping near the end where a skeleton of a man sat cross-legged on the floor. He had a wrapping of cloth around his legs and up and over his back. A prisoner's clothing, though not that different from what the man had worn when free.

The only thing that took Cain by surprise was Ezekiel's paleness. His flesh looked blanched against the chains on his ankles. The rune scars along his arms and shoulders looked like shadows in the torchlight. The man did not turn as Cain approached. He held a finger aloft to beckon him to wait, not dropping it until he had returned a marker to his book and set the tome aside.

Ezekiel turned to him. As always, the sheer intensity of the gray eyes, one flecked with yellow, one with green, were almost overwhelming. "Welcome home, Mortimer." Ezekiel's eyes narrowed at the sight of Isil. "I see you brought my warden." He grinned at Cain with mock-surprise. "Didn't you have more fingers last time?"

Cain clenched his fist within his glove. *How had the old man known? Don't worry about it. He's just trying to get to you.* He relaxed his hand. He couldn't be seen as weak here, not in front of the guards.

Ezekiel tilted his head. "If you're here, I assume the keys are back. We can't be erased. Kill as many as you want. Another will rise, though maybe difficult to find."

Cain ignored him. "Isil thinks time slipped."

"I'm sure he does. Does it matter? Or are you trying to justify losing the keys in the first place?" The hermit rose and turned to place the book in one of the nearby alcoves. He took care to make sure it rested in perfect alignment with the other texts. "What's important is they are on their way. Will you let them come?"

Cain nodded. "If fate doesn't intervene."

"I'd worry less about fate, and more about your pet witches. They know they're unwanted in your world." Ezekiel spoke with no regard to Isil, a former mage, standing in the chamber. "The longer you keep them alive, the more chance they'll betray you. They don't have our *vision*."

"I don't share your vision."

"You share a piece. You want the Titans gone. So do I. You want the witches to die. And I agree it's what they deserve. Yours is a simple, admirable, incomplete plan. Imperfect. I want more than the symptoms removed. But why should the wise Mortimer Cain solve the problem when he can work in half-measures?" Ezekiel cocked his head. "Or are you here to take my advice?"

Cain growled, "Your way leaves nothing."

Ezekiel sniffed. "It leaves the world, which some would argue is more important than even you. But enough of imperfect things. How goes your military conquest? Making a difference?" The hermit's eyes laughed at him.

Cain walked to the nooks. He idly picked through the books. "The Titans are moving south, as you predicted. The people are noticing. We are gaining believers."

Ezekiel said, "You must be proud of yourself. Your ends are justifying your means. But I think there is still a problem. The *number* of Titans, those aren't decreasing, are they? Those are growing. Ever more intense, ever hungrier. I know what you think, Mortimer Cain. Until the witches are all gone, it won't stop. And perhaps you're right." He tapped his knee with a jagged fingernail. "But it is just so *hard* to find them all."

Cain cleared his throat. "Enough. I have questions."

"Of course, of course. Answers are what I'm here for. Why else would I be kept?"

Cain folded his arms across his chest. "The keys, who are they?"

Ezekiel cracked a smile, his teeth shining white despite the years of being locked away, and however much time before that. "And how would I know? There is nothing written about who they would be. As counterpoint, I'd say they are unknowable, even to themselves. The legacy passes from hand to hand. Generation to generation. No one lives forever."

"I don't care about their families. I want to know their strengths. I want to know who I'm facing."

Ezekiel snaked around to meet Cain's eyes. "Who are they? They're *me*, you idiot."

Cain snapped backward. "What?"

He continued, "The keys are pinnacles of their orders: mage, wikken, monk, scholar, and hermit. At the time of the Pentarch, each was the undisputed master of their art. The keys may die or be born again. It doesn't matter. As the bond passes, so will their return to destiny. And when they find their place, they will regain the power of their forebearers. All I am is what they will be. And they are just as dangerous."

"You aren't so dangerous now."

"No. I suppose I'm not."

Cain set his jaw. He could feel the old man laughing at him, thinking him weak, ignorant, simple-minded. He felt the blood rising in his ears. The corners of his vision started to tinge with red. He could end it now. He could leap across the gap and bring his fist down onto the old man's throat again and again, until the bones splintered and cracked. His teacher would never speak again, and the hermit's key would pass to him, he supposed. But he couldn't. He shouldn't. He was to be the monk. Plus, Ezekiel had built up lifetimes of lies. What if the old man's mind passed as well? What if it overcame his own consciousness? What if Ezekiel, wearing Cain as a mask, sat at the controls of the Black Gate? No. He would wait. He must calm himself.

Cain met Ezekiel's eyes. "You speak of power, what is yours? When will I see it? All this time, and nothing. I doubt it exists."

Ezekiel snickered. "You ask me to play my cards. And as much as I enjoy making you wait, I know you are very, very busy, and very, very important. So, I'll do you this favor." The hermit smiled. "My power is objectivity. I look beyond individual lives to the greater world. You cannot understand society from within it. Only when you give it all away can you be free from influence. Listen to *me*, not these hypocrites."

"Now they're hypocrites? A minute ago they were just witches."

Ezekiel chuckled. "One breeds the other." The hermit turned his back. "Remember, Mortimer, no matter how many cities you conquer, towers you fell, and how many people hang on your words, only one thing has meaning. Atonement."

40

~ Cinq ~

Cinq looked at the pile of waterlogged, burned, and mangled books with anger and loss, but mostly guilt. Despite his protests, the wikken had dragged them through a series of waterfalls as they journeyed through the network of caves. Everything had been soaked. Now, he sat cross-legged on the cave floor and assessed the damage. He picked up the nearest volume and eased open the cover. The pages ran with ink, the words gone. He tried to turn the page, and great yellowed chunks came apart in his fingers.

Blue looked on sympathetically. "You're making it worse. We'll need a kiln, some dry grass, and as much grain as we can find."

Cinq raised an eyebrow. He hadn't adjusted to Blue's transformation from irritable guide to irritable academic. She might take a while to mature into her new role, but she would eventually. They all had. And the process was accelerating. Cinq could remember snippets of spells and lore he'd never studied. The most difficult concepts were becoming, well, *easy*. He hadn't spoken about it himself, but Yon indicated he was gaining skill without practice. And as for Nissa, whether she admitted it or not, he'd watched her ability to speak with the fey strengthen tenfold since they'd first met. Was this because of the Convergence, or from being in each other's presence?

"The grain's one way to go," he agreed, "but I think the issue is the ink, not the pages. I could probably put a spell together, but I'd have to improvise. And I suspect the wikken wouldn't react well to me using magic."

Cinq checked another volume before dropping it back into the pile. Nothing was salvageable. Schematics of the machine, lost. Details of building materials, gone. Diaries of construction, ruined. He and Blue—mostly Blue—had at least skimmed most everything before Gorenheim. In the end, it had all come down to just one journal: a small, hide-bound book written in careful script. This one he'd kept in a protected pocket of his coat. It, too, was damp, though not destroyed. And luckily for him, neither written in cipher nor ancient tongue.

He flipped through the journal, carefully opening each page and blowing gently on it. He traced the words to lock them in his memory, then moved on to the next. The subject of the journal was what the Pentarch called the "lockspell," the multiple safeguards used to secure his machine. It was more complex than Cinq had imagined. First off, there was the temple housing the Black Gate. It hadn't disappeared by accident. The Pentarch and his colleagues had deliberately built it in the desert in a wide-open pit. They *knew* the sands would cover it up over time—they were counting on it. The Pentarch wanted the Black Gate hidden until the Convergence came again. Secondly, the Black Gate wouldn't work without the Titans. That was Nissa's territory; Cinq hoped she'd learned something useful. Given that the Titans were manifestations of the fey, he assumed that meant he needed their consent. The last part of the lockspell was the keys. Five keys for five disciplines. According to the Pentarch, he regretted this part. He didn't think five people could make good decisions any more than a thousand could. In his journal, the Pentarch confessed that he needed to break the lockspell, so that he—and only he—could use the machine. The only person the Pentarch trusted was himself.

And there the journal stopped. If the Pentarch had figured out a way to pick his locks, he didn't confide it in these pages. And as far as Cinq knew, the answer wasn't in the damaged books either.

Cinq looked at the far side of the domed grotto where the others were sequestered from the wikken. Yon held one of the half-destroyed books, a manual detailing the Pentarch's ideas on martial techniques. Whenever Yon found a legible page, he studied it, occasionally frowning. He'd stand up, go through the motions, whether seated, balancing, or dancing, and return to his book. At first, Yon had practiced in the main cavern, until his many admirers drove him back here.

A smile crossed Cinq's face. The wikken had treated all of them quite differently. While he had gotten hostility, Blue received respect. Yon, though male, won their hearts in an instant. The wikken followed him around like puppies. Or to be more accurate, as if he were a puppy. As for Nissa, the wikken would only say she was safe. He hoped they were telling the truth.

Cinq straightened at the sound of footsteps padding through the inch-deep water. A moment later, a severe woman appeared wearing black leather pants and a halter. Her white dreadlocks were pulled back by a loose leather cord. Her skin was completely covered in wikken runes. Cinq stood as he saw Nissa following behind. His friend limped, and she had an expression somewhere between triumph, enlightenment, and distress. They ducked through the low, dripping entrance and stopped.

"Nissa!" Yon yelled. The boy dashed to greet her. Cinq and Blue followed immediately after so that Nissa was crowded between the three of them. She returned their hugs and introduced her companion.

Everyone, this is Tarra. She is the chief of the enclave and our warden. Did I say warden? I meant host." Nissa winked. "And she's going to help us."

Tarra muttered, "Within reason."

"Right, right, right," Nissa said. "The deal is that she helps as long as we get out of here as quick as we can and don't make too much of a fuss. She thinks we might confuse the sisters and their glorious mission. But first, introductions. Key number one, Cinq LeGarrec, mage in questionable standing from Eastwind Tower. I'm key number two. Key three, Yon, initiate of Open Eye monastery and a stand-up guy. And key four, Blue, of Alexandria, future scholar."

"Welcome to the enclave," Tarra replied. Her voice was dry, formal, unwelcoming. Cinq was used to this from the other wikken.

The five of them looked at each other warily. Nissa had introduced them as keys. That was telling, but Cinq wasn't eager to give much more away. He waited.

Tarra said, "Nissa, you said you had a destination."

She replied, "Oh, right, right. Cinq, do you mind?"

He hesitated, studying his friend for a sign to hold back. But she gave no hints of caution. "Very well." Cinq retrieved his long coat from where he'd suspended it to keep water from dripping on the books. He spread the coat on a dry patch of floor to show the map inscribed within. He oriented it with his compass and tapped the northern region. "This is us, outside of Gorenheim." He paused. "*Are* we outside Gorenheim?"

"More or less."

He held the Tracer to sight on the dimmest of the five lights. He didn't need to be precise; the measurement was the same as before. He tapped at a blank spot on the map where no mountains, forests, or even hills were etched. "The fifth key is here."

Tarra crept closer. She scowled down at the intersection. "In the Expanse? There's nothing there."

Yon asked, "You've been there?"

She shook her head. Anyone with sense goes around it. The witchlord has an outpost. It's where he used to live before his 'great ascension.' We sent scouts there, but an attack wasn't worth the effort."

Cinq smoothed the fabric of his coat. He remembered what Calladius had said. The witchlord had found the machine. Both the key and the Black Gate would be there. He thought it odd that this was a surprise to the wikken.

Blue cracked her knuckles. "Well, are you going to help us or not? Any advice? Or maybe a guide? We're running out of time."

Tarra traced a path through the mountains, snaking along a river and down the other side. She said, "These passes are poorly traveled. They'll be rough, but perhaps unwatched. I can get you there faster."

Nissa wrinkled her nose. "But? You're about to say, 'but,' aren't you?"

Tarra shook her head. "No, no 'but.' I promised I'd help, and I will. I just hope I'm not delivering you to the witchlord on a silver platter."

Cinq bristled. "You have a better idea?"

"Certainly. One of you stays behind. The others find the last key and bring her here. Then we decide next steps."

Cinq tried to keep his words calm, though his mind screamed in opposition. Even if they had the luxury of time, they had to stick together. He knew that more than anything. "We're not uniting the keys for fun. We need to unlock the Black Gate." He didn't know that last part for sure, but she didn't know that. He also knew he'd tell her anything she wanted if it got him out of this cave faster.

Nissa clapped her hands. "So… we appreciate the suggestion, but we're going to stick together anyway. Remember the deal?" She plowed ahead. "Now that that's cleared up, how big's our escort? Not you, of course, you can hide here."

Tarra stared Nissa down. "If you want to be fools on a fool's errand, I won't stop you. But I won't risk the others. Even the ancient fey make mistakes. And if you won't take my suggestion,

I need assurance. You must be willing to take steps against the witchlord using the Black Gate. Do you understand?"

"I understand. And I'm ready for that," Cinq said.

Yon nodded in agreement.

"Me too," Nissa said.

They all turned to Blue, stewing in the corner. "A suicide pact wasn't what I had in mind. But sure, I'll do what's needed. That good enough for you?"

Tarra regarded Cinq. He got the impression she wanted this stinking mage as far out of her sight as possible. She pursed her lips. "You want help? Then move quickly. Get your things and meet me at the exit. Nissa, my supplies are open to you. You have one hour. I'll explain later."

Nissa clapped her hands together. "Oooh! Mystery! Mystery! Mystery! The wikken are *soooooo* mysterious."

Tarra rolled her eyes and walked briskly from the cave. The four of them waited until the footsteps faded from earshot, each trying to read the emotions of the other.

Yon clasped Nissa's shoulder. "Are you ok? They wouldn't let us see you."

She smiled. "I'm fine. A bit banged up, but I'm fine. And, hoo-boy, have I got things to tell you."

Cinq said, "What happened, Nissa? I know you, and something happened. Is this about being back home, or something else? Did you find your fey?"

Nissa's eyes twinkled. "Yep. And it's a lot worse than we thought. You saw what happened to the otherplane? *Well...* turns out that was the Pentarch's fault. Actually, she said it was *my* fault."

Yon wrinkled his nose. "Wait. Whose fault?"

Nissa continued, "When the Pentarch pushed the worlds apart it took, like, all the magic in the otherplane. He sucked it dry; *we* sucked it dry—since we're the keys. If we tried to do the same thing again—that would be the end of the otherplane."

Blue folded her arms. "No otherplane, no Titans. Problem solved."

Nissa's voice rose sharply. "You're missing the point. You can't just destroy a *whole world*."

Blue replied, "You just said we could."

Cinq cleared his throat. "It's not a solution. Our worlds are connected, always have been. If one were to collapse—by whatever means—the other wouldn't survive. Morality or selfishness, that's *not* an option."

"So, what do we do?" Yon asked.

Nissa sighed. "We need to fix it."

"Fix *what* exactly?" Blue asked.

"I don't know! The otherplane, I guess. Or the whole vicious stealing magic cycle thing, or… Look. We didn't have time to get into specifics, and I kind of get the feeling she didn't know."

Cinq frowned. "This is usually where I say that it won't matter unless we find the fifth key."

"So, say it," Blue said.

"This time, that's not the right answer. If what Nissa said is true—which I'm not doubting—*how* we fix the problem becomes more important than when." Cinq locked eyes with Nissa. "But what about the Titans?"

She cocked her head. "What about them?"

"What do you mean, what about them? That's why we came here. We'll need four Titans to use the machine. Four. What did she say about that?"

Nissa winked. "Oh, that? That's not a problem."

Yon said, "How is that not a problem?"

"Because she said it wouldn't be. If we keep our promise, the fey will keep theirs." She shook her head. "I'm still trying to understand it all. But we need to get going, right? I'm going to say some goodbyes. We can talk on the road."

Nissa skipped away with Yon tagging along behind. Cinq stuffed the Pentarch's waterlogged book into his satchel. "All right, Blue. Let's get supplied."

* * *

An hour later, Cinq, Blue, and Yon stood at an iron gate near the mouth of the cave. At this point, a river ran the entire width of the opening, with the bars of the gate reaching down into the water as well as embedded in the ceiling. Cinq had put his worn coat back on, though he felt ridiculous to have it tucked up around his waist. His pants were hiked up, and his boots hung around his neck to keep them dry. He would be damned if he'd be traveling with wet feet.

Beside him, Yon and Blue had returned from the armory. Yon had found a woolen monastic robe like the one he wore at Open Eye, though much thicker. He'd also located a leather cuirass studded with bronze, which bound around his middle. A light armor, but more protection than nothing. He looked every bit the warrior monk, except for the hair growing on his head. Yon claimed that the northern monks kept enough up top to keep them warm. Blue had traded her garb out entirely, though the canvas pants, heavy travel cloak, and furs suited her as well as her sailor's garb. As long as her clothes had utility, Blue was at home. Maybe one day, when all this was over, he'd get to see her in a dress—if that's what she wanted.

Cinq gripped his staff. The wikken on either side of the gate regarded them with open disdain. That was likely his fault. He hadn't appreciated how much the wikken hated the mages until arriving.

A splash of footsteps caused Cinq to turn. At first, he didn't recognize her. Nissa had thrown away her worn traveling rags and now looked every part the huntress. Black leather leggings, a sleeveless top with iron plates woven throughout for protection. She resembled a wikken warrior of legend, and more like herself than she had since Ignaesdale.

Blue whistled. "Very nice, Nissa. I take it we're not blending in anymore?"

Nissa feigned surprise. "Oh? Well, this is just in case things get exciting. I got a traveling cloak, same as you." She unfurled the cloak and wrapped it around her shoulders. Nissa looked at Cinq and burst out laughing. "Cinq? Aren't you going to wear your boots?"

He looked down at his bare feet, then at Nissa wading through the river. He sighed. "There's a charm, isn't there?"

"Yup."

With a nod from Tarra, the guards opened the gate. The wikken chief passed through first with Nissa close behind. As soon as they crossed the plane, they vanished from sight. Cinq, having expected as much, followed behind. He held his breath as he broke through onto the other side.

Cinq blinked in the pale afternoon light. He stood on a pelt of soft, spongy grass. A gurgle of running water could be heard all around him. The river emerged from the mountainside several yards away. As the warm water mixed with the cool of the mountain air, fog drifted around them. In front of him, he saw the rolling hills of the northlands, and beyond that a black pillar of smoke. Gorenheim likely lay on the other side, still smoldering in the wake of the Titan's destruction. He looked back at the entrance. The enchantment made the mouth of the cave look like nothing more than a mossy wall. When Yon and Blue passed through, it rippled like water. Satisfied, Cinq sat down on the moss and put on his boots.

Nissa walked to stand beside him. She rotated her boot in front of his face to demonstrate that neither it nor she was at all wet. Cinq shrugged and continued to lace. For all he knew, the spell only worked for the wikken. Or specifically excluded mages.

Tarra stood on the edge of the cliff, her back to Cinq and the others. She pulled up the hood of her cloak. The faint green and gray blended well with the landscape. "We don't have much time before sunset. We'll need to be there by nightfall."

Cinq scrambled to his feet. He gripped his staff, feeling that once again the magic within brimmed over. Was that from being in the wikken enclave, or still something left from the otherplane? Or was it the impending Convergence?

Tarra set off, with the four of them close behind. Cinq quickly learned that the pace of a wikken in her homeland was not to be underestimated. He had to jog to keep up as they wrapped around the side of a mountain on goat paths and across fields of talus. After about twenty minutes, they rounded to the north side and entered into the shaded part of the hill. As they crested the next hillock, Tarra paused. In the valley below, the landscape changed from a grassy expanse to gray-black stone.

Cinq crouched to examine the rock. Unlike the sandstone around Ignaesdale or the granite slabs dotting the hills of Northwind, this rock had minute swirls, which snaked the surface in oblique curlicues. The slope of the hill had changed as well. The black expanse was nearly level, an unexpected plateau.

Blue traced the grooves with her finger. This is igneous, isn't it? Cooled lava. And it looks recent—in geological terms. She turned to Tarra. "Has this always been here, or was there an eruption recently?"

Tarra knelt to lay her hand on the rock. "This is the work of the Fire Titan. She brought us fire, not ice as for you. Follow me."

The wikken chief set off onto the lava field, a gradual descent as they made their way to the center. The shadows grew long against the mountains, and the gray of twilight stretched overhead. The poorer visibility made walking difficult, and all of them stumbled on the protruding ridges or misleading depressions in the rock. As they walked, the slick rock sloped further to become less of a plane and more of a funnel. Had the slope always been there? No play of light could obscure this type of depression.

They stopped at the end of the lava field where the earth dropped a dozen yards into a pit below. Tarra motioned for them to follow. She started a circumnavigation of the crater, only to step into a grooved path etched into the walls. Again, Cinq hadn't even seen the indentation before, but now observed that it spiraled around, no more than twelve inches wide, around and around to the floor of the crater. They progressed slowly, not wishing to make any misstep, and by the time they reached the bottom, the first stars had appeared overhead.

From the base of the crater, the walls around looked sheer to the point that finding the etched path once more proved difficult. More evident was that nothing was down here at all.

Nissa said, "Well, we are officially in a hole. What next?"

Tarra replied, "We wait."

Cinq fought to keep the smile from his lips as he counted the seconds. He made it to three before Nissa spoke again.

"Well… I'd ask you what we were waiting for, but I also want to know what made this hole, even though you said the Fire Titan did. But that doesn't explain why a Titan would be this far from a city in the first place."

"Just wait," Tarra grumbled.

Cinq tried to sound serious. "If you knew Nissa from before, you know she won't quit asking. So, save us all the pain."

Tarra replied, "Very well. Long before the witchlord came to Gorenheim, we heard rumors of what Madam Yanamadra had done in the north. She turned the fey into her puppets and murdered her enclave." She paused. "The wikken are not weak, mage. We have held our own for hundreds of years. But to see that kind of power… to see the fey used against us could not be ignored. We needed to be ready in case Yanamadra came for us. But if the fey could be wielded by our enemies, could we do the same?"

The four of them remained silent, waiting for Tarra to continue.

"The result was unexpected. We could call one or two fey with ease. But when we tried a greater call, a gate opened. The fey poured through from the otherplane. When they arrived, they changed, they joined to become the Fire Titan. She roared into existence and in doing so not only called for the lava that created these blackened fields but drew the life from the wikken. The Titan burned the wikken and the land. And then she was gone."

Cinq tapped his chin. "It didn't have enough to eat."

"What do you mean?" Blue asked.

"The Titans—and the fey—need magic to sustain themselves. The power of a city, thousands of people living and working together, each with emotions running hot, activity, love and hate. That's the fuel a Titan needs. When the gate opens, the Titan rushes out to gather what it can. It destroys until it simply burns itself out. Without an overlap to hold it in place, the Titans can't be sustained."

Tarra's face darkened. "And you, mage, are an expert on the fey?"

"Every day I learn more." He looked up at the rock walls. The pit was growing ever darker. He prepared his staff to act as a torch. "Now, why are we here?"

Tarra smiled thinly. "You are so wise, mage. You tell me."

Cinq paused from wrapping the rag around his staff. "If you put it that way, I'll guess. When you 'accidentally' summoned a Titan, it left a lot more behind than a hole in the ground. Some remnant of the otherplane is still here. We saw something of this in Alexandria. So, what was left behind? Or did you bring us here to prove a point?"

Nissa interrupted, "Well, I get the point. She's trying to say—without actually saying it—that she doesn't care if we succeed."

Yon said, "Huh?"

Nissa continued, "Tarra, and maybe the rest of the enclave, are ready to live in a Titans' Age. They think they can ride the wave and do just fine. This, *this,* is a subtle brag. How far off am I?"

Tarra fixed Nissa with a long, cold stare. "Perhaps I *will* welcome the Titans' Age, but that's not why we're here." She pointed at the rim of the hole. "I don't want you picked up by a reaver patrol, and I don't want you leading one to us. Now watch."

As she spoke, the hole grew darker. Cinq looked skyward to see that the stars that had appeared earlier had begun winking out. Cinq whispered to the end of his staff, which grew to a soft, white glow. The rags wrapped around it caught fire to become a torch. His breath caught in his throat.

All around, bored into the walls of the abyss, circular holes opened to tunnels. Cinq walked to the nearest tunnel. He lifted his torch to look closer.

"Careful, mage." Tarra reached down to grab a handful of the rocky volcanic earth and threw it at the nearest tunnel. When the rocks reached the opening, they accelerated, disappearing in a flash as they rocketed inside.

Blue advanced to stand beside Cinq. "It's a lapse of sorts. Are we in an overlap?"

Tarra said, "Not exactly. But you're right. Time within those tunnels barely exists. If you enter, not one minute will pass until the spell is broken."

Nissa said, "That doesn't make sense."

Tarra said, "The how is not known." She walked around the bottom of the hole, gesturing at runes that reflected the torchlight. Cinq didn't recognize the wikken script, but he could see that not all tunnels were marked. "We have explored about half of the tunnels. All are past sites of the Fire Titan. All are burned out husks of ruined cities." She stopped walking in front of one of the passages marked with a rune made up of five vertical slashes. She turned back to face them. "The Tannisong Stronghold."

Yon's eyes brightened. "That's a monastery! Master Shen trained there."

Tarra shook her head. "The monks are gone. The Fire Titan left no survivors. Since then there has been... unpleasantness with reavers. It should be empty now."

Nissa put her hands on her hips. "Should be? *Should be?* I'm going to need a bit more than—"

Tarra snapped, "You're out of time. *We're* out of time. Go."

Nissa stomped her foot. "Fine! And if we don't make it, good luck with your Titans' Age." She turned back to regard the opening. "So... any tips on using the magical zippy rock tube?"

Tarra growled. "Don't look back, and never stop running."

PART FIVE:

Convergence

41

~ Yon ~

Yon accepted the short, lit torch. He stared into the ten-foot-wide opening of the tunnel. Despite the perfectly cylindrical bore, the stone on all sides had been etched with the meandering ridges of lava rock. He had volunteered to go first, not out of bravery, but as a monk, it was his duty. He started to focus his chi when his memory of the otherplane stopped him. If he needed to, he would use that as a last resort, but not until. He crossed the threshold.

The first tentative step became a full-on run as he hurtled forward. Behind him, a great force pushed like a tailwind. Only by running—*sprinting*—through the tunnel could he avoid being caught in the tide. As he ran, the force behind him built and released, wave after wave of pressure. The torch ripped from his hand, ricocheting down the tube. But instead of leaving behind darkness, the individual embers traced through the tube in infinite streaks. Then even the embers started to fade. In a panic, Yon accelerated. He ran faster and faster, slowly overtaking the sparks as they brightened, until he saw the spinning torch itself.

Digging into hidden reserves, Yon ran faster still. His lungs burned and his muscles screamed in protest. But in the back of his mind, he knew that the slightest pause would leave him alone in the dark.

The world dimmed. The ache in his muscles diminished. Sound faded away. Though he ran, the movements felt distant, muted. Instead, Yon listened to the steady beat of his heart. The frenzy drifted from his memory until he was only dimly aware that his limbs moved at all. The dichotomy of extreme speed and languid awareness stretched on. Time passed. The approach and descent into the crater felt like weeks ago, Gorenheim an eternity. The suspension of awareness snapped away, replaced by the rush of air in his ears and the thud of his boots on stone. Yon could make out something in the distance, a white light that quickly approached.

He collided with the stone wall at a dead run, ricocheting off to collapse on a floor littered with the debris of animal bones, cracked pottery, and indistinct gravel. Yon lay still for a moment, reeling from the impact, before rolling to a seated position. His whole body ached like after an afternoon in the sparing yard. Thinking of his friends behind him, he retrieved the still-burning torch and crawled aside. He wasn't in a cave anymore. The walls—the solid walls—were of neatly mortared brick. On one side of the room stood the wall with which he had so abruptly collided. And on the other, a faint crimson glow. There were no other signs of the tunnel.

In a great blur, a second torch struck and rebounded from the wall, followed by Blue, who slammed into the brick but retained her footing. Dazed, she staggered aside to join Yon.

Next came Cinq, and finally Nissa. Each elicited an "oof" of surprise, but with the exception of minor scrapes, no one was injured.

Nissa held her head in both hands. She pushed her palms against her temples as if her skull would come apart. "I'm the last. Tarra's not coming."

"Oh." Yon's heart sank. "I hoped she'd reconsider."

Nissa released her head, though her face was still screwed up in pain. "Nope. Back into hiding for her. Good riddance. So… where are we?"

Cinq peered around, his voice low. "Looks like a dungeon." He paused. "No prisoners."

Yon grinned. "It's a root cellar. Can't you smell it? Monks aren't big on dungeons."

Cinq nodded. "Fair enough. Yon, lead the way."

Yon turned to look first one way down the corridor then the other, before setting off at a measured pace. His feet were noiseless as they tread through the thin layer of ash on the ground. He padded down the corridor of the root cellar, noting the scorch marks on the walls, likely the work of the Fire Titan. He heard no footsteps. He wondered if all the monks died in the flames, or if some survived until the reavers came.

The root cellar stretched along a long corridor, with small rooms on either side lined by rows and rows of shelves. Ash lay everywhere, disrupted only in places by piles of blackened and broken pottery. The only evidence of anyone else having been here were a few sets of footprints, though they could have been made long ago. Yon was seized by a thought that perhaps they had entered the wrong tunnel. But for all the utility of the space, a monkish hint persisted. On they continued, until reaching a narrow staircase that ascended into the dark. Yon turned to Nissa.

"Are any of the fey around?" he asked.

The wikken tilted her head to listen. "Yes…. but no one is talking to me. I can hear some murmurs, some whispers and such. But no real voices."

"Does that mean anything?"

Nissa shrugged. "Not necessarily. We're strangers. They have to warm up to us. I'll keep trying, but it might take a bit for them to answer."

Yon turned back to his ascent, grateful that the stone steps didn't creak under his weight. At the top of the steps, a heavy door appeared in the torchlight. Yon first pushed, then pulled the door to him. The charred wood groaned as he swung it just enough to peer through. Darkness. But not complete darkness. Moonlight shone through a soft covering, which a push indicated to be a tapestry. Yon turned and put a finger to his lips with a gesture for the others to stay put. He handed his torch to Nissa and slid past the curtain and into the room.

Silence and stench. Yon crouched low. He remained motionless as he strained his ears to listen for footsteps. All around, the remnants of crates lay smashed on the ground, the spoiled and moldy contents leaking out. The smell of rotting fish and rancid meat filled the pantry. Something had come in, ransacked the place, and left the remnants behind. A bear had once done the same at Open Eye, though it decided to spend the winter there in hibernation. The monks hadn't dared wake it until spring, by which time she'd become something of a mascot.

Yon poked his head back through the curtain. "I'll be back in a few minutes. Keep your ears open."

Taking care with his steps, Yon crept from the pantry and into a dining room. The exposed rafters, charred but not destroyed, curved up from the walls to connect high above him. In other places, the damage was covered by newer boards, or hanging tapestries. In the center of the room, a reaver soldier lay sprawled backward across a heavy wooden table, the shell of his armor cracked open like a crab. Dried entrails lay strewn about. Yon recoiled. His stomach twisted and bile rose in his throat. He paused, swallowed hard, and crept forward. The corpse had been deliberately arranged. Inexplicably, thick, black dirt was packed into the abdominal cavity. Panic rose within Yon. He wanted to run back to the others, but a tickling of awareness made him press on.

He put careful foot in front of careful foot. He focused so that his chi sat just at the edge of his awareness, ready at a moment's notice. He moved past the dining room and though an arched entrance into what must be the great hall. Back at Open Eye, the great hall had been small and multi-leveled due to the mountain slope. But here in Tannisong, the walls were of high stone, reinforced by enormous wooden beams, most charred, though a few looked new. The place resounded with immensity.

Yon paused. He heard a series of grunts and huffing coming from the next room. He dropped low to peer through the opening. On the other side, bodies lay everywhere. Most were dressed in the distinct armor of the northern tribes, complete with reaver insignia. He saw only soldiers—no cooks, no maids, no footmen. Either the witchlord didn't ascribe to that sort of thing, or the others had long fled. Each body had been laid in a similar fashion: armor shucked open, and innards replaced with dirt.

A creature hunched over a fallen soldier. It was massive, easily ten feet tall, and with the heavy, shaggy build of a bear. Its fur was partially white with streaks of blond and gray. Crimson smattered the beast's forearms as it continued with its work, grunting and hooting as it went. The beast pinned the corpse down with its foot and seized the plate armor with its massive hands. The claws, five inches long and translucent, pierced the armor. In a shriek of ripping metal, the breastplate parted. The beast threw the armor aside, then gingerly scooped the man's belly from his abdomen. The creature looked around for a moment before dragging a wooden crate closer. It filled the empty cavity with soil from the cart, then entrails, then more soil. It poked the top of the mound with one claw before placing something into the indentation.

The beast snapped around to stare at Yon. For the first time, he could see its face: a yeti. Large nostrils flared above a wide mouth, which the yeti opened to show rows of white, square teeth punctuated by massive canines. It growled and stood. Upright, the beast's arms were long enough to rest its knuckles on the ground. The yeti's eyes were an intense blue, like the sky in winter. It growled, the sound reverberating from the walls of the empty hall. Yon felt a stirring in the air, a disturbance in the flow of chi. The creature was focusing.

Yon's heart pounded in his chest. Still, he took a deep breath and stood. He stepped into full view. He kept his hands folded in front of him, not a stance of aggression, but one of readiness.

Slowly, deliberately, he focused his chi in the most unobtrusive way he knew. And in doing so, he could feel that the creature did the same. This wasn't just a beast.

"My name is Yon of Open Eye." He said the words slowly and clearly. "What is your name?"

The yeti responded with a howl of rage. Its jaws cracked open as it bared its teeth. It sprang forward, closing the gap between them in seconds. The creature raised one hand, chi surging through its body as it struck downward. Yon sidestepped the blow with ease. The yeti raised its other hand and then paused. In response, Yon lowered himself to the stronghold floor. He folded his hands across his lap. The yeti looked perplexed, and for a long moment seemed locked in indecision. It sank to sit across from Yon, hands folded as it mimicked the pose.

They sat across from one another, each wreathed in the thrum of chi, until the beast's eyes transformed from rage, to perplexity, to sorrow. The creature reached out with one massive paw and placed it heavily but gently on Yon's shoulder. A floodgate of emotion opened between them. Waves of regret, loss, and misery cascaded from the creature. The yeti emitted a low, keening wail, so different from the happy grunts of occupation only minutes earlier. Yon's eyes watered; tears ran down his cheeks.

The moment was interrupted by footsteps from behind them. Yon turned to see Cinq, with Nissa and Blue hovering behind him. Yon waved his friends off before turning back to the creature. The yeti reared up, but not in anger. It leaned forward, its nostrils flaring as it sniffed all of them in turn. Then the yeti huffed as it lumbered back to the body of the soldier. Yon eased to his feet.

Nissa dragged Yon close. She whispered, "What is that thing? And what is it doing?"

Yon replied, his voice low and unhurried. "It's a yeti. It's confused. I think it mixed up the reavers with the monks."

Nissa asked, "But what's it doing?"

Blue whispered, "It's a sign of respect. He's planting trees in their bodies. The saplings are to help the souls be reborn." She rolled her eyes. "You all have *got* to quit looking at me that way whenever I know things. I know things now, ok?"

Cinq cleared his throat. "Then what killed the soldiers?"

Yon walked back to where the yeti worked on the remaining corpses. When he grew near, the creature turned to face him. Yon pointed to the bodies, eliciting a grunt from the yeti.

When Yon rejoined his friends, Nissa asked, "What did he say?"

"It's hard to understand him. Maybe the other monks could, but—"

Blue interrupted, "Does it matter? Sure, intrinsically, it matters. The Fire Titan killed the monks and something else killed the reavers. The yeti is a coincidence, but it doesn't change a simple fact."

Nissa asked, "Which is?"

Blue gritted her teeth. "We shouldn't be here. Whatever it was might come back."

Cinq nodded. "I agree. We have enough fights ahead of us. Perhaps we leave this one be." He turned to the door.

As the others walked away, Yon went back to the yeti. He bid him farewell, receiving only a grunt of acknowledgment. The four of them walked from the great hall, no longer slinking through the shadows, and into the outside world.

Beyond the doors, the sky glittered with a tapestry of stars unhindered by a gleaming crescent moon. All around, the forest was a skeleton of charred sticks and burned husks of trees. Yon sighed in relief as he saw the stars and the moon's phase. They were the same as when they had entered the tube. Time hadn't slipped.

Cinq glanced at the Tracer and returned it to his pocket. He put a finger to his lips, then led them down the steps of the stronghold to continue along a road leading away from the monastery. Though only a crescent moon, the night was so clear there was no need to re-light their torches. They wound down from the mountaintop. After the monastery was well behind them, Cinq turned to step off the road. He led them along a dried creek bed, following the twists until out of sight from the road and protected on all sides by a jumble of granite boulders. He slung his pack to the ground and settled beside it.

He looked up at the others, his eyes sunken with exhaustion. His face was brushed with dirt, furrows from sweat creating tracks down from his brow. "We need rest. We're close, but we won't make it tonight."

Nissa shivered. "Can we make a fire or… No. Probably a bad idea. Never mind."

Blue settled beside Cinq. She rifled a bedroll from her pack and wrapped it around her shoulders. "Nissa, you ok?"

"Me?" The wikken looked surprised. "Why just me?"

Blue said, "The enclave. The wikken. The things they've done."

Nissa frowned. "I'm trying not to think about it. Tarra and those wikken crossed a lot of lines, a *lot* of lines. You don't just force the fey to do what you want. It's what they drill into our heads from day one."

Blue pressed. "But are you ok?"

"Yes! Yes, I'm ok. Why do you keep asking me that?"

"Because everyone needs a clear head. I'm not trying to be your mother." She lowered her voice. "And this isn't going to get easier."

Yon tried his best to smile. "Maybe not easier, but we are getting closer."

Blue scowled. "Yeah. Then we just 'fix it,' that's what the oracle told Nissa. Never mind that we're walking into a reaver camp. Never mind that they'll know we're coming if they pick up their Tracer. And never mind that we have absolutely no idea what we're doing." Her breaths were heavy, her eyes wild.

Nissa shook her head. "What about all those journals? Haven't you learned anything?"

Blue shook her head. "Nothing I haven't told you. We still need a plan."

Nissa pouted. "Well, we're not breaking the otherplane again, that's for sure."

"That's not an answer!" Blue snapped. "We need an actual, absolute plan. Right now we're just chasing ahead and following the pretty lights and hoping it all works out."

Cinq, who had been watching the exchange in silence finally spoke. "I have a plan. And Nissa's right, we can't do what the Pentarch did."

The three of them turned to look as he pulled a water-damaged book from his pocket. He peeled the pages open to a place marked with a thin piece of leather. "The machine will do anything we put our minds to, but not without a cost. We can't take too much from any one source to do what we need to do."

Yon asked, "Do what?"

Cinq snapped the book shut. "Close the gates."

Nissa replied, "Which gates?"

"*All* the gates. Every last passage between nearplane and otherplane. Every opening, every overlap, every thin place. If no one can cross, no one can steal magic from the other."

Blue protested, "No. That's not enough. What if a mage just opens another gate, or a wikken, or the fey? Anyone can if they know how. The Convergence will make it easy,"

Cinq gripped his staff with both hands. "Then we'll just have to make it harder. Reinforce the boundary or something. There has to be a way."

Yon felt a twist in his stomach. He barely whispered. "There's the witchlord's way."

"What?" Nissa spun to face him.

"If there weren't magic users, no one could open gates," Yon said. "I'm not saying kill anyone, but what if we changed people… a little. Or made them forget what they can do."

Blue shook her head. "There's still the fey. I don't think they'd live without magic… unless that's part of the plan."

Cinq said, "Well, it's all I have for now. You come up with something better, let us know. Now, if you don't mind, I need to sleep."

Yon bit his lip. "I have another idea. What if instead of closing the gates we opened them? If we shared our magic with the otherplane, they wouldn't have to take it. The fey wouldn't need to become Titans. Think about the yeti."

Nissa said, "You lost me, kiddo."

Yon replied, "Not the one yeti, all the yeti. They came from the otherplane, then they changed. They became *real*. They have families, lives. They eat fish and live in caves and sleep and talk and build and other things. They aren't just of the nearplane or just of the otherplane. Maybe more of us could be like that."

Cinq said, "Well, we've got two days to decide, maybe less. Time is running out."

42

~ Nissa ~

Nissa awoke to the dull murmur of the fey. She rolled over and untangled herself from her blanket. The morning was cool, damp with mountain air and the promise of blue skies above. In the distance, sunlight painted the top of the mountains before progressing down the slopes and to the valley below. A few feet away, Nissa saw the rumpled forms of Blue and Yon sleeping. Cinq, technically on morning watch, was nowhere to be seen.

The whispers of the fey tickled her awareness again. She rose slowly, trying to discern the source. She pulled on her boots and crept away from the camp. After a few yards, she noticed an imp-like creature seated cross-legged atop a rock, watching the sleeping party. The fey's skin was the same pale blue as the morning sky, with sage-colored eyes and gossamer hair. Her form was humanoid from her ears to the tips of her fingers and toes. She held something in her hands that she kept turning over and over again. A kind of nut, perhaps, or maybe an interesting pebble.

"Hiya," Nissa chirped. "Is this your mountain?"

The fey looked up, cocked its head, and launched into a series of high-pitched chirps, tweets, and whistles. She wanted to know why Nissa and her friends weren't on the road. The big people were *always* on the road. They didn't like to leave the road. And now they were here. Were they building a new road? What was wrong with the old road? Did it not smell good anymore? Wouldn't they rather go back?

Nissa nodded with interest. She made no effort to pry information, nor pretend to be anything she wasn't. Nissa wished she got to converse like this more often. She longed to go back to a relationship of happy coexistence, not dire circumstance. The daydream was interrupted by a singular crack, like a pulse of thunder. The fey sprang to her feet, her eyes filled with terror. A shriek ripped through Nissa's mind. The scream was both a cry for help, and something far greater.

The fey was gone. Not run away, but fled to a different shape in a different place. Nissa heard another shriek. Another cry of pain from another fey, then more and more, until the hills wailed in agony. Fey after fey, cry after cry, until the anguish was replaced by silence.

"Nissa!"

She twisted to see Cinq sprinting at her. He threw aside a bundle of plants in his arms to come to her side.

"What is it? Are you ok?" He held her shoulders tight in both hands, even as her body shook in fear. Yon and Blue were awake as well, both on their feet, eyes darting around, looking for the source of the problem. Cinq said, "You were screaming. Are you ok? A dream? Or something real?"

Nissa shook. The fey's pain reverberated through her mind. She rubbed her temples. "Real. I… I think it's real. Maybe a dream, or… The fey are scared. Something's happening."

Blue had drawn her cleaver. "Did something follow us?"

"No." Nissa shook her head. "It's not from the monastery; it's from that way." She pointed in the direction where the noise had originated, or more accurately where the feeling of danger loomed largest. Cinq pulled the Tracer from his pocket and glanced down. He didn't need to say what he saw. They all knew where they were going, straight into the storm. He cleared his throat. "We're almost to the Expanse. Is it coming from there?"

Nissa fought to breathe, to calm herself. "I don't know. They're quiet now." She swallowed. "I'm afraid of what's happening."

Cinq handed her his water skin, and Nissa took a few tentative sips. As the others watched, the mage backtracked to claim his bundle of foraged plants. He pressed pieces of roots, nuts, and small hard fruit into each of their hands. Nissa ate mechanically, though she had no appetite.

When at last they returned to the road, the night's sleep seemed only a memory. They set out once more. Nissa paced a dozen yards ahead of the others to listen, and not frighten off any nearby fey. They walked, dropping from high-alpine bushes, to blanched aspen forests, down into the thick green pines. The land grew hotter and drier as the landscape shifted into scrublands dotted with juniper and sage. Even here, the charred remnants of burned trees and bushes remained, though much had been replaced with new growth. The wilderness had claimed the land once more.

Nissa heard a distant pattering and stopped. She placed one hand upon the ground. The reverberation told her what she suspected. She dashed back to the others and motioned for them to follow her off the road until they reached a natural ditch. They hunched out of sight and waited. Moments later, the sound of horses, accompanied by frenzied shouting, first thundered near and then diminished to nothing. A cloud of dust rose from the road to hang in the air.

"You think they're looking for us?" Yon whispered.

Cinq replied, "Not us."

Nissa said, "So do we wait longer or…?"

Cinq shook his head. "No. Absolutely not. We have to move while we can. We'll stay just off the road, in case we need to hide again."

The pit in Nissa's belly remained. Sometimes, when the world was at its most hostile, the best thing to do was to charge ahead. "So… is anyone up for a run? I don't like not being able to see what's coming. Follow me."

Nissa made her way until the road was just in sight. Keeping it in the corner of her eye, she started out over the scrub, weaving through bushes and threading around trees. Her brisk walk became faster until she ran just as quickly through the wild as she had on the road. Every so often she would glance behind her to see Blue in her work gear and, more comically, Cinq with his long coat behind him and staff held upright to bat away branches. And then, the wilderness ended.

Before her lay the Expanse. Even after the snow-covered reaches of the Rendezvous and the dreamscape of the otherplane, something about the sea of pale sand disturbed her.

The landscape stood uninterrupted except for ridges formed by the coursing winds, and enormous spears of rock, which stuck out like the ribs of a long-dead animal. Nissa turned to where the mountain rose from the Expanse, the range running north and south as far as the eye could see, but in front of her—nothing. If they took another step, there'd be nowhere to hide, and no fey to warn her. Not a single voice whispered at her from the sands.

Terror crept over her, starting at the pit of her stomach and radiating up and out as her mind registered what stood in the distance. Three enormous shapes moved across the wastelands: distant, colossal. The first was like a mountain, hewn of stone swirled by cascading sand. One leg was amalgamated by boulders, the other made from chunks of granite that looked like gravel due to its size. The torso was mixed with rock, stones, and even sand, with trees bristling from its back. The Earth Titan.

The second entity reflected the pale blue of ice: hard angles and jutting shards. It glistened, softer and smoother than the one at Gorenheim, perhaps as it melted and froze again in the desert sun. A cloak of mist rolled around it. One arm and one massive leg were a fully liquid state, sloshing on one side, while churning like the breakwater of the ocean on the other. As for the other arm, it bristled with countless icicles that cut long grooves in the sand as it passed. The Water Titan.

The third shape frightened Nissa most of all. It was black in parts while smoldering in others. The surface drifted like pulsing embers, which in turn glowed or radiated flames. It drifted in color and intensity from red to orange to blue-hot, and even a dull umber hardly visible in the morning sun. Where the colossus tread, the ground froze, leaving behind snow and packed ice with every footprint. The Fire Titan.

Nissa heard the others walk up behind her. Soon all four of them gawked at the three Titans as they patrolled the Expanse. Nissa fought for words, but the enormity of the forces was too much to absorb. She stumbled, dropped to one knee, and vomited onto the parched ground. The taste of bile in her mouth and working through her nasal passages helped ground her.

Cinq helped Nissa back to her feet. He forced a smile as he wiped her mouth with the sleeve of his coat. He said, "On the bright side—if there is a bright side—I'll bet the reavers are distracted. And it seems the fey came as they promised. Only one to go." In a gesture that had become ritual, Cinq pulled the Tracer from his pocket and held it aloft. All five lights shone brightly, with only one a hint dimmer, and tracking straight into the Expanse.

Blue plucked the Tracer from Cinq's hand. She appeared to be choosing her words. "Two questions. First: Do you think the Titans are here because of us?"

Nissa winced. Her mouth was sour and wretched. "They have to be, right? The oracle predicted this—or maybe she promised it. The machine, the Convergence, us, *everything*. It's all happening."

Blue nodded. "Ok, ok. Second question: Are you *serious!?* Are you serious right now?" Blue asked in disbelief. "Look. Look out there! There are three *Titans* out there. Three! This isn't a matter of little bits of chance and theory and guessing. We are running into the center of the apocalypse, and we still don't have a plan. And before you interrupt, Cinq and Yon had *ideas* at best.

But it's plan time. What about the hermit? What about the reavers? Am I the only one that feels like our plan should have a few more steps?"

Nissa was stunned to silence.

Blue continued, "And look at Yon."

Nissa turned to see the young monk's eyes wide and unblinking. His eyes flitted back and forth from Titan to Titan.

"See?" Blue said. "He's not ok. None of this is ok."

Cinq gripped his staff with both hands. "Are you done?"

"Am I done? No. I'm not done. Are you done? We're all done."

Nissa braced herself for another onslaught but was surprised to hear Yon speak in a quiet voice, like someone forcing calm over themselves when they clearly didn't feel it.

"It's still the same plan," Yon stated.

Blue snapped, "What is?"

"We have to get to the hermit. And we will." He paused for a moment to take two shallow breaths. "The Titans don't care about us, not yet. We aren't important until the five of us are together."

Blue closed her eyes so tightly that her nose and temples furrowed. She sighed and opened them again. "Fine. You want me to buckle down and do my job? That's what I do best." She held up the Tracer in one hand and the compass in the other. "One thing at a time, so just ignore the primal forces of nature for a bit and let's be grounded. Does everyone see over by that first dune? See those rocks? That's the reavers' road. Those cairns must mark the way to the camp. If any reavers are stupid enough to be out here, that's where we'll find them."

Cinq said, "Is that a possibility?"

"Yes," Blue stated, "If we're stupid enough to go to the Titans, at least some reavers will be smart enough to run away. We'll have to go around." She paused, her eyes challenging. "If it's any consolation, as long as we have our Tracer, we can't get lost."

Yon asked, "And if a Titan gets near?"

"We run," Blue finished.

Nissa ventured, "Ok… but what if those cairns aren't just a path? Maybe they are about staying away from dangerous stuff that we don't even know about."

Blue said, "It can't be more dangerous than *that*. Any real concerns? Do we vote? That worked out so well last time." She rolled her eyes.

No one spoke. No one needed to.

They set out. With the first step, Nissa knew the travel would be difficult, each footfall an effort. Blue took the lead. She navigated with both Tracer and compass, sighting from dune to dune or between wind-sheared rocks. At first, the sun shone bright overhead. This far north, the heat was tolerable, but the intensity was still draining. And the specter of the Titans never ended. Usually, when a Titan appeared, it existed for only a few minutes. But these weren't going anywhere, except in their plodding circuit. Cinq proposed that there was a pattern to the movement, as steady as the stars and planets. Nissa wasn't convinced.

As afternoon set in, and the Titans grew close, they stopped at a jutting rock that offered a hint of shelter. The stone protruded at a stark angle from the ground, and they huddled on the far side from the Titans. Even so, their presence was unshakable. The reverberations from the Earth Titan's plodding gait were one part, but nothing compared to the spiritual buzzing around her.

After a few minutes, Yon scrambled to the top of the jutting ledge. "Hey! I can see the camp," he exclaimed.

Nissa climbed up after him, followed by the others. From atop the rock, she saw the last few miles of the salt flat. In the middle, a small forest of tents clustered in concentric rings around a large one. Between them and the camp lay the unerring path of the Titans. Cinq had been right. They weren't just wandering, they followed three defined routes. Each of the paths was distinct, whether packed sand from the Earth Titan, darkened mud from the Water Titan, or the frost left behind by the Fire Titan.

Cinq said, "At least they're consistent. Maybe we can time it right."

Nissa clicked her tongue. "So what? We make a run for it? Out of the fire and into yet another, smaller, angrier, and more vindictive fire?"

Cinq cleared his throat. "Or one of us could scout ahead."

Nissa nearly choked. "What happened to 'staying together and stronger together'? Now you want to split up?"

Cinq lowered his voice. "We don't really know what's over there."

"Yes, we do," Nissa countered. "Elemental terrors, unfriendly reavers, and Key Number Five."

Yon said, "We don't know for sure that—"

Cinq said, "That's my point. Blue's been saying it all along. We can't go in blind."

Nissa sighed. "Fine. I'll go ahead. Yon had the last turn."

Cinq shook his head. His face was twisted in pain. "No, I'll go. And I'm not going on foot."

43

~ Cinq ~

Cinq perched on top of the angled monolith. The topmost slope had been weathered by the relentless barrage of sand and wind to be ever-so-slightly rounded. The gradual leveling created a perfect vantage point for him to gaze across the desert. The wind had died down in the late evening, and the sliver of moon did little to interrupt the sea of stars overhead. Cinq looked up, absorbing the immensity of the sky. He looked across the sands at the flicker of campfires from the camp a few miles away. No one had ventured out since they arrived, no one dared.

The Earth, Water, and Fire Titans continued in their elliptical orbits. Even in the moonlight, the Water and Earth Titans were more easily heard than seen. The Fire Titan, however, burned dull and red as the coals of a campfire. Cinq felt the Titans pulling at the magic all around them as steadily as the moon pulls against the sea.

On the far side of the slab, Blue watched for Titans and reavers alike. They had rotated who was awake until now, and the time had come for her to take over. Cinq, however, had no intention of sleeping. He grabbed his staff and laid it flat across his knees. The polished wood thrummed with power. The quantity of magic was in greater abundance than Cinq had experienced in his whole life. Was this from the Convergence, the Titans, or the Black Gate itself? Nevertheless, after years of conservatism, he still hesitated to use magic unless necessary.

Cinq steeled himself. Was he conservative, or just afraid? He shook his head. There was no time to second-guess himself. A year ago, he wouldn't have dreamt of attempting this kind of magic. But recently, the most complex spells seemed simple. Time to find out for sure. He gripped the staff with both hands, holding it level with the ground. He felt the desert breeze against his skin, smelled the arid burn of the sands, and heard the beating of his own heart. One, two, three. He released the spell—

And walked barefoot across the sands. Cinq looked down, but of course his feet weren't there, so there was nothing to see. He held up his hands, but his hands, too, were still holding and drawing power from the staff on top of the rock. He pushed the idea from his mind. To concentrate on his lack of body would never help the projection. But recognizing that limits didn't apply could be useful. He quickened his pace, not his footsteps, but instead the movement of his mind through the ether. He sailed forward, threading in a matter of seconds between the gap of Earth and Fire Titans. When he reached the edge of the camp, he stopped. Cinq tried to blink, to force his eyes to focus on a world that was less than sharp at the edges. There were no fences here, no towers, nothing marking the perimeter. Instead, soldiers' tents dotted the area in orderly blocks of four.

Cinq drifted around. While most of the camp must be dozing, a few reavers meandered along the corridors. Some were on patrol, while others had the aimless stride of the sleepwalking or drunk. Cinq glided on, past the barracks to the epicenter of the camp. There, a large white tent stood apart from the others. Massive poles ringed it on all sides, staked down by ropes as thick as his arm. At the front of the tent, two pairs of guards stood on opposite sides of the doorway.

He glided closer to look inside, then stopped short. At the edge of the tent, the ground shifted. Where the sand beneath him looked normal, here it was different. The pale-yellow sand, the red splashes on the soldiers' armor, and even the banner of the witchlord were colorless. He watched in fascination as the guards paced around the tent, occasionally passing through that barrier only to see their color fade and appear once more. Cinq reached out with his mind to feel the ebb and flow of magic in the world. Just beyond that line, magic simply *wasn't*. A void. If he tried to cross, his astral projection would fail, or worse. Was the void in place to protect something, or to contain it?

Discouraged but intrigued, Cinq continued his search. He journeyed a full circuit around the camp, passing through several of the soldiers' tents. He wasn't afraid he'd be sensed, as anyone trained to do so would likely have been purged as a witch. And while he listened, the conversations were universally mundane. Cinq decided on another angle. There had to be more to this place. Where was the hermit? Or was he, as Nissa suggested, an unsuspecting reaver? Back and forth, back and forth, Cinq cut the camp in a grid. He studied which tents looked occupied and which were empty. He located weapons caches and the kitchens.

On his third cut through camp, something beyond the ring caught his eye.

Weary of sleeping soldiers, Cinq left the camp to examine the hovel. Four simple walls and a flat roof, it bore no remarkable feature other than its solitude. Cinq passed through the entry and was surprised to see a man cross-legged on the floor, hands folded in his lap. The man looked ancient, with scars running down both of his arms, a shaved head, and face covered in gray stubble. He looked directly at Cinq and nodded.

The man spoke in a gravelly, penetrating voice. "If you are to enter without knocking, spirit, state your reasons."

Cinq remained frozen. He did not speak, did not move.

The man smiled thinly. "Don't be surprised. I'm not here either. But this is my home, so I come back when I can. If only like this." To illustrate, the man passed his hand through a nearby stool. His skin parted like mist to reform on the other side.

"Can you see me?" Cinq asked. "Can you hear me?"

"There's nothing real of you to see, but I can hear well enough. Astral projection. Clever, exhausting, risky. You're not a wikken—too male for that. And you don't sound like one of Isil's protégés. A word of advice, there. Cain has mages amongst his followers. Careful where you walk. You are more fragile in that state than you know."

Cinq watched the old man. If he had a body, he would have been pacing. "Who are you? Where are you?"

"Where is easy, but that is two questions, not one. This 'where' is my home and has been for a long time. The other 'where' is not far away. I'm sleeping in my prison. They keep me there inside the void, but my mind still wanders. I don't need magic for a dream such as this."

"You're… dreaming?"

"In a sense. My body sleeps, my mind is not weary, and my soul never tires. I wander. I followed you, thinking you were a ghost. But most ghosts don't set to cross an army camp in perfect right angles and grid patterns as the tower-trained would. Lucky for me you came here, where I am familiar enough to speak."

"You didn't say who you were," Cinq stated.

"And you haven't introduced yourself either, Cinq LeGarrec of Eastwind Tower. But it doesn't take much imagination."

Cinq's ears burned and alarm shot through his body.

"No reply. That's all right. I didn't need one. What I do need is to be free of my prison."

Cinq hesitated. "You know me. But I don't know you."

The man's thin smile widened. "You don't know me? What a hateful thing to say. As far as I can tell, you've spent your whole life looking for me."

The tumblers clicked. "You're the hermit. You're the fifth key."

The man shrugged. "Fifth? Certainly not. I am the first. I'm only the fifth of *your* biography, of *your* collection." The man's voice turned grave. "Listen closely, Journeyman LeGarrec, as our time is short. We have much to discuss, but we can't speak meaningfully while I am captive." The man stared ahead. The effect unsettled Cinq as he knew he was trying to stare at him, but the man's eyes did not meet his own. The effect made the man look blind. "You've seen the Titans?"

Cinq nearly choked. "They're hard to miss."

The hermit continued, "Tomorrow morning, after sunrise, the last will join. That will be your chance. Come to the excavation site. Get in however you can. I'll be waiting. And one more thing." The man lifted his wrists to show thick manacles and chains. "Bring something to cut these. Something real. The tent is—"

"In a void, I saw."

The hermit smiled. "At least you're observant. I'd hate to think less of you." The man's eyes crinkled. "Don't wait too long. You won't get a better chance."

Cinq's pulse quickened. He felt certain, but he still had to ask. "It *is* here, isn't it? The Pentarch's machine?"

The hermit nodded. "Of course. And I've been waiting a long, long time. Don't make me wait longer."

"And do you—" Cinq began, but the man had blinked out of view.

Cinq cursed himself for not acting faster. A thought crept through his head. If the hermit could cross the void, why couldn't he? No longer bothering with the illusion of walking, Cinq turned and projected his mind across the gap between hovel and camp until he stood in front of the central tent once more, in front of the void. If this worked, they'd finally have answers.

Tentatively, he held up his hands, hovering just above the barrier where color washed to gray. He reached forward and was sent hurtling back into the Expanse.

44

~ Cinq ~

Cinq's eyes snapped open. He had returned to his body, now stiff from sitting for so long. Night was fading into dawn as an amber glow lit the eastern sky. Sunrise would come quickly. They needed to get moving.

He looked down at his hands. His knuckles ached, blood trickled from his palms. With great effort, he willed his hands to relax their grip. He extended his fingers and stared numbly at the welts. The void had burned him, not just sent him home. Cinq placed one finger tentatively on his staff. The wood no longer pulsed with magic. Gone, exhausted, and yet steadily refilling from the throb of energy all around.

Cinq unfolded himself and descended to where Blue waited next to his sleeping companions. He kept his fingers crooked so that he could carry his staff while avoiding the painful contact with his palms.

Blue looked up. "Did it work? Your spirit-walk, or whatever you call it?"

Cinq nodded. "Enlightening, though not without its effects." He extended his hands to show his wounds. "Some places I just couldn't go."

Blue clicked her tongue. "I'll wake the others."

"Thank you."

Blue roused Yon and Nissa, who were still groggy from having their sleep cut short. When they were all up, Cinq detailed what he'd seen: the camp, the soldiers, and the hermit. When he finished, he looked at the three of them. He felt exhaustion weighing down on his shoulders.

Yon asked, "Anything else?"

"The hermit—" Cinq began.

"I don't trust him," Nissa declared. "I mean, I wasn't exactly there, but I get itchies thinking about him."

Blue set her jaw. "It's way, way past time to quit now."

Yon asked, "Do you think it's a trap? Maybe that's why they quit chasing us."

Cinq winced. "I doubt they quit. But that's not to say they're not waiting. And something tells me that old man wasn't lying about being trapped. It's just that..."

Nissa said, "What, Cinq? What? We're all probably about to die anyway, so what's so important now?"

Frustration billowed inside him. "He looks like me," Cinq blurted. "And Yon, and Nissa, and even Elizabeth. Our eyes are the same, our build is the same. It's like I was looking at myself sixty years from now. Or maybe a hundred."

Blue looked back at him. Her eyes were cold, but not with criticism. She was working on the puzzle.

Cinq continued, "I noticed our similarities before, but I just thought it was a coincidence. Or that the people who were keys all came from the same place or were related. Then I go back to this." He pulled the journal from his pocket. "The last thing the Pentarch wrote, the *last* thing, was that he wished he'd never made the lockspell. He wished he'd kept control as he couldn't trust anyone else. There was too much at stake."

Blue eyes widened. She clucked her tongue. "I see where this is going."

Nissa exclaimed, "Well, I don't. Where are you going?"

"Maybe," Cinq grimaced, "maybe he did it all. He made the locks, he made the keys, he made it so keys could pass from person to person, and he even made the Tracers. He did everything he told the others he would do. But in the end, he still kept that control. And I think I know how." He closed his eyes and exhaled. "I think he split himself."

"Exactly," Blue stated.

Nissa shook her head. "I'm sorry, he what?"

Cinq tapped the ground with his staff. "Think about it. He didn't trust anyone else to do what he planned to do—to destroy one world to save another. But he'd made the machine so it took five masters—five keys—to operate. But he was a Pentarch. He was five masters all by himself. So, he divided himself, body and mind, into five separate people, one from each discipline. He took the place of the keys—the place of *all five* keys. And when he was done, he threw himself—*us*—forward in time. So, at the next Convergence, he could do it all over again."

Nissa folded her arms. "Um, except—assuming this isn't complete bullcrap—we couldn't even remember who we were, let alone follow through some master plan."

Cinq shrugged. "Well, maybe that was the plan. Maybe we weren't supposed to know until we were ready."

Yon opened his mouth, closed it, and opened it again. "Well… this is kind of good news. If we're bits of the Pentarch, and so is the hermit, maybe he's like us. He's bound to be on our side."

Nissa bit her lip. "Maybe, maybe. But can we go back to where we are *chunks of the Pentarch!* Because I am not—not, not, not, not, not—just taking that as a given. I'm a girl!"

Blue deadpanned, "One day, Nissa, I'll explain chromosomes. But if you need convincing, remember the Pentarch's tomb? All of you could go in except me. Remember how that shifty mage said it was warded against anyone but the Pentarch himself? And one other thing—"

Nissa rolled her eyes. "For the love of god, if I hear one more 'one other thing' my eyes are going to explode out of my head."

Blue waited.

"Well?"

Blue continued, "Want something more? I remember doing it. Just bits and flashes. But I remember making the choice, laying the spell, and going through with it. It's not clear, but I remember it in the same way I have snippets of Elizabeth's memory. And I don't think Cinq figured this out either, no offense. Your mind just finally got around to remembering what it knew all along. I don't know why it's faster for me. Maybe it's because I'm a new key, and you have been so all along. But it doesn't matter. We need to quit whining and think about—"

Blue's words faded to nothing as a thunderous roar rose behind them. Cinq snapped around, only to be hit by a gust of wind and the sting of airborne sand. The desert between them and the camp buckled upward, while at the same time the clouds above twisted and funneled down. Two spiraling tendrils, one of sand and one of sky, connected, then billowed, then grew. The tornado thickened as faces, limbs, howling mouths, and grasping arms lurched out from the roiling clouds even as they disappeared back within. Cinq squinted his eyes against the gale. His stomach dropped. The Wind Titan had arrived.

The Titan, though lacking a defined body, leaned back to howl into the sky. The action caused the three other Titans to turn and look. The wind picked up once more. In great waves, gales pulsed from where the Wind Titan stood, kicking up the desert surface in an enormous sandstorm.

"Take cover!" Blue yelled.

"No." Cinq shook his head. "This is it. This is our chance."

Sand howled across the desert. The temperature dropped; the air pulsed with heaviness. When the next wave hit, Cinq was nearly knocked over. He stumbled closer to the others to not lose sight of them. Soon all direction had been lost. They clung to one another in the formless void, scrambling to cover their eyes, ears, and mouths with strips of cloth. Cinq removed the Tracer from his pocket. He took the first step forward. Once again, he relied on his lodestar.

Step after step, he fought to maintain his course as the wind whipped crosswise. Cinq gripped his hat in one hand, and in the other, held one end of his staff while his friends grabbed it as well to keep themselves together. By the time they reached the camp, sand had filled his pockets, worked into his ears, and underneath his clothes. Fortunately, however, they encountered no guards. Cinq stopped at the camp's edge, searching for familiarity, but he recognized very little. He needed to collect his thoughts. He saw a small tent with a door tied shut from the outside. Hopefully, that meant no one was within. He led the way to the tent and ducked inside.

Within, the howl of the wind was replaced by the oppressive flapping of the canvas. The sides of the tent reverberated as wave after wave of sand pummeled them like a roaring waterfall. Cinq shook his coat to dislodge more of the sand and surveyed their temporary shelter. They were in a warehouse of sorts, with stacks of neatly lined wooden crates around the perimeter and in tight rows within. Using his knife as a pry bar, he opened one of the nearby crates and nodded to the others to do the same.

"Good scouting, Cinq," Blue exclaimed. She whipped the lid open to reveal helmets, tunics, and the leather armor common among conscripted men. Blue's grin said more than her words. With these, they could masquerade as reavers. The cheap garb may not provide much physical protection, but it should work as camouflage.

Blue passed the gear around and the four of them were soon dressed. Cinq rolled up his hat and tucked it into his coat. He covered himself in a tunic with a leather breastplate. He looked down. In another life, he could have been a soldier. He'd already been everything else. He strapped on a helmet, securing the chinstrap before wrapping his face again in cloth to protect against the windstorm. Cinq tapped on Yon's shoulder to get his attention over the howling wind. "How do I look?" He kept his voice just loud enough to be heard without shouting.

Yon replied with a smile and a thumbs-up. Then his face, too, disappeared in cloth.

Cinq pointed at Nissa. "You need to cover your legs."

"I'm wearing pants," she countered.

"What?"

Nissa spoke a little louder, "I said I'm wearing pants."

Cinq shook his head. "You're wearing skin-tight wikken leather. Cover it up. We don't want anyone looking too closely."

To his surprise, she acquiesced. Perhaps she wasn't interested in a fight or just couldn't hear him. But in another minute, the four of them looked like fresh recruits to the witchlord's cause. His gut clenched. He'd been so focused for so long, he hadn't allowed himself time to think. But now, he felt about to step off the precipice. His voice cracked. "Is everyone ready?"

Yon said, "I think the wind is slacking a bit."

That wasn't what he asked. But maybe that was all the answer he'd receive. Maybe readiness didn't matter. Plus, Yon was right. The flap of the tent had diminished, but whether constancy in a maelstrom was impossible or the Wind Titan was about to make another pass, Cinq didn't know. At least now they could hear each other.

Blue asked, "What about your staff?"

In response, Cinq lined up two crates held closed by a leather strap. He ran his mage's staff beneath the strap and tugged it upward. Yon responded immediately to grab the other end. Not only did the staff look like any other stick used to haul goods, but perhaps this would give a little more cover. Blue shrugged, less impressed.

Nissa said, "In case they see through us, any last words?"

Cinq nodded. "Only one thing. It's been an honor."

Nissa tackled him with a hug. She squeezed him tight and kissed his cheek through the face wrapping. "Right back at you, you skinny, weird, clone-twin-whatever-you-are." She turned to the others. "That goes for everyone."

Blue walked to the entrance and untied the flaps. She held the door aside while Cinq and Yon filed through holding the staff and crates. Once outside again, the wind surged and ebbed, sometimes settling, sometimes threatening to rip their burden away. Nissa and Blue joined them, holding the staff so that the four of them looked like pallbearers. They wove through the tent corridors and to the center of the camp.

Cold surged through Cinq's body. He took a sharp breath and cursed as he passed into the void. The presence of magic snapped away. No magic, no chi, no whisper of the fey. He felt alone, empty. He darted a glance at the others as they all gave a collective stumble, turning to meet his gaze. He nodded, and they started forward once more.

The flaps of the large tent parted as they approached to reveal that, despite the lack of guards patrolling outside, they had been watched closely. Six guards stood around them, armed with swords, clubs, and hand-axes.

One of the reavers spoke. His thick northern accent combined the guttural tone of a tribesman with the brogue of the working class. "Oy. You're dead crazy to be out in this shite."

Cinq pulled down his facemask to spit on the ground. He tried his best to match the tenor and tone of the soldier. "Think this is my idea? Think I chose it?" He hesitated for only a moment before continuing. "We're here for a sampling."

The soldiers exchanged skeptical glances. "Really?"

Cinq shrugged. "I didn't question it." He tried his best to look bored.

The soldier grunted and beckoned with one hand. He pointed to an opening in the center of the room. "You new here? You know how to use the winch?"

Blue walked up to the apparatus of buckets, winches, and pulleys just behind the reavers. She grabbed the first of the two crates and placed them into the open contraption, while Nissa and Yon worked together to position the second.

Blue said in a deep, gravelly voice. "You two, get down there and catch."

Cinq snagged his staff and took his first step to the ladder when he heard movement behind him.

"Wait."

He turned, trying his best to look not only calm, but slightly bored. His jaw clenched as he saw a glowing object in the reaver's hand. The soldier held a sphere between his thumb and forefinger. It was a miniature Tracer.

"It's them!"

Cinq moved first. He grabbed his staff with both hands and swung around with all his might. The reaver started to duck, but he didn't move fast enough before the engraved wood cracked solidly against his temple. As the man dropped, the other reavers scrambled to pull their weapons. Yon, Nissa, and Blue were in motion. A throwing knife from Nissa struck the second reaver, and he doubled over in pain, allowing Cinq to move in and attack with his staff again. As he did so, Yon closed the gap with the next two reavers. He lashed out with a crescent kick to the nearest one, followed by an elbow, fist, then knee. Blue was more direct. She swung her cleaver, once, twice, three times, disabling and felling the remaining soldiers. In a matter of moments, the reavers lay incapacitated.

The attack left Cinq wide-eyed and breathing heavy. He'd known exactly what to do. He'd never used his staff to strike a person in his life, and yet he knew exactly what to do. His disbelief gave way to panic. "What now?" He looked at the fallen and bleeding bodies. "Can we hide them?"

"No time," Blue barked. She darted to the ladder and grabbed the outside supports. She slid down without using the rungs.

They scrambled to follow her to the chamber below. When Cinq's boots hit the sandy bottom, he turned in circles, looking for where to go. The underground chamber stretched twelve feet tall, and because it was wide, the ceiling felt low. Arches of interlocked hexagonal stones fanned in all directions. A few had shovels, buckets, or other equipment piled in them, while others opened to rooms still filled with sand. In the center of the chamber, the winch and pulley system connected to the opening above. Nothing stirred. No reavers, no workers, no one who might have heard the scuffle. Was this due to the sandstorm? The Titans? Or was it too early for the work crews to arrive?

Nissa propped her hands on her hips. "Which way? Clock's ticking."

Cinq glanced at his Tracer. The fifth light pointed to the smallest door at the far end of the chamber and, for a moment, he wondered how it worked within the void. He gripped his staff, holding it ready to swing, and walked forward. As they passed through the entrance, the corridor sloped down. With the first step inside, a rusty smell filled his nostrils. He moved closer, step by tentative step, until reaching a room with an iron ring bolted into the center. A rusted chain led from the anchor to a seated man dressed in rags. He had a shaved head, gray stubble across his face, and arms covered in scars reminiscent of wikken runes. Around the man, three soldiers lay in crumpled piles, their necks and limbs at impossible angles. The captive looked up from his task of hacking at his chain with a knife. He grinned at his visitors with ivory teeth. He stood, folded his hands, and bowed deeply.

The prisoner said, "And then there were five." He looked up to meet their eyes. "I've been waiting so long." He looked around. "Cinq LeGarrec, Nissa al'Cedar, Yon of Open Eye, and... Where is Dr. Yimini? Where is the scholar?" He craned his neck to look behind them.

Blue replied, "How about you introduce yourself first? Then we'll talk."

The old man cocked his head. "Here, I'm called Ezekiel. To you, I'm the hermit." He peered at Blue. "And *you* have taken the scholar's burden. Good to see that it actually worked." Ezekiel looked her directly in the eye. "I know you have questions. I have answers, though perhaps not as many as you'd like." He glanced around. "But we must move quickly. The guard change will come soon, and we'll be discovered." He held up his chain. "Can you get me free?"

Cinq looked down at the metal band. "Blue, any thoughts?"

She looked from Cinq back to Ezekiel. "Sure. Here's a thought. We've got a strange man, old as time—maybe older—chained underground to the floor, surrounded by bodies, in a place where you can't use magic. They call this a red flag."

Ezekiel's eyes flashed. "I'm here because Mortimer Cain knows what I am, just as he knows about all of you. He doesn't want that machine started. He's afraid of what it can do. What *we* can do."

Blue replied, "Why didn't he kill you? Take out a key and problem solved."

Ezekiel said, "Keys cannot be destroyed, only passed." He lowered his voice. "Mortimer would prefer me kept. To him, I am known. But we must be in place before it starts. The Black Gate awaits."

Cinq nodded to Blue. She hesitated, then retrieved a metal club from one of the fallen soldiers. She threaded the weapon through one of the chain links and wrenched the handle. The link snapped in two.

"Leverage," Blue murmured. "Well, go on. Lead the way."

The hermit's eyes flashed in victory. He reached down to pick up the chain so that it didn't drag on the ground. He walked quickly past them, his bare feet padding on the sandy stones. When they returned to the entry hall, the hermit peered around the corner before hustling forward once more. He passed through the tallest doorway, plucking a torch from the wall as he entered. Cinq and Nissa followed his lead with Blue electing to keep her hands free.

Ezekiel paced down the corridor until it terminated in a solid wall etched with a great seal. A picture of a dragon with five heads occupied the center, an elegant script formed an inscription around it.

Cinq asked, "What's it say, Blue?"

She replied, "'Through fraternity, security. Tremble and consider the power within.' Promising."

Ezekiel crept forward. He caressed the seal with his hands. "Three hundred years of waiting. And here it is." He smiled coldly. "I've had the witchlord and his men spend the last year digging out a warehouse when the way in was right here. Kept them busy, though." He waved to the others. "Come, all of you. Find your mark and bare your palm." The hermit moved to one side of the seal where there was a small circle and a rune that Cinq recognized from his studies to mean "self." Ezekiel placed his hand on the mark, which elicited a sharp metallic click.

Blue folded her arms. "I'm not moving until he explains what's going on. He says he's hundreds of years old, and the rest of you can't remember your own mothers. You're not the same."

Ezekiel removed his hand, and the seal clicked again. "You need answers? Very well." He breathed deep. "I was once the hermit. Now I am the guardian."

45

~ Cinq ~

Ezekiel, the hermit, the fifth key, regarded them with eyes sunken into his weathered face. Despite his emaciated limbs, his disintegrating rags, and the skin that was both weathered and pale, he radiated with inner strength. And if the bodies in his cell were an indication, he was dangerous. He said, "I don't know how much you already know, or how much you think you know. So, I'll cut through the most common of lies."

Cinq started to interrupt, then thought better of it. He'd wait.

Ezekiel said, "Let's start with the Titans. They aren't just here to smash things."

Cinq nodded. He hadn't come this far to keep secrets, but he also wanted to test if they were being lied to. "We know they're the fey. We know they're trying to bring magic back to the otherplane."

"That's just the edges. Ironically, the first Titans *were* made to smash things. In the years leading up to the first Titans' Age, the mages wanted power. They built their machines to siphon magic from the otherplane. Ever wonder what they did with that power?"

Blue had drawn her cleaver and made a show of inspecting the blade. "Rule the world? That's what people use power for."

Ezekiel pointed to her. "She's a clever one, a fitting heir to the scholar. It was the mages who first created the Titans. They crafted them in the image of the elements—not the elements of science, but of the old mythologies. They forged monsters from the fey.

"But the fey… they learned from those who enslaved them. They learned of their strength when united. The mages taught them to fight, but the fey fought back. They emulated their masters, becoming Titans of their own volition. It wasn't the fey that started the war."

Cinq noticed the man spoke with such conviction that truth radiated in his voice. He found it hard to consider the words as anything but truth. It was like hearing his own thoughts coming from the mouth of another. After all, they were both aspects of the same person.

The hermit held up another finger. "The next thing to remember is your Pentarch was no saint. He was educated and accomplished, but not benevolent. The mastery of the disciplines made him practical. He also knew his ideas would be challenged, especially with regard to the Black Gate. Not everyone was as willing as he to push the worlds apart. The mages? They wanted the otherplane for its power, they didn't want it inaccessible. The wikken? They wished to commune with the fey. They wanted no separation at all. Even the scholars protested the loss of knowledge. Only the monks and hermits desired peace over opportunity."

Nissa cocked her head. "So that's why he did it. No one would go along with his plan, so he split himself up. He wouldn't disagree with himself."

The hermit didn't reply right away. He studied them. "How long have you known?"

Cinq answered, "I suspected it after reading his journals. But I wasn't sure until I met you. Then I couldn't shake the idea. It explained so much: our talents, our memories, even my fixation with the Tracer. Part of me always knew." He paused. "How did you figure it out?"

Ezekiel said, "I didn't. I remembered. But I've had more time to do so. I was thrown forward in time like the rest of you, but not far. Just enough to stay hidden. As a hermit, I was to be an observer, a keeper of memories. I was to be the guardian of the machine as I was the least tempted to use it. The rest of you inherited powers of mages, monks, wikken, or knowledge of science. Not me. I was given the time to remember what we had done. And if needed, to be ready to do it again."

Yon's eyes went wide. "Are… are *you* the Pentarch?"

The hermit smiled thinly. "No more than you. I'm only a piece. When I awoke, I remembered some of the past, but I had lost everything else. All memories or learning as a mage, monk, wikken, or scholar had disappeared." His face turned deadly serious. But now we're here, the five keys, together. And it is time to do what we were made to do. Are you ready?"

Ezekiel approached the seal and placed his palm on the open circle. The apparatus clanked as some unseen mechanism released. When no one moved to join him, he looked over his shoulder. "This isn't the machine, it's the front door. We're not there yet."

Cinq moved first. He found the rune of the mage and placed his hand in the circle, eliciting a second metallic clank. Yon followed, then Blue, and lastly, Nissa. When she found her mark, the seal rotated a half turn before separating into five portions that retreated into the wall. On the other side, a spiral staircase dropped into the darkness.

Ezekiel strode forward, only to stop at the topmost stair. "For years I have felt the heartbeat of the machine. Today, we see it together."

Cinq hastened after the hermit. "And then what?"

The hermit did not turn to answer. He dropped down step after step, passing carved murals of men and fey, Titans and monsters. The images washed past Cinq while sparking memories of long ago. Ezekiel said, "Perfect question. The pieces are in place: Titans, keys, and now the Convergence. The curtain between us and the otherplane is thin. What needs to be done, must be done *now*. We must right the great wrong." Ezekiel's eyes lit up. "Here it comes."

Cinq felt the wash of magic flow over him. They had descended past the magical void. He hadn't realized how much he'd depended on the aura of magic around him, even if reluctant to use it. Ezekiel looked elated. Not only was his expression one of contentment, but his appearance was changing. The years melted from his body. Whatever magic he'd used to prolong his life, and had been denied him in the void, returned. Ezekiel turned to Blue; his eyes danced with excitement.

"Scholar, can you set wards? I don't want anyone following us."

Blue shook her head.

The hermit's smile faded. "This is not my area of expertise, but I'll try." Ezekiel swirled his arms in elaborate patterns. His hands lit with a pale glow as they effused luminescent mist. He drew a symbol first on one wall, then the other, then again at his feet. The light flared, faded, and disappeared. He turned back, satisfied.

"I've been thinking about that one for a while. A nice surprise for the next one down those stairs. Come on! No time to waste."

As Ezekiel pushed by to retake the lead, Yon watched in awe. "You're… getting younger."

Ezekiel shrugged. "A monastic discipline, I know. And here you were expecting nothing from me but the hermetic. As I said, I've been around a long time. I've learned a few things on my own." He trotted down the stairs. "It helps knowing just how much of the world is knowable."

The hermit stepped lightly, spiraling around twice more before the stairs ended on a smooth, tiled floor. The polished slate fit together in perfect hexagonal patterns, extending the length of the antechamber and onto a mural at the end. As Ezekiel set another series of runes on the stairs, Cinq studied the picture. Silver inlay covered the wall to depict a wide-branched oak. At first, nothing happened, but when Ezekiel approached, the wall parted in the middle to reveal an immense open chamber. A suspended walkway protruded into the darkness.

Ezekiel set off without hesitation. Cinq gripped his staff with one hand and considered both the burgeoning magic within, and how easily he could tap into it if needed. As he stepped forward, he noted the walkway had no supports, either from above or below. Overhead, he saw the ceiling of the cavern festooned with stalactites, pulsing in a dull red glow. The faint light illuminated the stone beneath his feet. Far below them, a molten river bisected the darkness.

Yon skipped to catch up with Cinq. He spoke in a stage whisper. "Is this a volcano? We're actually in a volcano!"

Cinq murmured, "Don't get distracted. Be ready."

They followed Ezekiel along the walkway to where it ended in the center of the chamber. At the terminus jutted an enormous granite spire that rose from the depths of the cavern. The top of the spire had been sliced off, morphing into a carved pentagon, which was in turn topped with a stone dais. This seal, like the others, had been etched with dragons, men, imps, and fey. The pictures were formed from runes, woven together so tightly that individual characters faded away. The formation was an enormous relic. Layers upon layers of runes, conduits, glyphs, and wards, each stacked atop and amplifying the other. Cinq reached out with his magical awareness, then recoiled from the overwhelming complexity.

Ezekiel stopped at the edge of the dais. He turned to face the others. "Careful now. We don't want to be hasty." The hermit stepped onto the platform. He walked to the center and spread his arms. "See what is possible when the disciplines work together? Mages used their magic to sculpt the stone. The fey inscribed the runes as directed by the wikken, all while the monks stabilized everything with their chi. The scholars applied their own principles of capacity and resistance to set the geometry to align physical and metaphysical in one. The result: exquisite."

Cinq set his jaw. He studied the ancient man now turned, not young, but younger. He thought of the books in the Pentarch's tomb. Hundreds of people had labored across disciplines to erect this machine, each knowing that a Titan could appear at any moment. There had always been a piece missing in the construction, a piece of the puzzle never quite explained.

Cinq asked, "And the hermits? What did they do?"

Ezekiel's eyes lit up. "Ah, yes. A good question. Our discipline, the hermetic discipline, was never one of power, but of contemplation. That carries a stigma, of course. Just as wikken are accused of caring only about the fey when they care *also* about the fey, the hermits were accused of caring not about people, when in truth we cared about *not just* people. Others were tasked with building the machine. We had to decide what to do with it."

An itch formed at the back of Cinq's mind. Maybe it was a revelation, maybe it was the dizzying effect of having all five keys together. He felt thoughts drifting from one of them to the other. Was this still about being a key, or because—except Blue—they were aspects of the same person?

Cinq asked, "Do you remember the final decision? The sacrifice of the otherplane?"

Ezekiel nodded. His eyes were a pit of sadness. "I remember it, and I regret it. It was the greatest evil our world has ever done. In the early years, I convinced myself it had been necessary. But as the worlds drifted back together, I no longer believed it. That unforgivable action, that great sin, the destruction of untold living things: *that* is our heritage. It is something that we did together. We must take personal responsibility."

Blue shifted the waistband on her uniform. She was tensing as though ready for a fight. They were all on edge, but why was she so uneasy? The things the hermit said resonated with Cinq. But perhaps Blue, lacking the connection they shared, heard them differently.

Nissa cocked her head. "Whelp. Three hundred years is a lot of regret. You have a better plan this time? Since, you know, you've had so much time to think."

Ezekiel frowned. He paced the dais, inspecting the engraved stone. Larger glyphs, like those on the seal, marked the corners of the pentagon. He brushed away the dust on each. "The question, the question, the question. That is, of course, the question. Pushing the worlds apart—as we did last time—is temporary and futile, not to mention it requires more magic than we can muster. Neither can we sever the ties between our worlds. We are too tightly linked. And for this reason, if one world falls, the other will follow. We must use the machine to heal the otherplane, not harm it."

Cinq asked, "Will that stop the Titans?"

"Of course. They'd have no reason to come. Whether our worlds are close together, or far apart, there will be balance. The fey have no need to horde magic, not in the way the mages did." Ezekiel stopped in front of the last seal. He dusted it off and smiled. He took his right hand and placed it on the glyph. A low *thunk* of machinery pulsed through the dais. The glyph lit up with a sallow, yellow glow. "Come, take your positions: monk, mage, scholar, wikken. The time has come."

Yon spoke up. "Wait. But how will we do it? Is there enough magic in our world to make a difference? What would it do to us?"

Cinq had paced to the rune of the mage. He looked at it, Yon's words fading to a buzz in the back of his mind. He felt an overwhelming impulse to activate the machine, to turn it on and drink deep of a power his mind somehow remembered. He said, "We need to do this." He looked back at the hermit. "How does it work?"

Ezekiel tapped against his temple. "Just your mind, dancing on the fabric of reality. The five of us will enter a realm of infinite possibility. Our limits will be only that which we can conceive."

Yon persisted, "But where will we get the magic?"

The hermit looked up. His right eye twitched as he hesitated. He didn't get a chance to answer. Behind them, from the direction of the stairs, Cinq heard a hollow boom followed by screams of pain and anger.

The reavers were here.

46

~ Cinq ~

Green flames poured from the mouth of the tunnel, spilling out in rolling waves across the walkway where they dripped off the edge. Moments later, reavers staggered through the opening, their clothes charred, armor blackened, and limbs bleeding from Ezekiel's traps. The soldiers stormed across the length of the walkway, stopping just short of the dais where the five keys stood. Up close, their eyes radiated hate. Cinq gripped his staff.

"Ezekiel!" a voice boomed from the tunnel's entrance. Four people appeared in the doorway and marched through the lines of soldiers.

The hermit cursed. He turned his head to the others. His voice was low but urgent. "This is the time to act. Activate the machine *now*."

Cinq moved without thinking. He pressed down on the rune of the mage. The glyph illuminated and a *thunk* reverberated through the floor, followed by another, and another. A low whirring filled the air as unseen machinery clicked and ground.

Cinq looked up to see that Yon and Nissa had also activated their runes. Only Blue hesitated.

A man plowed down the walkway. He wore a steel breastplate draped in a dark cloak slashed with red. Scars crisscrossed his weathered skin. He glanced down at the border between walkway and dais, then stepped forward as though he expected to be stopped by an unseen force. When he looked up again, his eyes flashed with triumph.

"Ezekiel," the soldier rumbled, "what are you doing with my machine?" His eyes narrowed. "I should have watched you closer."

Alarm surged through Cinq in recognition of the woman standing just behind the soldier. He had seen her on the summit of the Rendezvous. Yanamadra lived. And that made the other man the witchlord himself. Cinq took hold of the magic within him. As he did so, he sensed the strength of the others. One of the other people trailing the witchlord was also a mage. More surprising was the intensity of the power within Ezekiel. Cinq had been so blinded with the thought of the man as a hermit that he hadn't considered him to be adept. Yet the amount of magic within the man was staggering. He was capable of far more than a few defensive wards.

The witchlord declared, "I am Mortimer Cain. These are my lieutenants: Isil, Golloth, and you have already met Yanamadra."

Cinq's eyes lingered on Yanamadra. She loomed in the ambient glow of the chamber—and she was changed. Burn scars covered her face, her mouth a thin line of fury. The hulking Golloth intimidated in his own way, a warrior covered in scars and tattoos. Isil, the mage, swirled with dark magic. Cinq noted the symmetry, he and his friends were four, as were the witchlord and his lieutenants. Ezekiel could tip the scales either way. Cinq prayed that his misgivings about the hermit were unwarranted.

Cinq steeled himself. "For someone who hates magic, you have strange companions."

The witchlord grinned. "Yes. But necessary. Of course, I needed to know my enemy. Magic has brought the Titans on us, and so I could not remain ignorant of that power, despite its abomination. But that is not why I have chosen them." The witchlord toed the engravings beneath his feet. "It's the machine, of course. The Black Gate. You are the keys, surely you can guess my reasons. I was once a monk, Isil a mage, Yanamadra a wikken, Golloth a scholar," he coughed, "of sorts. And we will be the keys soon enough."

Nissa held up her hand and wiggled her fingers. "Hate to break it to you, but you're one short."

"Am I?" The witchlord turned to Ezekiel. "Are you done with your theatrics, old man? We have an agreement."

The hermit folded his arms across his chest. "Actually, I've reconsidered."

The witchlord's smile dropped. "What do you mean? You're free, aren't you?"

Ezekiel nodded. "Yes. And thank you for that… temporary lack of supervision. But I prefer these kids to your butchers."

The witchlord narrowed his eyes. "You trust these witches? Impossible. You know who doomed our world. You were the one who proposed we purify it. No monks, no wikken, no mages—no one to reopen the gates. The Titans' Age will end before it can begin."

Nissa let loose a guffaw, which turned into a full-fledged howl of laughter. "You are so *dumb*. I mean, super-dumb. You can't just 'kill 'em all and no more magic.' Magic isn't just curses and fireballs and lighting. Magic is *life*. Mages and monks just shape it, they don't create it."

The witchlord growled. "Liar! The witches use more than they create. They can't do that dead." His voice dropped, once again eerily calm. "I will kill them all. Then we'll see who's right."

Ezekiel stared at the witchlord. "And so we're back to the beginning. The wikken is correct. Your solution, Mortimer, is incomplete. But you want to see for yourself? Fine. I'll show you." He turned to Blue. "Scholar? It's time."

Blue cleared her throat. During the discourse, she had drawn her cleaver and now slapped the blade methodically against her palm. She turned away from the witchlord and his lieutenants to Ezekiel. "Not until you tell me whose side you're on."

Ezekiel's eyes blazed in the cavern light. "I am on the side of justice, the side of balance. It is the only way we can pay for our transgressions. And if that means sucking all magic—and all life—from this world, so be it. Now, unlock that seal."

Cinq's stomach clenched. Ezekiel and the witchlord were both insane, and no amount of talking could change that. Their only chance was if he and his friends could control the machine instead of the hermit: four against one. If one of them were to fall, and be replaced with the witchlord's allies, then it might not be enough. They had to risk it. "Now, Blue, do it now!"

Blue's eyes widened with shared understanding. As she reached for the seal, the air pulsed with non-light. A distortion of air ripped from Isil to collide against Blue. She was thrown back, skidding across the stone, only to come up with her hand clenched on her cleaver and rage in her eyes.

The witchlord raised his weapon. "Stop them, all of them! Kill them and take their places."

Isil released another bolt of energy. This time Cinq was ready. He intercepted the threads of magic, redirecting it back at the dark wizard. Isil reeled from the blast but did not fall. Golloth, the warrior, charged to strike where Isil had failed. He collided with Blue, who desperately parried his attacks. She was clearly unmatched. Golloth's attacks drove her to her knees. Then his whole body stiffened. As he turned, Cinq saw three knives bristling from Golloth's side, with Nissa poised to throw a fourth. Golloth took a step toward her, while Cinq prepared his next attack.

"Stop!" Cain roared. "You'll damage it! Remember where you are!"

"Too late," Ezekiel sneered. The hermit held two fingers close to his chest. With his other hand he reached up to seize the air. He brought his fist down swiftly and violently to the stone floor. Power radiated in all directions. The witchlord, Yanamadra, Golloth, and Isil were ejected from the dais and sent skittering back onto the walkway. The hermit stood once more. He raised his hands above his head, and a sphere of energy formed between his open fingers.

Cinq called, "Blue, do it now!"

She dove at the last of the runes and slapped her hand onto the scholar's glyph. Thunder echoed as the etchings on the pentagon shifted to pale white. Yellow light snaked a maddening path through the maze on the dais from Ezekiel to Yon. The monk cried out as he was knocked to the ground, his body washed in energy. Cinq tried to help, only to watch as a second trace of power, this one an intense violet, twisted to meet him. Pain shrieked through his body, dropping him to all fours and sending his staff clattering to the stone. Electricity coursed through him.

A bolt of vibrant green energy engulfed Nissa, and one of orange encompassed Blue. Lastly, the power splintered in all directions so that each of them: mage, monk, wikken, scholar, and hermit joined with another, a star within a pentagon. Only Ezekiel remained standing. Potential crackled through his body, light poured from his eyes. Their bodies were becoming one, as were their minds. Memories tangled as they wove together: Yon awaking at Open Eye, Nissa with her enclave, Blue surviving the haggards, and lifetime upon lifetime of rage, anger, and regret from Ezekiel.

Rising from the ashes of so many lives, came memories of the Pentarch. There was a moment as a boy playing on the steps of the Open Eye Monastery, a swim beneath a waterfall in a wikken enclave, a late night in the archives of Alexandria, and seclusion on a moss-covered mountainside. Cinq choked on the flood of memory. He remembered the decision to build the machine, and the moment when they chose to sacrifice the otherplane. He relived crippling a world, and the lives lost in consequence. And somewhere—somewhere deep within their shared mind—Cinq touched the Black Gate. The machine was not physical, no collection of gears and counterweights, but one of energy and power, a latticework of runes, glyphs, channels, and threads that extended down beneath the dais to infinity below.

The framework wove through stone, lava, shifting sands, and underwater seas. Cinq felt the doors open in his own mind. His awareness had become a gateway, and he was not alone. Cinq, Yon, Blue, Nissa, and Ezekiel, each of them fought for control. But he could never win in this place. In this reality, Ezekiel was a god among infants.

Cinq knew what had to be done. He hurled his essence at the Black Gate. The others were pulled in with him.

47

~ Cinq ~

Cinq's awareness snapped to complete clarity. The chaos of joining minds with Nissa, Yon, Blue, and Ezekiel was gone. In its place: crystalline lucidity.

He stood in darkness and on darkness. A sea of obsidian sand stretched beneath his feet. This was the surface of the otherplane, and yet the great trees were nowhere to be seen. There was nothing but black and sand and sky. Was this truly the otherplane? A memory? A shared past or possible future? Cinq placed his palm against the sand and felt the hunger for magic. This was a dream.

Cinq took a tentative step forward. He was relieved to hear the soft crunch of his boot against the sand, the sound making the experience more real. He registered that he again wore his long pants, coat, and broad hat. The soldier's uniform was absent, as were the wounds on his palms.

He spun to look behind him but saw only the same featureless landscape. Panic rose in his chest. He needed something, *anything* to gain his bearings. His mind was too fragmented with memories of other people and other times. With great hesitation, he reached out to feel for the magic in the world. If this was the otherplane, it would react against him. He closed his eyes and calmed his emotions.

Beneath his feet, the sands pulsed with a thin layer of power. It lapped at his ankles in minuscule currents. He raised one foot, and with the slightest of focus, he brought his heel down hard.

Energy radiated outward, emitting a hollow tone as it traveled, growing so faint that he couldn't be sure if he heard the sound, or simply imagined it. The wave returned, this time from a different direction and with a different tone and pitch. Cinq walked in the direction of the echoing wave. When his bearings had faded, he stomped again. As before, a wave of power rippled out and echoed back.

He quickened his pace, but moving through the desert was difficult. His feet sank with each step, the fine sands giving way. With effort, he pulled his boots out again. He watched the black sand resettle so that his footprints disappeared. He struck the ground again. Once more the wave went out, but this time he saw the point of reverberation. He rushed forward to where a small mound rose in the desert. He dropped to his knees and dug. He recoiled in surprise as his fingers touched something solid. He lifted, and Nissa's unmoving body came free from the ground.

"Nissa… Nissa wake up. Wake up!" he cried. He put his ear to her chest and heard the faintest of heartbeats. Without thinking, he reached out for magic so that he might cast a spell of wakefulness. In this alternate existence, magic persisted around him.

Nissa's eyes rolled open. "Cinq? The hermit… he's too strong. There was…" her head lolled once more.

Fury welled inside him. He couldn't leave her here, and yet urgency consumed him. He hoisted her in his arms and started to run. He didn't think about her weight, he didn't think of the loose sands. And soon he was skimming across the desert in the direction of the next ping. The black sand and black sky left little horizon, and yet he could see a shadow made real. It rose, tall and pointed, as the sands hardened to packed dirt and then polished obsidian. The shape resolved into a low-angle pyramid, sharp ridges running in the direction of the peak. A man was silhouetted on the apex, dancing as he moved.

Cinq lightened his footfalls so that he approached more softly. Now the dancer was visible. He wore a turquoise robe that looped over one shoulder, the other shoulder revealing pale skin covered in the runes of the wikken. The form stopped and turned toward him: Ezekiel. All traces of the decrepit man had vanished. The hermit was muscular, vibrant. In this younger self, Cinq saw again the resemblance to Nissa, Yon, Elizabeth, and himself.

The hermit called in a clear and accented voice. "Cinq LeGarrec, welcome to our sanctuary. I wasn't expecting you to send us here."

Cinq carefully laid Nissa's body down. He stepped around to stand between her and the hermit. "Better us than those replacements."

Ezekiel laughed. "It's the same in the end." He tilted his head back and cast his arms wide. The Black Gate pleads for direction. The machine will have but a single master and a single mind. This isn't cooperation, it is a matter of strength. And whether you, or

Cain, or centuries of keys passed from one to the other, it is my destiny to be in control." He met Cinq's eyes. "True, your monk friend put up a fight, as did the wikken. But they are children. You're all children to me. And I am not limited by discipline."

"So, you *are* the Pentarch?"

Ezekiel shook his head. "*The* Pentarch? No. I started out as a fraction, just like you. I had to re-earn my mastery. I am certainly a pentarch, a master of five disciplines. But I am also myself." He dropped his chin. "And now we're all that is left. After you fall, the machine will be mine."

"And the witchlord? What about him?"

Ezekiel shrugged. "He was always a contingency. So many things could go wrong. I didn't know if you'd been trapped in the otherplane, and I didn't know if the machine would work again. Mortimer's way, though imperfect, would have been a first step." He tightened his lips. "I didn't expect him to turn on me."

A low rage boiled within Cinq. Not directed at Ezekiel, but at himself. "Was this always your plan? To destroy our world?"

"No. After the first Convergence, I was righteous, indignant. It took time to accept what the five of us had done. I had to make amends." Ezekiel's eyes burned into Cinq. "I'd like to show you the way, but we don't have centuries for you to see the truth." His face darkened. "I respect you, Journeyman LeGarrec. But this isn't about any one person. It is about what must be done."

Cinq darted his eyes around, hoping for some hint that would give him the upper hand. He had to keep Ezekiel talking. Maybe Nissa would wake up, or Yon, even Blue. "What is this place? It's not the otherplane, not really."

Ezekiel said, "This is my mind. It's what I see when I sleep. A ruined world, the ruination we wrought. I was never allowed to forget."

Cinq set his jaw. He reached out his hand and his staff appeared, created not from magic but from thought. He twisted it around to hold at the ready, one hand gripped high and the other low. He sharpened his awareness. If this was Ezekiel's mind, it was Cinq's mind as well. He had once spent years manipulating his dreams to remember his past. And though the effort had failed, he was stronger because of it. In the real world, he might be constrained by the supply of magic, but in his mind, things were different. Cinq brought his focus to the end of his staff. Blue light streaked toward the hermit.

Ezekiel sidestepped just in time. His eyes lit up. He crossed his forearms and his body surged with his chi. He darted forward, fists ablaze. And now Cinq was on the defensive. He swung his staff, shifting the air to a whip, which he used to throw the hermit skidding across the obsidian.

Ezekiel rose, his face flushed with rage. He reached his hands above his head and a beam of light crossed between his palms to become a staff of intricately twisted ivory. He flourished the staff once before settling into a stance that mirrored Cinq's own.

"You want to play at mages? You may have his essence, but I have three hundred years of study."

Cinq snorted. "I get it. You're old. Consider it noted."

Ezekiel howled. He swung his staff and a bolt of energy arced from the tip. Cinq raised his staff to intercept it just in time. The energy surged between them, and though the power would have overwhelmed Cinq in the waking world, this was his mind. A dream, nothing more. And if a dream, he needn't be constrained by the limits of knowledge—even against a pentarch. Cinq advanced. He wanted the hermit's focus on him for as long as possible until—

A tsunami of obsidian sand slammed into Ezekiel, sending him flying. Cinq shaped the dream made flesh. As he focused, the sand rose, piling upon itself, higher and higher to form legs, a torso, arms, and head. Cinq sculpted his dream, but he wasn't alone. His companions may have fallen, but their combined memories bolstered his focus.

The Sand Titan roared as it advanced on the hermit, its voice reverberated with all four of their aspects.

"No!" Ezekiel screamed as the black fist struck him. Ezekiel scrambled to his feet, furious. The sand swirled around him, rising as a pedestal on the ground. Ezekiel raised his arms, the staff bathed in lightning once more. An arc of energy seared from the starless sky above, redirecting to hit the Sand Titan. The Titan exploded into a black cloud.

Cinq set his jaw. Ezekiel may command magic far greater than Cinq could pretend, but it was only magic. He wasn't using the strength of the dream. Cinq raised his arms. This time he reconstructed the Sand Titan, infusing it with an aura of magic and the memories of he and his companions. The entity rose from the ground, twice as large as before. Ezekiel spun to face it. He unleashed another bolt, but this time the Titan absorbed the energy. It took another step forward.

Ezekiel backed away, not even glancing at Cinq. He must not realize the connection between Cinq and the Titan. Did he think this was his own nightmare? Ezekiel turned to run, but the Titan snatched forward with the speed of a viper. It held the hermit aloft, the sands on its arm twisting and swirling like a dark tornado. Cinq felt a wave of power as Ezekiel tried to focus his chi. The Titan devoured the energy as easily as before. Ezekiel howled. He reached out, grasping at the streams of his own power and extending far beyond. He wasn't using the power of his dream, he was deliberately tapping directly into the energy of the world—just as Ascertine had done.

Cinq reached for the sky. He carved a chasm into the earth. The Sand Titan plummeted down, dragging Ezekiel with it. A burst of energy, a column of blinding light, erupted from the chasm as the hermit transformed into pure energy. The light—and Ezekiel's presence—faded as the sands closed in around him.

Cinq dropped to his knees. He released the image of the Titan from his mind. The reverberation of the hermit's thoughts were now absent, though Nissa, Yon, and Blue remained. Their memories and feelings had become one—now absent Ezekiel's poison. From the ashes, they became aware of the machine. It opened to them. The power of two worlds lay at their fingertips. They had gone from five keys to four, but that didn't matter. They were of one mind.

And as one, they knew what must be done.

48

~ Cinq ~

Cinq lay flat on his back. The floor beneath him thrummed with the heavy cycle of machinery. Each pulse, like a distant drum, grew slower and slower until at last dying completely. In the following silence, he heard a susurrus, a rumble neither mechanical nor lithic. Sand drizzled from above. Not sands of obsidian, but a swirl of earth and dust, dank and organic.

His head throbbed. Something was changed—the air, the earth, the *world*. But his memories were in tatters.

His body hurt. Every muscle ached. His skin burned as though he'd broken through the ice and plunged into a frozen sea. Far above, stalactites hung from the ceiling, bathed in a pale glow like moonlight. Before, they'd been red. Why weren't they red?

Cinq snapped upright. He had returned to the underground temple; he was back atop the stone pentagon. The wasteland of black sand and obsidian steps was gone, fading as quickly as a dream. He sifted through memories of his battle with Ezekiel, the Sand Titan, and the merging of minds, worlds, and energy.

Cinq grappled for his staff and struggled to his feet. At the corners of the pentagon, Nissa, Yon, and Blue lay motionless. But Ezekiel was changed. Nothing remained of the hermit except charred bones. Cinq limped over to look. He toed the ash, skeptical that Ezekiel was truly gone. This could be a trick; he had to be sure. Cinq removed the Tracer from his pocket. The lights within brightened at his touch, but there were only four of them. Then those, too, softened and died. The orb became dark. Cinq opened his hand, and the Tracer fell to the floor. It bounced once and rolled off the edge.

He waited, listening for a rattle and crash that never came. Cinq's gaze drifted past the dais and to the suspended walkway. Empty. No reavers, no bodies, no signs of struggle. His first thought was of another lapse. How easy it would be for time to have slipped? Had days and years run by while they were within the machine? Or had time reversed? Had the battle yet to occur?

The cavern rumbled. Streams of sand and gravel fell from the ceiling, cascading through the black. Cinq looked up, his hand shielding his eyes from the debris. A dark mass descended from the ceiling. The shadow wriggled downward, curling and twisting until touching down on the dais. The colossal root found purchase in solid ground. Small, organic tendrils crept across the surface, stopping at his feet.

A voice called from behind him. "What is it?"

Cinq turned to see Nissa propped up on one arm. Alive. His heart leaped in his chest, the shock snapping him from his trance. He hurried to her side. "Nissa… are you ok?"

As he helped her up, Cinq's vision went white from the effort. He heard more rustling and saw that Blue and Yon were also awake. They stood and crossed to join with Cinq and Nissa, then stopped. They stared at the massive root now sending out smaller tendrils, which searched for cracks in the stone until spilling out over the edge.

Cinq's memories returned in shadows and flashes. Once Ezekiel had fallen, the machine opened itself to him—to all of them. They'd become one. They'd seen the entirety of two worlds. They'd seen the sickened mass of the otherplane and the billions suffering within. They'd seen an opportunity and given… a push.

Cinq limped back over to the root. He knelt and placed his hand on the knotted wood. As he touched it, he heard sounds at the edges of his mind, the murmurs, mumbles, and voices of countless fey. They filled his awareness, a blanket of consciousness that threatened to overwhelm him. The voices were not suffocating, but completing. They were a wash of color where before there had been gray.

Nissa touched his shoulder. She said, "They're here, Cinq. *All* of them. And… they're *singing*." She looked up at him. "And the magic… I can feel it. For the first time, I can feel it. What's happened?"

Cinq reached out with his mind. A glow warmed him from within. The current of magic, the current of life, filled the air in zephyrs and eddies. But it was neither of nearplane nor otherplane. He tried to grasp it, but it glided away.

"Stop!" Blue commanded. Cinq spun to face her. She had drawn her cleaver and stared at the suspended walkway. "That's far enough."

Someone was standing just past the edge of the pentagon, a man in a steel breastplate and a scorched cape. A gash ran across his cheek, the blood already drying. The witchlord rested his hands on the pommel of his curved sword. He gripped the hilt and probed the edge of the dais. As he did so, the air rippled and collapsed like an enormous bubble.

Behind Cain, the once-empty walkway wavered. What had been shadows became the fallen bodies of reavers. Some were burned, others dusted with frost, and still others impaled by their own weapons. None stirred, none groaned. Had they all been killed, or were these only those who remained? Cinq's memories flickered, or rather a memory of a memory. Ezekiel's last act before entering the machine was to ensure he wouldn't be disturbed. He'd left his estranged pupil behind as witness and testament.

Cain stepped onto the platform and walked to the husk of Ezekiel's body. With the side of his foot, he pushed the charred mass over the edge. Cinq realized what had been eluding him. The molten river at the base of the cavern no longer flowed red. It emitted pale blue light.

Cinq rapped his staff against the stone. He locked eyes with Cain. "There's nothing left. The machine is broken."

"I assumed as much."

Blue took a step forward. "I'll bet you did. But if you don't drop that sword, you'll be keeping your buddies company in hell."

Cain tossed his weapon to the ground. He nodded to the root. "You did something, didn't you? Of course you did." His eyes flickered to Ezekiel's remains. "He planned to kill us all."

"So did you," Cinq replied.

Cain waved his hand. "I was prepared to do whatever it took. Perhaps I was wrong about my options."

Cinq looked back at the root. His hand tightened on his staff. "The Convergence. It's complete. The worlds are at rest."

Cain said, "If that's true, I must hold myself accountable." He shook his head. "Perhaps there is monk in me after all."

"You have got to be kidding!" Nissa shrieked. "Mr. Witchlord says he's a changed man and all is forgiven? He killed thousands!"

Cinq tightened his jaw. "And what about us, Nissa? How many did we kill?"

She said, "But that wasn't really even us! That was us from before."

Yon said, "He should be forgiven. We should all be forgiven. Not just him, or us, but also the fey."

The last tumbler fell into place, and Cinq understood their new reality. Nearplane and otherplane were no more.

He swallowed hard. "It's time we went home."

CODA

~ Yon ~

Yon opened his eyes as the first rays of sunlight peeked over the mountainside to brush the skin of his face. He unfolded himself from his lotus position and rose to look over the red rock and vibrant green to Ignaesdale below. Across the once-barren desert, the massive trees of the otherplane stretched their branches. Newer and younger life, nearplane and otherplane alike, thrived in the welcome shade. In the town, people were already hard at work hauling cords of wood and shaping clay to make bricks. Yon would soon go into town to help, just as soon as his meditations were done. And, of course, he needed to check on his pupils.

Nissa stumbled up the path. Her hair was wild and frayed, pulled back in a bun, even if not shorn completely. The wikken marks covering her arms and legs looked comically out of place beneath the robes of a monk. She stood before Yon, rolled her eyes, and exhaled deeply. "*Master* Yon. Your presence is requested in the main hall." Sarcasm dripped in every word.

Yon nodded and smiled.

"And…" Nissa continued, "before you get too used to being high and mighty and smug, just remember that it's going to come back around. The enclave hasn't had a lot of boys in the past few centuries. You're going to want friends."

He raised an eyebrow. "What are you talking about, they loved me there. Wait a minute, are you trying to bargain with a master?"

"I will wipe that smile off your face, baldy. I don't care if you've punched a dragon. I. Don't. Care."

"I'm kidding, Nissa, I'm kidding. I'm just… happy you're here. And if it's any consolation, they're giving Cinq a harder time."

A grin cracked Nissa's face. "I know! But everyone here freakin' loves Blue, am I right? How is that fair?"

Yon shrugged. "She works hard. And she has a lot of good stories."

"Rope, tackle, sea shanties, and ancient history. She's the whole package."

Silence settled on them. They'd only been at the monastery for a few weeks, and despite the upheaval of roles and prestige, Yon knew this idea would bring them together. They'd each spend as long as it took to be fully accepted by their disciplines: monk, mage, wikken, and scholar. Would they go on to be hermits, each in solitary? That was still to be decided, or perhaps they would content themselves with being quadarchs.

For a moment, Yon forgot about the reality that spread itself across the desert and across the world. Nearplane and otherplane were now one. Fey roamed the streets and magic rang in the air, even if the mages could no longer wield it. Instead, they studied and appreciated, and turned their talents to a world content in its newfound symbiosis.

Because no one knew what would happen next.

453 ♦ Phil Coleman

Acknowledgments

This book would not have been possible without the support of my family. I am grateful for both their grounding and enthusiasm. Sarah, Ellen, and Maggie's passion for books and reading is one of the greatest encouragements in my life. They make me understand the power and importance of stories.

I would like to thank Amy Jo for her review of an early draft during a pandemic, as well as to Amanda, Leslie, Denise, Roger, and the rest of the Third Thursday gang for their no-holds-barred critiques and opinions. Credit must also be given to Liz for her meticulous review, honesty, and precision. Lastly, I'd like to thank not only my immediate writing community, but the larger community of book people, readers, artists, teachers, friends, and family who have helped and cheered along the way.

About the Author

After college, Phil left North Carolina for the west and then never managed to go home again. When not living and breathing books, he likes to hike, mountain bike, ski, and appreciate being where the air is thin, and the cows outnumber the people.

His books and stories are all about taking an idea and then pushing it far beyond the bounds of our own reality. After all, we have more than enough real life in our real life.

Phil lives in the mountains of Colorado with his wife and two daughters.

This is his fourth novel.

Web: https://www.philcolemanbooks.com
Facebook: https://www.facebook.com/philcolemanbooks/
Instagram: https://www.instagram.com/philgoodbooks/
TikTok: https://www.tiktok.com/@philgoodbooks